AN EYE
FOR DARK
PLACES

AN EYE
FOR DARK
 # PLACES

NORMA MARDER

LITTLE, BROWN AND COMPANY

BOSTON   TORONTO   LONDON

First Edition

The characters and events in this book are fictitious.
Any similarity to real persons, living or dead, is coincidental
and not intended by the author.

Lines from "To the Lost Child," by Brigit Pegeen Kelly, Copyright © 1988 from
To the Place of Trumpets by Yale University Press.

The author is grateful to the Illinois Arts Council, a state agency,
for a literary grant that supported the completion of this novel.

Library of Congress Cataloging-in-Publication Data

Marder, Norma.
    An eye for dark places / Norma Marder. — 1st ed.
      p.   cm.
    ISBN 0-316-54606-2
    I. Title.
    PS3563.A6442E93   1993
    813'.54 — dc20   92-38577

10 9 8 7 6 5 4 3 2 1

RRD-VA

*Published simultaneously in Canada
by Little, Brown & Company (Canada) Limited*

Printed in the United States of America

in memory of my father, Max Rajeck, 1904–1962

and for
Herbert, Michael, and Yuri
and my mother, Gertrude Rajeck Mintz

                                   . . . and
hands,
these things that find and belong
to each other, also move and carry like water
more than themselves, as they fly in their birdlike ways toward whatever small purposes
they have been given.

                              —Brigit Pegeen Kelly,
                                "To the Lost Child"

AN EYE
FOR DARK
PLACES

CHAPTER 1

THE BIRDS were limping, masses of them, limping and dragging their wings, bumping and recoiling, pecking listlessly. Sephony leaned on the wall above Trafalgar Square, cradling her package on the smooth, cracked stone. The fat gray things were ugly as aggressive weeds, a crossbreed of pigeon and quail, their long shabby wings useless, their heads twitching nervously like robos with defective wiring. Some hopped on one leg.

Limping birds, she thought, another bad sign. Like the peeling Triangle billboards.

Rain fell and the wind picked up, ruffling neck feathers. Head down, she ran with the crowd, holding the package close to her chest, her eyes stinging. She didn't wear an infrahelmet, there was no law against that. She shuttled from tube to hoverport and was home in half an hour, but with no time to study.

At the hall mirror she automatically patted down short triangles of hair. She didn't like her reflection; hadn't liked it in years. Not that it mattered. Lines feathering away from her eyes; a saggy, pinched look. She smiled for the mirror, as her daughters would; no, she wasn't like her daughters — nor were they like her.

She dashed to the kitchen and fastened an energizer collar around her neck, setting it to 4. Her pulse speeded. Her heart pounded. She ran to the larder, plucked meat wafers from the bin, ran to the sink, soaked the wafers, and tossed leek and potato flakes into the reconstitutor. Her feet skimmed the floor; she measured, poured, and stirred. Her arms jerked strangely and her hands fluttered like wings. In ten minutes a casserole was baking in the old Aga. She reset her energy level, partially unwound by cleaning up, then fled to the orange room and dropped into a recliner.

A muscle twitched over her left eye. Marek would be home soon and then the young. She loved them, oh yes, but she could never escape when they were home; she was bleached and spread through the house like white ashes. She was a manager, yet not one room was hers and hers alone. Nerves twanged in her wrists; her hand quivered like a dying fish. People damaged their adrenals from using energizers too often. But how else to accomplish everything? Calm, calm, she said to her twitching hands and they hiccuped into stillness. She breathed rhythmically and saw, through closed eyes, a towering ring of sarsens in a stony pasture, the dark boulders mixed with swaying black-shawled figures against a red sunset.

The front door slammed; sarsens smeared and vanished. Marek's footsteps thumped in the hall and the geese honked — the noises a heavy jumble of murmuring and honking. Ashamed of her irritation, she ran to the phone table and rearranged a bouquet of daffodils.

Douglas and Harold waddled into the room, tilting clumsily across the carpet. Douglas, the young gray one, nipped her hand.

"Bad boy," she said and stroked both their silky heads.

The room expanded around Marek, filling with forced heartiness. An aura of disappointment always clung to him after a day's work. He kissed her absently on the ear. She kissed his cheek. He dropped into the black recliner — a tall, heavy-boned man with large features — hair messy and face chapped.

"That bit of rain should help," she said.

"What rain?"

"About an hour ago."

"Too busy to notice, I suppose."

"I got through three chapters this morning," she said.

"Some sherry, if you don't mind," Marek said.

Across the room a hand appeared on the mantelpiece. It crawled carefully between the holograms and china candlesticks and came to rest with its fingers dangling over the edge, caressing a white bas-relief. She often saw hands. They clung to walls or attached themselves to light fixtures. They moved through space like dancers on wires. They rested on chair backs or dangled from table edges. Many women "saw things," although they didn't talk much about it. Her friend Peg saw barn swallows, her sister, Ari, saw begonias on the odd occasion, and Mums claimed to see eyes. Most men didn't see things and generally didn't believe in what women saw. In the early years of her marriage Sephony learned to keep silent about hands on chairs because Marek deliberately sat on them. Women are an idiotic species, he used to say, having had a girlfriend who saw moths. But if so many of us see things, she had argued, isn't there something to it? It's just psychological, he had said and laughed. It was a short laugh, a sort of bark, with the head thrown back. Dismissing her. The laugh hadn't worn well. It rang disturbingly in her ears during the last marriage review just as she signed the papers. Still she renewed, everyone renewed, one simply didn't know people who severed their marriages. Twenty-six years, three renewals, the last only five years ago. It seemed the longest, driest period. Perhaps the whole point of marriage review was perverse, it actually discouraged free choice. She shouldn't criticize. A liver-spotted hand crawled down the side of Marek's chair and disappeared underneath.

"And I picked up the new brainer," she said, handing him sherry in a fluted glass.

"You'll kill yourself one of these days and blame it on me." He sipped the sherry. "Lovely," he said. "Any messages?"

"Rolf won't be home this weekend. That's three in a row."

"Is it? Well, he's revising right and proper, doing it thoroughly. He won't fret over his exams the way you do."

"No, Rolf only frets over his laundry, I think."

Her retaliation fell short; he was already sinking into engineering problems. "The metal's going to crack on the test run," he muttered to himself. "That's it in a nutshell."

"Dinner in half an hour," she said.

At the table Simon, Dote, and Melani gossiped about their friends. All three were so careless, so arrogant, so beautiful. Sephony cradled her thumbs in her fists. Although proud of the young, she was harsh and critical. Simon was asthmatic — terribly attached to her and quite reclusive. Dote was gregarious in a bright, conventional way. Melani, at fourteen, was a spring-weather child. She came and went, now tractable, now sullen. Sometimes Sephony didn't know if she quarreled with the girl or with herself. She adored Melani and she was angry with her; she identified with her and felt alienated. Rolf, taking an engineering degree at Cambridge, had been away at school since he was eight. She scarcely knew him.

The morning was dim, promising rain. Sephony watched Alf, the farm manager, walking the weeder through the herbaceous border, holding it stiffly in front of him as it hummed and squirted. He was a Dull but, to her view, quite competent. She waved him to stop. Last week the weeder had confused ground elder with Michaelmas daisies, and six clumps of the lovely blue flowers had melted into a sodden mass of brown strings.

"Has that wretched thing been fixed, Alf?"

"Yes, mum, works like a charm, she do."

"I still think it's far and away safer to weed by hand."

"Works fine, mum."

"Well, all right, then, carry on."

How the Dulls liked machines. She walked up the path, past the empty barn, over the stile, and along the stream. Douglas and Harry materialized, nipping excitedly. They turned and waddled toward the pasture, honking at sheep who baaed raucous antiphonal chorales from their side of the fence. The hill was covered with bluebells. She sat on a log and looked out over fields and woodland, enjoying stillness and the pride of ownership. One hour was all she allowed herself.

Alf caught up with her at the vegetable garden. "Almond tree's got peach curl," he said.

"Well, we must make a note to spray it in the dormant season. There's no help for it now."

"No, mum."

"Well, then."

"Will there be anything, mum?"

"Tell Alfie to be sure to pour warm water in the parsley drill before he sows the seeds."

"Right, mum."

"You forgot to tell him last season."

"Right, mum."

"Well, then."

It began to rain again, the good soaking kind. She ran to the greenhouse, leaping puddles. Flats lay on the tables — white blocks containing cylinders of peat moss. She dropped pepper seeds into half the holes, runner beans in the rest, and marked the division. On her way to the house she snatched up some yellow primroses for her study.

They made a bright spot, bunched in a little vase on her windowsill. Melani shared the study with her — took it over evenings and weekends and left a trail. She tidied Melani's desk, stuffing biscuit foil into the rubbish hole and stacking disks. Satisfied, she scooted the swivel chair to her desk and watched the rain. Her carrel, nestled in the eaves of the west window, gave her a sense of completeness, like gardening. Everything compact and orderly — shelves of gaily colored fichebooks, the white aramid desk itself, so austere and smooth, and the glossy black fiche cube. She unwrapped the package and lifted out the brainer, a dark green box with two electrodes like pincers. She felt proud owning it — afraid of so many things and afraid of this too, but using it anyway, using herself. The small, slick box mocked her. Who knew what harm it did speeding up her mind.

The pink-stained rain fell steadily — a soiled curtain that hung from a wounded sky. Water had been changing for years, rivers greener and the sea darkening. Marek accepted the environment. He took medicines too, a tablet for every ailment. Can't change the world, he said gruffly, so get on with it.

She put on the electrodes, tapped 4 on the brainer, and felt the speeded mental pulse edge into her nervous system, clearing her mind, making it dry and clear.

A red light glowed on the fiche; amber sentences slid up the screen. Quickly she dove into the Neolithic period in western Britain, studying an ambiguous historical record rooted in the hard evidence of bones and tools. In that period people spoke to the invisible with granite and earth, forming grand mysterious statements out of megaliths, stone hoops, dolmens, and mounds. What might they mean?

She halted the text and dictated tensely to the little red light. "People in all times search for common denominators — they want unifying facts and ideas — some connection, for example, between snails and thunder, or birds and death. The Gauls had a sacred language that was austere, they addressed the unknown with earthworks and stone. The Druids, more modern in a way — certainly cruel — used human sacrifice as their supreme sacred language, burning men alive in wicker cages with a view to altering the fates of their heroes. They incorporated bird skins and wings into their clothing, were enchanters, and were said to be able to fly."

A hand materialized on the fiche cube, lounging arrogantly on the black plastic — a slim, graceful hand with manicured nails. Two muscular hands clung to the curtain rod. A spidery hand crawled across the sill, detouring around the primroses. She swiveled her chair. The room was full of hands. A few hands were a comforting presence, but more than ten offended her like accumulated dust. She appealed to them silently to disperse. Take turns, she coaxed, some of you can come back later. Rotate. Change the guard. She imagined a parade of hands marching in unison. She counted to ten. A brown pudgy hand crawled up the windowpane. On the ceiling several crept in monotonous circles. Sephony controlled her disgust. Druids, she commanded herself and mentally brushed the hands away.

She continued dictating, eyes closed. "The word *druid* means 'knowing the oak tree.' They were the learned class in Celtic society. Some were judges, others were seers. They were concerned with enchantment and sacrifice. Historians believe they are related to the Hindu Brahmins, and both are probably survivors of an earlier Indo-European priesthood. A Druid who committed a serious crime was punished by being barred from witnessing a human sacrifice."

A crowd shivered with suppressed tension. A crude wicker cage burned on a high rock slab. Charred hands writhed in the flames. Shadowy bodies shimmered and fell.

A wave of distress swept over her, a mixture of longing and anxiety. She looked up. The window was stretching and contracting, the vase horribly elastic — flat and wide, tall and narrow. The entire room heaved. She pulled off the electrodes, shocking her heart. The walls rippled. Long, slow swells undulated from ceiling to skirting board — rubbery and moist. She swiveled frantically to the opposite window. It grimaced. Something stabbed her knees and elbows; her head ached; her heart pounded. Testing the space ahead, she made for the door. It stretched upward, buckling the floor. She grabbed the bobbing doorknob, pulled the door open, and stumbled away from the mad, collapsing room, out into the hall, where the banister stood firm, solidly descending. The door clicked.

Grasping the cold metal rail, she stepped down the stairs, foot to foot like an invalid, her trousers ballooning, the soft fabric brushing leg against leg. She glanced out the window on the landing. The rain had stopped. At the edge of the lawn, the flowers in the herbaceous border smeared like bad video. Pink rhododendrons and white azaleas dripped. Iridescent grackles wandered across the lawn, limping.

Safe in the orange room, she curled on the couch — energy leaking, pores leaking — she would shrivel up. Tea, she thought. I'll take a cup of tea and replenish fluids. But the kitchen was as far as Aberdeen. What was happening? The kitchen, she said, and forced herself off the couch. She shuffled cautiously, adjusting to wood floors, carpets, and treacherous doorsills, dealing with doorknobs and doors, through the hall and all the way across the dining room, and arrived in the kitchen finally, out of breath. The teamaker delivered a plastic cup of tea with milk. She scalded her tongue. Her eyes were heavy, everything looked strange. The teamaker was precariously perched, canisters were about to topple, the microwave was on the verge of sliding into the sink. The sink, the lovely sink, the double translucent violet sink was buckling. Molecules were bursting from confinement, eager to dance. The world is coming apart, she said, and took another sip. Or am I coming apart? She sipped again. What's falling? What's what? She finished the tea hastily, but couldn't think what to do with the cup. Should she set it on the counter or toss it across the room? The second was the more attractive challenge. The cup fell from her hand. She stepped on it. It made a soft crunching sound.

The wind blew through a hole in one ear. Obviously, then, she must close the window. Alf, in the distance, was digging up weeds, pushing the fork into the soft earth, lifting it with short, sharp movements. She could imagine the thin, brown roots that he was dislodging. She noticed, then, that she felt quite well. It had passed. Whatever it was had passed. She took a breath. I'd better go outside, she said, and walk around a bit.

The young had cooked a lovely meal. To please them, she ate some cauliflower soup.

Marek chewed loudly. "I keep warning you about the brainer," he said with complacent affability that felt like punishment. "Pushing it that high."

He smiled, his mouth large and rubbery. He tended to repent after attacking her.

"How about a nice drive," he said, "to cheer you up."

"You'll like the sunset," Simon said kindly, always her champion.

"Pass the bulgur," said Dote.

"I wouldn't go back to school," Melani said, patting her arm. "Not me. When I'm done, Mumsy, I'll be done."

"We'll go directly after supper, then," Marek said. The day's whiskers grayed and roughened his face, aging him.

"Can I come?" begged Melani, as she used to when she was a child.

"Do your revisions," said Marek.

"She'll do them after," said Sephony, and ruffled Melani's boyishly cropped black curls.

The hovercraft was fairly new, a bright green six-seater with three rows of bumpers around the base. Sephony strapped herself into the front beside Marek. The seats were low and sloping. With a hum they set off over the vegetable garden and across the pasture.

Grass, like hair, curled away from the downdraft. The sky was a pleasant pale yellow.

"Make it bounce!" shouted Melani.

Marek bounced the craft. The rise and drop, usually exhilarating, nauseated her. Bounce, bounce. She opened her mouth to shout, but sound lodged in her trachea like a piece of aspirated carrot.

"Isn't this super!" hooted Melani.

The fish pond rushed to engulf them, then rippled away. They rose above the trees. Bounce, bounce. Sephony gasped for breath. Her eyes hurt, she couldn't close them. Poplars shivered among budding oaks. She flapped her hands.

Marek turned, laughing, then straightened the flight path with a jerk. "Hush up, Melani," he barked, "something's wrong with your mother."

Melani massaged her shoulders. The craft flew evenly, hugging the ground. Her breath returned.

"Thank you, Melani, that's lovely." She reached back and patted her hand.

"You always like bouncing," Marek said reproachfully.

"I'm sorry," she said, feeling guilty, as if she'd deliberately sabotaged his kindness.

He parked and they walked to the house in the twilight.

"Look," said Melani, "another of those limping birds."

"The square was full of them yesterday," said Sephony, "waddling about like hikers with gravel in their boots. Have they some disease?"

"They look queer," said Melani.

Sephony shivered.

"What, Mumsy?"

"Nothing. Anyone for tea?" Smile, she commanded herself. Do something.

The children dispersed through the house. She and Marek sat in their recliners, anchored to milky tea and soy thins. She held to the normal. How was your day? her voice asked. Any Triangle announcements? Is the county getting its waste pod? White noise drowned his answers; hands swung from the ceiling on invisible threads.

"I'm sorry I'm not better company," she managed to say. "My mind seems to be racing."

"Off you go, then," said Marek. "I'll close up."

She lay awake long after he fell asleep, icy with fear. Ill, perhaps. A brain tumor. Hooded figures swayed in a circle of stones.

Chaos and uncertainty leaked through everything, as if one leg were shorter or the floor had holes. Words bunched on the screen and letters dropped away. Green beans shattered in the slicing and half-done tasks bled into the sink. Branches clawed her as she hurried down the orchard path. Safety was the couch in the orange room, where she curled for hours on her side, waiting for tremors to subside.

After a week she persuaded Dr. Easton to see her at home.

"Not epilepsy or a tumor, no need for tests — not even a full-fledged nervous breakdown." He was earnest and never prescribed unnecessary medication. "It's mental tension, my dear." He looked at her severely.

"Well, that's not too bad," she said uneasily.

"If you rest."

"Oh, I haven't time. Exams are coming up."

"No studying for a while. No reading. No video. Complete rest for the mind and the body. Let's say, two weeks. Stay in this room, since you like it. Or it likes you." He laughed.

She felt relieved and guilty.

"I can't," she said.

"Listen to music."

"What about my degree?"

"Classical music would be best. Mozart. Haydn. The logic of the baroque can be very soothing."

"Exams are in a month."

"Were you using a brainer?" he asked sharply.

"Yes."

"How high?" he demanded.

"Three. Sometimes four."

"Damn those pulse boxes," he said. "You're spinning, my dear. Give yourself a rest. No body pulser, either. Agreed?"

So that was it.

"It will take some getting used to," she said.

When Dr. Easton left she lay on the couch, her head on her hand. Afternoon light cast long shadows on the floor. She imagined stepping onto the shadows, following them out the window and up, up, through the trees and over the orchard. How tired she was. Rubbing the small of her back, she trudged up the stairs to the bedroom. When had night come? She lifted an edge of heavy curtain and was stung by daylight. She sat on the bed, kicked off her slippers, and idly scratched the nap of the blue and gold medallion carpet.

Something hummed. A presence was in the room. A shadow eluded her, a stain in the corner of one eye, moving just behind her head, just out of sight. It was a large presence, and — odd that she knew this — round. Firm and nebulous, like the idea of life at the beginning. The presence called

"Come." It did not call, it implied "Come." Should she follow? Follow what? Where? Something terrifying was implied. Her thoughts spiraled in self-defense.

The carpet gave way. There, in the heart of the medallion, in the circle of flowered petals, something darkened just beyond her toes. A hole opened there, deep as a well and edged with moss. A light glowed deep within and a thin, metallic ladder set itself shimmering against the curve. Quickly she withdrew her feet, her heart pounding.

"Come" meant, in a quiet, definite way, "Climb into the well." She sat suspended. The light glowed in the deep distance, beautiful and intriguing. A breeze kissed her left shoulder, a delicate pressure, like a baby's touch. It almost moved her.

"No," she said, aloud. "No, I can't. I'm afraid."

The well sucked itself closed. The presence retreated slowly and reluctantly. Was that a reproach, that chill on her shoulder? Slowly it backed across the room and vanished.

She stared into the center of the medallion. A scorpion in geometric calm faced its mate. Something marvelous had been possible, something ineffable. Gone.

Hysterically tempting the presence and herself, she screamed inwardly, "Come back," and bit her lip. She threw herself on the bed, crying for this loss and a lifetime of losses. What if it returned? She listened, terrified. Nothing.

She ran downstairs and phoned Peg, her only close friend.

"I'm dying," she cried, "I'm going mad."

Peg arrived quickly and brought a tray of tea into the orange room. She was energetic and unhappy, with a brilliant nervous manner and comprehensive interests.

"How immensely exciting, seeing something new," she said briskly, passing Sephony a cup. The steam smelled of mint. "The voice must have something to do with hands."

"No . . . I don't know. I didn't see it, for one thing. Then, hands don't want anything. This expected something. It still does."

"Ah . . . a messenger."

"I don't know. Something extraordinary."

Peg paced to the window and back, then threw herself into a chair. "It just might be interplanetary," she said.

"Peg . . ."

"From a competing realm of influence."

"Rubbish."

Generously undaunted, Peg waved her long graceful arms. "Or a belief system."

"Don't."

"Some people still belong," Peg said, her violet eyes bright and defensive.

"Oh, but they're even more peculiar than you — they believe in reincarnation and that sort of thing."

"There you have it, my love. That could have been your father's voice ordering you about, true to form."

Peg's blunt humor was relaxing, so bleak and off the mark. Other people found her irritating, but Sephony liked the irony that accompanied her quirky passions.

"What an immense opportunity you have," Peg said, "for sharing the universe . . . you may be a sender or a receiver."

"What if I'm crazy?"

"Don't . . . Please, my love, don't turn a gift into illness."

A gift. Druids and Gauls — questions to the invisible. "Well, I might look into a belief system," she said.

"Why not? What religion were your ancestors?"

"Ah, Jewish, I think. Do you know yours?"

"Buddhist and Church of England . . . who knows what they were before — Plutonian, probably. Shall I make some inquiries?"

"If it won't get you in trouble."

"What will you tell Marek?"

"I don't know. Am I crazy?"

"Do you think you are?"

"I wanted to call it back, but if it had come I would have refused again."

"You'll get another chance," Peg said, her voice husky and focused.

"I'm so tired, so very, very tired," Sephony said.

"Sleep in Rolf's room. Come along, you can't stay here."

"I'm comfortable."

"You won't be for long." She tugged her out of the recliner and put an arm around her.

Upstairs in Rolf's room Sephony lay down on his seldom-used bed, on top of the covers. Peg drew the curtains and found a duvet.

"I'll leave a general sort of message for Marek," she said, tucking the duvet around her. "Ring me tomorrow."

"Thank you. I don't *feel* as if I'm crazy."

"You're not." Peg kissed her forehead.

"I don't know what I'd do without you."

Sephony slept, half woke a few times, heard voices, dreamed, and forgot her dreams.

She woke out of sorts and stumbled to the nearest lavatory. Her teeth were furry, her breath tasted foul. The house was empty. What did the family think of her, what message did Peg leave? She showered and dried on a blast of warm air.

Someone had set a breakfast place for her with an orange.

She ached as if a friend had died, as if the house had burned and she lost all the cassettes of the children's voices.

She had no appetite. Listen to music, Dr. Easton had said. She went to the computer in the video room and called up the classical music file. Adams, Cage, Johnston, Mahler, Messiaen. She chose Mozart's Quintet in G Minor, synthesized by Wen Qi, and entered the code. Music Service was a private, reliable system and the relay was swift. She lay on a floor pillow. The music was cool and clear; she slipped into melody and harmony, passing through tones and time, rising and falling, bewitched, but not content. Afterward she took a walk. She ate toast and the orange and listened to the first act of Gluck's *Orpheus*. The day passed; she was idle.

"Well, now — how are you?" Marek asked, when he came home.

"Sorry about yesterday," she said. "Sleeping through like that."

"No problem. I spoke to Easton. He says you're not even to cook this week. We'll manage."

"I don't see how," she said.

"Don't worry," he said heartily, "you're not needed at all."

"I can't say I like that."

"Why not? I'd be glad of a rest if it were me. I could bloody well use a rest."

"What did Peg say?"

"Headache . . . I don't know . . . who can read that woman's handwriting. What happened?"

"It was very strange. I'll tell you later."

Marek patted her on the head. "Are you allowed some sherry?"

She drew away. "I'd better not."

At supper the young were respectful and solicitous. Dote and Simon had cooked the main dish. They served her while Melani dashed about the kitchen making salad.

How beautifully they could behave when they were feeling generous. A patch of uncritical affection swelled like pincushion moss, perfecting the young into lively and clever beings. Then her emotion dried up and they stood exposed. Callous. Mocking their friends. Wheedling their father. Annoyed with her. She saw them clearly, like dull stones in a dry riverbed.

They made her think of ordeals, of feeling drugged on sugar — of the Great Drought and refusing to eat her puddings and being forced to eat sugar. Two years of forced feeding. Whatever was allowed under food rationing, her mother had argued, was nutritious. Fridays after lunch the kitchen robot — a tubular kiro named Edwin — brought to the table a little silver cup embossed with hideous vines. Her mother watched while Sephony escaped mentally, traveling through the universe as she swallowed the granules spoonful by loathsome spoonful. What did it have to do with the young?

She crumbled a piece of blue cheese. The others ate biscuits.

After dinner Sephony and Marek sat in the orange room. "You'll think I'm daft," she said.

"It won't be the first time," he said dryly. "Tell me what happened."

Sephony looked down at the Shirvan carpet — at stylized birds with wings like forks, and red flowers in their bellies.

"There was something in our bedroom. A kind of presence." She glanced at Marek. He looked severe and incredulous.

"Well, it was," she said defensively, "a presence and a well with a shining ladder. The presence wanted me to climb down into the well. I was terrified. But after I said no, I felt simply awful, as if I'd lost something irreplaceable."

"Good grief, Seph."

"Don't you believe me?"

"If you ask me, you should never have gone back to university."

"That's not the point."

"A mysterious presence in our bedroom . . ."

"I felt it, like you in this room, I could almost see it."

"That's rubbish."

"Things exist that can't be touched or fixed," she said desperately.

Marek gave her a suffering look. He clasped his large hands. "What do you want from me?" he asked softly, neutrally.

"Nothing," she said, forcing herself to sound firm. "It's quite all right, I'm sure I'll be fine in no time."

"We might take a holiday. Go to Korhogo." He tugged her out of the chair. "A good night's sleep and you'll feel better in the morning."

Inwardly she screamed in protest.

She put her arm through Marek's, her spirit careening down the hall, while she leaned her head against his comfortable, alienating shoulder.

Sephony walked along the stream in a fine rain, the geese waddling beside her. Shadowy trees dripped, the tall grass bent, mud squished underfoot. Vigorously, she slogged through the cow pasture and climbed Lilac Hill by way of the fish ponds. The rain cleared for a moment and she stopped at the top to smell the morning.

Closing her eyes for a moment, she saw an image of a riverbank and a swan scratching its tail. A forgotten figure appeared in profile, hands in pockets — a thin young man, shoulders hunched forward, intent on the swan. Amazed, she squinted at Aaron, her first love. Why did he arrive? The shining well was more important, the voice and the question of belief systems — that's what she needed to think about. But the images persisted. Aaron held out his slender brown arms and they strolled through Regent's Park. Burgundy tulips blazed; the rosebushes had been cut back. She lay with her head in his lap and they listened to Keats.

Where was memory stored? Some said it was outside the body, a file of personal and collective experience that one cued up. Others said memory was in the brain. Whatever, outside or in, people didn't waste time dredging up the past — life moved forward. Yet the past was one of the interests they had shared, it set them apart. She'd forgotten Aaron was linked to that aspect of herself. Thirty years ago.

Leaves hung, dark and wet, chestnut branches opaque and separate. Rain weighted berries and sky, the whole forested and pastured slope to the house pressed and dripped.

Home, in the grip of memory, she sat at her desk, cradling a steaming cup of tea.

"You are not permitted to marry him," her mother had said, "a family of criminals."

"What do you mean? They're the loveliest people."

Her parents had sat stiff as Egyptian royalty, their faces hard and glistening.

"They're Minos," her father said.

She had sunk into a chair, molded to its form, trying to connect her beautiful dark-skinned Aaron with the Minos in history videos — limping albinos, the human refuse of the

Norwich minoxine disaster, pale young bodies slumped in derelict housing blocks.

"That's ages ago," she'd said, "the Minos all died out."

"Sixty years is not ages," her mother said. "Bad blood will tell."

"But it was a dominant trait."

"Our grandchildren would be tainted."

"Don't you understand about genetics?"

"You see how thin he is," her mother had said, cold and triumphant.

Why hadn't she defied her parents? She sipped tea and judged her weakness, remembering the heavy perfume of guilt. There was something she hadn't done or had done — what was it? Something worse than cowardice, but she couldn't remember, only that she had crawled backward into darkness, into a many-years-long fall into despair.

She looked through her disks for a volume of Donne, slipped it in the cube, and cued "A Valediction: Forbidding Mourning." A thin, sexless voice intoned:

> Our two soules therefore which are one,
> Though I must goe, endure not yet
> A breach, but an expansion
> Like gold to ayery thinnesse beate.

Aaron had married a friend of her second cousin and disappeared from her life.

And if it was true, that their connection thinned without breaking? Their two years together rose to the surface, shadowy with vivid details, and she allowed herself the pain and pleasure of remembering. She longed to ring him up. I'll meet you in London . . . we can have lunch.

A vague memory nibbled and winked, of breaking with him in Regent's Park — his eyes hard with pain, her thumbs hiding in her fists. She bore the shame for an instant, whole and clear, but her words drowned in a sickly light. She couldn't remember what she said, only that she'd lied.

Perhaps after all these years she should ring him up.

Perhaps this was a time to tend the untended. Although surely he'd forgotten her, as in an hour she'd forget him again.

The hour passed and she didn't forget. He hovered in the doorway, a tall young man with jade green eyes and an ironic, self-deprecating smile. She remembered them making love. What was this preposterous indulgence, these immoral feelings? Why was she thinking about Aaron and not about the voice and the well? The answer was ridiculous. Marek didn't love her. What an absurd thought, after so many years.

The geese chased each other into the meadow, tromping the daffodils, clumsy and argumentative.

"Your belief system is run by a man who calls himself Reb Nacht," Peg said. "He's soulful and crabby, my informant says, and carries a positive aura."

"Reb Nacht?"

"It means Rabbi Night."

"How sinister."

"Do you think so?" Peg asked, surprised. "I thought you'd like the resonance."

"Don't you think belief systems died out for a good reason?"

"Life is cyclical."

"But surely we shouldn't have them again . . . religion and elections and all that?"

"I'm formed by the present cycle too, but yes, I can imagine others . . . yes." She glowered balefully. "This is hardly a perfect world."

"Hardly. If I go, what about Marek?"

"Include him, I suppose, to keep the peace. Although he'll be a fish out of water."

"He'll make an effort, he really will . . . he'll be a steady hand at the wheel."

"At what price," Peg said grimly. "I agree, though; you have to ask him. Getting involved on your own, well, it's better for you, but it works hell with marriage."

*   *   *

Limestone wrinkles mocked Sephony from the mirror. Strange face, strange eyes — those hooded blue gems — not hers. Something watery shimmering as the face filled the mirror to the edges — aging, widening, wrinkling — spreading beyond the frame. Sephony blinked and her own face snapped into the glass, her own brown eyes and smooth ruddy cheeks. Terrified, she tucked her hair behind her ears.

She lost her will; nothing surprised her. She was in the greenhouse sowing tomatoes in flats and found herself wanting to confide in Marek. She had a fantasy of phoning him at work, the digit lights slow, the connection delayed; even in fantasy the Triangle didn't care about utilities. The fantasy started positive — Marek glad and fascinated — and ended in despair — Marek resentful, asking was she ill or had she swallowed poison.

After dinner, though, she proposed a walk. He was wearing loose white coveralls — his clothes were always loose, his large frame hidden in folds of cloth.

They climbed to the top of Lilac Hill and sat on a log without speaking. She straightened her legs. The left ankle was thicker than the right.

Down the path, between chestnut trees, grackles limped and pecked, their feathers catching violet and black light.

"I'm getting used to the damn birds," Marek said.

Her tongue surprised her. "Do you remember Aaron?" she asked.

"Who?"

"You met him years ago at Andrea's wedding. Director of research at Genco."

"Tall chap?"

"Very thin."

"Ah, yes."

"We wanted to marry, but Mums and Dads wouldn't allow it." She said it flatly.

Marek looked stunned. "Marry who? What? That tall, thin fellow?"

"Yes, we planned on it."

"Odd, you never mentioned him." His voice was strangled.

Her thumbs tucked themselves into her fists. "He was a biologist . . . we loved poetry, history, old things. Aaron and I were different from everyone . . . I was different then." She sighed.

"What did your parents have against him?" He looked at her sharply, angrily, but she went on.

"They, ah, didn't approve of his family."

"Why not?"

She hesitated. "You know how Mums and Dads are."

Marek shifted explosively. She wanted to contain him; she had a perverse hunger to entice her own husband with this story. She told him about buildings she and Aaron worked to preserve, poetry they'd read. Aaron's name shattered on her tongue, shadows of buildings toppled; poems vaporized. But she couldn't stop.

"You certainly could have told me years ago," Marek said. "You didn't have to keep it secret."

"I was afraid you'd be hurt that I loved someone . . . oh, like that, not practical . . . that it would be a criticism of you."

"Well, it is, isn't it?"

The grackles limped toward the bank of the stream, pecking nervously. Telling the truth was exhausting.

"We've done all right," Marek said, "we get on all right, don't we?"

"Not really," she admitted in a small voice. "You're distant, absorbed in yourself, in your work. I didn't realize how distant you are until Aaron popped into my thoughts. There he was . . ."

"Well, I do have to work —"

"And as I thought about him it seemed to me that . . . you know . . . that you didn't love me. I was comparing, you see, remembering — oh, what it had been like." Her voice trailed away, but she looked straight at him. So often she stared off to the side, at his ear.

"That's nonsense, my dear," he said briskly. "You're not the least bit interested in what I do. You think I'm a clod because I don't listen to poetry." He reached out protectively and covered both her hands.

The heavy flesh felt oppressive, like a low ceiling or too many blankets.

"Next thing you'll be wanting to see him," he said with complacent humor.

"I've thought of it," she said earnestly. "The end was such a muddle."

"Ah." Anger reddened his face for a moment. "Was he offended by . . . whatever your parents objected to?"

"I didn't tell him," she whispered.

"You didn't tell him." He paused. "Must have been something horrendous."

She nodded.

"I can imagine the tone, at any rate."

"You've had your share."

"What was it about him, exactly?"

"Oh . . . an awful idea they had about his family."

"So I was second best."

"Who can say. That's meaningless."

"I hope I haven't been too much of a disappointment," he said.

"You've been a dear, really you have."

"I want to take care of you."

"Ah," Sephony said, "that's not what I need."

Marek looked baffled.

"I'd rather you . . . if only you would notice me instead of — oh, imposing yourself on me."

He turned away in silence. She wanted to withdraw her fingers from the cave of his hand, but she didn't want to hurt him. Best to change the subject.

"Peg wants me to make an appointment with that belief system leader in London, Reb Nacht," she said. "Would you go with me?"

"Is that what you mean by noticing?"

"In a way."

"Well, it's a lot of nonsense," he said gruffly. "But if you want me to, I suppose I could keep you company. As long as we both realize it's nonsense." He tucked her hair behind her ears, slowly, stroking each ear. "You look very nice."

"Do I?" She flexed her fingers; they were damp. "You haven't told me that in years. You look very nice, too."

"But sad. You look sad, Sephony."

"I need to think for a while," she said. "I'll stay here."

He stood up. "Shall I come back for you? It's getting dark."

"No, unless I'm not home in an hour. Unless I, you know, drift off."

"Right."

She watched his broad back receding down the hill, the geese waddling beside him. A gloved hand crawled under a patch of ivy.

Automatically she conjured up Aaron. He lurked, no longer "gold to ayery thinnesse beate," but a dry onion skin, lightly resting in her mind and ready to blow away. Clouds sailed into the afterglow. She rose, dusting the seat of her trousers, and started down the hill in the fading light.

The path tunneled and twisted, sending up shafts of light ahead, trees closing in, the ground lumpy and uncertain, her heart straining, tumbling her forward.

She ran into the garden and hid against the moonless side of a copper beech, setting her memory band to diary, holding it to her lips. "When you tell a secret," she whispered, "it becomes thin and gauzy. I've lost Aaron. Marek has him. I gave him away. All I have is his ghost. Why did I do that?"

CHAPTER 2

SEPHONY keyed her mother's phone number, the connection lights barely blinking between the last two digits. She unrolled a partially worked needlepoint belt in shades of blue, a present for Dote, and stretched it over her knee, waiting for Mums's voice to crackle through the gooseneck speaker.

"Sephony, my dear, I was beginning to worry."

"It's only five past, Mums."

"I was sure you'd forgotten. Well, I'll expect you Sunday at one."

Sephony pressed a folded strand of midnight blue wool between thumb and forefinger and pushed the eye of the needle over it. The belt was composed of small interlocking triangles shading from dark to light, midnight blue to sky blue, in waves of increasing and decreasing intensity.

"And the young will come?" Her mother's voice swooped, cracked, and fell.

"They're dreadfully busy with exams, you know."

"I don't want them to feel obligated, of course."

A cluster of puffy white hands crawled across the table, bumping into and over one another like newborn mice.

"How's Jason?" Sephony asked.

"His hip is worse, my dear, but he's using a stouter

cane. We found a marvelous carved one, a genuine moun-
taineer's cane — you know the kind, centuries old. Jason
adores it."

"I'm sure he looks dashing."

"Jason's not dashing. You can't call Jason dashing. Your
father was dashing, but not Jason, my dear."

"I think he's rather sweet."

"Sweet, yes, but not dashing."

"Mums, I must ring off now. Shall I make a strawberry
flan for dessert?"

"No, my dear, the menu is well in hand."

"Plain strawberries, then."

"No, no, your sister is bringing Irish moss. Sunday at one,
my dear, be punctual. Cheeribye."

Sephony sewed furiously, stabbing the needle into the
grid, pulling the stitches too tight. Irish moss, she thought, the
most drab, tasteless pudding. One puffy hand crawled up the
curved white neck of the speaker. The others scurried back and
forth as a group, tumbling over one another in manic blind-
ness. They used to tap Mums's face in the old video days.

Mums was a cold force — custodian of the right way,
dispenser of morals and traditions. Repressed anger coiled
through her like poison in the fine hairs of nettles. Within the
family she raged operatically, displaying emotional extremes:
benevolence and malice, generosity and greed, devotion and
cruelty. But her true weapon was silence. Sephony had holes in
her spirit. She thought of herself as a sieve, pocked by ab-
sences — withdrawn love, withheld gifts, and unanswered
questions. She couldn't penetrate Mums's sheen, couldn't
soften it; she had no influence whatever. The natural magne-
tism that should operate between mother and daughter was
disrupted. They flew apart. Yet she was held in check.

She threaded a strand of cobalt.

After breaking off with Aaron she'd worked on a reforesta-
tion project in Devon and had come home with a broken
wrist and hair so knotted it was cut to remove the tangles. Did

Mums's disapproval harden then? She returned to university but didn't finish; she married Marek — solid, respectable, and comfortable as a cousin — and switched loyalties.

Gauzy nets of fog flew past the window, ripped by the wind.

She shouldn't blame herself anymore. No blame, said Peg, an idea she got from the *I Ching*. Easy to say. Her parents were — what was it? Lazy? Fearful? When she and her brother and sister came of age they found themselves playing roles that had been prepared, without their realizing it, since infancy. Mugs was established as the wise son and Ari the good daughter; Sephony was cast as the ungrateful one, her sense of fair play taken for malice and her opinions twisted into reproaches. No escape from roles after marriage; two disputes with Mums sealed her — sealed them all — like insects in amber.

When she and Marek married they spent their first Christmas with her family on schedule. Dads was ill that year — his first illness — and festivities were canceled. She and Ari read to him while Mugs and Marek played endless rounds of Virtuality. Was Mums bored without her joints of lamb and black puddings, did she feel empty without that glittering silverine tree? Christmas was such a frenzy. Lost in antiquity was the pagan's defiance of the winter solstice. Lost in history was the birth of a child. Christmas defeated darkness by celebrating accumulation, and since the family business — Brackett's Stores — profited, her parents were usually very merry. She wished at the time and since that they could always have such a peaceful holiday, free from devouring enthusiasm.

Nearly a year later — it was autumn — she was having tea with Mums. She remembered holding a rose-patterned cup in both hands.

"This Christmas," her mother said, "will make up for last. What do you think of a New Year's Eve party — costumes, perhaps, and music . . ."

Sephony had sighed into her cup, both pinkies jutting stiffly like horns. "Marek and I are spending the holidays up at Whittles."

Her mother's eyes glittered dangerously. "Dreadful name," she said.

"Remember we're taking it in turns," she said tensely. "One year with you, one year with Marek's family."

"You didn't spend last Christmas with us," her mother said flatly, both fists on the table edge.

"We were there — only Christmas was missing."

"Your father was ill and now he's much better."

"But it's not your turn. Last year was your turn."

"Surely you value family tradition."

"Next year, Mums." She poured another cup of tea and forgot to strain it. Leaves floated on the milky fluid.

"Nonsense. We'll expect you on the twenty-fourth." Her mother snapped a biscuit in half and laid the pieces on her dessert plate, nervously brushing her thumbs across her fingertips.

"I'm sorry, Mums, but taking turns is part of marriage."

"So you're renouncing your obligations." Her mother's chin made rigid folds against her neck.

"What about Marek?" she asked.

"He owes everything to you. You brought a very substantial portion to the marriage."

"What has that to do with obligations to his parents?"

"You see, you respect his obligations, but not your own."

With a tiny silver spoon, she scooped tea leaves onto her saucer. Some sank and floated up again, like flies' wings. The soggy heap on the saucer oozed brown. She stared into the flecked, milky liquid, her nerves scraped by the sound of her mother chewing a biscuit.

After Sephony returned from holidays with Marek's family, Mums was as watchful as a betrayed woman, her declarations of love harsh and tinged with bitterness.

The second dispute was even more trivial.

Ari was only sixteen at the time and adored Sephony. It was a Saturday, bright and clear, and an expedition was organized to the ruins at Highcliffe. While Marek helped her parents stow lunch in their craft, she and Ari leaned against the shed, their faces raised to the sun like sunflowers. They wore white and held hands. Dads backed out of the shed; Mums got in beside him and adjusted her hat. Ari gave her hand a little squeeze, folded herself into the craft and plopped down in back beside Mugs. Across the driveway Marek waited in their little beige Minitro. Sephony waved to her family and walked toward him, shielding her eyes against the glare.

A window hummed. "Where are you going?" her mother called.

"Pardon?" she said, turning.

"Where are you going? Get in."

"I am," she said, tapping the hot bonnet of her craft.

Mums leaned her elbow on the window frame. "I mean with us. On a family outing we fly together, the five of us."

"But that's ridiculous," Sephony said.

"Marek?" her mother trilled. "Sephony is traveling with us."

"No, Mums," she said, "I'm going with my husband." She felt childish and pedantic using the possessive.

"Your husband," said her mother sarcastically. "Your husband. Where's your loyalty to us?"

Her father turned off the motor and strode across the driveway, nervously stroking his bald head. He was a short man with a narrow brown mustache.

"Sephony, this is important to your mother. We're seldom together, anymore."

Like a baby toddling to freedom, Sephony stubbornly walked around the helmet-shaped craft and sat in the passenger seat. Marek patted her knee, isolating her in a heady, uncertain alliance.

Marek leaned out his window. "The route past Portschurch should be fairly clear," he said affably.

"I always obeyed my mother," her father drawled. He turned smartly, hands clasped behind his back.

At Highcliffe Mums sulked beneath her hat brim while she and Ari gathered stones on the beach. They climbed the cliff to the ruins and raced like goats along a tree-shaded ridge.

Later in the week she rang Ari for a cooking report.

Ari's face was orange and brown on the failing video screen, cheeks and chin askew, sliding to the right. All video screens were failing.

"Was the meal a disaster?" Sephony asked.

A ripple transformed Ari into a cubist portrait.

"Mums and Dads liked the chicken sauce for a while. Then Mums asked did I have the recipe from Guides and I said I had it from you. And then she wouldn't eat it. She pushed it off to the side and ate kelp and rice."

A whiff of family air came from Ari's troubled face, like the acrid air in a damp room where shoes are moldering.

"Anything else?"

There was a click of suppressed thought.

"Uh, that's about it."

"I see . . . we'll try something else Saturday," she said lightly, afraid of Ari's reply.

"Mums says I'm to have Virtuality lessons Saturday afternoons."

"But that's our day."

"I have to."

"Oh, Ari, it's so stupid."

"You know what she's like."

Sephony pushed, but only slightly. "When will we see each other?"

Ari chewed a hangnail. "Maybe after school or something."

The smell was strong.

"Must run now," Ari said.

"Oh, yes, so must I," she said, having already begun to slip backward.

Their relationship stiffened. Ari visited occasionally, her conversation guarded, her face tense.

"Mums says you're a bad influence," she admitted.

Their love turned to embarrassment, then apathy, then hostility. Heirlooms Mums had promised her went to Ari for wedding and birthday gifts — a jade bottle, two jade horses,

and a Tiffany lamp. Defiantly, she began collecting Ch'ing dy-
nasty jades more exquisite than the lost inheritance, including
a snuff bottle with a delicate chain dangling from the handle —
the entire object miraculously carved from a single stone.

Sephony folded the belt and tied the skeins of wool. The
hands vanished. Outside the window a delicate pink rain fell,
a dry rain that left the earth parched.

Isn't Mums adventurous, she thought charitably, approaching seventy-five and having a lover. My friend . . . my
friend Jason. So discreet. Jason, age ninety-three. Never acknowledged as her lover, never invited for the main courses
when the family comes to dinner. My friend Jason, how nice of
Jason to drop by for dessert and coffee.

Sephony went out to the greenhouse. The seedlings were
doing well. The beans would be ready to set out in a day or
two, the green peppers in about a week. She pinched tomato
leaves. I'll fly down to Portschurch, she thought, and get stones
for her birthday — brownish stones like potatoes. They'll be a
nice change from granite.

Mums's painting wasn't serious, although she spent so
much time at it. What began as therapeutic doodling after Dads
died became an obsession, requiring a studio. Mums painted
circular designs on smooth stones — bold disks ringed by
lighter or darker bracelets — bright red, for example, ringed
by yellow, then purple, then black. The colors were symbolic
and their placement significant. White meant truth; yellow was
optimism; red was power; blue, secrecy; orange, courage;
green, growth; purple, deceit; and black, nihilism. Each ring,
Mums believed, had a moral effect. As for repetition, all artists
have recurring images, she said, look at Albers.

Why does Mums draw circles? Sephony wondered, wa-
tering trays under the seedlings with a thin hose. Why does she
like repetition? A composer named Erik Satie wrote short repetitive phrases and ate only white foods on white plates. It
had something to do with control. She left the greenhouse and
walked across the lawn. The rain had stopped, petals were

falling from the apple trees. Something eluded her, something that would be clear if it weren't about her mother.

Since telling Marek about Aaron, Sephony felt a craving now and then to tell him her thoughts. It was a kind of narcotic, a hopeful repetition, an experiment in forestalling despair.

They flew in the outside lane over green earth parceled by hedgerows. Coming up was the town of Ufton Nervet, clusters of red brick and tile.

"I was thinking about Mums, how she holds us in our places," she said. On a rubbled field, twin towers spewed thick clouds of white smoke.

"Mothers are like that," Marek said.

"Yours isn't."

Inside her a cylinder opened and closed its curved door, opened and closed, to talk or not, to reveal more or not.

"Do you like her?" she asked.

"My mother?"

"Mine. Do you?"

"Hilary's a decent old girl. Lots of backbone." He paused. "One doesn't like your mother, one respects her. Of course, I keep my opinions to myself about all those damned cows' eyes she paints. I suppose you like them."

"I can't stand them."

"You never told me."

"I was just thinking the other day they express the worst side of Mums — glossy and rigid."

"Oh, yes, pink plus purple equals honesty, that sort of rubbish."

"Not pink," Sephony said. "She doesn't mix white with anything. No mixed messages."

"You actually know what all the colors mean?"

"Yes," she drawled.

"Amazing."

"She tells everyone."

"But who listens?"

"Her painting is good value. It keeps her busy and she gets attention and even money."

"Which she doesn't need," said Marek.

They were silent for a while. The Thames curved below. Sephony clasped her hands and stroked a knuckle with her thumb. Having begun experimentally, she risked continuing.

"Do I hold on to the young?" she asked, her voice light and nervous.

Marek looked startled. "Well, I suppose you do . . . yes, I suppose you do." He nodded as if entertaining a problem in metal fatigue. "Asking Rolf does he eat properly and where does he wash his clothes. At twenty-two and about to be married." He laughed his short barking laugh.

"That's not what I meant by holding on. I mean, do I make them afraid of me?"

"Afraid of you?"

"Why, yes."

"Who could be afraid of you?"

"But I'm so critical."

"Oh, people get annoyed with you, but afraid? No . . . no one's afraid of you."

"Well, that's good," she said.

"Can't be afraid of a rabbit." Marek laughed. "Wait a minute. The geese. I think Doug and Harry are a tad afraid of you."

"Marek, really. You're making fun of me."

"Quite right, my dear."

Sephony continued, her cheeks hot, "I'm afraid of Mums, no doubt about it."

"But you take your own stands."

"Yes, and then it falls."

"What falls?"

"The rod."

"Ah. Just a moment. Fellow is passing too close. There now, what rod? Another of those things you see?"

"I don't see it, but it's there. It hovers in the air about two meters above my head, horizontally, a sort of croquet stick." Her voice was breathy.

Marek raised a bushy eyebrow.

"It's there all the time," she said.

"What does it do?" he asked flatly.

"It hovers."

"It hovers," he repeated.

"So I hunch over a bit, you see? If I were to stand up straight I wouldn't be ready for it. Whenever I disagree with Mums, it strikes right here." She touched the back of her neck.

"Enough real things to be afraid of without imaginary croquet sticks."

Sephony slitted her eyes. "I remember when it was gone, it was lovely to stand up straight and breathe freely, just lovely. When I was pregnant the first time. I don't suppose you noticed Mums was different when I was pregnant."

"No, I couldn't say so." He cleared his throat.

"Everything I did was good," she said softly. "My ideas about a nurse, about decorating the room, the clothes I bought — everything I thought or planned, all my little methods, she approved of." She stopped, but her tongue went on. "At first I thought she'd changed. I'm a grown-up woman, I thought, I'm pregnant, there'll be harmony between us, we'll be equals. I remember we laughed together. And even after Rolf was born she was lovely while I was getting used to tending him. But after five months we disagreed about weaning and I insisted on my way and suddenly her face closed and she stood straighter than usual and there it was, the stick had snapped into place and I hunched over and buried my nose in Rolf's soft little neck."

He frowned. "How do you remember all those details, my dear?"

"It was the same with Simon. All light and love until he started walking, and then snap, the stick was back."

"What's the point, then?"

"Do you remember how nervous I was after Dote was

born? How we had to go away and leave her with the nurse for three weeks?"

"Yes, indeed. After Melani, too. We went to some island or other."

She spoke softly. "The stick was going to hover, like cancer after remission, like madness after an interval of sanity." She paused. "That's when I understood she didn't care about me at all. She was protecting the unborn — that's what her niceness was all about — she didn't want me to miscarry."

"Don't turn her into an ogre. She's just your mother, and quite old."

"She wants us all to be extensions of her. The row about my not flying to Highcliffe with them — do you remember that one?"

"No. Probably she doesn't either."

"Flesh of my flesh, blood of my blood. The newborns were very important to her. I was done with, used up. It makes me feel all twisted knowing my mother loves our young more than she loves me." Sephony bit her lip. "It's a queer feeling," she said softly, "it goes very deep. It's rather like jealousy."

"Oh, come now, Seph. Jealous of our own children."

"Something like that. Just a tiny feeling, a little apple pip of a feeling. I think that's why I'm so critical of them. On the outside there's a razor edge of hostility. I love them very much, but I'm very critical."

They turned off the A42 airspace and flew along the A19.

She felt self-conscious. She'd made a fool of herself, talking really to herself. What was she going on about? "I shouldn't bother you with all this," she said.

"Bit difficult to listen and drive," he said, and seemed relieved. "You analyze too much, my dear. But it'll pass when you're feeling better."

She grunted softly in the back of her throat.

They rotored up her mother's drive and nosed the fence.

"I feel a mess," she said.

"Well, if we sit here too long they'll think we're quarreling." He patted her shoulder.

She took a deep breath. "Where's my jacket?" she asked.
"That it behind you?"
"Right," she said briskly.
They walked to the house, space between them.

After lunch, while Mums was in the studio with Jason, they sat around the blue aramid coffee table and planned her birthday party as if it were a surprise, balancing rose-patterned china cups on their knees. Ari took charge in a sweeping way while her husband, Gus, nodded agreeably. Mugs and his wife, Psilla, so thin they could fit on one chair together, radiated critical intensity.

"Starting over each time," said Mugs. "Why can't I persuade you to keep records?"

Her brother had no facial hair. There was something repulsive about his smooth skin — his face so much like hers, except for the flat, tight mouth. He was a perfectionist. He wore gray. His hands repelled her — wide with short fingers, their smooth muscularity suggesting monstrous efficiency and some hidden obscenity. He had inherited Brackett's Stores and was accustomed to ruling with calm, absolute authority.

"I'll do two main courses and two desserts," Ari said, ignoring him. "And Gus will order the wine. Psilla?"

Psilla, pale and ethereal, spoke as if reciting poetry. "Creamed lobster," she intoned, emphasizing each syllable. "Cauliflower with tofu. Raspberry Pavlova."

"Super," said Ari. "Seph?"

"There's just the first course, then," she said gallantly. "Pâté, possibly, or do you think soup?"

"Soup is a good starter," said Gus. "I like soup."

"Soup, then," said Sephony. "Breads, of course, and pureed peas with mint. And a wheel of Stilton. I'll see to the basmati when we arrive. Shall we all bring our silver serving bowls?"

"No, everything comes with the service," said Ari.

"How many are we inviting this year?" asked Marek.

"Forty-six," said Ari.

"That's not too many for the reception room," said Sephony, hoping for elegance rather than a windy picnic.

"We're hiring a tent," said Ari.

Sephony dwindled and contracted, checked by a shrug or a twitch of the lips. Mums would say "Didn't Ari do a splendid job?" with brief nods at Mugs and herself. A limp hand settled beside the biscuits.

"Pity Mums doesn't trust robos to serve," said Mugs. "They're much less expensive."

"You don't want that," Marek said. "We went to a dinner last week and the robo dropped a whole platter of fish — the main course — fillets and sauce all over the floor."

"Who was that?" Ari asked.

"The Watleys, do you know them?"

"The Triangle is stagnating," said Gus. A placid man, a dealer in gems, rugs, and rare cassettes, he sharpened aggressively over economic issues. "Standards are met, yet products deteriorate. We move ahead and go backwards at the same time."

"There's a chap in Dorset," said Marek, "who could produce domestic robos — made some prototypes — but he can't get a building permit."

"And the phones," said Ari irrelevantly. "The time between digits gets longer and longer."

"The Triangle has its ways," said Sephony, "but still, the phones . . . yes." The collective mood called for an offering. "You start keying and all goes swiftly and you think, thank goodness, there'll be no wait this time, and then there's a bit of a wait before five and a still longer one before six and an interminable wait before seven."

"The phones are only an aspect of — I'm sorry to say — the Triangle's worst problem," Gus said calmly. "Production depends on a wider utilization of the Dulls."

"The Dulls," said Ari. "Who wants human machines wandering about? — don't start in on that."

"They're only half monsters," Gus said with a teasing look at Sephony. "Good workers, aren't they, Seph?"

"They're just fine," she said uncomfortably. She was rather fond of Alf and Alfie.

"The Triangle has its ways," said Marek, echoing Sephony. "You can't question or the whole system falls apart."

"It *is* falling apart," said Gus.

"Not the system itself," said Psilla, "the system is intact."

"We wouldn't want a return to elections," said Sephony.

"France does," said Gus.

"I agree more Dulls should be released into the private sector," said Mugs sharply. "If I could use them instead of robos, I wouldn't have had to sell off those two shops in the North."

"They're small and horrid," said Ari.

"Well, enough of that," said Mugs. "Bring in Mums and Jason."

Jason filled the doorway as he came through, a ninety-three-year-old hairy giant with a blunt red nose and rimless glasses. He leaned heavily on a stout cane.

"My little conspirators," Mums said brightly. Her blue eyes darted aggressively as if searching for enemies. Wrinkles feathered her cheeks from eyes to jaw.

"We have to hope it doesn't rain," said Ari.

"It never rains on my birthday. Jason, my dear, sit down."

Jason dropped his weight carefully into a white pedestal chair with a red seat, placing his cane across his knees. He was kind and generous — content, in his old age, to adore a woman for her vitality.

"Some coffee, Jason?" asked Sephony.

"I'll do it," said Ari, snatching the jug.

"A few sweets, Sephony," said Jason, his glasses magnifying his eyes into an indeterminate expression.

"Your new cane has splendid carvings," she said.

Ari returned with the jug. "Sephony wanted the party indoors, Mums," she said, "but I said you'd prefer the tent."

"Oh, yes, it's so wonderfully old-fashioned to have a tent party, so like the garden parties one reads about. A lovely old-fashioned tent party. Even though July is not as warm as it used to be, but we don't mind, do we? We're made of sterner stuff. Who said that? 'We're made of sterner stuff.' "

"Churchill," said Jason in a gravelly, high-pitched voice. "Or Spencer-Martin. Same house, you know. Or was it Kipling?"

"Well, thank you, my dears, for taking so much time for your poor dear mother." Her smile faded. She looked away, absorbed in some unpleasant thought.

"What is it, Mums?" Sephony asked warily.

"I was thinking about that poor woman who vanished in Regent's Park on Thursday."

"I heard about it," Ari said. "Out walking her dogs and they all simply vanished."

"None of us is safe," said Mums.

"I don't know why they don't simply raze the damn Jungle," Marek said, "it should have been done years ago."

"That wouldn't help," Mums said. "We'll never feel safe."

"And there was that young man beaten to death," Psilla whispered.

"Such a grand zoo it was," said Mums emphatically, "with lions and elephants. And giraffes. You loved the giraffes, children. And now the ghosts of all those murdered animals are taking revenge on us. I'm not a foolish old lady, any number of perfectly sensible people agree. Don't they, Jason?"

He cleared his throat. "Yes, my dear, but I'm certain there's a criminal element in there."

The Jungle, Sephony thought, was one of those horrors everyone ignored, right in the heart of Regent's Park — quietly dangerous like radioactive waste. During the Great Drought, when food and water were scarce and foreign animals were an unaffordable luxury, the zoo was closed. Everyone saw the killings on video. Lions backing away from the laser, chimps smiling in terror; one animal after another facing death — tigers, elephants, gorillas, rhinos, gone in a flash and a hiss. "For the good of the nation," the newsreader had said. Everyone felt guilty, as if they'd massacred the animals themselves. Only the small foraging animals were saved, sealed in behind a plexiglas wall. News reports said they were well and reproducing and everyone felt better. And then, somehow, people forgot. Somehow the zoo turned into the Jungle, a fearsome place. There was a menace inside, nameless and horrible. Some dreadful miasma seeped out and wafted over the wall, some loathsome quality that made people hurry on when they came within sight of it. What lurked inside? An insane asylum? A prison? Diseased people? Diseased animals? Mutations? Something leaked out. People disappeared. Mutilated bodies were found near the wall. Were any of the stories true?

"It's four o'clock," said Sephony. She couldn't bear to hear Mums go on about the Jungle.

"You're always the first to leave," said Mums, holding out a veined hand that trembled slightly.

"We promised to help Melani with maths."

"Such a dutiful mother."

The family walked them to the door. From the driveway Sephony looked back at them, clustered under the portico. They were a marine aggregate, a sea anemone waving tentacles. Sephony waved back. The craft, scattering puffs of dust, rose into the air.

Melani called as they came into the hall. "Mumsy," she drawled, loping down the stairs, "you had a phone call." She looked like an impatient boy, toes pointed inward, hands in pockets.

"From?"

"I don't know. He was rude, he wouldn't leave a name."

"Oh! What sort of voice?"

"Deep. Stodgy. Something weird about him."

"For me? Not for me or your father?"

"For you. I asked his name and he said he'd ring again."

"How did he refer to me?"

"Mrs. Berg-Benson."

"A salesman, most likely," she said. "Have you done your maths?"

"It was such a lovely day, I took Plumsie for a gallop." She looked defiantly hopeful.

How odd, a child of hers in love with a horse. Almost no one rode horses in their district. Some were left years ago, and Melani asked for one and trained the animal by instinct.

"That won't get you a high score," Sephony said. "Off with you. I'll start dinner." She went into the kitchen. Who had called? How annoying to have loose threads.

Over the next few weeks the call came again, always when she was out. Each time the caller asked for Mrs. Berg-Benson and refused to leave his name. Dote said he sounded neutral, she didn't think he was a salesman or anyone they knew. Simon said he sounded mysterious and a bit hostile, but that was pure Simon.

Sephony and Peg splashed through puddles left by a June shower, Peg wearing yellow boots and Sephony green. "Surely the voice that said 'Come' wouldn't need a phone," Sephony said.

"But it might *like* one," Peg said, "it might be mischievous. Or it might be adapting. A spacecraft using ultra- or infra-sound frequencies would be inaudible — and if it had a different color spectrum it would also be invisible . . . the voice could actually be hovering overhead this very moment."

"Very poetic. An invisible being calls directly into my phone line, adjusting his sound frequency. And why me?"

"I think one of your other selves may be living in its own continuum."

"In space?"

"Possibly . . . or the enthusiast in you is alive on earth — perhaps she's an orange or a goat. Or perhaps her husband was forced into a space migration and he's miraculously escaped and is trying to contact you."

"You may have any number of selves, Peg, but I have just the one."

Undaunted, Peg scanned the neighborhood, her large violet eyes glinting wickedly at the Cartwell house, a large Victorian brick house with two wings — an eighteenth-century thatched cottage on one side and a twentieth-century ranch on the other. A bubble enclosed the structure, with its incongruous roofs and windows. There was sharp disagreement in the neighborhood over bubbles.

"Roger Cartwell could be phoning desperately and secretly, so infatuated he's barely civil to you at council meetings . . . have you noticed what an adolescent he is? On the other hand, odd people do wander about. Someone might be making a nuisance of himself."

"Watching me leave, you mean, and phoning when I'm out."

"Boring, too boring," Peg said, waving the idea away.

"I tell you truly, Peg, your ideas aren't as crazy as my own — I don't believe it's a real person."

Peg laughed, a deep husky laugh. "You see? The enthusiast lives. Is a spirit phoning your children?"

"Perhaps."

"But the spirit in your room didn't actually speak."

"No. And the voice on the phone is a real voice. And the young hear it. So it's not the same. But I'm convinced it comes from somewhere else — I wouldn't dare say it to anyone but you, Peg, they'd think I was daft."

Peg ran her nervous fingers through thick brown hair and kicked a stone into a puddle.

"Things lose their skins, sometimes," Peg said softly. "Sometimes I'm afraid to touch a cup because it's swarming with horrid little black filings."

"Yes."

They exchanged a look. "Are you dreading your mother's party?" Peg asked.

"Ari says she has a surprise, some people who haven't been before. Maybe it won't be so tedious."

"How about Reb Nacht?"

"I'm sorry . . . I haven't phoned him yet."

"All the belief systems have their offices in the same house. It's called the Society for the Preservation of Ancient Thought."

"I like that."

"Get in touch with him, don't moon about it."

"After Mums's party."

"You could tell Reb Nacht about the phone calls."

"Oh, the voice will be quite enough for him."

They walked in silence through a patch of forest. Slender oaks grew beside their elders. Chestnuts and copper beeches arched overhead. A few tardy bluebells struggled in the undergrowth beside a cross-hatching of fallen branches. Stunted blackberry bushes hedged the road, filling ditches that had once drained runoff. They emerged from the fragmented shadows. On their left, grazing land and cropland stretched to the A4. On their right were houses. The sound of craft grated on the wind.

"How's Veronica?" Sephony asked. "Is she going to pass any subjects at all?"

"Lunar geography barely but music with high marks. I think she may have perfect pitch . . . I'll have her tested. With her remarkable sensitivity to all kinds of music she could focus on flute and then all those other subjects won't matter."

"She'll sort herself out in the long run. She lacks confidence mainly, don't you think? I have faith in Veronica."

Peg bit her lower lip. "If I can just keep her interested in something . . ."

They said good-bye at the garden gate. Peg strode away with the tension of a former dancer — in a short padded jacket and tight black trousers, her head down and her shoulders hunched against her private demons.

The Society for the Preservation of Ancient Thought. Sephony went up to her study. Terrible thoughts were preserved in Veronica's sensory memory. Peg didn't talk about it, only told the story once. Returning home early from a dance tour, she heard ratlike squeals from Veronica's room — and found the child naked on her grandfather's moving lap, her face screwed in pain and disgust, an expression she still wore. I'm not doing anything, Peg's father said. Molesting her? Trying to rape her? Peg couldn't say. The bestial negation went beyond rape and molesting — her own father perverting her child's basic impulses for life, forcing her into a state of nonbeing, gouging her, emptying her. Peg gave up dancing. Veronica's trauma was buried, never discussed. She became fearful and demanding; ate bark and grasses; ripped her clothes.

Sephony nervously lined up cassettes on her desk. She too carried such a touch in her flesh — not a devastating violation, but one that nagged like an old splinter. A hungry and insistent imprint on her arms, a soft jealous imprint from an old man with incomplete emotions, needing to touch a girl child. Why face him now? He was dead, harmless. She hadn't thought about him in years. Let him sleep, why make a fuss about it?

Roughly, she pulled out the slide album and called up an old photo.

The little screen brought up Cousin Maurice and Aunt Hazel, stiff in their wedding photo, taken by Dads. Aunt Hazel, whose innocent look lasted years after the wedding, clutched a womb-shaped purse embossed with daisies. She wore a jacket embroidered with tiny pearls and a cap of braided feathers. Cousin Maurice smiled smugly and sadistically, fat jowls pressed into his neck. Thin gray hair shone on his scalp. His egg-shaped body was encased in a tight brown coverall.

As a child, chastised for grumbling about him, all she could say was "I can't stand Cousin Maurice."

He was the bête noire of her childhood, the shadow that terrifies — expanding and dwindling, advancing and retreating in the dark. In front of her parents he assaulted her with smiles and pats. As she grew older he reached up into her sleeves, stroking and pinching the flesh just above her elbows. He held her between his knees, smiling hungrily, his eyes stony behind gold-rimmed glasses, asking questions about school, his voice insidious and loathsome.

"He's a dear," her mother would reply, "and unmarried and will remember all of us."

At fifty-seven Cousin Maurice married a woman his age, a Miss Hazel Hill, daughter of the lord mayor of Oxford. She was timid and had liver spots on the backs of her hands and grieved for the children she would never have. She wanted to adopt an orphan. Cousin Maurice insisted that Sephony visit them in Oxford for a week, and her parents forced her to go.

She remembered everything, beginning with dinner. Cousin Maurice and Aunt Hazel were stationed at opposite ends of a long table; she was flanked by empty chairs. They made conversation. An ancient clock ticked. She ate the main course.

"You haven't finished your peas," Cousin Maurice said softly.

Four dull peas lingered on her plate.

"That's a good girl," he said.

She speared one awkwardly.

"And the next one. Good girl. You want to be a good girl, don't you? Doesn't she, Hazel? Eat the last one, my pet, that's the way."

The following morning she played the piano for Aunt Hazel's aged mother. Lady Hill lived in a darkened room among plants that grew without sunlight. Trailing ivy grew there, and ebony spleenwort and maidenhair fern. Pampered by damp warm air, the plants were self-absorbed like sick people. Lady Hill herself was as ghostly as an Indian pipe, planted in a wicker armchair under ivy, her translucent hands quivering lightly on cane-wrapped arms.

Commanded in a low, quavering voice to play something, Sephony had tiptoed through plants and shadows to a curved box on thick legs, afraid to disturb the exhausted living things. She lifted the lid. The keyboard looked familiar. She struck a key. The sound died. She struck another.

"There's something wrong with it," she had called politely.

Lady Hill had gestured impatiently toward the base of the instrument at three brass pedals.

Haltingly, on this strange piano with dying tones, she played two short Bartók pieces, striking the keys with much effort. She did not like old music; it was about human life, about activities and feelings. She liked modern music, which was about cosmic things — the colors of a sunset, the seasons, and planetary movements — expressed in sound clusters that dissolved and little high-pitched melodies that winked. She tried a simple piece by Wen Qi, doing her best with the sustaining pedal, but the tones were truncated and she could not get any satisfaction. Her fingers felt clumsy and tired.

"I'm sorry," she had apologized. "I'm used to a synthesizer."

Lady Hill sighed. "I will be happy to hear you play again tomorrow," she had said. "Don't be afraid to repeat yourself. I shall not mind. I shall not even remember. Good day, my dear."

She held out a pale translucent hand.

The way out was through a video room between Lady Hill's room and the hallway. Cousin Maurice was pacing up and down, wearing only his underpants. He had thin hairy legs and a puffy belly. She had never seen a grown man in trollies, certainly not her father. She wanted to run, but she was transfixed. Where was Aunt Hazel? Her eyes dropped to the part of his body she least wanted to see. His trollies were white and very short; thick black hair curled around the edges. He clasped his hands behind him and rocked back and forth. She tried to concentrate on his glasses, on the gold rims and grayish lenses, the stony eyes obscured by reflections. But her eyes kept dropping to his pubic hair.

"I have to go to my room," she said.

He came toward her and stroked her arms, standing well away, bending slightly at the waist.

"That's a good girl, that's a good girl," he said.

Sephony turned off the slide album.

Hands. Hands. Her father's hands were larger than life. Her mother's hands were slender and knobby. Cousin Maurice had puffy fingers, white and sadistic, like slugs. She looked at her own clasped hands, the hands of a keen gardener, the right thumb stroking the first two knuckles of the left hand. When she saw hands, whose were they?

CHAPTER 3

THE PINK PARTY TENT on Mums's perfectly cropped lawn billowed and exhaled in the breeze. The herbaceous border shone in triumphant state — red pom-pom dahlias, fuchsias, purple foxglove, and a stand of rare red-heart yellow gladiolus. The roses were in exhibition form. Sephony wore a lime green cotton shirt and pale blue trousers that floated around her ankles. It was a lovely day, sunny and cool, the party was certain to be a success.

Having given instructions in the kitchen about heating the soup and vegetables, she found her mother in the drawing room with Marek and the young and a handful of relatives. Mums was elegant in a long-sleeved black silk tunic and white silk trousers, her silver hair a radiant, rippled cap. She wore her pearls.

"So there you are," said her mother, gesturing with outstretched arms. She radiated nervous energy.

"Happy birthday, Mums," Sephony said, kissing her on each cheek. "The roses look spectacular. Even the Snowfires bloomed just for the occasion."

Her mother smiled, holding Sephony at arm's length, critically looking her up and down. "An interesting combination . . . blue and green . . . I would never have thought of it."

Sephony fought against feeling reduced.

Mums glided away. Drinks were being served on the terrace as well as in the drawing room. Near and distant relatives arrived, old friends greeted Mums and one another. Soon the room was quite full. People moved outdoors, those who had been outdoors came in. There was a nice steady hum of voices. Sephony leaned against a table, sipping sherry and talking with her brother-in-law, Gus. She felt a chill. There was a chill coming from somewhere.

"Do you feel it?" she asked Gus.

"Feel what?"

"The chill."

"I was thinking it's too warm in here."

"Oh," said Sephony.

Gus stepped back. "You're not getting ill, are you?"

"I think not. Just a bit chilly."

She had been staring at the back of a man who was talking with her cousin Andrea. A narrow back, a trifle stooped. A long neck jutted forward, the head was capped with curly black hair. The ears were rather prominent. The man waved his arms when he talked and nodded his head for emphasis. She had seen all that before. He turned, smiling. Her fingers froze around the stem of her glass. Her feet too were frozen. She did not know how it had suddenly become winter. He saw her and his smile disappeared. They looked at each other calmly across the room. He said something briefly to Andrea and came toward her. He was crossing the tundra, there was a snowstorm, winds blew against him, making his way difficult, but he came, slowly, and then he stood in front of her. He took her hand, the one that was not frozen around the stem of the sherry glass.

"Hello, Sephony," he said, as if it had been yesterday.

"Hello, Aaron," she said.

"How are you?" he asked. His pale green eyes were glowing.

"Cold. I mean, fine. Very well, in fact. And you?"

"It's good to see you. I knew I'd see you."

"I recognized you from the back."

"Did you?" His eyes flickered.

"Yes."

"You look . . . you've scarcely changed."

"Neither have you."

"Can I get you some more sherry?"

"No. No, thank you." With an effort she set the glass on the table behind her. He let go of her hand.

"How is Marek?" he asked awkwardly.

"He's fine. And Sybil?"

"Fine."

"The young?"

"Fine. And yours?"

"They're all here for a change, even the eldest."

"How many do you have?" he asked.

"Four. Two boys and two girls. And you?"

"Three girls. The two younger ones are here."

There was a bubble between them but their voices were ordinary. That was what struck her, even as they spoke; on a day in July we're chatting about this and that and our eyes are formal and our voices are normal and although time is a bit slow, there's nothing unusual about it.

"I'm so pleased," she said, smiling.

For a moment he looked startled. "Tell me about yourself," he said. "Shall we walk outside?"

They left by the side door. "I'm finishing my university degree," she said.

"Didn't you finish . . . ah . . . then?"

"No," she said, embarrassed. "I'm studying ancient history. It's fascinating, but very difficult."

"I shouldn't think you'd find history difficult."

"Not the material. Finding the time, you know, to do everything. You know how it is. Meals and the young and the farm and committees and all. You know." She smiled up at him, blinking, feeling a tightness around her mouth. None of it was what she wanted to say.

"Oh, yes," he said. "Quite."

They chatted about his work, his daughters. She mar-

veled at how well they functioned. There was an upper layer of
language that covered the moment adequately. Subjects were
limited to the present; ideas tinkled like crystal. They talked
about gardening, the economy, and their health. A bell rang for
lunch.

"I made the soup," she said.

"It will be delicious," he said. "Now I must be off and find
my . . . family. Awfully good seeing you again."

"Yes, awfully good."

They both hesitated.

"Let's talk again later," he said seriously. "After the meal."

"I should like that very much," she said earnestly.

He waved as he turned, a gracious salute.

She waved too, then clenched her hand and let it drop.
She needed a moment's privacy, she was not fit for company.
But Aunt Helga materialized, firm and obstreperous, Mums's
elder sister.

"Sephony, my dear," she sang, "who's that charming man?
I never forget a face, but names, names."

"That's a lovely suit, Aunt Helga."

"Did you hear what I said?"

She choked. "Aaron Limorrz."

"I know him from somewhere."

"Do you?"

"Oh, Sephony, you sly girl . . . That was your young man
. . . he hasn't changed a bit . . . still thin as a noodle. Hilary
never told me you kept up."

"We don't. Ari must have invited him."

Aunt Helga looked greedy and suspicious.

"Auntie," she said desperately, "let's try the soup. I made
it myself. Shall we?" She crooked her elbow for the old woman.

"No, thank you, my dear, I'll run along. You'll want to eat
with your husband."

Sephony found Marek sitting in the tent, alone in the
rose-tinted shade at a table set for four.

She sat down and he leaned toward her, his expression
baffled, his eyes blank. "Was that who I think it was?"

"Who?"

"The man you told me about." He cleared his throat and said "Aaron," pronouncing the name as if it were in a foreign language.

She nodded. The name had its own resonance; it belonged to its own time. Out of context, it jarred.

They talked. Food arrived. Her face was drying, her skin was drying, she heard it crackle when she smiled. She must be careful not to tear it — talking, smiling, eating — she must move in small ways to keep the paper from tearing.

"I said, do you want bread with it?"

"Bread? No. No, thank you. Just a bit of soup."

Eyes in the walls, she thought, watching my gestures, every finger watched, every bite, reading my lips. Her blouse was lined with cactus spines, they kept her alert.

Melani and Simon joined them. Where were Rolf and Dote? Food came and went. They were eating creamed lobster; everything in the tent was tinted pink. Outside on the grass stood three long tables, their white cloths weighted at the hems. Servers in red suits glided from table to table, filling wineglasses. Voices droned, silver clinked on china. Sephony was picking at chunks in sauce when a familiar touch pricked her shoulder.

"Sephony," said her mother, "I must talk with you, just for a moment. You won't mind, my dear, will you?"

"I should love to finish the lobster, if you don't mind."

"Certainly. Shall we say ten minutes in my studio?"

"Is it a must?"

"In my studio, Sephony. And you, my dears," she said, taking hold of her grandchildren. "Are you enjoying the party?"

"It's lovely," said Melani.

"Awfully good," said Simon.

"Well, cheeribye," said Mums, striding between tables.

Sephony exchanged a look with Simon.

"What does Gramma want?" he asked.

"Blood and bones," said Sephony, wiping her lips with a serviette and pushing back her chair.

Her mother stood by a window overlooking the formal gardens, drumming on the sill. Paint spots on her worktable made a chaotic base to cups of dried color and battered tubes; brushes flared in a vase. On the shelves hundreds of varnished stones faced forward, their brilliant suns and rings glistening like kohl-rimmed eyes. Sephony cast a friendly glance at the unpainted stones in the corner. Gray and dull, they rested on one another in a congenial heap.

"A fine celebration," her mother said, coldly. The light fell on half her face, exaggerating the lines.

"Yes, it is," Sephony said cautiously, leaning against a stool.

"A very . . . diversified group. How nice to see so many people."

"We did our best."

"I'm glad everyone is happy."

"I'm sure they are."

Her eyes widened. "And am I supposed to be pleased to see that man, that Aaron?" She glared like a hawk.

"It was such a surprise," Sephony said calmly, hoping to avert unpleasantness.

"Oh, indeed, quite a surprise. On my birthday, no less. Where everyone can see. Your behavior . . ."

"You didn't expect me not to speak to him . . ."

"It's very cruel to use my party as an excuse, or is it revenge . . ." A warning lit the fierce blue eyes.

"Revenge?" She was shocked.

"What have you got against me? Do I dare trust the food? Did you poison my soup as well?"

"Mums — I didn't invite him."

"It's a public slap in the face."

"Perhaps Ari . . ."

"Now you blame Ari."

"I'm not blaming anyone —"

"I find it hard to believe that one little word didn't pass between you."

"I didn't invite him!"

"Sometimes your memories are just too convenient, Sephony. I know all too well the state you've been in lately."

"You don't know anything!" She was a child, her nose was full of tears.

"Your motives are clear," her mother said, her face twisted with rage.

Sephony rushed to the far end of the studio and picked up an unpainted stone. "For years you've been accusing me!" she shouted. "For nothing!" The stone was smooth and speckled with black.

"I'll ask Ari who invited him," said her mother. "But she's not one to make mischief."

Sephony turned. "There's no pleasing you!" she screamed. "Aaron's just someone from long ago! He's not a weapon or a problem!"

"For you he is," her mother said, squinting.

She wanted to drop to the floor, wanted to clutch the hems of Mums's trousers and cry "Take me back, I'll be your good little girl." Hands appeared everywhere — on the table, the stones, the floor, the window. She looked up and around as if to chase them.

"What is it, Sephony?" her mother asked, alarmed.

"Why do you hate me?" Sephony shouted and ran from the room.

In the library she fell into a large chair, appalled at herself, holding the stone to her diaphragm and feeling its agitated upheavals. A grown woman, screaming at her mother. Fallen so low.

When she was calmer she walked to the tent, passing the lawn tables. Aaron looked up, a forkful of greens suspended. Their eyes linked, his greens still suspended; then he looked away and brought the food to his mouth. Sephony went into the tent. Marek was alone at their table.

"Where are Melani and Simon?" she asked mechanically.

"Off with the cousins, making room for dessert. What did she want?"

Sephony placed the stone to the left of her plate. It looked lonely. She cradled it in her lap.

"She accused me of inviting Aaron."

He looked speculative, puzzled. "You didn't, did you? I mean, I wouldn't think so, but after our talk, you might have . . . No, I shouldn't think you would."

"Never."

"What happened then?"

"I shouted at her."

"You didn't." He was teasing, mocking.

"I did." She caught the grim humor in it.

"How splendid," he said. "How splendid of you." He threw back his head and laughed.

It was infectious in a painful way. Laughter was like crying; her lips were tight and her chest hurt.

"I even took one of her precious stones," she said. "I wanted to toss it through the window."

"I'd like to heave the whole bloody lot through the window."

A server interrupted them, handing Sephony a small pink envelope. On the back of a silver art card was a scrawled message: "Sorry, my dear, it was Ari." Ashamed, she handed the card to Marek. Perhaps she didn't give Mums enough credit.

"You don't usually win," he said.

"It's not much of a victory." She felt empty. Her outburst hadn't counted; hate had no more effect than love.

She ate greens and meat that must have arrived during a lapse in attention; the wine was cool. Behind the transparent pink wall Aaron sat at a long table. She waited for the meal to end. She waited for the next opportunity to talk with him. She sent her thoughts backward while she chatted with Marek.

Wedges of filbert cake arrived with coffee; she ate Stilton. Marek excused himself. People were stretching, walking around the lawn and gardens, breaking out of family groups. Rolf strolled out of the orchard with his ladylove. How handsome he was — tall, large head, broad shoulders — looking down at the girl, touching her elbow. Her son. It was too personal. She stepped out onto the sunlit lawn and glanced at the table where Aaron had been eating. It was empty.

He was standing with four men by the house. The curve of his back and chest suggested thoughtfulness and modesty. He ran his hand through his hair. His hand lingered and stirred the air as it came down. In profile he resembled the Egyptian king Akhenaton — hollow cheeks and soulful eyes with a pointed nose and chin. He turned and saw her. Would he make some excuse, leave the men? He patted one on the back, shook hands with another, waved and left, saying something over his shoulder. This time he arrived on wings.

"Well," he said, "can we take a walk?"

"As long as we don't disappear. The spies are out."

They walked slowly through the orchard. Their arms brushed.

"Do you still listen to poetry?" she asked.

"I haven't much time for poetry these days. Some. Why?"

"I hardly talk about literature with anyone. You know, that clear mental space. I miss it," she said simply, sadly.

"I'm surprised to hear that. I really am. No friends, Sephony?"

"One, but she's not that sort."

"Marek's a good person, I've heard."

"He's a practical man," she said. Discussing Marek seemed disloyal. For an instant she saw him as an ancient shroud in their hands, exposed to fatal air, yellowing and crumbling.

"So we both lead busy lives," he said, putting his hands in his pockets.

"You know . . . it's very strange — you've been on my mind. I'm very glad you're here. I've been, I've been, well, let's say, in a fragile state, not my usual self at all, having strange thoughts, seeing things . . ." She looked at him questioningly out of the corners of her eyes.

"Yes, go on. Please."

"There are things I should have told you years ago."

They walked in silence. His desire to speak, she thought, was as loud as words.

"There are secrets that color our lives," she said, sadly.

He looked at her speculatively. "Sephony? If I gave you my office number? Are you ever in London? You must be."

"Often."

"Phone, then, any morning before ten and I can arrange to meet you for lunch. Would you? Would that be all right?" He lifted her wrist and dictated his number into her memory band. She tensed at the pressure of his fingers.

"What's the stone?" he asked.

"A talisman. Would you like it?" She handed it to him.

He caressed the stone with his thumbs. "How will I carry it?" It didn't fit in his pockets. He looked at her helplessly. She held out her hand.

"We should go back," he said, placing the stone gently in her palm.

She touched his arm. "Aaron?" The name, like a lozenge, lay on her tongue; her hand was aware of itself.

"Yes?"

"You didn't phone recently, on account of the party, per- haps, phone and not leave your name?"

"No, I never thought of phoning. I considered not coming, but the thought of seeing you, well, I couldn't not, could I?"

"But you didn't phone." She withdrew her hand.

"Why do you keep saying that?"

"Someone's been phoning lately, a man, always when I'm out."

"How very peculiar. Although, without knowing . . . It really is strange, I assume."

"Very."

"What do you make of it?"

"Oh, it's hard to say about such things."

She looked up at him, her cheeks hot. "It would be awfully nice if we could be friends, you know, just friends." Her voice was breathy.

He touched her shoulder. "Yes," he said, "I should like that very much."

They separated.

Pleasure, like suffering, strained her nerves. For the remainder of the afternoon she felt heightened and keen, but superficial. Impressions stung and flew off. Ari said something nasty; Mums bent over a small child to accept pansies; Jason arrived very late. She was observant, but not thoughtful, a person living only in the present.

Standing alone in the shade of a walnut tree, she watched as Aaron, his wife, and two plump daughters said good-bye to her mother. Shards of late-afternoon sun glittered behind the copper beech. Mums was stiff and regal. Aaron's thin body curved like a new moon over her outstretched hand.

When he left she felt ill and exhausted. A gritty disappointment dragged at her spirit. She could not make conversation. She found Marek at the pool with Mugs.

"Hello, my dear," said Marek. "We're arguing about the filter system again."

"I asked Dote to fetch you," she said irritably, "but she was so busy giggling with Enid she wouldn't lift herself off the grass."

Marek patted her shoulder. She winced.

"I don't ask that much of them."

"You're overwrought, my dear," said Marek.

"I'll wait in the library," she said. " 'Bye, Mugs." Brother and sister kissed formally.

The library was dark and cool. She sank into a wingbacked leather chair, the sort people die in unnoticed. Paintings and hollies lined the walls — pastures and hillsides, lakes and country houses — each a little window into a landscape from another era. A portrait of her great-aunt in profile was discordant, staring into its own distance: harsh, noble, and sharp-nosed, like herself, like Aaron. Past and present were convulsing. Aaron lived in the open again, out of memory's control, wobbly, on a turbulent field. She rubbed her knuckle. She was in an earthquake — houses tumbling, walls cracking, windows popping out of their frames — she was running and falling, all in an eerie silence, while blue flames leapt out of deep cracks in the earth.

CHAPTER ⚡ 4

A BLACK AND SILVER ROBO opened the door, gleaming and graceful.

"Reb Nacht," Sephony said distinctly.

"Reb Nacht," repeated the robo in a fluty imitation, twirling on his stem. "Room seven — room seven." His arm flashed toward a corridor.

"My word, a Russell Four," said Marek.

"I haven't seen one in years," she said. "It's a good omen."

They walked on threadbare carpeting past scarred doors with polished brass plates. Number 7 was "The Society for the Preservation of Ancient Thought — Judaic Studies." Below was a note, "Enter without knocking."

The room smelled of old paper — the walls covered with books and the chairs and floor heaped with manuscripts. A man slouched behind a desk, eyes closed. Thinning hair curled limply above his forehead and bushed around his ears. He wore brown. Marek cleared his throat and the man half opened heavy-lidded eyes.

"Just a moment," he intoned abstractedly, "one brief thought."

A little furrow twitched above his nose. He reminded her of a sleeping Pekingese. Suddenly he looked up, still grappling inwardly, and made an effort, it seemed, to take them in.

"So," he said, sitting up with a little jerk and rubbing his hands together, "you made good time?" His voice was soft, a bit nasal, and sad. There was a little gap between his front teeth.

"Are you Reb Nacht?" Sephony asked.

"Yes, please sit down, please sit down," he said.

He was studying them, looking from one to the other, a deep, impersonal sorrow in his hooded protruding eyes.

He had apparently cleared two chairs for them.

"I'm sorry to be interrupting your work," she said.

"No, no," he said, "I've been waiting — veritably on pins and needles. Are you comfortable? Just give those papers a little kick. Good. Tell me already," he went on, his grief congenial, "I don't mean to rush you . . . Tell me, please, all about your religious experience."

"Oh, I'm not sure that's what it was," she said.

Reb Nacht put his hands beneath his chin, palm to palm, resting his lips and nose on his fingers.

She began with the doctor's visit, then the voice and the well. The story, having lain dormant and accumulating hope, felt alien; it told itself with too many details — it was distorted, passionate, limp. If the presence was listening, she thought, it wouldn't recognize itself.

"It seemed to mean something," she concluded lamely, cheeks burning. "But, you know, time has gone by."

Reb Nacht slapped the desk.

"You see," he said, "the Triangle is wrong, every time they are wrong. People come to me with such stories and yet we are not supposed to believe. A remarkable experience," he said passionately, "what a remarkable woman you must be." His lids flickered. "What sort of religious training have you had?"

"None, of course."

"Of course," he said sadly, "naturally." He sighed. "There's no doubt about it — you received a visit from the Almighty, from some aspect of the Almighty."

"I beg your pardon?"

"Do you think the idea of an Almighty is ridiculous?"

"There is no such thing."

"Ah, but my dear, your experience tells you otherwise. Why did you come here, of all places?"

"A friend suggested it."

"Not many people see Him anymore," he said, almost to himself. "Even the people in my congregation, my small, defiant congregation. It's many years since I've been so blessed. But here and there . . . now and then . . . come living proofs — like you . . ."

"That's a rather swift judgment," Marek said brusquely. "Considering she probably imagined the whole thing."

"Who knows the ways of the Almighty? She was accessible. A vessel."

"But . . . if so . . . why me?" Sephony asked.

"Who can say?"

"My husband is right . . . I could have been hallucinating."

"No, no. Such things really happen."

"And if I had gone — down the well?" Her breath caught on the question, it was so absurd.

"You might still be there."

"There? Where?"

Reb Nacht shook his head. "Who can say. You are one of the treasures of this world. I can arrange for you to meet a few others. Would you like to?"

"Well, I don't know . . . I don't think so. I just wanted to talk with you . . . privately, you know." Her loyalties split; she was aware of Marek.

"You will feel comfortable in our study group, Mrs. Berg-Benson. We would be honored to bend our minds and hearts around your questions — and you could do the same with ours."

Sephony laughed. "That's very kind of you, Reb Nacht. I can hardly say no to such a charming invitation."

"How do you define your profession, exactly?" Marek asked gruffly, suspiciously.

"You mean, how does a religious teacher survive in the

benign shadow of the Triangle? It's simple. What the Triangle doesn't understand doesn't exist. You'd be surprised what curious freedoms lurk in the nooks and crannies. Perhaps not, perhaps the Triangle thinks we serve a purpose. Who knows?" He grimaced and rubbed his hair as if to shake something loose. "My congregation, a hundred families in the whole of England, pays a modest salary. The study groups pay small fees . . . people come from all over Europe. Would you accompany your wife to meet some people who believe in the old ideas?"

"That's not my cup of tea at all. It's not my wife's either."

"At the end of the month we're spending a weekend on a farm near Horsham. We'll be discussing experiences of the spirit, how to bring them into our lives, how to pray and meditate."

Marek flashed her an exasperated look. "You could go without me, my dear."

"Ah." Reb Nacht thought for a moment. "What are you interested in, if I may ask?"

"Machines. Farming. Fishing."

Reb Nacht rubbed his hands and smiled, satisfied. "Very good. You can putter about with Ansel. Ansel runs the farm, he has oh so many theories and lots of equipment. You can fertilize cabbages while your wife meditates on eternity. Not to be left out. Very important, not to be left out. You know what I mean?" His protruding eyes were hooded, he pointed a finger at Marek. "For you, very important."

"Ah," said Marek uncomfortably.

"Good, good," said Reb Nacht, "then it's settled." He rummaged among his papers. "Here," he said, handing Sephony a battered notebook. "The address and the time. And the fee, which is trivial." He smiled. "We look forward to seeing you. Very much."

Sephony dictated the information into her memory band and returned the notebook. They rose. Reb Nacht was quite short. He wore a brown robe made of heavy cotton. Frayed bits of white showed at his neck and wrists. They shook hands.

Outdoors, she put her arm through Marek's.

"What did you make of him?" she asked as they turned onto Grove End Road.

"Fertilize cabbages," Marek spat, "for a trivial fee."

"It really isn't much," Sephony said, squeezing his arm. "I thought he was rather sweet after a while. Didn't you find him rather sweet?"

"He's not our sort."

"I know."

"Do we have to spend time with people who are . . ." He stopped.

"Go on."

"Who are weird."

"I'm weird."

"But I'm used to you."

"Well, you'll have your, what's-his-name . . . Ansel. I'm sure I won't like the group. But let's give the weekend a try. I'll prepare food in advance for the young."

"How are you feeling?" Marek asked her.

"Very high." She laughed.

"I'd better get you home before you fall."

"Perhaps I won't," she said.

At home a message in Dote's handwriting said the mysterious caller, abbreviated M.C., had rung at two-fifteen.

Ansel's farmhouses stood among copper beeches. Three geodesic domes, made of white fiberglass, were pocked with tiny, square windows; the whiteness, contrasting with the trees, had a pale, temporary quality — very modern, very simple, balancing heaviness with buoyancy. Sephony pressed the doorbell and the door swung open into an atrium filled with hanging plants and works of art. Marek dropped their bags on the floor. A *fu* dog grimaced from a wooden pedestal. A large mirror was framed in cowrie shells. Holograms lined the walls. While Marek stalked around the spiral staircase and peered into open doorways, Sephony looked at the art. The holograms were magnified parts of things — a spider's leg, fork tines, a naked elbow — mysteriously depicting an inner physical reality.

"You'd think someone would be here by now," Marek snapped.

"We're quarter of an hour late," said Sephony.

"Bloody impolite," said Marek.

"And whose fault is it —"

A woman with frizzy gray hair appeared. "I'm sorry," she said briskly, "the bell is rather faint. I'm Bess Apple." She fidgeted with a heavy silver necklace. "We're just about ready to begin. So if you'll just pop into your room and pop down again . . . you'll hear us . . . your room is upstairs, second door on the right."

The room was pleasantly disorienting, Sephony thought, its simple furnishings enhanced by a magnificent silk carpet whose pale geometric forms glowed like jewels. She recognized the pattern. It was called an Asian bird carpet, although the motif was really leaves and flowers.

"Usak," she said, squatting to study the design, "eighteenth century, I think, look how marvelous . . ."

"Domes are never adequately insulated," Marek said, taking his pound of flesh.

He left the room and she traced stylized yellow leaves attached to flower clusters by beaklike stems. The whole carpet was floral, yet one could not help seeing the leaves as nectar-sipping hummingbirds with primroses in their bellies.

"Water pressure's low," Marek reported, returning from the lav.

"Let's go," she said, and wondered if she would have been wiser to come alone.

The house breathed its intriguing otherness — another person's house was like a strange city — hallways gossiping and rooms hoarding smells. As she followed murmurs in the distance, her hopes rippled. Was she about to meet extraordinary people? Would they have some rare familiar quality, like the voice itself?

Reb Nacht and a small group of people sat on the floor in a bare sunny room, chatting comfortably. Reb Nacht rose, looking pleased and worried, and she apologized for being late.

"Not too late, not late at all," he said. "This is Sephony and Marek Berg-Benson," he announced. "Bess, please start the introductions." He led Marek out the door and left it open.

Sephony caught Bess's husband's name — Harold — because it was said first; the other names passed by and vanished. Mats were spread about, and a table or two held books and ornaments. She looked out the door. Across a sunny, graveled yard a thick, red-bearded man emerged from a barn, wiping his hands on his coveralls. Framed in two doorways, Marek relaxed and shook hands. She turned back to the group. The people were of various ages, seven of them sitting in a circle, wearing ordinary clothes. They looked like a committee that met regularly. Did they know one another outside this group? Did they discuss their families? There were five women and two men, all but one older than herself. What lay behind their ordinariness? Why were they off the beaten path? Had they all heard voices like hers?

"Please take a mat," Bess said, twisting her necklace.

Sephony took one of the shiny blue mats to a gap between a fat woman wrapped in a shawl and a vigorous white-haired man. They shuffled to make space for her and chatted a bit about sitting cross-legged and getting stiff. The man was in his seventies and had an intelligent, ironic look. The woman had an accent she couldn't identify. Harold sat directly across from her, smiling like a porpoise. He was in his late fifties — a puffy-eyed man with a large head, clipped gray mustache, and wet lips.

Reb Nacht returned. "Everyone looks ready," he said, settling himself beside a sturdy, freckled woman. "The study group," he said to Sephony, "combines practices from many spiritual movements, our aim being to liberate the spirit in and around us. We begin with breathing in unison. Let us all join in. Crystal," he said, "if you would lead us, please."

"Is everyone comfortable on their sit bones?" Crystal was

an elderly humpbacked woman with piercing blue eyes, her voice surprisingly deep and husky, a man's voice.

Hissing sounds rattled in the room like dry pods in the wind. Crystal gave encouraging instructions. As the group inhaled and exhaled, Sephony caught the rhythm.

"Thank you, Crystal," said Reb Nacht. He looked around the circle. "For our guest, I will explain the guided meditation, which is the focus of our morning's work. It is an ancient technique for centering the mind, an experience in obedience, in following visual paths to the quiet center of our being. All you need to do is enter the leader's vision and give yourself up to his voice. Who conducts the meditation today?"

"Harold," said Bess.

Harold riffled a pile of note cards and smiled eagerly and damply at each person. Sephony rehearsed a description of him for Peg as she politely smiled back.

"This meditation is a series of gardens," Harold began in a nasal voice. "I think you'll find some part of yourself plus a universal truth in each one." He shifted a note card. "Imagine yourself outside a square, on a gravel path bordered by silvery hedges." He spoke through his grin, his teeth large and yellow, and sucked saliva back into his mouth with loud slurps. "Close your eyes, please. The hedges are very prickly and close. What's on the other side? It has only one color, gray, the color of gravel. You walk round and round, not knowing where you're going. This is the garden of ignorance. Actually it's not a garden."

Eyes closed, Sephony walked in the garden of ignorance and felt a wave of anxiety.

Harold continued, "You come to a gap in the hedge. It was there the whole time and you just didn't see it. You step through into a small, rectangular garden of lovely yellow daisies."

"Daffodils," said Bess.

"Daffodils," said Harold. "Thank you, dear. Clumps of golden daffodils, swaying in the breeze. This is the garden of questioning. We wonder, where are we? Does this garden lead somewhere?" He stopped and slurped.

Sephony stood uncertainly in the yellow garden. Daffodils brushed her legs. Optimism, that's what yellow was in Mums's system. This garden should be important, for her inner self was indeed a garden of questioning.

"If you imagine facing south then the next opening is in the east hedge. You notice I said east. Orient yourself." He chuckled.

Mentally Sephony turned left.

"The next garden is a large blue triangle, a blue garden. There are Michaelmas daisies around the edge and clematis and gentians, and the grass is drowned in a sea of ageratum." Harold sounded pleased with his metaphor. "Blue is our active life, all the things we do. Think of the things that keep you occupied, work and family and so on."

Sephony peeked at Harold. His eyes shone and he wiped his mouth with the back of his hand. She could not enter this garden. She saw the forlorn weeder robot after it killed her Michaelmas daisies.

"We will go on, we will go on. The next garden is brilliant orange. It's shaped like a half-moon. Pass into the center. Pick some marigolds, look at the wallflowers and azaleas. This is the garden of sensual pleasure. Azaleas are very sensuous! And pick some honeycomb dahlias. Aren't they superb?"

Harold certainly was cavalier with the growing seasons. And how were the beds arranged? Did the flowers grow helterskelter? She didn't care for azaleas, they were vulgar. Midget dahlias had a nicer cap than giant hybrids. She tried to be tolerant of Harold. What would Mums think of his analogies?

"We're feeling relaxed and stimulated, but good things don't last, not at all, they don't last. Even all the gardens aren't beautiful. Let's walk through a narrow hedge into a garden that's all brown. Just bare earth, hard and cracked. This is the garden of achievement. The garden of worldly nothingness. Consider the thirst that follows accomplishing something. What does it mean? Are you satisfied with what you earn? How do you feel about winning and losing?"

The soil was dry and desperate, it begged for attention. A

dark life breathed through hummocks and cracks. She wanted to turn over the crust and set in seedlings and water them until they budded. She stepped on a spade.

". . . brilliant red roses in a circle. Red is emotional. The flowers are pure feelings — poppies, tulips, geraniums, and rhododendrons. Think of all our feelings, how powerfully they toss us about. Anger and fear, you know, love, jealousy — flowing like blood in our veins." The metaphor excited Harold, he was drowning in saliva.

She had barely begun — she was still digging when she was torn away, jangled. And there were mistakes in Harold's floral language. Hands crawled up a shadowy undulating wall. Aaron strolled out from behind a bush and disappeared. Peg had done guided meditations that didn't sound in the least like this.

She withdrew and let the drone fade. Purple shaded into lavender, lavender into pale blue. She drifted and emerged at forget-me-nots.

Harold's voice had become insidiously soft. "Slowly, don't rush, stroll into the garden at the center, the white garden, the circle in the heart of the square. The garden of belief, isn't it perfect? All those white flowers — zinnias, daisies, and calla lilies. The sun is bright. We know there is a presence here, a presence that watches over us. We feel it at the heart of ourselves, the being who is all in all and over all."

Sephony waited. The presence was not there. It was a thing of darkness. Perhaps it had been in the brown garden, waiting beneath the soil. Here were only sunlight and daisies. She thought of the Jungle, overgrown and malevolent.

"Thank you," said Harold.

The group woke from its trance. People shuffled and stretched. Sephony straightened her legs and flexed her feet. She had taken a risk, letting someone tamper with her mind.

People were arguing, talking at once. Some liked the meditation, some felt alienated. Two women apparently believed in ghosts and had seen them hovering in a garden she missed. The devout skeletal one was Elly, her voice high and childlike. The fat passionate one, Nuncia, was thanking Harold for calling up her dead aunt. The older man was Charles.

Reb Nacht nervously pushed back the hair that hung over his forehead. "I think your ghosts, Nuncia, are indeed preludes to a heightened spiritual condition. Personally, you know, I don't believe the dead perform marvels of resurrection, but I believe people can construct visions that appear corporeal. And this can be a source of enlightenment."

Visions. Sephony's heart pounded at the thought of speaking. "You know how women see things," she said cautiously, her face hot. She looked around the circle; the women nodded. "Well, are ghosts different? And what are hands, or bats, or whatever we see? Are they really there?"

"The question arises," said Reb Nacht, "for those who are so fortunate as to have a spiritual life."

"Or unfortunate," muttered the woman beside him.

"Anna is our cynic," Reb Nacht said. "She sees God but would rather not."

"I didn't choose either," said Sephony, "if that's what it was."

"To get back to your question," said Reb Nacht. He tilted his head. "What do you see?"

"Hands," she said.

"That's very unusual. Images of power. What do they do, your hands?"

"They crawl about . . . like spiders," she said flatly.

Anna laughed.

"I, for one," continued Reb Nacht, "don't see things. But I am interested in the visions of others."

Anna twisted a strand of long black hair. Her face was deeply lined, yet freckled like a young girl's. "Do the same hands appear over and over?"

"I'm not sure . . . perhaps they do."

"Do they remind you of real people?"

"I don't know — I've wondered . . . they seem to be just hands."

"Whatever we see is real," said Elly, "because we see it."

"Whatever we touch or hear is real," said Charles with a chuckle. "I don't know about visions."

"Different people seem to value different senses," said Reb Nacht. "Sephony's life, as it happens, has been disrupted by a vision. We can sympathize."

He summarized her experience thoroughly and accurately. She heard it as if it were about someone else and felt embarrassed, almost humiliated, to be eavesdropping.

"The well puzzles me," he said. "The Almighty shines a light from below. We usually associate God with the heavens above — what is on high is good, what is underground is evil."

"We don't have to think that way," said Anna. "There's life within the earth and the sea. The deep is a fertile, fruitful place."

"Like the womb," said Crystal hoarsely.

"They used to bury people," Charles said with measured authority, "so the earth was identified with death."

"God spoke to Moses from a burning bush," Elly said raptly.

"Why locate God at all?" asked Crystal. "Why does God need a place? Can't it be everywhere? Although I admit I feel a pull to look up as if God were thought, and thought were superior to instinct."

"Just because we have brains," said Anna, "doesn't mean we can't think with our feet."

"In Neolithic times," Sephony said, on safe ground, "people believed stones and trees could think. They talked to the earth."

"Nobody knows that for a fact," said Bess. "We have to know where God is when we pray."

"And that place," said Reb Nacht, "can be in a teapot or behind a bush. We needn't argue about it. I think we would agree the voice that called 'Come' was the voice of God. Which means, for you, Sephony, learning a great deal of history."

She felt discouraged. The discussion, by turning on a single point, had left out her whole experience. "History interests me a great deal," she said politely.

"And now," said Reb Nacht apologetically, "we should have a bit of lunch."

He rose clumsily. The others followed.

"Feeling stiff?" asked Anna as they walked outside.

"A bit." Sephony liked her.

"I suppose your husband went off with Ansel," Anna said.

"Is that the customary thing?"

"Oh, yes — Ansel's the resident baby-minder for bored family members."

"So you're the odd one also, in your family."

Anna laughed and flashed Sephony a wicked look. "Yes, definitely odd. Two of my children are around someplace."

"How many do you have?"

"Five."

"And your husband?"

"Ex-husband."

"I'm sorry."

"We severed four years ago," she said defiantly.

A severed marriage. She felt a flicker of insecurity, as if she'd been reproached.

They stood on the lawn, adjusting to the noon sun. A simple lunch was laid on a long table under a canopy. Marek strode toward her, exuding the energy of the outdoors, his testiness gone.

"How was your morning?" she asked.

"Excellent. Excellent. It's very reassuring to know that different farmers have the same problems. How was the group?"

"Oh, I don't know."

"Do you want to leave?"

"I'll stay the day, at least. Anna?" She stepped back to make a triangle and introduced them.

Anna gave Marek a bold, suspicious look, a mixture of coquetry and hostility. "How did you get on with Ansel?" she asked.

"He's a very knowledgeable chap," said Marek.

"Does he own this place?" asked Sephony.

Marek nodded. "Built the house with his own hands. His father's in your group. That white-haired chap."

"Reb Nacht is going to say a blessing," said Anna.

"Well, I don't have to, do I?" Marek laughed.

"Don't be rude," said Sephony.

Reb Nacht stepped under the canopy, accompanied by the tall, bearded Ansel. He bowed his head. The others bowed their heads. Sephony watched.

"Boruch ato adonoi, eloheinu melech ha'olom, hamotzi lechem min ha'oretz."

"Amen," said the group.

Sephony remained silent. Ancient, shawled women swayed in a circle of stones.

"What does that mean?" she asked Anna.

"Praised be the Eternal One, our God, Ruler of the universe, who brings forth bread from the earth."

"Well, then," said Marek, putting cheese and bread on his plate, "I'm going to have some."

"There are my children," said Anna, and walked away.

Sephony and Marek sat on the grass. The sun came and went. People were dotted on the lawn, eating, like figures in *La Grande Jatte.* Harold and Charles, Elly alone, Nuncia and Bess, Anna and her children, Crystal alone, Ansel and Reb Nacht. She sensed their separateness.

The afternoon session began with Reb Nacht's invitation to pray silently. Beside her mat was an old black book, its title, *The Holy Scriptures,* glowing faintly in gold letters. The book was heavy and flexible, the soft leather cover bending with the weight of thin gilt-edged pages. Everyone sat quietly, hands in their laps, eyes closed. Sephony wondered what they were doing. Like so many things, prayer was understandable when she thought of someone else doing it. One petitioned a being for intercession or ransom. One asked for harmony in the universe or gave thanks. But how? And to whom or what? She closed her eyes and imagined a point of light in the center of her forehead. It slipped away. She centered it under her chin. It glided up past her nose to the center of her forehead, hovered, then flickered out. She tried repeating the word *God* over and over, but the short, harsh syllable dripped like water from a faulty tap. She needed a musical word like *Daphne* or *Theona*.

"We trust God has heard," Reb Nacht said quietly. "Now — if you will open to Genesis, chapter twenty-two. The story of the binding of Isaac. Please read and stop after 'Abraham dwelt at Beersheba.' "

The print was tiny and she identified with Abraham. Horrified, she took her dear Simon and a kitchen knife up Lilac Hill to "offer him there for a burnt offering." Surely the sacrifice would not happen — the voice was not so terrible — Isaac would live. To her relief the knife was withdrawn and a ram was sacrificed instead. It was just a test, after all.

Reb Nacht cleared his throat. He glanced around the circle, enthusiasm shining through his mournful look. "So," he said, rubbing his hands, "God commands Abraham to sacrifice his child — a calamity, you might say, although not unusual in that age. We will speak of the historical context later. Why is Abraham prepared to kill his beloved son? Elly?"

"He knows Isaac will live forever as a spirit." She spoke wistfully and kindly, her face twisted with private suffering.

"Nonsense," said Charles. "The Hebrews didn't believe in transmigration or metempsychosis. In Ecclesiastes it says — hold on — 'The dead know not any thing, neither have they any more a reward.' I'm afraid your view isn't supported by the text."

"If Abraham didn't expect Isaac to die," Crystal said, "the story would be pointless."

"He does live on as a spirit," Elly said.

"I've never read the Bible," Sephony said hesitantly. "I'd hate to offend . . . you don't read it literally, do you?"

"No, no," several voices said.

"Wouldn't be any discussion," muttered Harold.

"There are many approaches," said Reb Nacht.

"I wonder, then," Sephony said, "if the story can be read as a fable . . . you know, as moral instruction about personal sacrifice. If you want to stay close to people — children, for instance — you have to give them up. You can't possess people — or things, either. And giving to a deity is the purest giving because you can't prove there is one. This is not my son, he is yours. I love him dearly, he is my one and only, but I will give him to you. Giving for the sake of giving." She wondered if she would remember what she had said. Her thumb rubbed nervously against her knuckles.

Bess purred, "What could you give up?"

Aaron on the riverbank watching a swan scratch its tail. "I don't know," she said. "But the idea of sacrifice applies generally . . . when we hold tightly to things we're crippled, whereas if something or someone is more important than ourselves . . . Oh dear, that sounds terribly materialistic, doesn't it, as if generosity were selfish."

"I agree with you completely," Harold said complacently. "Belief is useful, especially for small people like us. Suppose I can't decide whether to stock up on tubing or filters? Limited space and how can I guess what customers'll need? I used to chew my nails, but now I tell God the situation. I say, 'It's in your lap, Friend,' and eventually He tells me what to buy. So I give up my decisions to God. Don't I, Bess?"

"You're not sacrificing anything," Crystal said dryly.

"Yes, he is," Bess said hotly, "he's giving up the freedom to decide."

"Hardly," Crystal growled, "since he had trouble making up his mind in the first place. He's using God to serve himself whereas Abraham was serving God."

"Was he?" asked Bess. "Abraham ended up with quite a profit. 'In thy seed shall all the nations of the earth be blessed.' "

"He didn't know that in advance," Crystal said.

Reb Nacht intervened. "The question is, what *did* Abraham know in advance? They walk up the hillside. Father and son. Isaac carrying a load of partly burnt wood. Abraham carrying a knife and burning torch. What is Abraham thinking? Could it be that although he is a fairly primitive man, he knows that God, by his very nature, has attributes of goodness and justice? I must show my faith, he thinks, by agreeing to sacrifice my son. But if God is good He won't require the sacrifice. Thus Abraham can honestly say to Isaac, 'God will provide Himself a lamb for a burnt offering.' "

"You think Abraham was bluffing?" asked Charles.

"No, Abraham was thinking about the nature of God. Not even thinking — knowing. Knowing that God exists and God is good — a single perception. Contained in the Divine decree would be a Divine way out. If God were not good, God would not be God and Abraham would not have believed in Him. Do you see the paradox? I am suggesting that God, by His very existence, promises that the thing which is asked is not asked." Reb Nacht tipped his head, birdlike, and rubbed his hands.

"That's too subtle for me," said Harold.

"God is bluffing," Charles chuckled, "in a transcendental sort of way."

Anna glanced appreciatively at Charles. "I keep wondering about Isaac," she said. "What's going on with him? I imagine him a very precocious ten-year-old, very suspicious. He says, 'Behold the fire and the wood, but where is the lamb for a burnt offering?' And Abraham answers, 'My son, God will provide Himself a lamb for a burnt offering.' Does Isaac trust his father the way Abraham trusts God? Is this an education for him — is his survival guaranteed by the way the situation is constructed? After all, Abraham is exceedingly old, even by biblical standards, over a hundred years, and Isaac is his only son, not counting Ishmael. So is God giving Isaac, also, a lesson in absolute faith?"

"Divine magic on every level," rhapsodized Nuncia in her strange accent. She wore a puffy wig of stiff black curls.

"Poor Isaac," said Charles. "Deceived by his father and then by his son. He's not a child, by the way, he's at least thirty years old."

Reb Nacht rubbed his hands. "Let's consider the binding of Isaac from the historical perspective. What were the customs of the time? Abraham was a primitive man, closely connected to his neighbors, but a mental step higher. He was the first monotheist, the first to conceive of a single Supreme Being. In that context, the old commentators tell us, the story has a positive and a negative aspect. The strengthening of Abraham's faith is the positive aspect of the story. The negative aspect lies in God's teaching Abraham what *not* to do. What's astounding is not that God *asks* for the sacrifice of Isaac, but that he intervenes and *prevents* the sacrifice. Abraham's neighbors worshiped multiple deities and that worship included the sacrifice of sons in the springtime to the goddess Astarte. So when God tells Abraham to do the same thing, he's not surprised — that's what gods and goddesses do, they ask for human flesh. But when he puts the knife against Isaac's throat, he hears the voice of God's angel say, 'Lay not thy hand upon the lad . . . I know that thou fearest God,' and in that moment Abraham understands God is not asking for a human sacrifice, he is asking for a spiritual sacrifice — indeed, he has already received it. God's primary purpose was to teach Abraham and his descendants that sacrifice of humans is abhorrent to Him. And thus the idea of symbolic substitution is born."

"And that idea circulated and developed throughout the world," said Charles. "And was dramatized by Christianity."

"Do you believe God literally exists?" Sephony asked.

Reb Nacht's half-hooded eyes were sad. "God is and has always been. Unity and eternity, the great mysteries. Wearing different faces in different religions created by different peoples. Lost now." He sighed. "As for Abraham, he represents a stage in the development of human thought. He is one of the great mediators. God exists as Abraham perceives Him. God is not, after all, revealed to everyone. He — or She — or It is interpreted by prophets and leaders. The collective human mind reaches a higher level when Abraham understands that God requires a symbolic sacrifice, when he draws back the knife from his son's throat. A high culture develops from that moment and the idea, as Charles says, circulates."

"So you really believe in an active deity," she said, trying to fit the idea to the presence in her room.

"I do. Most do not. It is eternal and varied. He-She-It is Buddha, Allah, Ishtar, Jehovah, Zeus, Isis."

Elly leaned toward Sephony. "I light candles Friday nights," she whispered, fingertips at her throat. "Fire opens the heart." She glanced fearfully at Nuncia.

"Ghosts," declared Nuncia, "open the mind."

"Good grief," said Anna.

"I am always amazed," said Reb Nacht patiently, "at the varieties of religious experience. We are united by our roots in the Hebrew belief system, but they are old and for many of us obscured by lack of continuity. I myself am from a family that has continued the practices. The same with my colleagues in Christianity, Buddhism, Islam, and the other belief systems. What you want to know is what was in your room."

Elly raised her arm. Her delicate skin was taut across her cheekbone, her eyes half rolled up. "Was it light or dark, Sephony?" she asked in a reedy, childlike voice.

"What?"

"The presence. I know you didn't see it. Was it light or dark?"

"I think it may have been light."

Elly gasped through clenched teeth. "Over which shoulder?" she asked.

"The left."

Elly gasped again.

"What does that mean?" asked Sephony, embarrassed.

Elly's eyelids fluttered. "What did it say?"

"I didn't actually hear anything," said Sephony. "I understood it to say 'Come,' but I didn't hear anything." She turned away; Elly's fear was too strong. "What's troubling is why it happened to me."

"You're a medium," declared Nuncia.

"Sometimes a crack appears in one's consciousness," Anna said carefully, "and God falls in. I don't believe in God, I have no use for It and I wish It would go away. But it's like Reb Nacht says, God is always there. Who knows why? A crack opened in me and I heard voices. I thought I was schizophrenic, explored that for a while, and now I no longer know what schizophrenia is. Maybe it means hearing God's voice. So

I try to accept voices the way I accept flowers that grow in lamps and old shoes."

Sephony laughed. "Like my hands."

"Right," said Anna.

"I see veils," said Nuncia.

"No one can tell you," said Reb Nacht kindly, "if the message 'Come' originated in your mind or with God. It could be that what Anna calls a crack in the consciousness opened and a new idea dropped in. Or it could be that God was offering you a specific and incomprehensible invitation. Who knows? You feared death or some other extreme change. Perhaps someday, when you least expect it, you will climb down the ladder."

"And wind up somewhere else," said Charles.

"What?" asked Sephony.

"Nothing," said Bess, "an obscure rumor."

"What?" asked Sephony, turning to Reb Nacht.

Reb Nacht looked at his fingernails. "Have you ever heard of beings in another dimension?"

"Oh, one hears such stories all the time. What sort of beings?"

Reb Nacht shrugged sorrowfully. "I myself am very curious. Be careful if the well appears again," he said.

The stillness took on a suspended quality; a group of masks stared at her, peculiarly frozen. Then they breathed and turned to one another and conversation hummed.

Reb Nacht waited until the group became quiet. "I would like you to consider," he said quietly, "how you can incorporate the psychological and spiritual aspects of the binding of Isaac into your lives. Sephony has presented us with the paradox that if we hold on tightly we risk loss. To let go is to have. But to truly let go — to lose oneself serving a requirement greater than any we set ourselves, as in times of persecution we give up our lives, one must let go in a state of thankful humility. I give this up, I give it away. Not so completely as to lose touch with this world, that is not how we interpret God's will, though other belief systems may do so. We are, as Harold says, small people. For some of us prayer is the only sacrifice we are capable of, and in praying we sacrifice the thing most dear — our reason. I will leave you with that thought. Let us rise, join hands, and sing 'Adon Olom.' "

"Were they pious?" Marek asked as they strolled around the farm before dinner.

"No. They're like the county council, only they talk about God. Two believe in ghosts."

"You don't say."

"Most of them are quite nice, though." She lowered her voice. "Except Harold, who led the guided meditation. He's a fool — and his wife. And Nuncia just wants attention."

"Do you actually like any of them?"

"Anna, you met Anna. Crystal. Charles . . . he's honest and reliable . . . a scholar, I think. And Elly, who believes in ghosts . . . and suffers terribly . . . she's genuine. Do you like Charles's son?"

"Good chap. Quite excited about improvements and things."

"Then there's Reb Nacht, who loves ideas and interprets the Bible from many points of view."

"But they haven't explained your little voice, or you would have said so." Marek's eyes shone with cruel mischief. "What do you say, my dear, shall we pack it in right now? Shall we chuck the rest of the weekend?"

"No." She was startled. "Although I could regret it to-morrow."

"Another guided meditation from Harold, you mean."

"Or Nuncia."

"Did you participate?"

"I had some ideas about the story of Abraham and Isaac."

"Who are they?"

"Patriarchs of the old religion."

"They founded it?"

"Religions aren't corporations. They evolve."

"I see. And these chaps, what's their names?"

"Abraham and Isaac."

"What did they do?"

"Abraham was the first to propose the idea of a single god."

"How does anyone know, my dear? Was the whole world keeping diaries?"

Sephony laughed, feeling a twinge of betrayal. "You're right. We talk about Abraham as if he were one person, but he could be many people. And events which take place in a day might have taken place in a hundred years. Anna says I must read a book about religions and the telescoping of time."

"Really. Well, do read it, my dear, and tell me all about it."

"You don't believe anything, do you?"

"I believe in the road underfoot, I believe in the stream and the trees. I believe in machinery even if I don't understand all the parts. But God and Abraham, no, I don't see any point to it. If it makes you happy, dear, I'll keep you company, but I don't believe it."

"You wouldn't."

"Why do you put it that way?"

"You're a practical man."

"You always call me that," he said defensively. "That's the proper way to be. That's the way most people are."

"So they are," said Sephony.

"Come along," said Marek briskly. "You're doing what you want and I'm keeping busy, so we'll have a good time. One more turn around the oak, then it's time to dress for dinner."

At night they lay in the double bed, Marek turned away, absorbed in playing Quizzet. Sephony's pre-sleep images tossed and blew like flailing branches. The hand-held game hawked and chirred. Something was wrong — some discrepancy between the presence in her room and the god of Abraham and Isaac. She tapped Marek's shoulder.

"What?" He shrugged her off.

"Sorry to interrupt."

"What is it?"

"Are you listening?"

"I'm listening," he said, rolling onto his back. "Why aren't you asleep? I was winning."

"We're going home tomorrow."

"Are you ill?"

"The presence in my room wasn't the god they're talking about."

"You're not going to go into it now, my dear, are you? You can wait till morning?"

"Yes, yes, I just wanted you to know we're leaving, that it isn't right for me, this god in the sky, I don't know why, but even saying 'God' seems wrong, God as authority, there's something wrong with the idea. I'm sorry, I just had to interrupt you."

"Quite right. No gods in the sky."

"I think I would lose something if I stayed, the idea of a god might cancel out or absorb the other thing." She kissed him on the cheek. "Good night. Go back to your game."

"Mmmmpf," said Marek and rolled away, his shoulder jutting above the cover.

CHAPTER 5

CUTLETS, she was going to make breaded cutlets. The wafers had soaked long enough. She hit them with a heavy mallet, enjoying the slap, slap of wood against moist flesh. The Watleys were going to be late, the Watleys were always late, and she was going to be late; everything was going to be late. She never did like the Watleys. She sipped a bit of sherry, coughed, and patted her chest. Lots to do and no energizer. She beat two eggs with water in a shallow bowl, poured flour on one plate and bread crumbs onto another, sliced the cutlets into strips, and dipped them according to a family recipe, her fingers heavily breaded.

Even here, in the kitchen, there was a murmur of voices, to the left by the window. She could see the sound — a diaphanous material, like gathered curtains — lifting and wavering. She rinsed her fingers, the thick coating peeling away down the drain, and set the platter of cutlets on the counter under the window. The sun was bright, though the day was cool. The bricks glowed and the left side of the hoverport disappeared in the glare.

A man was coming down the garden path, wearing strange black clothes and carrying what looked like two slaughtered chickens, one under each arm, their heads swaying on limp necks. He came right toward her, to the window, and banged his forehead against the glass, his nose and hat brim flattened against the pane. She waved him away — he would break the glass, he would fall in, right onto the counter with his chickens and his smile. He stepped backward and, with a cheeky smirk, walked off. She lost sight of him and then the door opened and he stood in her kitchen, in a loose black coat, yellow shirt, and baggy trousers. His shoes were muddy. He must have come past the pond. Like a robot clown he nodded and smiled.

The shape and order of life turned fragile and gauzy. She was alert to space — to light and distance.

"What do you want?" she asked, hearing Mums's poisonous drone: none of us is safe.

He lifted first one dirty white shoe, then the other, examining the soles, then stood at attention, expectant. Nothing to fear. He was rather good-humored, a tradesman out of his zone — harmless, she sensed that.

"Tell me what you want," she said firmly. "Or out you go."

The man offered the chickens, their heads dangling stupidly and softly. One white, one yellow. Legless market chickens, with tiny, atrophied claws.

"No, no," she said brightly, "you probably want the Cartwells. They're past the horse chestnut trees, second house on the right, big bubble."

The man offered the chickens and smiled.

What a bother, she would have to call Alf. She started toward the farm communicall but the man stepped sideways and blocked the little red plate.

She turned to the dining room and he was ahead of her, on the other side of the door. She turned and he stood by the kitchen door. In the dining room — in the kitchen — like crawling hands — smiling and holding out his chickens.

Panic arched wavelike, a deathly wall of water, arching and hissing. Desperately she visualized stillness: walls solid, molecules still, the teamaker in place.

The man was dropping chickens in one of the sinks. He

carefully removed his shoes and put them in as well and ran the water hard.

Light and space, light and space; the gauzy murmur sweetly lifted and swelled. Boldly ignoring him, she went into the larder, switched on the light, and carefully chose three nice bunches of broccoli. She switched off the light and peeked into the kitchen. He was still busy at the sink — a figure from historical holograms, the music hall entertainer or the poor wedding guest, squashed stovepipe hat and scraggly blond hair. She expected him to dance, right there in her kitchen. But he was washing his shoes.

And she needed to wash the broccoli. Light shimmered in the kitchen between here and there and she walked through it, nervously approaching the man who was, after all, no more than a large, absurd hand. She stood beside him, gauzy voices humming, and reached for the tap. Arm brushed arm, or so it seemed; she hoped she was imagining it.

He winked at her boldly and swung the tap. Clean white shoes rested on top of wet chickens, laces tangled hideously with necks.

The wave arched and hissed. Deliberately she carried the broccoli to the cutting board, cut off flowers and woody ends, and peeled the thick skin, taking a firm hold at the base of each stalk and pulling upward with smooth strokes. She sliced the stems, each piece notched and curved, the cross sections beautiful and original. Halfway through she glanced toward the sink and then around the room. Well, that's over, she thought, but the gauzy voices hummed in a minor key. Mushrooms. She walked into the larder, switched on the light, and stopped. There was a large hole in the center of the floor.

It was a sort of dry cistern, the sort of thing one uncovered occasionally on the farm. Not at all like the well in her vision — just an ugly black hole in the middle of the larder floor. She squatted and passed a hand through to make sure.

Well, then, a hole in the floor. Would it last or pucker away? She waited. Cover it, then — find something in the barn — more important than slicing mushrooms. Yes. Cover it up. Wouldn't want the young to fall in. In the entry she reached for her padded jacket hanging on a hook, but found herself putting on her brown wool coat instead — a supple coat with large patch pockets, rather long and old. How big was the hole? She went back with a metergun, passing through the kitchen, where the atmosphere was heavy and expectant as before a storm. Cutlets on a platter, broccoli flowers and slices on the cutting board, everything waiting and holding its breath.

In the larder the well was wider and more defined. It contained two ladders.

This is mad, she said coldly to herself — and the metergun fell into the potato bin. It's not mad, she said, I have another chance to go away. She was trembling. The world was reorganizing itself; she put her hands in her pockets for stability. The family will be furious, she thought.

The man startled her, materializing at the edge of the hole as if he'd been sitting there cross-legged all day. He was her age or younger, his face lean with broad, high cheekbones and thin lips. He was impudent and very foreign, like someone who'd been on a space voyage for years and come back knowing absolutely everything, whom one dislikes yet trusts with one's life. His eyes blazed at her — a fierce crystalline blue. He rolled over and wriggled into the well feet first, inviting her with a hopeful expression. He was confident, yes, and a bit sad and tired, and she noticed he wore his shoes. Gallantly she said silent good-byes to the larder — to cheeses and vegetables in colorful heaps on orderly shelves, to eggs in a tray. She wriggled into the well and stood on a ladder. They stood back to back.

It would be even better if the ladder shone, she thought with a twinge of exhilaration, but then, it isn't the same well. It was rough earth or stone and the rungs were corrugated and something like wood. She twisted her head. The man nodded and began to descend. Not a talker, that one. She followed his movements, the hem of her coat flapping around her ankles.

It was a tedious way to travel and hard on the knees.

What lay ahead didn't matter — she had a sense of rooms spreading from the distant, invisible base of the ladder, places that existed in old literature. She felt gleeful, escaping like a child, a woman like her, with all her responsibilities. And thinking ahead — part of her mind swirled — she had neither comb nor toothspray, therefore no one intended her to stay long. Perhaps she would be home directly after dinner — had anyone found the hole or the chickens in the sink? She looked up. Above glowed a circle of light; she'd left the larder light on.

Down, down, continuing down. She imagined Marek and the young as tiny specks with tiny legs, moving about upstairs with the Watleys, arms flapping, heads nodding, but tiny, like poppy seeds. Upstairs was a shadowy place, a circle of light no bigger than a ceiling lamp, and diminishing. The man behind her was oddly substantial. She needed a name for him. The chicken man, she thought.

Pale green specks began to glow on the surface of the well and she smelled a pungent vegetable odor like garlic. She marked distance by the circle of light above, now the size of a duck's eye.

The green specks merged into patches that shone like moonlit water; home was a dot. It stayed a dot, like the North Star, and the farther she went the more she depended on it. When the dot winked out she panicked and rushed up a step to bring it back. Down a step, up a step, she couldn't go on. The chicken man tugged at her coat.

Attentive, then, to the green spreading and taking on dark, glowing colors, she thought of things decomposing — death generating energy and energy becoming light. Bands of blue and purple pulsed like the ribs of sleeping animals, like the bellies of captive fish. For the first time she looked down. A few rungs below, the ladder itself was glowing. Awed, she stepped onto the first radiant rung and climbed down a silver ladder, shining and cool, looking up to darkness and down to light.

As they neared the last shining rungs the chicken man at her back pressed against her; there was barely room for them both. She twisted in alarm. He had swelled enormously. His belly caressed the ladder and he grew fatter with each step, wedging them tightly together. And her own body? She felt dizzy — the air was strangely compressed and rushing without wind.

On solid ground, they sidled through a portal into a dim, wavery space. Was she limping? Her legs felt uneven; her hands tingled. The chicken man, immense and silent, was swollen into his coat.

She flexed her limbs but the air rushed on. She felt as if she were traveling although everything was still, as if she and time moved at different speeds. Could she dissolve the phosphorescent twilight in a breath and a shake of the head? Was she in the kitchen slicing mushrooms?

The chicken man took her hand. His was fleshy, the palm rough — a large, warm hand exerting a firm, soft pressure. Her hand was surprised — shocked, she might say. He was calm and concentrated, looking at something far off, paying no attention to her, his jaw muscle twitching, his thin lips tightly compressed. His skin reflected the bluish-green glow. At home the meal must have been abandoned. They were looking for her. The poppy seeds were scurrying.

"What is this place?" she asked.

The chicken man smiled. Although he didn't answer, his calmness was contagious. On the other side of the portal the ladders had faded — the way back was vanishing, closing off — it seemed the well had been sliding away since they stepped out of it. Four archways yawned in the dim place.

The chicken man, with an elaborate flourish, delivered an apple from nowhere, looking impish and pleased with himself. A gesture of hospitality, a welcome to where? His land? But she couldn't eat, she couldn't possibly eat. She accepted the apple — a pippin — cupped it briefly, and returned it as if the gift went both ways. The ceremony seemed to satisfy him. He blew on the apple and it vanished.

Still wordless, he took her hand again and they entered a darkly luminous tunnel. Green and blue phosphorescence

flowed and bubbled. Space was so deceptive she couldn't tell
kilometers from centimeters. She was a child dreaming about
frustration — cutting the string that frays and frays, and
searching corridors for the loo. The splendid silence was cold
and brilliant: the silence of dreams, a hypnotic, oppressive
silence.

They passed through an archway into a spacious cavern,
gray as twilight. A gray beach surrounded a lake; the air was
cool and damp. Gray stones poked through soft, lumpy soil.
They headed for the water.

He's home, she thought, now he'll speak.

"This is lovely," she said, "and very restful." A slender
pole stood in the water — plastic or wood, she couldn't
tell — on a clover-shaped base. She let a handful of soil run
through her fingers. Grit clung to her palms; she thought of
clams.

The chicken man dug at the water's edge, his dark jacket
taut from sleeve to sleeve, and brought up a rough, ribbed
shellfish, which she took, hating its mute pulse, and dropped
to spin away in a whirlpool of dust. Complacent, the man sat
on a flat boulder, like a waiting sumo wrestler.

She rinsed her hands. The lake was as blank as rocks and
sand, blank as cavern walls, gray-surfaced and blank. Obsti-
nate surfaces, impenetrable as neighbors, showing nothing.
Silence gnawed like hunger; she screamed inwardly for release
from muteness.

"I'm certain you understand English," she said.

By the rock jetty, agitated splashes churned the water.
Then silence again. A current rose up, a humming without
sound or content, thickening the air.

"Perhaps we should move on," she said.

"Or stay," he said.

He stood and placed both hands on her shoulders, his
blue eyes shining with a strange, fierce light. Like a balloon
losing air, his body lost its excess flesh, his face grew lean, his
stomach flattened and his clothes hung, shabby and wrinkled.

"Or stay," he said again, and smiled.

"What are you?" she cried.

The chicken man laughed. "Flesh comes and goes," he said.

"No."

"Like that." He slapped his thigh.

"No," she said.

"Flesh comes and goes. Voice comes and goes."

"Is that why you were quiet for so long?" she asked.

"Quiet?"

"Why you didn't say anything."

"Oh, voice. That." He laughed. His hands were still on her shoulders.

She didn't know if he sounded odd because he galloped through logic and grammar, or because of his intensity. He rather resembled a robo; his pronunciation was correct, but the circuits were alien.

"Sephony," he said.

She winced.

"Sephony, Sephony." His voice was deep and musical.

"And may I ask yours?" she retaliated.

"Ask."

"Your name."

He hesitated, looking up. "Claro."

"Claro."

"Also, He Who Was."

"Hehoowas?"

"He . . . Who . . . Was. Also Dartri, Amos, and That One."

"Well, I had quite a different name for you."

"Another name?" He bowed his head politely.

"Chicken man."

"Oh, very good." He laughed. "Very good." He gave her a penetrating look. "Now food." He brought a wedge of hard cheese from his pocket, breaking it in two. His hands had strong tendons and, surprising in a fair-haired person, black hair on the fingers.

They sat on adjoining rocks. "Where are we?" she asked. The cheese was sharper than cheddar.

His teeth clicked as he chewed. "Here. There," he said, and vanished, materializing immediately across the lake. She shivered, and he was sitting beside her.

"Are you . . . are we . . . two places at once?"

He rubbed his jaw under the ear where the muscle was tight. "I think 'there.' "

"Is that how you arrived at my kitchen?"

He nodded and she bit off some cheese. She thought he was still eating, but realized he had finished some time ago and was mimicking her chewing with clownish enthusiasm — a kind of language.

"What if I spoke Senufo?" she asked. "Would we be able to talk?"

"With words?"

"Obviously."

He looked at her critically, his eyes blazing with the light of different circuits.

"When you know the language," she said kindly, "words matter a great deal."

He sighed. "We sleep now."

Sleep. Going was one thing, but staying was quite another. She looked around the cavern, at the high domed ceiling and rock walls. She imagined her family worried sick and felt entirely responsible. She would pay — no doubt she would.

"My family aren't like me, you know," she said. "They couldn't possibly understand." Recklessness bubbled up at the thought of them, of Mums.

"You came," he said. "You must sleep." It was an offer, not a command. He was generous, this strange creature; his attention made a claim on her loyalty.

"Arms around my neck," he said, "we fly."

He clasped her rib cage, his fingers seeming to extend like a net across her back. On a humongous breath and a lift they rocketed upward, spiraling over the lake and on up, circling high under the rough dome, then wafting down and landing by the cavern wall.

"Well," she said, stepping away from him, laughter bubbling up again. An immense, painful confidence rolled inside her, like a coil or a huge ball of fuzz; she wanted to laugh and laugh.

The rough wall was pocked with deep sandy-floored caves. Claro squatted in the entrance to one, shaking open a yellow cloth like a sheet, totally engrossed in the simple task. A fierce focus came off his haunches and the curve of his back; he shook out the cloth as if it were the most important task in the world, as if it were the only task, as if he and the cloth were one. She was relieved when he stood, breaking the tension, dusting his hands on his trousers. He bowed ceremoniously and stooped into the next cave.

She curled sideways on stiff fabric with little slubs. Her lower legs, where the coat didn't cover, felt uneasy, as if they might detach themselves and float away. The air was warm enough, but her legs ached for weight. She tucked her feet under the coat, alert to whispers of stone and sand. Out in the darkness every little sound split and crescendoed.

She closed her eyes and sensation vanished. A triangle and a circle appeared on her pre-sleep screen. Completion, she thought, her mind floating. The triangle is solemn; the circle is mischievous. The triangle is the government, all secrecy and authority. The circle is zero and infinity. The triangle stands firm. The circle rolls under the bed, gets lost in the shrubbery, irritates the eye. The triangle is birth, maturity, and death. The circle rotates and balloons. The triangle is entrance and exit, the mysterious number three, harsh and precise and sharp as a knife. The circle is a full moon.

She slept and heard distant splashing, as if someone were tossing stones. Half-awake, she turned onto peculiar softness. A shadow was waddling toward her in the shadows, a small gray thing — a sort of penguin without a face.

"Help," she called thickly, paralyzed in a nightmare. "Help."

The blank gray creature waddled closer and her memory flickered. She opened her mouth to call Claro but he was already sitting there, rumpled and yawning.

"A nudge," he said.

It stood outside the cave, a naked sexless creature with skin like a whale's.

"Even robos have eyes," she said, yawning.

Claro reached out a lazy hand and it waddled into the cave and sat down, crossing its little legs. Claro touched the nudge's head and the nudge stroked Claro's cheek with three stubby fingers. Sephony sat up.

"Touch nudge and think Hello," Claro said.

She put three fingers on the nudge's knee, on its rough damp skin.

"Think greeting," Claro said.

She thought, *Hello, how are you, so pleased to meet you,* saying it over twice to make sure.

A greeting washed over her in return, a pleasant, watery greeting that began as an idea and turned to actual words in her mind.

She decided to reverse the process. Touching the nudge on its puffy, three-fingered hand, she asked, *How do you see?*

Nothing. Its blank head seemed self-contained and hostile. She repeated the question.

"It doesn't answer," she said. "I asked how it manages to see."

"Ask, How do you know where you are?"

She put it that way and the answer came as if from her own mind — it had sonar perception of shapes and distance.

Where do you live? she asked.

Rock caves in the lake came the answer as if it had been her own idea.

Claro laughed. "Nice, very nice," he said. "You're getting on."

The nudge reached for her cheek with its three fingers, its touch so cold and penetrating her gums hurt. The nudge was saying *Come.* She shivered and said, *No,* the resonance of invitation and refusal falling into the mad fretfulness of middle-of-the-night nerves. *I'm very tired,* she said/thought, *I should love to come in the morning.*

The nudge leapt to its feet, flapping its arms and jumping hysterically.

"What's the matter with it?" Sephony cried.

Claro jabbed a hole in the sand. "Nudge lives now, not tomorrow. When you say no, nudge is, how do you say? . . ."

"Frustrated?"

"Frustrated." The nudge jumped and flapped.

"But I've only slept about an hour."

"Many nudges will come in this cave. Many more nudges. Better to visit by lake."

"Calm him down. I can't stand to see him jumping like that."

Claro touched the nudge on its palpitating belly and it dropped cross-legged on the sand, its head tilted to one side.

"Why isn't it impatient anymore?"

"I said yes."

"That pacifies it?"

"Pacifies. Yes."

"How very familiar," she said dryly.

A pulse rippled across the nudge's chest, bubbling under the rough gray skin.

"It seems very nervous," she said.

Claro looked at her blankly.

"Do they have a sense of humor?"

He frowned and drew designs in the sand.

"You don't know?"

"One nudge is like another."

"You mean, they have no personalities, they're all alike?"

"To me, yes. To nudges?" He shrugged. "You will see. When you are with nudges the only voice you hear is your own." He looked at her questioningly. She noticed he was speaking much better.

"All right," she said.

Claro touched the nudge and, rising with a little leap, it waddled ahead, sickle-shaped arms swinging in unison.

Up ahead shadowy figures massed like penguins on a

snowy shore. A few separated from the flock and waddled toward them, clustering and quivering, competing for touch. So many greetings. She answered as many as she could.

Led and pushed by the emissary nudges, they waded into the flock, which nervously scrambled for places, bumping and crowding into Sephony's mind. *Do you fly upright? Where is your flock?*

Nudges touched her coat, tested her pockets, and counted her fingers. She was explaining hovercraft when fingers reached up under her trousers and stroked her leg. She shook them off, but the touch was repeated. "Let go my leg," she snapped. All the nudges nearest her jumped and flapped their arms, beating the air with their little hands. A blow landed on her knee and she cried out and kicked. It did no good. A nudge reached up under her trousers and patted her leg from knee to ankle, the swarm gyrating like spoiled children.

The touch was impersonal, exploratory, testing the material. Her leg not her leg, but an object of curiosity. Why did she resist? Held apart, set apart, kept hard and sealed like a container of poisonous fluids. Afraid of contaminating people. Violation of privacy wasn't the only issue, but her fear of contaminating.

She thought *Wait* and sat down experimentally. She gave in, gave them something — yielded to their curiosity — the absence of resistance strangely important. A nudge clumsily removed her left shoe and sock and studied her toenails while the squirming crowd bobbed with excitement.

She absorbed it, child and mother, doubly examined.

"Claro?" She held her foot still.

"Yes?"

"When I'm thinking, to myself and not to them, just thinking, they don't seem to read my thoughts."

"Who can say."

The pressure of bodies and minds suddenly lifted. Nudges were turning away and waddling into the lake. The nudge examining her foot joined the others in a mass exodus.

For a few moments heads bobbed on the surface of the lake, little hands splashed, then they were gone and the lake was still.

"Well," Sephony said, putting on her shoe, feeling a quickening, an easing, "no good-bye, no thank-you."

Claro laughed. "Nudges understand nudges like my people go from here to there. No nudges in other parts."

"Parts of what?"

"Domino."

The name echoed and spread.

"What is Domino?" she asked, brushing sand from her coat and trousers.

He waved his arms in spirals.

"Where are we exactly?" she insisted. "Is Domino a patch under England? Is it everywhere?" They walked to the caves.

He smiled, if she could call it that, his lips stubbornly compressed, turning silence into a moral imperative. "Tomorrow we travel," he said. "We see a beautiful garden and my village." She was so finely tuned to gray that the rough walls and rippled soil had nuances of color. Or perhaps she was just sleepy.

At her cave they said good night — she with words and he with an elaborate spiraling gesture — and she curled on the yellow cloth, facing the lake. She smelled fresh air, as if through an open window — night with a promise of tomorrow, a childhood freshness. Curled in safety, she sensed something unknown before her; it was a long time since she'd looked forward to tomorrow. She closed her eyes, suspended, and saw poppy seeds rolling on the kitchen floor.

CHAPTER 6

OVERNIGHT the pole had sprouted into a showy white spike. Glorious foxglove bells big as daylilies nodded busily, spitting tiny seeds that bounced off the petal bars and rained into the water, making tinkling sounds, faint as clicks against glass. Nudges swam hysterically just below the surface and the cavern seemed lighter.

"Flowers grow every morning," Claro said. Rumpled and splotched with sand, he splashed water on his face and drank hungrily.

"Is it safe?" she asked, knowing the hazards of strange water.

"Is good," he said.

"What a difference," she said.

"Every morning flower seeds become one with water . . ."

"Dissolve?"

"Dissolve."

He brought water for her and she drank from his cupped hands.

"Like raspberries," she said, thanking him, and squatted by the lake for more. It was so full of life this morning — flowerbells quivering, seeds falling, and nudges churning the water like a school of mackerel. A flower fell. More flowers fell, tumbling mouth first and floating sideways, wreathing the pole in widening circles. Soon the lake was adorned and the pole was bare. Nudges fed relentlessly and Claro was flying over the lake, a swimmer on air, coat drooping — she held her breath at his ease and grace — zooming like a herring gull, snatching up handfuls of flowers. She laughed. As eager to feed her as a doting human mother, yet able to fly. What else could he do?

The petals tasted like artichoke hearts. She ate slowly, savoring the delicate aftertaste, and when she finished he flew over the water and harvested more. She trusted he knew what was digestible; she had to trust that. We had flowers for breakfast, she would tell Peg, and Peg would ask, Didn't you worry if they were poisonous? And she'd smile wickedly and say, Yes, but you know, one has to plunge right in.

She studied him. He was sturdy and muscular — his shoulders broad, his arms and neck thick and somewhat short. He carried himself proudly, coiled inside himself, holding energy and thoughts in reserve. A soundless current emanated from him, on the verge of randomly turning him, she thought, into something unpredictable.

She draped her coat over a rock, washed her face and arms, and rinsed her teeth. A few flowers drifted by, yellow pistils peeking through the bells, soon snatched under. What sort of life did the nudges have at the bottom of the lake with their single mind like a mushroom fungus?

Claro smiled a thin, crooked smile, and held out his hand for them to move on.

The tunnel, with its green glow, was a touch of home, a touch of yesterday, though eons ago. She could walk forever, neither leaving nor arriving, marking time on a fog-shrouded islet hovering between sea and sky. But they did arrive. The place was lovely in an austere way — a vaulted crossroad where four Gothic arches yawned into neutral light.

"A worldmaker carved this," Claro said. "Choose which one goes to my village. Choose which one we take."

Each tunnel pointed in a different direction.

"Surely you know the way."

"Oh, yes." He laughed. "Choose." Their voices were absorbed by stone.

The space filled with hands — gray and gaunt and bony as crabs, crawling across the beautiful vault to its pinnacle and down the ribs. One hand, more aggressive, came to rest on an archway. Was it a warning or an invitation? It fluttered into a fist, opened and closed, and whirled hysterically. Sephony stepped toward it.

"Done," Claro said, and propelled her by the elbow.

The tunnel was crimson and warm, so narrow she touched red phosphorescence and was stung, as by poison. Something malevolent oozed into the air, something monstrously casual and inviting. The tunnel breathed like a sleeping creature, its walls moist and swollen, its malignant dome closing in.

Claro tightened his hold on her elbow and hummed a monotonous little tune over and over, the same maniacal notes in a low register. Dots of pain blinked on her fingertips. His profile was grim in the crimson light; he seemed on the verge of swelling again.

She ran — she had to run — and he kept pace, enduring his own misery. The noxious air silenced her, so heavy on her larynx and chest. The moist redness blurred and exhausted itself and then she was out in the nasty twilight and drew a deep breath.

"What? What?" was all she could say, feeling alone and twisted. She was afraid he would hum again.

Claro was terrifying. His face loomed, enlarged and isolated, a hard-edged secretive face lit from inside, hanging remote from her and stony in itself.

"How will I get back?" she cried furiously, "how will I get back?" He seemed to be snapping his fingers in her ears. She struggled to shrink him to his proper perspective — it was more than a trick of light — but his detached face hung between her and the now-complacent red tunnel. His jaw muscles twitched; his eyes were hooded.

He began to sing enthusiastically in a language full of vowels — a raucous song sounding wildly out of tune — from deep in his throat. A touch came alive on her shoulder, a baby's breath of memory of a grand presence full of light. All the while Claro sang loudly and solemnly as if staring at death and shouting it down.

The song ended on a descending flourish and he stood whole and full.

"I am only Claro," he said sadly, and took her hand.

A sexual rush flared into her hand as if her palm were a breast. Astonished, she closed her eyes and the sensation vanished. She opened them and it flared again, flowering and branching. She had a curious sense of settling in, of resting on a nugget of pure self — a nugget that could, if it wanted to, say yes.

"We can fly," Claro said, and she wondered why they couldn't earlier. "Not to my home — to a Muzid garden — they make beautiful earthworks. Arms around."

The ground shifted and her body grew feathery. She nestled into him, moved by the contours of his chest and belly, his vinelike arms, his jaw against her ear. She flew in a haze, eyes wide open.

They landed in a park plumed with trees at the horizon — a contoured garden whose only colors were shades of green and gray. They walked, linked, merging with the intense and limited spectrum. Every species was heightened and exaggerated; every plant was either bursting with life or on the verge of dying. Enlarged liverworts and swollen mosses. Brilliant green slime molds and pale gray cacti. Monumental ferns.

The garden vibrated through Claro's hand as they tugged each other from tree to tree. Behind a fat clump of jades she found a miniature garden and marveled at dainty fringed stalks tiny as thorns; she touched a halo of baby hair around a berry. Passion flared in every node and branch. She was a blue-tongued leaf, a transparent bulb on a wavering stalk; she was the undulating lawn and the web of prickly hair. If she could find a smaller garden and a smaller one, each complete and large in itself, she would put it in her pocket, carved on a cherry stone.

The garden was theirs until a group of creatures appeared around a bend — Muzids, she assumed — moving stiffly and jerkily like vertical crabs. Bare-chested, they wore long narrow skirts in bright colors.

Two Muzids approached, one brown-skinned and the other reddish, gesturing excitedly with bony fingers, squealing "Eelie, eelie." Claro spoke with them in a high-pitched chatter. In the center of their foreheads was a lump that quivered and seemed to be alive; something within rolled around under delicate and blue-veined skin. An eyelid, yes, an extra eye. Their bald heads were small for their bodies and their jaws long for their faces. They had tiny nose holes. The extra eye appeared to be useless, while the pairs of eyes, deep and cat-like, glistened expressively in answer to Claro's introductions. The brown Muzid had flat triangular breasts; the red Muzid, Sephony thought, might be female.

"With two eyes," said Claro, "they see in light. The third eye sees into shadows and other darkness."

"Ah," said Sephony uncomfortably; perhaps her mind was one of the dark places into which the third eye might penetrate.

"They invite us to visit them," Claro said, "when the garden closes."

"I look forward to seeing your home," she said, nodding formally to the woman.

Claro translated. The Muzids squealed "Eelie, eelie" and stalked away, waving their rodlike arms.

"I shouldn't like to be forever without the sun," Sephony said. They sat on a log under bearded palms like trolls' heads.

"Or without rain," Claro said.

"I shouldn't like any one weather for long."

"You are a . . . traveler."

A heady, comfortable thought. "You wouldn't happen to

have a bit of food," she said. He vanished and materialized in a minute, proudly dropping greenish-gray spotted pears into her lap.

"They are safe," he said.

He didn't grow fatter, but his presence increased; a sense of him enveloped her with every bite. She hungered to ingest the juicy pear swimmingly like an amoeba. She ate down to the core and nibbled around the seeds, ate another and another, faster, watching Claro devour his pears in savage bites, seeds and all. She remembered a story about a culture in which sex was performed in public and sharing a meal was the ultimate intimacy.

Whistling and clanging shattered the quiet. Muzids in rotorized caps flitted through the park, vicious as hornets. One blew a whistle, another hammered on a cymbal, shooing a group of their fellow creatures, reversing direction, and somersaulting toward Sephony and Claro.

"Noisemakers," said Claro. "Guards, you would say."

The noisemakers glared at them, rotors spinning — extra eyes spinning.

"Have we broken a rule? Is eating not allowed?" She suffered a flash of sympathy for strangers routed from Regent's Park.

"The garden closes," said Claro.

They rushed for the exit and joined the Muzid couple at the gate. She wished she were a single spot of light, invisible and observant, so she could see a third eye in action. It would glow, she thought, and penetrate like acid.

Together they crossed a plaza where creatures milled about, chirping like cicadas on a summer night. The plaza floor, etched with geometric designs and figures like Joshua trees, feathered off into fog. Creatures crisscrossed and disappeared.

Through the mist a hill appeared, pocked with arches and stairs. Their sector, the Muzids said. Sephony and Claro held hands in a black tunnel, led like children on a rope. A door creaked open and they went through. Still complete darkness — no phosphorescence. Sephony bumped into something solid, passed between what might be pieces of furniture, and eventually found herself sitting beside Claro on a fabric-covered bench.

They sat in the dark, hearing domestic sounds. No light for visitors, she realized in dismay, no light of any kind.

She should have guessed. The third eye sees in darkness, Claro had said. She should have asked, What of it? But facts were surrounded by walls and only when she bumped into them did she stop, ashamed, and think, Ah, yes, consequences. Facts dazzled her, they were so powerful she took them at face value. She didn't speculate. Marek used to accuse her — used to, that was strange — used to accuse her of failing to abstract and synthesize. You babble all the details, my dear, he used to say, why don't you just pick out what's important? Perhaps out of her milieu she became stupid; perhaps intelligence is the ability to think of thinking while life is in motion.

"You might have warned me a Muzid house is totally dark," she said.

"You would not have come."

"What are we going to do?"

She felt him shrug.

She hoped her eyes would adjust, but eyes open, eyes closed, she saw only darkness. Claro breathed evenly beside her. From the distance, perhaps beyond a wall, came gentle clicks and thumps and high-pitched chatter. She moved closer to Claro, felt him solidly connected to her. Her own breathing was rapid and unbearably loud.

"They could kill us in the dark," she said, half seriously, "we'd never know it was coming. What do you suppose is that thumping?" She beat the rhythm on his thigh. "Like that. It's very loud."

Claro laughed. "Oh, that's your heart."

"Do you hear my heart?"

"I hear mine."

She leaned back and tried to relax. The seat was covered with rough cloth like burlap. Her skin prickled, it was trying to see through its pores. Perhaps this is how Muzids evolved, she thought; eons ago they were driven by a need to see in the dark and developed a third eye, whereas we discovered fire.

Footsteps and voices approached; something clattered by her feet. She felt embarrassed about being seen while she was blind.

Claro chattered and the Muzids replied antiphonally.

"Which voice is which?" she asked, determined to understand the music of their speech.

"Miga, the man, has a high voice. The woman is Lersch."

"What are they saying?"

"They're sorry you can't see their paintings. Lersch is putting a plate on your knees."

Paintings, well, she was sorry too. She touched the plate and picked up a cold slice of something bitter like cauliflower.

She and Claro in the dark. Their hosts in the light. How did blind people avoid self-consciousness, under scrutiny like protozoa? She stared alertly at the voices, trying to interpret lilts and clicks.

"Claro," she said. "Can you get us a microtorch?"

"Good. I go home."

An exchange of chatter, a tap on her shoulder, and he vanished. And if he didn't return? She would develop a third eye, see Muzids as flames, prowl their tunnels growing long-jawed and squeaky, developing a language of touch. The air quivered and Claro was back. With a click the room sprang into being, softly lit by a bouquet of nodding fibers.

Murals blazed along the upper half of the walls. Enormous leaves and brilliant flowers broke into lozenges, one form traveling into another — a journey of golden stamens, red and blue petals, and green stalks — abstract and energetic.

"Who did these?" Sephony asked.

"Miga and Lersch," said Claro.

The Muzids alternated speaking through him. Sometimes shadows brought one of the extra eyes to life and it drifted lazily in a bony socket. Their arms and long fingers wove patterns. Sephony could almost understand the weaving, the flap of emotions. But the single eyes had a secret, hovering quality, as if they looked inward as well as outward.

"Our family does painting work," said Lersch, her single eye brilliant orange with a dilated pupil.

"How does a person change to different work?" Sephony asked.

Miga and Lersch twittered in painful agitation, pausing nervously between phrases, making some strange appeal.

Sephony tried her simple question again. "What if a rock worker wants to plant trees in the beautiful garden?"

They laughed, a collective unto themselves. "No, no," they said. "Trees are the gardeners' work. We are painters."

Whistling and clanging gnashed and grated out in the corridor, dwindling, gnashing and grating again, then vanishing.

"Bedtime," said Lersch. "When we sleep, others work."

"We had better leave, then," said Sephony. "You've been very kind."

But they were caught in regulations; everyone in the sector was obliged to sleep. Miga and Lersch rose; Claro carried the lamp.

"You're very kind," Sephony said again.

She felt exhilarated and disloyal. Her hips swung. Patched into this stony house, she carved out a brittle sensation of freedom. She flitted from thought to thought, then realized she had been avoiding precisely those thoughts that were essential, for the Muzids, with profuse waves of their arms and squeals of "Eelie, eelie," left her and Claro in one small room.

She laid her coat on a carved chest, under a leaf pattern in muted shades of violet, green, and brown. She tried to think of something to say, something to take up time.

Claro stood across the room, looking gaunt and troubled. Muscles twitched in his jaw, his blue eyes glowed. Sephony ran her fingers through her hair; her mind fled from her body and rushed back to connect with it, in waves of contradictory desires.

He vanished with the lamp and returned on a breath,

having found, he said, a lovely bath for her. And it was — a grotto with a small, rock-rimmed pool of running water.

He left her there with the lamp and she sat, knees up, gratefully splashing away sand and sweat. With one finger she wrote messages to herself in the water — fragments that she forgot as soon as she wrote them, the words swirling as they drained away. She dried herself with a patterned cloth and dressed, hating the touch of her dirty clothes.

She tiptoed back to their room. Claro was lying on one of two padded platforms, arms pillowing his head, legs crossed at the ankles. He stared at the ceiling. Sephony set the lamp on the floor between them, lay down on the adjoining platform, and covered herself with her coat.

Sexual tendrils grew in an instant, a jungle of vines and morning glories quivering between their bodies.

"I don't know how to switch off the light," she said.

He swung his feet over the platform and squatted beside the lamp, his face fiercely shadowed.

"Leave a bit on," she said.

He dimmed the light, then slowly, heavily, stepped over the lamp and sat on the edge of her bed. He took her hand. She sat up quickly.

"I know," he said.

"You know?" She spoke thickly, dumbly.

He touched her head tenderly and stroked her hair. She closed her eyes.

"Then what will we do?" A small voice was dragged out of her, as fish-laden seines are dragged from the sea.

Shadows flickered on his face. He took her hand in both of his, stroking each finger from the base up over the knuckles to the tip. She tried to penetrate the concentrated face, silent with strangeness. What did he feel?

"What are we going to do?" she repeated.

He kissed her. His lips were strong and elastic, thin as the edge of a cup. Slowly, shamefully, she put her arms around his neck. He drew away.

"That is all," he said, mournfully.

"What?"

"I can do no more."

"But why? I can't bear it."

He shook his head. "Is impossible." He took her face in both hands and kissed her again.

"Impossible?"

"Impossible."

"Which is worse, to be unfaithful or to burn?" she asked bitterly.

On her cheeks he sketched delicate spirals across invisible hairs.

"We are different," he said.

She hugged her right leg, her forehead on her knee, rocking from side to side.

"It's better we go to sleep," he said. He stepped over the lamp and she heard the rustle of cloth as he lay down.

She curled on her side away from him, drawing her feet under the coat. Wave on wave, the currents rolled. She was attached to a warp of thin filaments. Every movement brought electricity, her hand sliding beneath her cheek, her knees changing angle; she was tormented, rocked as bell buoys rock in a storm, lights twinkling, bells ringing, weighted at the base and buffeted from side to side. She remembered lying on the grass with Aaron, stretched on their sides, knees entwined, the hot youthful touch. After that, intermittent cold.

The bed was hard and grew warm, as the bed in her house grew warm when the mattress current was too high. She threw off her coat. Why was he so scrupulous? She hadn't expected him to be, not Claro. Her nerves sang a mad song, the sound echoing along corridors lined with abrasives and needles, a grating song, wild and furious. Tossed up and down, she fell asleep between breaths and dreamed of nodding foxgloves stroked by disembodied fingers.

In the morning she woke to the sight of Claro tiptoeing past the foot of her bed, wearing only trousers. Startled, she glanced at his bare torso. She shouldn't stare at him, she shouldn't even see; she glanced swiftly, in stages, and finally took it all in. He paused, hands on hips, posing for her.

She thought of a zebra. Plumes of black hair flanked a black band that striped his chest, rippling over a pleated diaphragm. Pectoral muscles, high and rounded like loaves of bread, had no nipples. She was embarrassed, stung by the glare of intimacy. Muscles and tendons shaped his flesh in peculiar patterns.

Claro turned around and faced the wall. "You see," he said softly.

The black plumes on his back curled away from knobby, pale blue vertebrae. His shoulder blades bulged and humped, round and dimpled like granite boulders.

"I feel you look," he said, still facing the wall.

"I . . . yes, well, you are quite . . . different from what one is . . . accustomed to."

"Am I ugly?"

"Oh, no. Not really."

"I am different. More different than you see."

He turned and crossed his arms just under the nippleless pectorals, looking down at her sternly, sadly — a yellow-headed blackbird, the light of different circuits blazing in his narrowed blue eyes.

"Are you married?" Sephony blurted.

"Am I? . . ." He stared.

"Married. Are you married?"

Claro sat down at the foot of her bed, hitching up his trousers.

"Married," he said, feeling out the word.

"You are?" Nervously, she rubbed her right thumb against her left knuckle. Claro turned up the lamp.

Two hands crawled along the floor and up the edge of the platform to Claro's bed — puffy hands wearing jeweled rings.

"Yes." He laughed. "Married."

"Fine," she said, relieved.

"Or not." He slid closer and separated her hands, giving each a little shake. "Are you?"

"Well, of course. You know I am."

"Ah. Here?"

"Always."

"Ah." Claro caressed her knuckles with his thumbs.

"Please don't do that."

She tried to draw her hands away. On the other bed the puffy hands were dancing, pirouetting around each other in mirrored phrases.

"It's not nice?" he asked.

"It's too nice, rather, but under the circumstances . . ."

He brought her hands to his lips and kissed each knuckle tenderly. She closed her eyes. "Please, Claro, this is impossible."

"For you it is impossible."

"But last night you said —"

"Oh, that . . . that is impossible."

A storm flashed through him, of rage or suffering. His pupils disappeared — his cheeks puffed and collapsed — he bared his teeth and snarled, exuding a fierce convoluted energy. The storm vanished as swiftly as ball lightning.

"Please," she said, "I'm sorry . . ." She must have made some terrible blunder.

On the other bed the hands bowed to each other.

"Quickly," she said, "do you see anything? On your bed?"

"Dancing hands," said Claro.

A giant boulder rolled off her, moss on top and dislodged earth beneath. She clutched his head and kissed him with her whole heart, just below the cheekbone.

Claro stood and drew her with him. He held her against him, kissing her, his cup-edge lips pouring light and heat. Her fingers curled as if she'd been burned, she could not keep her hands on his shoulders, the intimacy was too extreme; although she craved something, some continuation or some release, she could not tolerate the silky, dimpled muscles. She tried to draw away.

Claro looked hurt.

"Please," she said, miserable with desire and revulsion, "please, could you put on your shirt?"

"You do not like my skin," he said, stepping back.

"I'm so sorry, I don't know what's the matter with me, or rather I do, it's not you, not your skin." Again her voice swam up from deep within her. "It's not anything you are, but it's so personal. Why, for thirty years I haven't so much as held hands with any man but my husband. So touching your skin . . ."

"Hands is skin."

"Yes, but they're out in the open. Your back and shoulders are usually covered, they're private, I feel as if I'm breaking the most awful taboo touching them."

"Taboo?"

"Things one is not supposed to do."

"Lips touching is not taboo?"

"Yes," she cried. "Why do some things bother me and not others?"

He pulled on his shirt. Sephony averted her eyes from his blue-spotted armpits.

"For me," he said, tucking in the back of his shirt, "is part of marriage here. One kind."

"Oh, but marriage exists in time," she said, "it's a condition, a contract, a law."

"How many marriages do you have?"

"Just the one." She looked at him suspiciously. "And you?"

He thought for a long time. "I think seven."

"You have seven wives in your house?"

Claro laughed and drew her to him, belly to belly. He kissed her ear, her forehead, the top of her nose, her cheeks.

"No, no, please," she protested. "I don't see, what is there? . . ."

"Seven wives," he chuckled. "They would laugh."

Troubled beats and pulses surged through the curve of Claro's abdomen — muscle and flesh not mingling with hers in total familiarity, but separate like electrified sculpture. She gave herself up to the exchange through layers of clothing, skin reaching skin, pores touching. They kissed and as Claro's intensity flowered in her she had a dim, strange vision of Alf in a field plugging the squat weeder robot into a brainer. No, no, she wanted to cry, they will cancel each other out. The robot quivered, the brainer twitched, both machines shook wildly, their different voltages and incompatible circuits clashing. The robot's arms burst from their sockets, the brainer smoked, and the machines shuddered to a halt, panels hanging open, burnt wires dangling, melted tubing dripping on the grass.

Sephony sobered suddenly and rested her head on Claro's shoulder.

"I see you from inside," she said.

CHAPTER 7

THEY LEFT THE LAMP for future guests and tip-toed out. The gray plaza was misty and noisemakers grated in the distance.

"I will speed you to my village." Claro looked uncertain.

"I think 'there'?" She mimicked him.

"What can happen to you, I ask myself."

"But you know everything."

He turned away, pained.

"Let's do a test," she said. "Carry me a short way — just across the plaza."

His face brightened. He squatted and she climbed on his back, clutching with her knees, his hair tickling her cheek.

"Not tight," said Claro. "I move with breathing."

As his ribs expanded, heavy wind pressed for a second and the flight was over.

"We can chance it," she said, and they plunged into nothingness.

As "gold to ayery thinnesse beate," she thought, as "gold to ayery thinnesse beate," fighting for breath, compressed in a metal vise with ice clogging her ears. So cold, so heavy. Pain in every limb. She gave up and lost consciousness.

She woke, soft and dizzy, lying cradled in ropes, in a hammock. Night. Faces hovering — eyes and cheeks blurring with fluty voices and long hair. Light glowing through leafy branches. Something above was softly luminous. She was under a roof, but the hammock was attached to the branch of a tree. A figure stood by the rope, swinging her gently. Was she dreaming? Where was Claro? Nauseated, she drifted into sleep.

When she woke again Claro was touching her forehead tenderly.

"Are we there?" she asked.

"Yes." His blue eyes were searching, worried.

"I'm fine," she said.

"Some juice?" asked Claro.

"That would be lovely."

She twisted sideways. The floor was luminous too. Outside, beyond branches threading the darkness, two large disks hung in the treetops — a glowing floor and a dark roof — connected by poles and shaded by leaves.

He gave her a heavy cup and she sipped a tart, thick juice.

"This is my house," he said proudly.

She swung her legs out of the hammock and finished the juice. The radiant floor was soft and insubstantial, like flour. When she stood, she sank, but not far.

"What are we standing on?" she asked, setting the cup on a table made from cross sections of a tree trunk.

Claro picked up a handful of the shining substance and poured it into her hand. Thin flakes, warm and silky, slipped through her fingers. They were too bright. She poured a stream of shining sparks onto the floor.

"And beneath?"

"Trees. Rocks. Water."

"No, I mean what's the actual floor made of? You know."

"This."

She squatted and dug, pushing aside soft, satiny flakes that cohered after separating. She dug and dug and reached no hard surface, no floor. Thin flakes whispered against her wrists.

"But you don't fall through," she said, standing.

He laughed and gestured to the grove. Beyond the adjoining house were other suspended glowing houses. Figures moved, shadows among shadows of leaves and branches, their feet bathed in light.

"It's very beautiful," she said. "It's where you would live. A circle of light in a tree."

"Come," said Claro, pressing her hand gratefully. "Meet my family."

The spell broke. Where could she run? The room was small and sparse. A pole with pegs held her coat and some strange clothes. The hammock was suspended between the pole and a branch. She appealed to him silently to wait; she wasn't ready to meet his family.

But he led her around a partition into the next room, if one could call it a room when there were no outer walls. Four people were sitting on a rug, around a low table. They stood up to greet her. The women were tall and slender with long hair. Theirs were the eyes that had hovered over her.

His wives, she thought. She did not know how to behave. Claro's arm was around her shoulder.

"Wife, Orta." A tall, pale woman with a taut face and blond hair nodded graciously. A delicate vein pulsed in her right temple; her skin was translucent.

"Wife, Leuma." She had an expressive, soft face and light brown hair. They spoke words of greeting.

"Daughter, Mimi." Mimi gave her a cold, inquisitive look.

"And brother, Grask." He was impassive.

So this was Claro's family. Part of it, at any rate. All had Claro's intense blue eyes and wore identical pants and tunics in pale colors. They were very handsome, these people who belonged to him. She felt lumpish, as with her sister or with Peg's friends. She could barely meet their eyes.

"Very pleased to meet you," she said, trying to smile.

Leuma stepped forward. "You are hungry," she said, and took Sephony's hand, her fine fingers softening the resentful flesh.

The yellow-wood table held bowls of nuts, grains, sliced fruit, and a loaf of brown bread. Light glistened through the weave of the rough, geometrically patterned rug. They made a place for her beside Claro. Orta and Leuma sat opposite, Mimi at the foot, and Grask facing the forest.

Here she was, a strange woman in their house, sought out by their husband. If only there were some apparent difficulty for them, some edge of discomfort. She was perplexed by their hospitality: food heaped on her plate, pleasant voices, an air of quiet acceptance. Suddenly hands crawled out of the radiant floor — hands with three fingers, spidery hands, blue hands, arthritic hands — crawling up the partition and over the table.

Mimi gave Sephony a sharp, startled look. Her hostility, if that was what it was, was a relief. A lanky blue hand tiptoed across the fruit, balanced on the bread, and leapt onto Grask's shoulder. He took hold of it and threw it out into the night.

"Wait!" she cried. "What does it feel like? I've never touched one!"

Grask frowned and conferred with Claro, their language excited and multitonal. How monotonous English was by comparison, using so few pitches. "Old," he said.

Taking courage, she glared commandingly at the flock of hands and they scurried to the edge of the house and collapsed in a ragged row, fingers quivering at her reproachfully, rustling the shiny flakes. But she waved them away, feeling a bit mean-spirited as they crept off.

The women tossed their long hair, their necks lined with blue veins. Which was Mimi's mother? Or was her mother one of the other wives? Seven, he'd said, good grief. They talked in their musical language, leaving pauses and looking at her expectantly.

"The bread is delicious," she said.

Leuma broke off another chunk and offered it.

"Where does it come from?"

"Village kitchen," said Leuma. She spoke haltingly, as Claro had at first, but with more words. "Visitors like our bread."

"Ah. And are the gardens communal?"

"You are sad," said Mimi matter-of-factly.

"I should like to see your gardens during the day," Sephony went on.

"Day?" Mimi giggled.

They dipped their fingers into the serving platter and she did the same, scooping out mouthfuls of nut-flavored grain.

"It *is* day," said Claro, patting her thigh. "And night, too."

"But no noisemakers," she said.

"No," he said, and everyone laughed.

She hadn't intended to make a joke. "What sort of clocks do you have?"

They laughed again.

"Memory and hunger," Leuma said.

"Time does not walk in a tunnel, nose in front," Orta said.

"We go to work," Grask said roughly, and drew a diagram in the air that was oddly satisfying. They stood fluidly, Claro too, and chatted. A sound twanged in her mind, like snapping violin strings, the pitches overlapping. She took a handful of nuts and ate one that resembled a filbert. They stopped talking and made chewing movements with her. When she finished they resumed talking until she began eating another, then they stopped and chewed with her again. She dropped the remaining nuts in the bowl.

Grask and Orta vanished, then Mimi and Leuma, who waved just before she went.

"Oh, what a muddle," Sephony said, when she was sure they were gone.

Claro dropped to the rug and put his hand on her knee. "What is wrong with my family?" He stroked her knee with his thumb.

"Nothing. Everything. You're so quiet with them. Are they angry that — how shall I say it — that you brought me? They don't seem to be jealous . . ."

"What is jealous?"

"Oh, a sour feeling when another person has something that belongs to you . . . or something you want."

"Oh yes, *having* people," he said sadly, "and *having* feel-ings."

"Is it wrong? Marek and I belong to each other because we've lived together a long time and raised our young and —" Her voice strangled and turned squeaky. "You're possessive, too . . . you say 'my family.' "

"Everything is my family." He gestured outward to the grove.

"It's hard to imagine not being possessive," she said. "One would have to be very confident . . ."

He compressed his lips and puffed out his cheeks, stub-born and affectionate.

"Ah, Claro," she said sadly, "belonging is very compli-cated. Very lonely." On a dim sculpted pedestal a stone woman reclined, bready and muscular, with squared feet and a hole for a belly.

Claro's cheeks deflated. "Come to the forest," he said.

She put her arms around his neck, her cheek resting on his warm chest. He held her as if they were a single creature. She felt dark and hollow, dark and weightless, flowing out to him.

They landed beneath the house, beside a shallow brook flanked by stones and bushes. Light from the floor above glis-tened on the water.

The house rose slightly like a feather on the wind. Did she imagine it? It was such a slight movement. She marked its position by an adjoining branch. The floor settled, was a bit lower than the branch, then higher, as if it rose and fell on breath.

He drifted up and lay on his back like a lazy swimmer.

"I wish I could do that," called Sephony.

"I'll take you," he called.

"Why can't I do it myself?"

"You can if you find the field."

He arched and slid through the air headfirst, muscular and acrobatic but, in the baggy yellow shirt and black pants, ungainly. He reminded her of a large mollusk, observing life from inside himself, only his eyes peeking out, impudent and intense.

They took a path through the bushes to a large, dark pool like an onyx, ringed by stones. Moss padded the cracks.

Claro disappeared and returned with a pile of neatly folded fabrics. "For drying and wearing," he said, dropping them on a flat rock. "Call when you have done." He rose past the branches and disappeared in the house.

Sephony undressed and walked into the pool. It was knee-high at the edge with a bottom of small, sharp stones. She waded to deeper water and dove in — washing and swimming, drenching her hair — ecstatic to be buoyant, alone, and clean. When she was refreshed she washed her clothes, rubbing fabric against fabric, using her knuckles as a scrubbing board, dipping and wringing as ancient people did before machines.

This was the pleasure of solitude. Freedom to bend and rise without comment or compromise, at ease with stone and shadow, leaf and water. Desire oozed from her; she wanted nothing but this pool, these mossy rocks, these simple gestures. She could live here and hang her clothes on a limb. She was a particle, a stone, a tree; she was the motions she made, bending and rising.

The clothing Claro had brought consisted of loose drawstring trousers and a wing-sleeve tunic with a hole for the head. The fabric was thin and pliant, neither woven nor knitted, but all of a piece like beaten bark and textured with little slubs. Pale colors overlapped randomly — pinks, blues, and violets.

She carried her wet clothes to a shrub and draped them over branches, her best green shirt and blue trousers.

"Claro," she called, looking up.

He appeared at the edge of the house, dressed in the clothes of his people, and drifted down, shifting to avoid branches, his tunic ballooning around his thighs.

He frowned at the laundry, stately in his own clothes. "They can't dry here."

"Because it's not permitted?"

"Because it's always wet," he said, plucking her knickers from a branch.

"That's quite all right, I'll do it." She reached for her clothes, but he held them bunched and drooping.

"Arms around."

They flew over cobalt blue umbrella roofs to a clearing where rows of identical tunics and trousers hung like Indian madras drying in the sun. Heat rose from crevices; the air was dawn-colored. Her alien clothes, so bright and reminiscent of parties, hung on a vine. Birds twittered and high above were clouds — the atmosphere without westerlies giving the illusion of infinite space, an outside that was inside.

Back in the house, sitting on the rug, her elbows on the table, fluffing drying hair with her fingers, she felt the alienness of clothes. Claro, pacing back and forth, a storm brewing in him again, was serious and prophetic in his own clothes and his own place. She was the clown, the one in costume — the cloth soft but not supple, pressing in the crook of her elbow, her breasts hanging heavily.

He paced, lips compressed, growing heavy and thicker, his jaw muscles twitching.

She saw a wave crashing against a rock, the spray foaming up and subsiding.

"I want you to tell me," she said, confident of the moment, "how you brought me here."

"Very difficult," he muttered.

"How did you do it?" she insisted softly. "Why me?"

Another crested wave shattered against the rock and a ragged fog drifted in from the horizon.

"This is how it was," he said, dropping cross-legged with a sigh, giving her a strange, fierce look. Reluctantly he cupped his hands, one above the other, as if holding something fragile. "I saw you, open inside, like limping birds. So sad . . . broken. In another field I saw you in a bottle of air, on fire, your whole self burning."

She was shocked.

"Sometimes the air was black and I thought you were

gone . . . sometimes blue, not so bad . . . but mostly it was gray and I watched you and knew you have one foot in Domino, and I brought you down through holes which are always here . . . many holes."

He smiled proudly, his chest swelling. "I am a ladder builder." He patted his chest. "Ladder builder. Keeper of wells. My family are well diggers and ladder builders."

He was gaunt and intense again, his eyes blazing.

"Can you see other people?" she asked urgently. "Anyone at all? Could you do it right now if you wanted to?"

"Ah, Sephony."

"How?" She touched his arm.

"Oh, I see them. So many . . ."

"How do you see them?"

"People come through. Like sickness coming. Or a bad spirit. The same people come again and again."

She felt as if her life depended on knowing more. "Do it and tell me what you see," she said passionately.

He grew thin and old, the skin of his face was parchment on bones. He closed his eyes, concentrated and pure as if he were about to die. His voice was quiet and hollow.

"This I see now. Thick, gray clouds. Holes in clouds. Air bottles dropping through, holding people. New people dropping through. Man running in place, child banging head against wall, young woman biting fingers. I see them, they do not have foot in Domino. Many bottles. People broken. I move, find people I see many times. Naked old man with brush and can of black paint . . . paints on himself, forgets to eat, black legs, black stomach, hair, face — forgets everything. Young woman with baby, in room full of things, cannot find chair, no place to sit, no place . . . scratches elbow, spot grows thick from scratching, bleeds. Blind man . . . inside him is himself smaller, and again himself smaller, and back and deeper, a tiny man he tries to touch."

Claro took a deep breath and shuddered. Flesh returned to his bones. He lifted his head. He was worn, spirit drained, blue lines under his eyes. Sephony clumsily drew him to her and kissed his cheek. He was stiff with weariness. She took his face in her hands and kissed him on the mouth, a dead mouth shaped like lips, the face hanging like a full moon.

"Claro, Claro," she cried, "come back."

She helped him into the hammock, his legs limp and heavy, and rocked him gently, feeling ashamed. She had asked too much and he had not reproached her. She was selfish and greedy.

He was still sleeping when Orta, Leuma, and Mimi returned. They took no notice, came and vanished, changing clothes, bringing food, moving partitions, passing in and out like stars on a windy night. Their language was soft and melodious and they gestured intricately like dancers.

Leuma woke Claro for supper by whispering in his ear. Sephony was locked into herself, a useless guest with no place of her own, watching Claro swing his legs over the hammock and look at Leuma with eyes emerging from dreams.

Sephony went to him and touched his shoulder lightly. "Does it always make you so tired?"

"When I saw you it was worse." He looked up humbly. "Much caring. Much caring."

His meaning stunned her; she could not address it, even if they had been alone.

"Do all of you see visions?" she asked.

His smile was sweet. "Many can. Orta sees, but not Leuma. Mimi is too young."

Leuma frowned. "I see clouds, pale shapes. Eyes not strong."

"Rather like me, then," Sephony said with a deprecating laugh. She exchanged a look with Claro. What did it mean that he cared about her? Love? Aaron had loved her. And the young when they were small. That was all. Claro was so strange, his suffering so private, such a solitary excavation. She had hurt him, her existence had hurt him. And he was satisfied. Is that what he meant by caring?

And Orta and Leuma ignored it, set out supper, and toward the end of the meal set out their own plans for her, a bit partisan, a bit competitive.

"We want to show you what Claro cannot," Orta said.

"Where women go," said Leuma.

Claro drummed on the table.

"I should be happy to," she said.

"Arms around," Leuma said. They drifted over the edge, knee to thigh, ear to cheek. Leuma was thin and angular, her arms vines across Sephony's back. One of Sephony's shoes came loose; she gripped the insole with her toes.

They landed in a clearing by a rock wall. Women were dropping from the air, tall and stately and identically dressed. Sephony wished, as when she was a girl, that she weren't so short. Keep your eyes open, she heard Dads say, watch where you're going. Greetings rose and fell like flutes and oboes, the same phrase repeated.

An antechamber led to a magnificent gray and pink cavern with a floor of polished marble. Women were dancing — it looked like dancing; they moved, yet gave an impression of stillness, waving their arms in angular, complex patterns. Orta and Leuma took her with them to a group of women in motion. Were they a family? They looked so much alike, so cold and austere.

She was truly the new girl at school. Except for Leuma there was not a friendly face in the group. She didn't know what to do, how to move or communicate. She felt heavy and exposed — her hands clasped in front of her, fingertips pressing knuckles in a convulsive embrace.

Clusters of women danced together. Her group made an archway of raised arms, and Leuma, with head and eyes, directed her to walk beneath. She passed stiffly under the canopy. The women made a circle around her. Bewildered, she looked from one to the other. Each made expressive gestures and expected her to imitate them. Sephony's bones were glass, her joints were lead. She could not mimic the winglike motions, the tapping and brushing patterns. She looked frantically beyond her circle and saw that elsewhere movement was picking up, legs were in motion. She longed to take Leuma aside and beg to be released from performing when she didn't know the steps. The group danced around her, exhorting her to imitate a raised foot, a spiraling hand, scooping motions. Orta drew her into the circle, arms linked across shoulders. She was too short, she reached up and they reached down and glided round and round. This she could do, it was even rather pleasant.

They separated. Women were spinning like tops, eyes closed, arms curved away from their bodies like wishbones. The room hummed with spinning bodies. One of the women in her group looked at her gravely. One by one everyone began spinning, and finally, with a sigh of acquiescence, Sephony closed her eyes and spun also. She gave herself up to boredom and fatigue. She became a dry leaf drifting in slow circles, spinning not because she willed it, but because it willed her; the spinning spun her feet, lifted her arms. She was soft and feathery, her bones hollow reeds. Light sang in her joints and around her elbows and down to her fingertips. The air too had changed. It was dense and powdery, she could lean against it. She spun and spun and time collected her and carried her to a place where motion was balanced and effortless, where everything was perfect.

And then it was time to stop. Just as she had said no to the voice that called "Come," she said no to oblivion. Beyond the movement, beyond the perfection of balance was a call to spin forever. She yearned toward it and pulled back. She sank to the floor while the room spun and she floated like a feather up, up, ineffably up. The feather hovered, floated down, and she opened her eyes and saw that everyone was lying on the floor, chests heaving, limbs collapsed. She smiled and dozed.

They all left together, rising into the air. This time Orta carried her. In the house they stood enraptured and suddenly all three laughed at nothing. She noticed a similarity in Orta and Leuma, the shape of their mouths, a proud expression.

"Are you sisters?" she asked.

"Yes," said Leuma.

"Oh, my sister and I could never . . ." She didn't even know how to phrase it.

"You spun well," said Orta. She had a slight lisp; her tongue pressed against her front teeth, as if to censor some excess.

Too energetic to sit, they paced the small room, kicking puffs of radiant flakes.

"Claro is different from you," she began.

"Speak," said Orta, "he is not here."

"He's so serious, like a stone, whatever I think or do goes to him and is weighed. It's that look in his eyes, as if he were going to die any moment and it wouldn't matter."

The sisters nodded.

For an instant she glimpsed a terrain punctured by holes and bottles of air, where time meandered and thought exploded. Where light sparkled on the intersections of a perfect spiderweb for centuries and centuries, crystallizing into connected dots. Where an intricate lattice of sunlit dead branches brought life into the forest.

"Are you both married to Claro?" she asked.

"Is different here," said Leuma mischievously.

"I can see that," she said.

"Can you?" asked Orta.

"No, probably not." She rested her head on her hand. The long day was taking its toll. She felt heavy-limbed, her cheeks dull. She walked to the edge of the house and stared into the treetops. "It never rains here," she said stupidly.

"Arms around," said Leuma and took her under the house. They washed their hands and faces in the brook and cleaned their teeth with leaves.

"If I were a good climber," said Sephony, looking up along the dark line of the trunk, "I could come and go on my own."

"No trouble," said Leuma as they rose.

Sephony sat on the hammock and took off her shoes, settling them carefully onto the luminous flakes. Orta laid her old clothes on a table. Claro appeared with Mimi. For a moment his maleness was obtrusive; he was an object, something she'd been talking about. She felt disloyal.

"We had a nice time," she said. She looked at the four of them as they spoke in their language and was glad to feel neutral, neither included nor excluded.

"We all sleep," Leuma said.

Claro frowned. "They made you tired," he said.

"I'm just fine," she said, yawning and twisting back into the hammock.

He touched her forehead lightly and disappeared with his family, leaving her cradled in the music of their conversation, a soothing sound like waves and distant birds.

CHAPTER 8

TOSSED IN THE AIR like a sick goat — she was tossed up and down — tossed and caught. She closed her eyes and was back in the dream, weightlessly flying; opened them and was tossed.

"Good, good," Claro said, "lie on the field." Or so it seemed; everything was garbled.

"Stop it!" she whispered, catching him around the neck. He muttered about lying straight and feeling the current, about needing to fly — looking fixed and stubborn like a boy gripped by a plan.

"Put me down, Claro."

"Words matter a great deal," he muttered, setting her down.

She sat on the hammock's edge and kicked flakes of light, fully awake; what had she said in her sleep? "I had a war dream," she said, "crushers were vaporizing people and houses . . . I was on fire . . ."

"I know," he said, slapping the rug impatiently. "I sat right here."

"You sat right here," she repeated uneasily. "What were you trying to do?"

He looked hurt. "I helped you . . . 'Fly, fly,' you cried, 'I must fly.' "

"I couldn't climb over the wall," she said. "I tried and tried . . . so I set myself on fire . . . and then I did fly, I remember feeling free."

"Yes," he said, and she gave him credit. He lay down on the rug and held out his arms. She lay down beside him and they interlaced themselves, kissing each other gently. His body was hard under a layer of softness, as if he wore many sets of clothes.

"I wish I could take you where tiny yellow pillows grow on stones," Claro said into her neck. "We would ride on the field, turning together." Why such sadness in his voice? He kissed her and her breasts hummed. She stroked the back of his head, his hard flat head.

"Today you will go," he said abruptly.

"No!" she cried, pushing him away. "I'll dig wells. You can make me a ladder down from the house and I'll come and go. Claro?" She kissed him, pressing her body against him, losing herself. "I don't want to go back."

"Impossible," he said, "impossible."

"Well, I could visit, couldn't I? You could come for me now and then."

"Never." He struggled, word exhuming word. "You are my shadow . . . you are the spirit of things, like hands." He kissed her forehead. "Your life is stronger than my own life. But now you go." He was gaunt, lines of suffering along his cheeks, his eyes blazing above deeply etched hollows.

Hearing Orta and Leuma chirping beyond the partition, they sat up, embarrassed. Grask drifted from a branch, carrying breakfast to the other side.

"Do you believe in life after death?" she asked.

"There is no death," he said flatly.

"Of course there is . . . you're not millions of years old."

He held still, his face very close. She looked into his eyes into a forest where ancient gnarled trees clung to a hillside — one tree split in two, moss and saplings growing in the crotch, the trunk bifurcated, hanging left and right.

"No," she said, turning away. "It doesn't make any sense."

He nodded solemnly. "I will sing to you now and then. You will remember."

Out in the grove, leaves curled against a glowing floor; children dove into the air, chasing one another like swallows. She printed them in her mind. Claro's family drifted out.

She and Claro sat opposite each other at the low table.

He tore a chunk of bread. His hands were strong and hairy, the tendons prominent, black hairs on the fingers. Hands shaped by hard work and thought, something fine and vigorous in the way they tore bread and brought it to his mouth.

"You're not simply going to disappear," she said. "We must send messages."

He became rigid and utterly alien; veins pulsed beneath his eyes.

"Come in dreams," she said boldly.

"In dreams." He slapped his chest and laughed. Black hairs peeped out from the neckline of his tunic. "I will try," he said.

"Time is so short, so terribly short," she said. "I want to see more of the village — the kitchen and where you work." She would prolong the day.

He laughed again, his eyes a warm greenish blue; she swam in them. And then he left her under the house with her own clean clothes and she swam in the dark pond. No tears, no release; she stored her sorrow. She dried carefully, memorizing each movement. "Good-bye," she said to the mossy rocks and trees. "Good-bye," she said to the pond. Claro floated down, like a herring gull on the wind. He smelled damp and clean. They flew up to the house.

He lifted her coat from the peg and she put it on. It was so heavy and stiff — she wondered why she'd brought it, why it had seemed essential.

They threaded leafy branches and swooped to a warm and bustling village kitchen. She memorized spice-scented grains softening in stone pots on beds of concentrated sparks. She memorized loaves of brown bread nestled on latticed shelves. Perhaps leaving soured her — it was too lovely, all that harmonious bustling making tracks in the glowing floor and in the many rooms circled around a tree.

Claro stuffed a chunk of bread in her coat pocket.

"Now I'm the chicken man," said Sephony.

"Oh, very good," he said.

They flew over the forest and drifted down at a desolate quarry where the illusion of infinite space was corrected by a narrowing and darkening. Stepping into a dingy, unfinished tunnel lit by fiber lamps, they watched people scraping rock, exposing phosphorescent veins and casting gigantic shadows, their tools making dry, metallic scratches and clanks.

"I start the wells," Claro said. "I know where to dig — how to catch the air. I tell others . . . there is a vein . . . and they say how do you know." He smiled wryly, one side of his mouth turned down. "Not too many mistakes."

In a crowded workroom Grask was fitting rungs into a sidepiece while Orta and Leuma worked at another table, whittling and gouging. Poles were stacked against the walls.

The women moved to a quiet spot between stacks.

"Mimi is gloomy today," Leuma said. "She will not say good-bye."

"But gloomy makes her happy," Orta said.

"Who is Mimi's mother?" Sephony asked.

"I am her first mother," said Leuma.

"I am her second mother," said Orta.

Sephony wondered what that meant, exactly.

They stood quietly for a while.

"I dread going home," Sephony said. "Having to explain. What can I tell them?"

"Do you pour out all your thoughts?" Leuma asked.

"Certainly not," she said, "but I can't keep this secret, can I?"

A jagged landscape approached in the distance — pieces of chairs, bushes, and doors — jagged fragments issuing acid ripples. And family faces, flattened on shards of glass. Glowering, shouting.

"It's possible, even quite easy," she went on, "to tuck some things away. But this would be enormous. . . ."

"They will not hear," Leuma said.

"They will not want to hear," said Orta.

"I hope you're right," Sephony said. "Do you know, you're the most tolerant people . . . how well you must get on with Claro's other family."

They looked puzzled.

"We are Claro's family," said Orta.

What could he have meant? Seven marriages. At the last moment she had blundered somehow.

"I must have misheard," she said, and they embraced.

Claro handed an auger to his brother. Like a bear in winter, he was fattening into a saddened fullness — his cheeks soft, his eyes veiled, his movements slow. He put a thick arm across Sephony's shoulder. With a twinge of distaste she felt the side of his body like a goose down coat pressed against her as they walked out into the dark, unfinished tunnel.

They walked leisurely, hand in hand, and stooped through a rough opening into a cave — the bottom of a well, she supposed. Tools lay beside a ladder, a lantern glowed. Everything was brown.

"Don't you have seven wives?" she asked.

"This well is not finished," he said.

"What did you mean, then?"

"Seven marriages, not seven wives. You are a marriage. Work is a marriage."

"I'm a marriage?"

"Oh, yes," he sighed.

She stroked his cheek high on the bone, the smooth skin, feeling a simple, tremendous happiness. Sorrow crowded against it.

"I can't bear to leave," she whispered.

He held her against his padded softness; it was all the comfort in the world. She wanted to rest here forever. She mustn't cry, crying would be humiliating.

"Where will I come out?" Her jaw was frozen.

"Wells do not go the same place each time."

"But where . . ."

"London, I think. Not Brussels."

"Ah. And the other well, the one to my house?"

"That well goes someplace else now."

"That's fine." Her voice was unnaturally high. "It'll seem more . . . natural to be coming from London."

"I traveled," Claro said. "To travel you must like the future."

"I want to give you something," she said, taking off her memory band. "It's the only thing I have . . . you won't be able to use it, but . . . please." She stretched the bracelet around his wrist.

"It's my treasure," he said sadly.

"Arms around," she said.

Her knees clasped his thickened waist like a dancer, unashamed. Beyond desire, she was grafted onto him. Their upward flight began with a jolt, a moment's dizziness, then a slow, uneven drift. They talked a little, kissed occasionally. She would have liked to remain in this state of prolonged languor, as in the hours preceding her father's death, when time was coated with thick snow and each minute was an extended step through drifts. She could not hold time, could not coat it with snow, it rushed like wind in a chimney and soon they were on a ledge against a ladder, holding each other. Claro was lean again and his cheekbones flared.

"So," he said.

"So," she said, tracing lines beneath his eyes.

"Who knows what I will learn," he said. "If I'm very sad perhaps I will come as the chicken man."

"I'll look forward to sleep," she said. "Night will be my best time."

"You go to a new life, I go back to the same."

"I'm sorry."

He stroked her hair, leaving imprints on her scalp.

"You can bring someone else down," she said lightly. "There are ever so many needy people where I come from."

"No." He was drawing into himself, becoming very gaunt.

She stroked his face, his eyebrows, she outlined his mouth, all memory concentrated in her fingertips. He put his hand on top of hers and pressed it against his cheek.

"So," he said.

"So," she said.

"Can you smell it?"

She shook her head, puzzled.

"London," he said.

"Not yet," she said.

"I'll wait here," he said.

For the first time she looked up. Above was a circle of light the size of a ceiling lamp. What did it represent? A street? Someone's house?

"Go," said Claro. They kissed. The snow thickened as they clung to each other, pore to pore.

Grief propelled her; she tried to rush without looking back, but he was calling in silence; he and all his world still loomed behind her. She climbed and turned, climbed and turned. His foreshortened figure grew smaller and smaller and finally, when she could not bear to see him dwindle altogether, she gave him up. She cried then, perched on the rungs while the sky — it was sky — yawned overhead. Her feet were lead, her mouth was dry.

Some traffic noise. A hiss of wind in branches. She climbed the last rungs apprehensively. Earth at the rim, bushes and trees beyond. It appeared to be a fairly private spot. Someone's garden? A park? At least it was empty, that was a bit of luck. She clambered out of the hole and when she dusted herself off and looked back it was closed. Shocked, she tested the spot. Solid earth, grass and weeds.

CHAPTER 9

"I'LL BRING OUT the sherry, Seph," Marek said, striding into the kitchen. He stopped. The kitchen was empty, everything orderly but unfinished — cutlets on a tray, broccoli on the cutting board. Water dripped from the tap. He turned it off.

"Sephony!" he shouted. Emptiness answered.

He jabbed the communicall and reached Dote.

"Have you seen your mother?" he demanded.

"She's in the kitchen."

"No, she's not. Something's wrong here and the Watleys are due in a minute. The table's not set. Dinner's not cooked. Go look for her."

He ran out the kitchen door, calling her name all the way to the stable. Inside, Alf crouched beside an ailing sheep.

"Have you seen Mrs. Berg-Benson?" Marek asked.

"No sir, haven't seen her."

"You've seen something, Alf."

"Something happen to the missus?"

"Why do you say that?"

The old man looked up with veiled eyes.

"Come now, Alf. Mrs. Berg-Benson isn't where she ought to be. What do you know about it?"

"Why me, sir?"

"You know damned well," Marek snapped. "You see everything."

Alf stood and dusted his hands on his coveralls. He was short, white-haired, and muscular.

"Seen a chap in the orchard."

"What?"

"Over at the north end. Wearing black he was."

"Why didn't you call me?"

"I thought he was one of them inspectors."

"Damned stupid. Was Mrs. Berg-Benson with him?"

Alf looked surprised. "No, he were alone."

"When was this?"

"Maybe twenty minutes ago."

"Twenty minutes!"

A craft whined and landed. "Damn," Marek said and raced around the drive to the front door. Simon was greeting the Watleys.

"Simon! Is she upstairs?"

"No. We checked every room."

The Watleys rotated their heads a few degrees, acknowledging some slipping in the machinery of manners.

"Excuse me," he said, "bit of a problem." He turned back to Simon. "Alf saw a stranger in the orchard. Get Dote and Melani, will you?"

"What is it?" asked Twyla.

"I'm terribly sorry, most irregular. Ah . . . we can't find Sephony, she seems to have disappeared. At least we think she has."

"Well-well," Britt drawled, stroking his slender mustache.

"She hasn't done the cooking, I'm sorry to say."

Melani burst through the door, trailed by Dote.

"I think we should ring up Peg," Dote said.

"Good idea," Marek said without enthusiasm. "Don't tell her anything special, just be casual about it."

"She could have gone for a walk and fallen, twisted her foot . . . or something," Twyla drawled. "There's about an hour of light still."

"We'll help you look for her, of course," Britt muttered.

They split in pairs after Dote reported Peg hadn't seen her all day. Marek and Britt searched the apple orchard and around the pond, and they all met in the orange room after dark, discouraged and confused.

"What are you going to do?" asked Twyla, picking at a biscuit.

"It's ridiculous. I shall have to call the police."

"Damned inquisitive lot," said Britt.

"Maybe she's been kidnapped," said Melani.

"Please don't worry about us," Britt said judiciously, "anything we can do to help, you know."

"She would have screamed," said Dote. "She couldn't have been kidnapped without screaming."

"Be a dear," said Twyla, "look in your mother's room and see if anything's missing — cards, personal things . . . you know."

"Mum was feeling better lately, I thought," Simon said almost to himself.

"Hasn't she been well?" asked Twyla quickly.

"Nothing serious," said Marek. "A bit tired. Too much studying."

"I see," said Twyla suspiciously.

Marek stroked his chin. "A bit of a breakdown. Doctor said she was to rest a lot. Heard voices, that sort of thing, cried a lot."

"How long?" asked Twyla.

"Since the spring. Since April, I think, about five months. Too many machines, always speeding herself up, all those papers she was writing. On top of her responsibilities."

"Well-well, old man," said Britt, "it must have been rather rough on you."

"An adjustment," said Marek, "it was rough on all of us."

"Rough on Mum," said Simon quietly.

"His mother's champion," said Twyla.

Dote returned. "Nothing missing that I can see. Her currency card's in her bag."

"That settles it," said Marek, pushing himself out of his chair. "I'm ringing the police."

He walked the Watleys to the door. "Sorry the evening wasn't quite up to the mark."

"Don't apologize," they said.

Two policemen arrived, young and efficient, asserting themselves and blanketing him with authority. Captain Waintree was pale and humorless. He and his silent assistant began in the kitchen, red recorder lights glowing on their chest pockets. They moved into the larder, staying within cooking territory. Every vegetable and egg in place.

"What do you suppose the metergun is doing in the potato bin?" Melani asked.

The captain's nose reddened. "What indeed?"

"My mother wouldn't measure anything in the larder."

The metergun — an orange, snub-nosed thing — had a cold precision, lying on its side among the potatoes.

"Where is it usually kept?" Captain Waintree asked briskly.

"In the entry," said Marek, reluctantly, as if he were betraying Sephony. "Don't waste time on it — she gets absentminded."

"Don't tell me my job," Waintree said, his nose reddening again. "Call your employees. I want everyone around this table."

Being ordered about was another jolt. Recorder lights winked. The inquiry was cold and official. Marek's sense of authority drained away; he was sucked into a vortex of violent plots, forced to waste time. Kidnapping. Murder. All of them were suspects.

The assistant took the children to search the larder and the house, while Marek, controlling his anger, followed Waintree into the clattering search craft. The detector panel reduced the topography to a series of line drawings; the officer shouted matter-of-factly about shallow graves and corpses.

"We'll put out an alert with her body code," said Waintree when they landed, "and check the nearby hospitals. If she's been kidnapped or injured we'll find her. Nothing else to be done now."

"Right," said Marek, his jaw tight.

The policemen left and the house was quiet. It was very late. Marek wanted to smash something, run somewhere, do anything but sit with the children at the kitchen table, anger churning. He sucked on a stomach tablet.

"Waintree took the broccoli and cutlets," Simon said, "and printed the potato bin."

"She hates the Watleys," said Melani. "Maybe she had one of her fits."

"Don't call them fits," said Simon.

"It's so eerie," said Dote, "like those awful stories Gramma tells."

"Go to bed," said Marek. "Go to sleep."

"Have you a theory, Dad?" asked Simon.

A suspicion like mucus lodged in his throat. Did she run off with a view to seeing that old flame, Aaron? No one would do such a thing in the middle of cooking. Why did he think she had run off?

"What makes you think I have any theories?" he muttered.

"I'll be awake all night," said Simon. "She could be walking around with amnesia."

"We've all gone a bit round the bend," said Dote, "ever since Mum started her degree."

"You can't expect her to cater to you all her life," snapped Simon.

"I don't expect to be catered to."

"You do, too," said Melani, "more than any of us."

"Because I get less," Dote said, glaring at Melani.

"Go to bed," Marek said, "and I mean now."

He sat at the table and grew old. He had no thoughts. His head was heavy and empty; his stomach ached. He went up to the bedroom. No scent lingered here, no breeze of return. Sephony was gone and the room was barren. He sat heavily on his side of the bed and dropped his shoes on the floor. He was not good at reconciling conflicting emotions or balancing opposing points of view. He had no patience with ambiguity. As he cleaned his teeth he swung between fear and a desire to break the mirror. Sephony had been gone a few hours, but it seemed years and a terrible loss. He imagined scenarios of her return. He held her tightly. He shouted at her. He scattered her ashes on the pond.

Curled on his narrow side of the bed, not daring to stretch out toward the center, he fell asleep immediately, but woke to a feathery touch on his cheek. He rolled onto his back, eyes wide open and heart pounding. He knew, as if a message had just been delivered, that Sephony was all right. He touched his cheek. It wasn't knowledge, it was some mental trick. Yet he was as certain of her safety as he was certain that he lay in bed. He tried to summon anxiety; it would not come. He talked to himself — objected that his mind, under stress, had created its own consolation. Another voice seemed to answer: Sephony is all right, no need to worry. All clues are false. Trust in her return.

He woke with the same certainty and tried to dismiss it on the way down to breakfast. Simon was hunched over the table, peeling an orange. Melani and Dote were frying bread.

"How did you sleep?" Marek asked.

"Bloody awful," Simon said.

"That so?" He took some tea and sat down heavily.

"I feel really rotten."

Marek cleared his throat. "I, ah, I had a peculiar experience. Rather like a message."

"About what?" Melani asked quickly.

"That your mother is . . . ah . . . all right."

They took a while to absorb it.

"Maybe I'm dotty," said Marek, watching the young console themselves with breakfast.

"What if it's true?" asked Melani.

"What if what's true?" asked Marek.

"What if she sent you a telepathic message?"

"Mum's not the sort," said Dote, with a warning glance at her sister.

"She sees hands," said Simon, spreading bean paste on his toast.

"That's accidental," said Dote. "Telepathy's a discipline. She's never studied telepathy."

"Maybe she has a gift," Melani insisted.

"Maybe she does," said Simon. "Maybe if it happens again, it's proof. What do you think, Dad?"

"Rubbish. I'm going to ring up Waintree and see what they've learned." He knew what they were thinking. Even if she had sent a message, he wasn't the sort to receive it.

Waintree came midmorning, with a new unnamed assistant. He took Sephony's body code from a tea towel and handed out decoders, directing them to search the farm. They hiked through fields and woods, holding the decoders over footprints, bits of clothing, or freshly dug earth. Marek's dream had taken the edge off his anxiety. Afraid of his complacency, he searched with extra zealousness.

They met for lunch; no one had much of an appetite.

"Have you called Gram?" asked Melani.

"Certainly not," said Marek.

"And Rolf?"

"Is there any point in bothering him?"

"He'll feel left out."

"Then call him, but tell him not to come home."

The day passed. Marek tinkered with an old robo. He saw Peg come down the road, hesitate at the gate, and walk on. Captain Waintree reported no signals at the airports.

Monday morning the young went to their classes. Marek rang up his assistant and said he was ill, hating himself for lying, hating himself for being ashamed of Sephony's disappearance. A hologram of her mocked him from the mantelpiece; she stood in front of a flowering rhododendron, her hair fluffy, dressed in blue. He clenched his fists to keep from smashing it, imagining her out there in the void. His mind skipped from one scene to another. Disappearance is worse than death, he thought angrily, from the point of view of the one who waits. She was responsible for his paralysis, for his shame.

Should he ring up her old flame, Aaron? Out of the question. Confide in her family? In her friend, Peg? Bloody hell. Tomorrow his mother-in-law would ring up and if Sephony weren't back he'd have to tell her. No telling what Hilary'd stir up. Forget it for now. He needed to do something, talk to someone. He couldn't spend the day puttering about, imagining things.

Reb Nacht. The little man with the big eyes. He should have thought of it immediately. She could be involved with those people and their bloody belief system. Perhaps she'd been doing things with them in secret.

Reb Nacht's voice was thin and reedy over the speaker.

"Reb Nacht, do you remember me, this is Marek Berg-Benson."

"The husband of Sephony. I hope she is well."

"Look here, old chap, I'm not accusing you of anything, you understand, but you wouldn't happen to be hiding my wife, would you?"

"What are you saying, Mr. Berg-Benson? You speak in riddles."

"No, of course you wouldn't, silly of me, just an avenue I had to explore. I'm terribly sorry."

"Something has happened to her? You don't know where she is?"

"Saturday she was making dinner for guests, return-obligation sort of thing, you know, no enthusiasm." His anger returned. "I went down to say I'd serve the sherry and the kitchen was empty — the food was just lying about. What do you make of it?" He was belligerent, but he couldn't stop himself.

"Make? What do I make?"

"I don't know. Mysteries are your business. The police are

useless. Apparently a stranger was wandering around the orchard. I thought if you knew of some group . . ."

"Did she leave a note?"

"Nothing."

"Her disappearance has nothing to do with our work, I assure you, Mr. Berg-Benson, nothing at all."

"The police think she may be kidnapped . . . or worse. I don't know why, I think she just left." He cleared his throat and felt calmer. "Sounds queer to say it, but I'm sure she's all right."

"You have an . . . ah, intuition?"

"You might call it that. Melani, our youngest, suggested telepathy. Tommyrot, of course."

"You had some . . . ah, idea?" Reb Nacht asked sharply.

"Saturday, in the night. Like a message."

"Take comfort from it," said Reb Nacht slowly. "It's not a coincidence. She's thinking of you."

"You'd trust that?"

"I'd trust it."

"Would you ask the police to stop looking?"

"No," he said, "I wouldn't go so far. But I wouldn't expect the worst. I would be reassured about her safety."

Marek sighed. "How do I get through the day, Reb Nacht?"

"That is difficult. Waiting — and you don't know how long. I will phone Anna — do you remember Anna? — they got on very well, there was a bond. Anna understands strange things. I will call her."

"Thank you, awfully good of you."

"How was your wife's state of mind recently?"

"Not too bad. More able to handle things — this dinner, for instance, I thought it was a good sign that she was willing to make a dinner."

"She didn't just wander off. You would have noticed if she were vague and abstracted."

"I think so, but I don't notice every little thing. No, she

wasn't like last spring — wait a minute. This summer some chap kept ringing up for her, always when she was out. Never called when she was in. The children kept leaving messages about a mysterious caller. Unnerving to Sephony. I wonder I didn't think of it sooner. I'll mention it to the police."

"If you think it's relevant."

"Do you?"

"Difficult to say, knowing so little. Possibly. Are you implying surveillance and kidnapping?"

Marek hesitated. "Or she planned on leaving."

"Very strange . . . for her."

"Quite."

"What can I tell you? Let us go back to the problem of passing the time. Are you a keen gardener?"

"Not as keen as Sephony. Look, I hope you don't mind being imposed on like this. Our family and friends are rather a straight lot. The ones who came to dinner thought the whole episode quite mad. Helped us search a bit and then were glad to leave."

"So there are people, besides the police, who know."

"Just the Watleys. Not the sort of thing one wants to talk about, you know."

"Do you like music?"

"No, my wife's the one. I don't go in for art."

"Ah."

"Sephony calls me a practical man."

"Even practical men must have resources in times of perplexity, Mr. Berg-Benson."

"I'll find something that needs fixing." Marek paused. "It's not knowing. How do you live with not knowing?"

"An old question, an old, old question."

"Yes, but this is specific."

"I don't mean to trivialize your anguish."

"It's not anguish, it's anxiety."

"The hands must be occupied. Do some hard, physical work. Gardening. Call me tomorrow."

The hands must be occupied. He was unraveling, he

didn't know what to do. He rang the office, but could make no sense of what he heard. He sent Alf away before the morning farm report was half-finished. He had no appetite.

In the afternoon he sat cross-legged in the herbaceous border, weeding ground elder from the Michaelmas daisies. He did it properly, the hard way, digging up the daisy plants and separating roots from rhizomes. Dreadful weed, one never got rid of it. Farther down the border, leggy roses needed pruning, and a waist-high clump of grass was overtaking a spot where poppies and red-hot pokers were due in the spring. He scrabbled in the soil for the rhizomes, feeling satisfaction as he tugged out handles of blight. By late afternoon five stands of daisies stood clear of weeds, their tight buds quivering above serrated leaves. He trundled the wheelbarrow to the clippings heap and dumped the mass of elder leaves and roots.

While Dote and Simon prepared supper he climbed Lilac Hill. He thought of parents whose children had disappeared, who tortured themselves imagining the children were starving and cold. It was horrible being attached to a void, like having pain in amputated legs. She wasn't dead — he was sure she wasn't dead — he'd always been sure he would die first. He sat on a log, breathing heavily. After all the pain on her behalf his anger returned, sure and grudging. How could she do this to him, how could she make him suffer? Was there a Sephony who could just run off? Impossible. Was she kidnapped, in silence, unseen? Improbable. Perhaps she'd met a man who was mad and was seeing him secretly. Were the phone calls a code? He dropped his face into his hands. Was she in trouble or was she punishing him? Did she have a secret life that excluded him? He couldn't go far with it, he wasn't interested in why people did things, but how. He was a decent chap. Damn.

Tuesday morning he attacked the roses, reducing the tall spindly bushes to squat, aggressive stumps. He forked the soil around them, tearing out the pernicious ground elder. It was a cool day, but he worked himself into a sweat, wielding the secateurs angrily, snap, snap, off with their arms, off with their legs, thorns piercing his gloves as he threw clippings into the wheelbarrow. He stomped the fork into the soil, thrusting the tines deep to lift out the roots, tossing huge clumps of elder and grass into the barrow. He moved down the border and tore out the ugly patches Sephony let grow between the plants. How much better each species looked when it stood clear and distinct. He could never get her to agree on that. He lifted out some feathery green stuff and something thicker, like centipedes. The motion of his arms made him angry. He had to move a certain way; if the fork missed its thrust or the earth resisted, his hands and arms surged with nervousness. He made mistakes and mistakes enraged him.

The phone rang in the greenhouse. He stomped to it and threw down his gloves.

"Hello," he shouted.

"Why, Marek," said Hilary's carefully modulated voice, "are you ill?"

"No, I'm fine," said Marek, wiping his forehead with the back of his wrist. "Just, ah, taking the day off. Doing a bit of gardening."

"A bit of gardening."

"Pruning the roses."

"Are you doing it together?"

"With Alf?"

"With Sephony. You know she hates your bare-earth policy."

"Well, we don't see eye to eye on everything, do we?"

"Let me talk to her."

"I'm afraid that's not possible."

"Is she ill?"

"No, she's fine, just fine."

"Call her, would you be a dear?"

"She's not here."

"Sephony is always home on Tuesday mornings."

"Not today, I'm afraid."

"Where is she?"

"I . . . ah . . . do believe she went hiking with Peg."

"Hiking with Peg."

"Um, yes."

"On a Tuesday morning."

"Um."

"I always ring up on Tuesday morning. Are you aware of that?"

"Ah . . . really? Every Tuesday? What a stickler you are for routine, Hilary. And you say Sephony is always home?"

"Always."

"Well." Marek felt he had a good grip on the conversation. "Today she isn't."

"Then something is very wrong."

"Perhaps she . . . ah . . . felt a need to break the routine."

"Why would she want to do that?"

"She's not the automaton she used to be, you know, much more independent. Comes and goes."

"Comes and goes, you say."

"Yes," Marek drawled.

"Well," Hilary said stiffly, "when she 'comes,' do ask her to ring me."

"Be happy to."

"Cheeribye."

"Good-bye."

He smiled craftily, a little twitching at the corners of his lips, as he drew on the soiled gardening gloves.

He finished the roses and took a bit of fruit and cheese for lunch. Food did not want to go down. He resented this shrinking of pleasure, the constricted throat, tight stomach, insides that wanted to contract and disgorge. He didn't like it, didn't like any change in his personality, he had been accustomed to himself for fifty years. He sipped half a cup of tea and rang Waintree, who made an appointment for two o'clock.

He hesitated before calling Reb Nacht. What did he expect?

"I hope I'm not being a bother," he said. "I need to hear a sane voice."

"No news, no news," Reb Nacht intoned mournfully. "I

spoke with Anna. She had no thoughts about the disappearance."

"Neither do I. No thoughts."

"How are you spending the days?"

"Weeding. If Sephony is gone much longer, the garden will be fit for a Horticulture Society tea. Pruned the roses this morning."

"Good work. I'm glad you're keeping occupied. Any further, ah, messages?"

"No. I've got no appetite, but I slept soundly last night."

"Good."

"The awful thing is the police. It's not that Captain Waintree accuses me of anything, mind you . . . but he implies I'm responsible."

"Are you?"

"Am I what?"

"The cause of her leaving?"

"We're not Siamese twins, you know."

"Well, it was just a passing idea. We make conditions, we create the Other. Isn't that what is meant by love?"

"Are you married, Reb Nacht?" Marek asked wearily.

"No, I'm not."

"You wouldn't preach if you were. I've never had the influence on Sephony that her mother has."

"We're getting into an area where I shouldn't probe," Reb Nacht said hastily.

"I don't mind. Beastly family, actually, sister who's barely civil, secretive brother, lots of wealth, love of power. Never saw the point to it, myself. They don't much approve of me, think I'm idle because I dabble at being an engineer and enjoy running the farm. Should be aspiring to something more, you see, something in a big way."

"I didn't picture you, if you don't mind my saying so, as humble."

"Humble? No, I'm fairly confident. I'm respected. How did we get onto this?"

"You were complaining that the police made you feel guilty."

"I'll sort it out with Waintree this afternoon. In the meantime I'll tinker with the old kiro for a bit. Edwin, we named him. She liked Edwin."

"I wish I could be of more use."

"Appreciate our being able to talk."

Marek stood by the workbench. The robo lay on its back, its chest open and its silvery arms and legs neatly laid out in segments. The circuitry was off in a dozen places and there were mechanical problems. Sephony used to urge him to buy parts on the black market, but the arrangements were so damned unpleasant. He was softening a piece of plexiglas for a kneecap when Alf knocked.

"Police, sir," he said, looking stern and suspicious.

"Damn," said Marek, laying aside the kneecap and turning off the burner.

He ambled into the front driveway. Waintree was staring at the shrubbery.

"See you have a basement," Waintree said, without preliminary.

"Early, aren't you?" said Marek.

Waintree stroked the tip of his nose. "Didn't know you had a basement," he said, nodding toward a small opaque window behind a braid of wisteria branches.

"Dates back to the twentieth century."

"May I take a look at it?"

"You mean no one looked in the basement Saturday night?" Marek asked, his voice rising.

"You didn't say there was a basement," Waintree said coldly.

"Good grief, man, let's go. When you said the whole house had been searched, I thought you meant the whole house. We never go into the basement."

"You seem very upset, Mr. Berg-Benson."

"Shouldn't you be? Damn it!"

"After you," said Waintree calmly.

They walked down the back hallway to a white door with an opaque glass panel, indifferent and menacing like a drugged eye. Marek tapped a button and a dim light illuminated the glass. He turned the knob.

A narrow stairwell sank into darkness. Space yawned on either side.

"Hold the handrail," said Marek.

At the bottom a cord hung in front of his nose, reminding him that the basement had no switches. He pulled it and a light blinded him. Ahead was a trail of cords; he walked from one to the next, more or less illuminating the area, Waintree behind him.

It was not foggy, but it might have been. The lights glowed feebly, leaving corners and edges in darkness. Stuffed chairs were indecently coupled, seat to seat, legs in the air. Ghostly tables slept with a moldy settee, blanketed by dust. Shelves held encrusted plates and wine bottles, an old burner, brushes with cracked handles, and tangled wires. The ceiling was supported by slender pillars.

Marek touched a wall. Something green came off on his finger. He picked up a small object and dusted it — a child's metal hovercraft, still bright red. He returned it carefully to its clean spot. Huge, plastic-sheeted forms lurked in the shadows.

Waintree was plodding around the perimeters with his torch. A red light glowed in his chest.

"Sephony is terrified of the basement," said Marek. "Only one in the family who has never, and I mean never, been down here."

"Nor your man in black, either, if that's what you were concerned about. We may be satisfied for the moment that unless someone had, ah, disposed of your wife and had the facility for simulating dust, which is doubtful but not impossible, then this search is fruitless."

Marek reversed the circuit, tugging the cords one by one, until darkness trailed behind them. They went up the narrow stairs. The door was a hideous dark green on the inside.

"People do not disappear," said Waintree.

"That has generally been my experience," said Marek dryly.

They sat opposite each other in recliners, Marek leaning back, Waintree perched on the edge of his seat, his hands clasped between his knees, his recorder light faint.

"They go away by themselves, carefully, but never cleverly enough. Or they are taken away. Or they are disposed of. Which do you think happened to your wife?"

"The second."

"Really," Waintree said, stroking the tip of his nose.

"She wouldn't up and leave and certainly not while preparing a dinner party."

"So you incline to the stranger in the orchard."

"In some way. Don't you?"

"Yes and no."

"Did you inquire in the neighborhood?"

"A stranger wearing black clothing was seen in a few places, briefly, not clearly."

"By whom?"

Waintree lifted the recorder from his pocket and rewound. "Cartwell, Archer, Gries-Hughes," a voice droned. Waintree switched ahead and the red band glowed. "Know these people?"

"Mrs. Gries-Hughes is nearly blind."

"Didn't say so."

"She's proud," said Marek.

"It's a common fact," said Waintree, "that when a 'mysterious stranger' is mentioned, suddenly he's sighted all over."

"You don't believe Alf saw him?"

"I don't believe anything, Mr. Berg-Benson."

"I think you bloody well do."

Waintree's look vibrated along Marek's nerves like a dentist's laser.

"You are not being charged, Mr. Berg-Benson, not yet, but I think — since you insist — that you know where your wife is."

Marek heaved himself to the front of his chair. "Do you know why people like us don't call the police? Do you know why we investigate livestock thefts ourselves? Do you?"

"Why?" asked Waintree sardonically.

"Because when the police can't find the criminal they accuse the victim. It didn't use to be that way."

"Do you know how often people report a theft when it's actually embezzlement?" Waintree asked.

"Do you know how often the police harass people into admitting a crime they haven't committed?"

"Calm down, Mr. Berg-Benson. We are still searching the length and breadth of this country. Neither your wife nor any companion will escape us. Unless your wife is dead. And the stranger does not exist."

"I appreciate your efforts," Marek said stiffly.

"She can't board any public transport in England without setting off a nerve coder," said Waintree, standing. "But we're concentrating on the area around Greenham Common."

"So close?"

"This chap, if he exists, has no craft, we assume he has no craft. She's in the company of a walker and hasn't gone far." His expression hardened. "Unless the entire assumption is wrong."

"There you go again."

"Now, now, Mr. Berg-Benson. We will find her, we always do." He tapped his recorder; the red light shrank and went out. He left.

Marek stomped to the workshop. Murderously, he reached into Edwin's gaping chest and tore out wires and chips. He forced an arm backward over his knee, the wrenching and cracking feeding his strength. He broke the other arm, and threw the legs against the wall. He felt like the man Waintree saw in him, guilty as if he had done whatever Waintree suspected, pushed backward into a torturer's box that reshaped him. Edwin's eyes glittered; he pressed them down into the sockets. He collected the parts, threw them into a bin, and kicked it under the table. Damn Sephony, for putting him in a false position.

"I'm not going to school tomorrow," Melani said at dinner. "I can't concentrate."

"Well, buck up," Marek said. He was tired, sapped, impotent. "They think she may be around Greenham."

"Did you ring Reb Nacht?" asked Simon.

"Nice chap, but he has no ideas. Your grandmother called."

"Oh-oh," said Melani.

"I, ah, said she'd gone hiking with Peg."

"Well done," said Simon.

"What if Gramma rings again this evening?" asked Dote.

Marek nourished a worm of irritation.

"We'll say she's out," said Melani, brightly. "We'll all lie."

"We'd better," said Simon gloomily.

"We can stall her till Saturday," said Marek.

"Maybe we should all remain home," said Simon.

How much Simon looked like Sephony.

"You don't want to hang about here all day," Marek said, still irritated.

"We'll see how we feel tomorrow," said Simon.

In the night Marek woke light-headed, his body adrift on the mattress. A faint light burned on the ceiling like a coating of ice on muddy ground. There were patterns in the ice — swirls, depths, and thin cracks. He was comfortable, even happy, he had not known such security since he was a child. And yet, comfortable as he was, he wanted to step out and up, put his feet on the ceiling, step through the thin ice, not to smash it, but to see what lay on the other side. He smiled, settled his hands under his head, and snuggled into the mattress. The patterns on the ceiling changed and developed. A frozen eddy swirled into a spiral. A slight roughening, like mackerels' breath on the sea, danced away in a lingering line. Caught up in this vision, he rose, helium-filled, closer and closer to the icy swirls and patches. He was just close enough to look into the ice and see, for a second, a tiny blurred figure. And then he was in bed and the room was dark.

CHAPTER 10

LOSS IS NOT DEATH, she muttered, loss is not death, but it felt like death. Even this garden was in a dreadful state — unkempt, the ground scruffy and poor. Ragged azaleas and stunted broom grew between oaks and beeches. The ground was littered with fallen branches. She picked her way over them, forcing herself to leave the spot behind. There was a clearing ahead, shrouded in mist. And a house? She pushed through scratchy yews, heading for lawns and stately oaks. Something smacked her straight on, jolting her, and she fell back into a pile of branches. Dazed, she looked up. What she had taken for mist was a scratched plexiglas wall, about five meters high.

She sat in the branches that had broken her fall, willing time to reverse itself. It's someone's estate, she said to keep panic at bay, a large estate outside London. Brown hands leapt among the twigs like toads.

Scrambling to her feet, she pressed against the wall, looking desperately through scratched plexiglas for a house, a street, people, some sign of domestic life. Mature trees cast late-afternoon shadows on the lawn. Paths curved around colorful flower beds, and far off at the horizon, roofs and towers rimmed the sky. Familiarity, a deathly familiarity, a slightly different angle, her position just slightly askew. Regent's Park.

Gloucester Parkway in the distance. Panic arrived in full force. She had come up in the Jungle.

Wells do not go the same place each time, Claro had said. A few more meters and she'd be on the other side. Another day or another hour would have made all the difference. A nervous, bony hand crept over her foot. She grabbed the index finger — it felt like a withered carrot — and twitched it into the underbrush. The hands scurried away.

She walked along the wall. If she could find a tree close to the wall she could climb it and work her way over. She kept walking. Way in the distance people were strolling before dinner and children played on the grass. Was there one brave person among them who would come close enough? Her heart pounded, she walked faster. On her left the canal wove in and among a grove of stunted trees, a cold blue line. Were the gates really sealed? She'd heard rumors they were merely overgrown.

She could almost feel Claro's hand on hers, almost see his intense blue eyes. The memory steadied her; she nourished herself with it, as if it were fruit. She picked up a good stout stick.

A gardener was bound to come along eventually. She had just to keep moving, keep a sharp lookout. She felt cold and unbalanced, attentive to roots and hummocks, to stiff branches and sinkholes. Then fear nudged her mind and she froze. Deep in, the trees grew thick. Would she know if she were being watched? She listened for rustling, for animal or human noises. Anything could attack her. It was so quiet. She remembered rumors of underground bacterial labs and a quarantine camp. Why was life punishing her the moment she returned? She forced herself to keep moving.

Three people were coming along a path from the canal — two adults with a very small child. What extraordinary luck. She beat on the wall with the stick and shouted. They stopped for a moment and looked toward her, frozen while she made encouraging noises. Then they turned the child as if it were a knob and hurried away. Only the child looked back, a small solemn face, from beneath the adults' arms. When they disappeared, Sephony sat on a log and imagined herself in their place, imagined hearing her own hoarse shouts and running away.

The sun was going down, creating anxiety in birds who wheeled and settled, scraping the air with their cries. She reached in her pocket for the bread. Something had happened to it — it was hard and stale. Would her hair turn white, also, would her heart stop? No forebodings. She would have to spend the night here, stifle her fear and hope for sleep. Then in the morning a gardener would pass by, or some other park employee, and would be persuaded to lower a basket from a pruning machine and that would be that. What would she say? How would she explain?

— I came up through a hole in the ground. — A hole, lady? — Well, you see, it closed up after me. — Very dangerous to tunnel into the Jungle, lady, how did you manage it without being discovered? — It was, you might say, an accident. — The police will have something to say about that. — I simply found myself here. — It's forbidden, absolutely forbidden.

The light was fading. The birds wheeled and cried. What was that groaning?

"I'd better prepare a shelter," she said, addressing a birch sapling. She searched for a spot that seemed right, parallel to the wall, in a thicket. She made a nest, building up the sides with branches and lining it with dry leaves, and set aside a large, leafy branch for a roof.

"There," she said. "What do you think?" Dusk was settling on the birch, absorbing it, blurring its dingy white bark.

She crawled into her nest, tugged the roof branch over her, and lay down, hidden at least, and protected as well as she could protect herself. The nest smelled of autumn and the ground was lumpy. She felt unreal, her limbs belonged elsewhere, they were numb and disjointed.

She shut her ears or they shut themselves. Hoots and screeches grew faint, all her senses were closing down. She felt nothing. Only her mind was active, imagining animals creep-

ing out of the bushes, sniffing round her. Had the small foraging animals survived? Did mad people wander freely? An
eerie stillness said no. It seemed to her that the place was
uninhabited, a wilderness. The emptiness was overwhelming,
she was in a vacuum, listening for sounds that never came,
only the faint sounds of wind and birds. The zoo had turned
into the Jungle. How did that happen? As she thought about it,
feeling sick as if someone were forcing her to believe something against her will, it seemed that the transformation was
deliberate or at least opportune, that the Jungle existed so that
people could believe it was horrible, so that a new generation
could grow up with a deep aversion to it. She'd heard mothers
threaten — "They'll put you in the Jungle." Was the Triangle
manipulating them? There was no way to know, only a pro-
found sense of being alone.

When she woke it was night. She lay in a pit of sound —
howls, cries, and barks passing overhead, spiraling and rising
to the stars. Points of light caught in the branches. She sat up.

On the other side of the wall, people were dancing and
singing. Lanterns stood on the ground, casting shadows on
painted faces and bizarre costumes. Antiphonal choruses raged
back and forth. She clambered out of the nest. Two girls
drummed in a spot just outside, their hair falling over their
faces. She rapped on the wall. The drums reverberated loudly,
the women seemed to be in a trance. She rapped again.

"Hello!" she shouted several times.

The light did not penetrate, the drumming persisted. A
young man danced with spastic frenzy, head jerking, flailing
himself. His howling was answered by other howls. From
within the Jungle? Sephony couldn't tell. She edged along the
wall, crouched near a lantern, and rapped again. A young
woman looked up, startled, and met her eyes. She tugged at
her companion's arm and lifted the lantern. Sephony looked at
them hopefully. The woman shouted; the dancer woke from
his fit. Silence fell as people gathered forward, their faces hostile and inquisitive.

Sephony stood up. The group backed away.

"Hello," she called. "I need help."

Silence.

"Not me," a man grumbled, "I ain't asking it nothing."

"What are ya?" someone shouted.

"Get me out," Sephony called. "I'm trapped in here."

"What are ya?" another voice repeated.

"I've had an accident."

"Y'see," a girl screeched, "there's loonies in there. I told you there was."

"Get some ropes," Sephony shouted. "Please. You could pull me out."

"They've done her over."

"It's a spirit," someone said.

"No, I'm not." Sephony spread her arms. "See?" She felt absurd, having to reassure them. "I'm trapped in here."

"Looks nasty t'me."

"Her colors ain't good."

"If you could get some ropes . . . some equipment . . ."

"Her eyes are burning."

"Please help me out of here."

"Spirit woman!"

"Get me out! Please!"

They snarled and shouted, slapping the wall, their faces ugly. Only two people on the edge of the crowd were silent, a man and a woman. She tried to get their attention, but they slipped into the dark. She wanted to kill the others for not believing her, only the wall stood in her way. She beat on it, screaming in rage, then sank to the ground. Their hostility was so much stronger than hers — penetrating the wall, beating her down.

"Leaves growing in her head."

"Spirit's going, can't see her no more."

"Let's sing, maybe we killed her."

Sephony crawled back to her nest. Jeering voices called for her, the drumming resumed. The birds continued their night music. The air was cold and damp. She huddled inside her coat, tense and angry. Eventually the people left, their lanterns twinkling across the lawn, and the night grew relatively silent. She pulled the branch over her head and after a long time she slept.

An early morning vapor rose above the trees, their uppermost branches clotted with scarves of webby moss. Doves cooed far off, ravens croaked. She edged along the wall, fighting roots and branches, the wet dawn in her bones, searching for a gate.

No point in planning conversations with a parks gardener. No one would believe her, no one would sympathize. She was tainted by the Jungle — a monster, a madwoman. What an awful way to look at herself, like being on trial and falsely accused, all the circumstantial evidence damning her. If she didn't take matters in hand she could starve to death in the middle of London — seen, heard, and ignored.

A blackberry hedge blocked her way. She pushed around it, thorns catching her coat and hair. Misty light wove through a grove of trees, touching fallen trunks and saplings. A terrible luring tune came from the interior, from just beyond a huge upturned root where the light was clearer. Shaking off caution, she walked stubbornly over the underbrush, every step terrifying and absolutely necessary.

On the other side of the root was a clearing — rather scruffy and gray, the ground dreadfully uneven. It seemed isolated, complete in its emptiness, a clearing in a wilderness. And yet there were human signs. In and among clumps of leggy stalks and patches of clover and ground elder, earth was spaded and worked, and raw earth had been recently turned. She stooped and picked up a stone. It was white and oddly shaped, more like a bone fragment. The sealed-in animals, what happened to them? She threw the bone away, shuddering, and pulled up her collar. What grew here? For whom?

The more she walked around the clearing, the more purposeful it seemed. From some angles the lumpy ground was orderly — mounds, actually, in rows. A good way to plant vegetables, but why was part of the clearing grassy and part freshly turned? A path, too wide for an animal track, snaked into the forest. The trees closed in; the clearing shrank and grew dark. A faint and ominous humming came up from the damp earth and shivered the grass. Frantic, she leapt over mounds and brambles and was back at the wall, beating on it with a stick she didn't remember picking up. Her hands were scratched. Could she dig a hole under the wall? What could she use?

In the distance a thin figure in dark clothing emerged from the mist, zigzagging through the shadowy trees. It was a young woman with long wet hair, coming resolutely across the lawn, carrying a sack over her shoulder. Sephony shouted. The young woman saw her and ran toward her, saying something. She came up to the wall and set down the sack.

"Morning," she called, astonishingly casual and friendly.

"Good morning," called Sephony.

The girl stepped back and looked Sephony up and down, apparently satisfied. "I didn't think you was," she said, or so it seemed. Her voice barely floated over the wall.

"I can't quite hear you."

The girl raised her voice. "You're not a spirit. Or a loony, neither. You didn't seem like one or the other."

"That's very kind of you."

"I'm gonna get you out," called the girl. "Can you hear me all right?" She was pale, not pretty, with hollow cheeks and an undernourished, determined expression.

"I remember you," Sephony called jubilantly. "You stood back last night. You didn't shout at me."

"Right."

The girl opened the sack and lifted out something made of ropes. "My bloke gave me his ladders. He wobbled about it, but I said I wasn't gonna let you rot."

She loosened a length of rope, its free end weighted with a stone.

"Watch out," she called, "I'm aiming where there ain't no trees." The stone cleared the wall on the girl's second try, the rope and part of a ladder snaking behind.

"Pull it in now."

Excited, Sephony reeled in the ladder while the girl shook out tangles. A square of red plastic among the rungs snaked upward and they tugged it on top until it hung evenly, the ladder dangling from both sides. The girl pointed a remote and the red square clamped tight to the wall.

Claro, Sephony thought, are you watching?

She climbed swiftly, balanced on high and maneuvering over the top, blindly agile, fear giving her wings to fly from one side to the other, and landed outside, in Regent's Park, hysterical with relief.

"You're super," she said. "Absolutely super. That was a tremendous thing to do."

The girl looked angelic, dazzling; she shook off thanks. "Pull fast," she said, snapping the remote. "Any park inspector seen that, they'll blink the bobs."

They rolled up the ladder and stuffed it into the sack.

"You've saved my life," said Sephony. "Sorry to be so wobbly."

"Let's skin out."

"Would you mind telling me your name?"

"Lela."

"I'm Sephony."

They walked toward the canal. The gray sky was beautiful as sunshine.

"Festy's a topper," Lela said. "He's new. Climbs over sometimes and does a look-around. Bloody deadly. How did you get stuck there?"

"It was an accident."

"What kinda accident?"

"I, ah, came up from underneath."

Lela slowed and shrank back. "Through a tunnel?"

"In a way."

"Crikey." She twisted a strand of hair, her look cold and suspicious.

"And then it closed up," Sephony said, hearing how strange that sounded.

Lela gave a little laugh. "Them things happen," she said, and they walked on companionably. "Where d'you live?"

"Near Basingstoke. But I have to ring first. And I don't have my currency card."

The teahouse wasn't open yet. They sat on a bench under the overhanging roof. Sephony wished Claro's bread hadn't suffered, she would have liked to share it. And she was very hungry.

"I brought you a couple biscuits," Lela said. She had a red mole on her lower lip.

"Oh, thank you."

She rummaged in the sack and gave Sephony a handful. "They're real tasty."

"Anything would be."

The girl's long hair fell across her cheeks. She wore a dark blue tunic and her shoes were coming apart.

"What a night, last night," she said, nibbling a biscuit. "They'll see spirits for years zimming out of the dark . . ."

"But you didn't see me that way."

The girl tossed her hair back with an intense, nervous movement.

"You didn't have a spirit aura and you wasn't a loony. Festy said I was the loony one. He wasn't gonna have nothing to do with rescuing you, except he gave me them ladders."

"I'm very grateful."

"I don't belong with them muckers no more. It's exciting and all, but I can't get lost in it like I used to. I used to feel mad and zimmed up, like everybody was last night." She frowned and the mole on her lip darkened. "You know what you looked like? You looked like the animals we see sometimes. Even Festy said that."

"I didn't see any animals."

"Don't know what they are. Seems like they wanna talk, they're so sad, pressing their noses into the wall."

"Couldn't you be imagining them?"

"Nah," she said contemptuously.

"When I was a child, it was a zoo."

"G'wan, you wasn't alive then."

"It's only about forty years ago."

"Crikey. People say it was hundreds."

"No, no, during the Great Drought."

"The what?"

"Don't your parents talk about the Great Drought?"

"I don't have none."

"Oh, I'm sorry."

"That's all right. Lots of us don't have none." She licked her lip, lingering over the mole. "You was lucky. People go in and they don't come back," she said.

"Oh?"

"Lost my bloke Jed that way — that's why I come got you. About three years ago he climbed over and didn't come back. We hadda pull in the ladder. And he didn't come back the next night. So this other guy goes over — Purvy his name was — and he don't come back neither. Scrawny mucker, took a knife with him — didn't none of us have lasers — lots of talk after, that we shoulda got one. Nobody else went in. Every night for a long time we hollered. Heard strangling sorts of cries, made your skin pop. I dunno. They must've gone loony or the spirits got them . . . or maybe they got et."

"Then I was lucky . . . that nothing happened."

"I wanted to hunt Jed myself," Lela said bitterly, "and then everybody said let Purvy. And he went instead."

"How awful."

"Yeah."

"What happened when you reported the two missing boys?"

"Oh, we didn't," she said, surprised, "we would've all got messed up."

"They could still be there, for all you know," Sephony said carefully. "Someone lives inside, I think — there's some sort of garden. Hasn't your friend said?"

"Festy ain't seen nobody," Lela said, and picked up the sack. "We better shove on. I'll be late for work."

"What do you do?"

"Cleaner. Mostly I work for Daly — she's been dying for

years. She don't like her nice old robo, so I wash her up and dust and cook and put on her legs and take her out. For Mo I sort of straighten up his shop when he ain't there — Festy's friend — he makes hollies. Where you headed?"

"I'm not sure."

"You could come with me."

"That's very sweet of you," said Sephony as they crossed over the canal. "Someone I know lives nearby. I think I'll go to Grove End Road."

"I'll walk you."

"Have you ever heard of the Society for the Preservation of Ancient Thought?"

Lela looked at her sharply. "Yeah. Daly has one of them old crosses with a dead man hanging on it over her bed. Makes my skin pop. Why . . . do you see auras?"

"I see hands."

"Wild. I see auras."

"In color?"

"Yeah, with little beads inside and waves. That's what's nice about being at the Jungle — seeing auras around my friends, all them lights, and it's like seeing their secrets. Yours was pale brown and it shivered all up and down your arms and around your head. A very sad brown with some specks of red in it."

Sephony walked in silence, imagining her body outlined in a quivering brown light.

"Lela," she said, "would you like to know where I've been?"

Lela looked at her sharply again. "You mean how you got in the Jungle?"

"Yes." Some tension released in her head. "I was . . . it was . . . how should I say . . . in a different world . . . underneath — Well, not underneath . . . outside."

Lela gave her a startled, radiant smile. "Mo's been someplace like that."

"What?"

"Everybody says he's making it up, but me and Festy believe him. What's the name of the place you were at?"

"Ah . . . Domino." It sounded ridiculous.

"No, that's not it. But it's someplace. You want to meet Mo?"

"Yes." Sephony walked faster. "Yes, of course."

"I'll tell him."

"How . . . ah . . . long was he there?"

She shrugged. "We don't see him that much so we didn't know he was gone."

"Ah. With my family it will be quite different."

The day was brightening. A metrocraft passed. A few people walked by. Sephony stopped. Reb Nacht's house was around the corner. Everything was large and potent — the street, city sounds, standing here with this girl.

"How can I get in touch with you?" asked Sephony.

"Crump. On Gloucester Road. I'll say it in your band."

"I'm afraid I . . . ah . . . left it behind," she said. "But I'll remember." She took Lela's wrist and recorded her own particulars. The girl's hand was bony and strong.

"You don't look like them sorts who live in Basingstoke," Lela said. "Such a warreny city."

"I live in the country, on a small farm."

"That sounds nice."

"You'll come visit, then."

"Will you ask me?"

"Of course I will."

"People forget."

"I don't."

" 'Bye," said Lela, tossing her long hair. "Tonight I'll knock up Mo and tell him about you."

"I owe you my life," Sephony said, hugging her. "And thank your friend Festy."

She entered into the little cul-de-sac and rang. Oddly, it felt like home, and the silver and black robo gladdened her.

"Reb Nacht," she said.

"Room seven — room seven," sang the fluty voice.

"I know," she said.

The robo twirled away.

She knocked at the scarred wooden door and Reb Nacht's nasal voice murmured "Come in."

He was dressed in brown coveralls, engrossed in his scanner, retrieving something, ensconced among stacks of books and printouts and smells of mildew and tobacco. He sighed, turned away from the machine, and glanced up at her — his eyes penetrating and sad, but not surprised.

"Sit down, sit down, my dear, make a space, just put those on the floor, that's right. I'll be only a minute. Haven't been able to reach archives for days. Ah, there we go. There it is." The ancient printer began a furious scratching back and forth; paper flew up and rolled backward.

"There," said Reb Nacht, rubbing his hands excitedly. "An account of the Mesopotamian flood. Very interesting, all the accounts of the flood. And you? Your husband has been frantic." He looked at her steadily from beneath hooded eyes.

"Ah." The other side was starting its grind.

"Let me get you a nice cup of tea. The Episcopalians down the hall always have tea."

The frenzied printer poured paper onto the floor in pleats. On the shelves old books split from their flaking bindings. She opened her coat and tried to touch the imprint of vines on her clothes.

Reb Nacht returned with a plastic cup of steaming tea and a sealed thimble of milk powder. "They're out of sugar."

"Thank you, that's lovely. I never take sugar." She set the cup on his desk and opened the milk.

Reb Nacht sat down heavily. The printer halted, whirred, and stopped.

"Now, then," he intoned, folding his small hands under his chin. "Your husband thought you might be here."

The tea tasted of raspberries. "Lovely tea," she said, flowers on her tongue, and sipped again. "Do you remember last spring," she said, "when some people spoke of interdimensional travel?"

"Where have you been?" he asked, his expression quick and curious. He leaned across the cluttered desk, his tobacco smell reaching her, warning her — so comfortable in this cluttered oasis of paper, dust, and history — that exposing her private life could flake it dry, like tobacco leaves or onion skins.

"I've just returned from . . . I don't even know what to call it," she said.

Reb Nacht sighed and leaned back, lips and nose resting on outstretched fingers, his large eyes grieving.

She said nudges . . . Muzids. She confided, described, held back. (What were Claro's other names? — Amos, she remembered.) Her story sounded totally mad, a truth that felt like lies, an excavated fresco crumbling when brushed by fresher air, a raised ship from antiquity cracking after centuries underwater. She marveled at her swift deceptions and inventions, so much happening at once, future tellings already a bitter metallic taste on her tongue.

Reb Nacht interrupted frequently. He was greedy for details about the third eye, the glowing floor, the spinning women. He was restless, alight with despair. His devouring interest almost silenced her.

"This Amos, a mythological figure, surely, of great presence. How did you feel about him? Your — as you called him — your inappropriate guide."

A brilliant yellow lichen exploded in a puff of light. "I got used to him eventually," she said.

"We will invite the study group," Reb Nacht said, his voice quivering. "We will discover the meaning of your wonderful experience."

Fond as she was of him, and grateful, she would give him some other gift — tape a description of the landscapes, perhaps.

"What can I tell Marek?" she asked.

"The truth, of course."

"You don't know him very well, do you?"

"He phoned twice."

"To say he won't believe me is an understatement."

Reb Nacht pursed his lips. "But you must try."

"Oh, yes, a hole opened in the larder floor, of course it did, won't you lie down while I ring Dr. Easton?"

"I agree, talking to a nonbeliever is frustrating."

"Annihilating, you mean."

"Then we will have lunch first. I'm ordering some eggs and rice."

She was hungry, starving, actually, but when the food arrived she pushed time away by eating slowly. Her lunch rested beside a stack of books. She read the titles — *Leviathan, Major Trends in Jewish Mysticism, Zohar: The Book of Splendor,* and *Zen in the Art of Archery.*

"You'll find your husband at home," Reb Nacht said. "He hasn't been going to work." He unearthed the phone, took her food box, and left the room.

The phone reproached her; she could not press the call buttons, could not violate its privacy. Her heart pounded and swelled up into her ears.

Melani answered, close and resonant.

"Hello, Melani," she said, wanting to cry.

"Mum?"

"Yes. How are you?"

"Dad!" Melani shrieked. "It's Mum!"

"Melani . . ."

"Hurry, Dad!"

"Don't shout so . . ."

"When did they let you go? Where did they take you?"

"What? I'm calling from Reb Nacht's."

"Hello, Sephony? Sephony?"

"Hello, Marek. Melani, be a dear and let us talk in private. I'll see you ever so soon."

"Well," said Marek.

"I'm at Reb Nacht's."

"The bloody bastard! I trusted him. He said he didn't . . ."

"Calm down. I've just arrived."

"Where've you been?"

"It's a long, complicated story, Marek, I can't tell you over the phone."

"You're all right?"

"Yes, yes. And you?"

"But where the hell've you been? The police thought you were murdered. They even accused us, the bloody fools. Oh, it's been quite a time, I assure you."

"You didn't call the police!"

"What did you think we'd do?"

"I just assumed you'd, ah, know I was all right."

"Well, I almost did, damn it, in an odd sort of way, I had a feeling . . . Came in my sleep, more or less. Couldn't explain it."

"Do you want to pick me up?"

"I'll fly down straightaway." He paused. "Although actually you'll be home faster by train."

"Quite right." She was unaccountably disappointed. "Reb Nacht can get me on with his card."

"Take the two-fifteen. I'll pick you up at the station."

"All right."

"I'll call the police and tell them you're back. So they don't catch you on the train."

"Catch me?"

"Body code bleeper. You're registered on all public transport."

"How awful."

"You weren't in one of those mental clinics, were you, where they don't give out information?"

"Nothing like that. Dear me, no."

"Well, we'll be all ears," he said caustically.

They clicked off. Sephony's fingers drummed in a hollow

of consciousness between being and returning. The door opened a crack and Reb Nacht peered into the room.

"How did it go?" he asked, rubbing his hands.

"He called the police," said Sephony dully. "My body code is registered on all public transport."

"But you disappeared, my dear. Vanished. Anything might have happened to you."

"It's . . . indecent. One never calls the police."

"Some people think nothing of it."

"Not us."

"Why do you find it humiliating?"

"I can't explain this to the police."

"No, of course not, you'll have enough difficulty explaining to your family."

"Exactly."

"So." Reb Nacht rubbed his hands and looked around the room as if books and papers could give advice.

"Suppose I tell the authorities I was on a spiritual journey," she said, "and I can't talk about it."

Reb Nacht sat on the edge of his desk and tapped his fingers against his mouth. "Yes . . . good . . . they won't understand the meaning of 'spiritual.' "

"The serious problem is Marek and the young. And my mother."

"Tell them the truth."

"Marek will say I'm crazy as a one-volt robo. Anyone would say I'm insane — I could say it myself. Could he . . . legally . . . put me in a mental clinic?"

"Do you think he would?"

"I don't know. If he were frightened enough, or threatened . . ."

Reb Nacht tapped his mouth impatiently. "If I remember from . . . ah, Elly's case . . . two doctors must declare you a danger to yourself and/or others. I suggest you stay calm, as you are now."

"Poor Elly . . ."

"You couldn't keep such a secret, could you?"

"Not easily. I don't know. Maybe I can. It seems the lesser evil."

Reb Nacht leaned his nose on his fingers. "I think," he said wickedly and wisely, "you might procrastinate."

Sephony's spirits lightened. "Yes, of course. Too tired, I'll say. Not ready."

"A lot of control in taking time. And speaking of time, my dear."

"The train. You'll have to get me on with your card."

"Anything else?" He rose and looked at her mournfully.

"Not that I can foresee. Just the basics. You've been wonderful to put up with all this."

She felt very calm. Reb Nacht punched her destination at the tube and she traveled to Paddington by rote, scarcely noticing where she was. In the train she stared into the window, lulled by the free-fall and smooth ride of the frictionless system. She saw a shadowy woman crawling out of a bog, pulling herself laboriously onto dry ground. Then the train ascended from the tunnel and glided into Basingstoke station and she was thoroughly anxious.

She slipped her exit card in the scanner and passed nervously through the split beam behind a couple marching with brisk little steps. No bleeps betrayed her. She breathed in relief and entered the west bubble. The moving walkway wobbled underfoot; the railing glistened filthily with oils and sweat. People scurried in and out of the membrane, an ugly, alien species — heads jutting forward, faces contorted, movements angular and nervous. Dispensing machines droned instructions while war games bleeped and buzzed, their gaudy lights and manic jingles overlapping in hideous dissonance. Outside, craft generated dirt and fumes.

Marek strode through the membrane, frowning, his padded jacket hanging crooked, his hair uncombed.

She couldn't speak.

"No hello?" he protested. "No hello? Really, Sephony."

He looked — untended. "I'm sorry," she said. "The machines . . . civilization is so jangling."

"Well, you don't want to be picking a quarrel with me about it."

"No, of course not. Hello, Marek." She couldn't touch him.

He turned away. "The craft's not far," he said stiffly.

The motor started. The craft lifted. Sephony looked out the window and back to Marek's profile. Long nose, thick chin with flesh doubled beneath, high forehead, messy gray hair. His lips were clamped tightly. Such a familiar, utterly strange face.

Marek cleared his throat. "Who was it?" he asked in a stifled voice.

"Who was who?"

"Who you went off with. Although how you managed to organize it so badly, I don't know. In the middle of preparing dinner for the Watleys, of all people. Well, Sephony, don't keep me hanging."

She almost laughed. "Oh, it's a terribly long story, and you're going to need lots of time to digest it. It's nothing like what you imagine."

But it was, in its odd way, she thought, and that part, which Marek suspected and dreaded, was what she would leave out. She looked at him again. Had he aged?

"Marek?" she asked, shuddering at the thought. "When did I leave?"

"Don't you know what day it is?"

"I'm not sure."

"You've lost track of time?"

"Just tell me."

"You left on Saturday."

"This past Saturday?"

"Yes."

"And today?"

"It's Wednesday."

"Four days," she said.

"Seems longer," he said.

"It does."

Marek looked at her. "You weren't kidnapped?"

"No."

"And you say it wasn't a clinic."

She shook her head. "Don't guess. You can't."

"You've got grass in your hair," Marek said.

CHAPTER ⚡11

EVERYTHING was veiled and unreal. Claro floating toward her, enormous and ballooning, the family shrinking to doll size. Claro floating forward, the family receding — big and small, big and small. She pushed lamb wedges to the edge of her plate and ate cauliflower and bulgar, waiting for a taste, a texture, something concrete.

"Aren't you hungry, Mum?" Simon asked.

"It's quite the biggest meal I've had in days," she said.

"Same here," said Dote.

Some details stood out. Melani's thin hunched shoulders, tufts of Marek's hair drooping over his ears like dry cordgrass. Something wrong with Simon's hands — a nasty aura oozed from them and made her think of illness. She patted his shoulder and he looked at her reproachfully. They all looked reproachful.

"It's not as if I died," she said, or thought she did, she couldn't hear her voice.

"Tell us what happened, Mum," said Melani, frowning, exasperated. "Why don't you tell us anything?"

"It's very complicated," she said.

Dote brought the fruit bowl. Sephony pressed the cutter into an apple and the segments fell away like petals.

She took her plate to the orange room and sat on the

floor, leaning against a pillow. Melani and Dote flopped cross-legged beside her. Marek and Simon perched on chairs.

"Why did you take your old brown coat?" Melani asked.

"Oh, I needed it," she said.

The emotional atmosphere churned and frothed, her memories rocky islets against which their expectations broke and fell back, their mutual disappointments crashing and recoiling like waves at high tide.

The girls looked her over, pursuing her.

"You're not wearing your memory band," Dote said.

"I gave it away," she said.

"You can't give away a memory band," Dote insisted.

"As a gift," she said, and they looked wounded.

"I'm sorry," she went on, from a great distance, "for not telling you anything yet. But I won't be pressed."

The young drifted away, sullen. Sephony and Marek climbed the stairs to their room. They slipped into bed from opposite sides, the sheet bunching into a ridge between them, and lay on their backs in the dark.

"Are you trying to drive me crazy?" Marek asked. "Is that what you're doing?"

"The third night," she said generously, "I dreamed all your heads were shiny plastic sculptures on pedestals."

"I'm not interested in your dreams."

"They melted . . . and when they hardened again your faces were all distorted and abstract — they had a rather grotesque gaiety."

Marek cleared his throat vigorously. "Nothing bad happened, I take it," he said testily.

"No." She smiled in the dark.

"Well, damn it!" He rolled on his side and struck the mattress. "It's bloody not fair! Not fair!"

"Shhh, no need to wake the young."

"Why should I be on the rack while you take your time!"

"I'm very tired. I haven't been in a proper bed in days."

"Where have you been, then?"

"I can't say. Please, I'm home. Can that be enough?"

"Maybe it isn't."

"Let's go to sleep."

"I can't sleep."

"Oh, Marek, don't be a baby."

He rolled away from her. She was tempted to rub his back to placate him, but her hand remained on her stomach. She would disintegrate if she touched him.

"Good night, Marek," she said. "We must watch out for Simon."

"What do you mean?"

"Something is going to happen to him."

"What?"

"Illness, I think. I don't know. Illness, yes."

Marek rolled over again, his body lumbering and slow, and put a hand on her shoulder. "You're sure you're all right?"

"Very sure. But I do need to sleep." His touch was tender, but heavy.

"Good night, Sephony." He patted her.

In the morning, alone in the house, the family at school and work, Sephony showered. She felt volatile, unmoored. She passed from elation to anger. At what? The house irritated her, being alone in the house made her angry. Well, then, that was specific enough, a basic problem, never solved. A single domestic issue. Why not take it up? Since she needed a room of her own, she would take one. She dried energetically with the blower on high. Take a room without asking permission. As a child she had felt the same clear conviction, running across the lawn, arms outstretched, into a driving rain. And again when she climbed into the well. She put on her clothes and laughed inwardly, guiltily, at the thought of herself as a troublemaker.

After breakfast she considered the possibilities. The upper floors were all bedrooms, baths, and storage. On the ground floor the video room certainly wasn't available and neither was Marek's study — his desk cluttered with equipment, his rifles hanging on the wall under glass. She walked through the laundry area, the orange room, sitting room, dining room, kitchen. She went back to the sitting room. It was austere and elegant — furnishings from the nineteenth and twentieth centuries, a Turkestan carpet, and a bay window looking out on the willow garden. Taking it would insult everyone's sense of propriety, including her own. A desecration, her mother would say. Still, they almost never used it.

She called Alf on the communicall. He appeared in the doorway, awkward and restless. By Marek's account Alf had seen a stranger from a distance. It made for a curiously distressing connection.

"I'd like you and Alfie to move some of this furniture out to the orange room."

"Alfie's in the pasture, mum."

"After lunch, then."

"Move furniture?"

"Most of it goes in the orange room, then my desk and things come down."

"Need to be careful of them tables and lamps, mum."

She saw fear of the indoors in his face and gnarled hands. Something was wrong with his hands, they made her feel anxious; like Simon's, they made her think of illness.

"Get Mason's boys to help you. And Alf," she asked hesitantly, "are you feeling well?"

Alf squirmed. Two of his fingers were permanently bent.

"You should take off a few days, perhaps. It's a bad season for being laid up. I'll mention it to Marek."

"Oh, not me, mum, you know that, mum."

"Well, think about it."

By four o'clock everything was in place. She scrupulously kept only those pieces that she had inherited, bought, or received as gifts, such as the walnut inlay cabinet now holding fichebooks. Her desk stood in front of the bay window. The room was spare, she liked the feeling of space. And it was hers. As for the orange room, well, for now it just had to be cluttered.

Sephony closed the door. The catch clicked. Nervously she stroked a jade bottle. In the shadow of the peaked hedge, orange dahlias bent their ruffled heads; pink and red asters glowed. She lay down on the Turkestan carpet, a gift to her from Aunt Bess. Digging her fingers into the velvety nap, she hugged the room to herself. "Claro," she whispered. She waited, a catch in her throat. Then she dared it again. "Claro." The word clung to the wall like a butterfly on a flower. "Claro," she said, softly.

"Sephony?" Marek's voice trumpeted from the orange room.

She leapt to her feet. Marek brayed again. She went out, carefully closing the door behind her.

"What's all this?" he stormed.

"Guess," she said.

"Don't play games with me."

"Try."

He glowered. "Redecorating?"

"No."

"I'm damn sure there's no leak again."

"No."

"Then why the hell is all the bloody sitting room furniture out here?"

"Not all of it."

He strode past furiously as she followed him into the room that was becoming her study, pressing her lips together to keep from laughing.

"You can't do this," he shouted, flinging his arms to encompass the travesty.

"But I have," she said.

"It's preposterous, Seph. We can't have a house without a sitting room."

"We almost never use it."

"You might as well close off the kitchen."

"Have you another suggestion?"

"For what?"

"For a study of my own."

"You don't dismantle a room without discussing it."

"Is this my home?" The question flared up.

"What a stupid question."

"Everyone else in the family has a room."

"You have the whole bloody house to yourself during the day."

"We've discussed this a zillion times."

"Well, don't you?"

"How about your study, Marek? It sits there, like your old rifle collection, uselessly yours."

"I need a quiet place to work when the occasion arises. And my possessions are my possessions."

"Quite right. And I respect that. So there you have it."

Marek hesitated. "Still, the proper procedure would have been to wait and discuss it."

"I've been waiting thirty years. We can renovate the game room eventually . . ."

"Oh, yes, when fortune falls from Mars."

"All right, let's discuss it." She pointed ceremoniously to a chair. "Now," she said, perching on the edge of her desk, "what do you suggest? Mind you, this room is far from perfect, as far as quiet goes."

Marek frowned at the carpet, his thick eyebrows nearly touching. He tapped one thumb against the other. She watched him think, imagined him mentally taking her morning's tour and waited for him to arrive at her solution.

"What if you kept your old study?" he asked. He looked cold and resentful, forcing himself to attend to her.

"The whole point . . ."

"For yourself, I mean."

"Where would Melani do her schoolwork?" she asked, surprised.

"In the kitchen."

"That's not fair."

"Do you like that room?" he asked, still with that cold, forced expression.

"Well, yes," she said grudgingly.

"You wouldn't feel shortchanged if you went back to it?"

"No, not at all."

Marek spoke slowly, heavily. "Melani can move in with me."

"I don't believe it."

"She can put her desk in my study and the upstairs room is all yours." He looked baleful. Was he asking her to reject his offer? Give him credit for nobility and reject the offer?

"You'll resent it."

"I'll resent this more."

The long windows caressed the dusk. Tomorrow she would be content in the old study, but now, in a mood brushed by exultation, the idea of moving back was disappointing, even disgusting.

"I'm going to take the jades and the white lamps upstairs," she said stiffly. "And my carpet. It goes to waste in here, no one ever sees it."

"It's too large." Fury glittered in his eyes.

"It will fit just fine."

"I don't understand this new distinction between yours and ours . . ."

"I'm sorry it offends you."

"Are you going to question everything, all our premises, all our values?"

The question shook her. "Yes, I think so. Our life is so awful, it's been awful for years."

Marek's face sagged; he looked baffled and weary, like an old, tormented bull.

"Where were you, Sephony?" he asked. "What happened to you?"

"I appreciate . . . you sharing your study," she said.

"Oh, I'll manage," he said, smoothing hair over his bald spot.

"It'll all be replaced tomorrow," she said. "Let's see where Melani's desk can go."

Home almost a week, she tried to get back to work in her strange and lovely room. Out in the gray day shafts of light dropped from a tiny patch of blue sky onto a distant field —

furrows and moraines textured with golden hair of grain. Some obstruction kept her from working, a muddle as gray as the gray fields not touched by the fingers of sunlight.

How was she to live?

She flipped through slides of old realist paintings and stopped at *The Proposition,* by Judith Leyster, seventeenth-century Dutch. A bearded fur-capped man solicits a woman while she sews, touching her shoulder and offering a handful of coins. Her candle illuminates their faces — his expression quietly insistent, hers quietly contained. She embroiders, focused on the canvas in her lap, her green gown shading into the chair, forming a huge dark mass from which her toes peek out. Their hands, each pair close together, speak their dialogue — his hands ask and promise favors; hers stitch and say no. The space around them is blank except for their shadows. He asks her to turn and accept the coins. She confidently refuses, radiating internal worth that cannot be bought.

My own sacrifice, she thought bitterly. For years I turned around and took the coins. What now? She straddled two lives. What did she owe because of her privileged journey? And to whom? Who might benefit?

She churned, scraped. Talk to Peg? Not yet. Peg would annihilate her with understanding. She would take the tube to London, buy a new memory band, and ring up Lela.

The communicall buzzed a rapid staccato. She ran downstairs. Marek could ignore buzzers; she always worried about missing something.

A policeman stood at the front door, a sallow young man with a thin face and red nose.

"Would you be Mrs. Berg-Benson?" he asked with mock deference.

"Yes."

"I am Captain Waintree, in charge of investigating your disappearance. Your husband told you, I am sure."

"No, he didn't."

"May I come in, please?"

"I was about to leave."

"Just a few routine questions."

She led the way to the orange room. Waintree perched on the edge of a recliner, a red recorder light glowing on his jacket pocket. Sephony sat on a hard chair and gripped the armrests.

"We cannot understand, Mrs. Berg-Benson, why we found no trace of you."

"Ah. Well, it was very good of you to take so much trouble on behalf of my family."

"Perhaps you would care to tell me where you spent the period from Saturday, thirteen September, until Wednesday, seventeen September."

"I would not."

"Beg pardon?"

"I wouldn't care to tell you."

"Mrs. Berg-Benson, you seem unaware of regulations. When you call in the police to solve a crime . . ."

"I did not call and no crime was committed."

"All parties must contribute to the solution. The case is not closed until we answer the question."

"And if I choose not to answer?"

"Creating a disturbance is a misdemeanor punishable by a fine of two hundred pounds."

"I didn't create a disturbance."

"The effect of your action, however private its intent, was to create a disturbance. We do not take it lightly."

"If only my husband hadn't been so hasty."

"What was the purpose of the metergun which was left in your potato bin on thirteen September?"

"Metergun?"

"Do you know who left it?"

"Oh . . . I must have been careless."

"Was it a signal to a subversive organization?"

"No, it wasn't."

"Did it reflect a personal aberration?"

"I suppose you could say that."

"Yours?"

"I don't know how to answer such silly questions."

"Your farm manager saw a stranger on the premises Saturday afternoon, thirteen September. Did you see this man?"

"Yes."

"Did you go somewhere with this man?"

"Yes," she said softly.

"Were you taken by force?"

"No."

"Did you go willingly?"

"In a manner of speaking."

"What do you mean?"

"I went, but I wouldn't say I willed to go."

"Perhaps, Mrs. Berg-Benson, you are ready to tell me his name?"

"No, I am not."

"Or where you and this man went?"

"I can't."

"You do not remember?"

Sephony hesitated. "I can't tell you."

"You choose not to."

"You wouldn't understand."

"Leave the matter of understanding to us, Mrs. Berg-Benson. The facts will be sufficient."

"Captain Waintree, if I must pay two hundred pounds in order to avoid further harassment I'll do it. I'm sorry I inadvertently caused so much trouble." Her face was hot, she spoke rapidly. "We've been paying for police services all our lives and have never had occasion to use them. Consider that our obligation is quit."

"You do not make regulations, Mrs. Berg-Benson. We are interested in subversive activities, our job is security."

"I don't belong to a subversive organization."

"It is still a matter of great interest how you arrived in London without being detected. Since your companion had no craft, we assume. And surely you did not walk."

"My companion, as you call him, didn't go to London. I went there alone."

"That is equally interesting."

"Is it?"

"Where were you on fifteen September?"

"What day was that?"

"Monday."

Sephony considered. "In a forest."

"Ah, so you were in the countryside. Near Greenham?"

"I don't know."

"You don't know where you were?"

"Strictly speaking, no, I don't. That's all, Captain Waintree. My travels were private. They don't concern the authorities. Now, if you'll excuse me . . ." Sephony stood.

Captain Waintree touched his pocket and the red light winked out. He nodded ceremoniously. "Whether you are subject to prosecution on the grounds of creating a disturbance and failing to cooperate is up to the local Triangle. If you do not hear from us within two weeks you can assume the matter is closed."

Sephony walked him to the door. "Thank you for your efforts," she said.

"My pleasure," said Captain Waintree.

Sephony was in London within an hour. As usual the Strand was dense, the pace brisk and regular. The helmeted crowd flowed toward Trafalgar Square, two lanes for walking, one lane for shopping. Sephony remembered as a child dropping a little metal star and trying to stop to pick it up and Mums tugging her and hearing the crunch as people stepped on it. She slipped into the shopping lane and leaned against a window that featured Norwegian silks. There were so many people, purposeful and hurried, so many of them, their faces plasticized in clear molded helmets, parading like lines scratched across the surface of the city. How could she consider any purpose worthwhile when people were scratches and life was as impersonal as the earth spinning on its axis? García Marquez compared people to dry leaves — a whirlwind of random patterns that eddied into a family, a town, a railroad station. Did it matter, then, if she wrote a dissertation or planted a garden? Hammersmith would go on being a wasteland no matter what she did. Could she do anything of value?

On impulse she headed for the call tube on the corner. A fat young woman stood inside, encased in shiny green tights. When she spoke she was animated, when she listened she chewed a finger. She raised her palm to Sephony; was she asking for patience or signaling the end of her call? Her hand expressed illness, like a facial expression, like Simon's hands and Alf's. It was disgusting, sluglike, with raw fingertips and a sinister miasma. The person on the other end apparently had the last words, for the woman bit one finger after another. She left the tube, head down, helmet tucked under her arm.

Sephony found Genco's code in the battered computer and spoke it into the phone, propelled by a wind at her back. She heard her voice say "Limorrz, please," waited, and heard Aaron's voice say "Three-seven-seven-six" and heard herself respond, "Aaron, this is Sephony," and froze until he said, "Sephony? How lovely," and she said, "I was in the city and wondered if you would have lunch with me," and he replied with pleasure and confidence, "What a splendid idea. When do you mean?"

"Right now, actually. If it's not too short notice."

"Where are you?"

"Near Aldwych."

"How about, ah, Gill's in ten minutes?"

"Super. See you then."

Her face was hot. Under the jacket her blouse clung to her armpits. She stepped out of the tube and turned down Arundel Street, away from the crowd.

The street outside the restaurant was grimy. Bits of plastic lifted and eddied, metros huffed by, settling to pick up passengers, scattering debris. She paced in front of the entrance, her eyes beginning to smart. The air had been clean in the Jungle, the park only a twenty-minute walk from here, but it might be miles away and years since she came out. Memories buzzed like a fly on bone china; already people looked less alien. Yellow coveralls were popular and those dreadful silverglas helmets that reflected the street. A pregnant woman waddled past with a one-armed man. Across the street a shabby metro shelter was filling. She felt self-conscious standing here, and anxious in a hopeful way. A group of people blew around the corner from the Embankment, trousers flapping. Was that Aaron towering behind them? She looked away, toward the Strand, and he materialized, filling the space with his presence.

"It's good to see you again," he said. "Why aren't you wearing a helmet?"

"Don't you mind being suffocated?" she asked.

He cupped his hand gently around her elbow. She opened the door. The anteroom was dim and fresh.

He uncovered his head and stood beside her like an awkward schoolboy, shoulders hunched to minimize his height. Black and silver hair curled softly and evenly on his head like a cap.

She slipped back thirty years.

"Didn't this place have the salmon cakes?" she asked.

"Salmon . . . I can't remember when I last had oily fish."

The people ahead of them passed through.

"Where else did we use to go?" she asked.

"Gyngle's," he said mischievously.

"Oh, that dreadful hiccup music," she said with an old combativeness.

"But the best chick-peas with sausages."

The host beckoned, an old man with a humped back and bright, dark eyes; they followed him into a crowded room, sectioned by counters and levels, smelling of fish and vinegar. Standees clustered along the counters, eating or playing Virtuality. They were led to a small table against the wall. Aaron's knees touched hers briefly as he settled into the chair opposite. The host extended his hand and Aaron recited his code into a ring.

His eyes had their old effect, like jades found in a dusty shop — pale green eyes drawn by age deeper into their sockets. It took some adjustment. His presence was familiar and strange — a shy, elegant man, still youthful despite silver hair at his temples and creases in his neck and earlobes, leaning forward in a dark brown shirt, alert and fleet, suspicious of wind and terrain.

She found the noise oppressive, the crowd like nudges, a single organic mass.

"Shall we get our food?" he asked.

They sidled between tables to the dispensing counter. A row of color-pics advertised the selection in line drawings more stylish than the usual holograms. Sephony chose food they used to eat; a plate slid onto the counter in a transparent red box, complete with utensils. Aaron carried his box and a beaker of wine and she picked up glasses on the way back to their table.

Aaron poured. "Cheers," he said.

"Cheers," she said.

For a moment they were young, and she sparkled against the margins of his being. Then he cut the tip of his pie with a fork and thirty years divided them like hedges. It could have been a week since they were lovers, or a lifetime. Their relationship was elastic, as mercurial as the weather, as certain as early morning. She clung to her meal, to fish, beets, and salad.

"How's your pie?" she asked. His hand was brown and veined.

"Rather fishy," he said.

"They used to make good pie," she said.

He sipped wine. They talked about family and work.

"I hate repetition," he said with a tense smile, "and administrators do nothing but."

"You enjoyed solving problems . . ."

He crossed his arms and tipped his chair against the wall. "Some administrative work came my way, I was flattered to be asked. My research wasn't going anywhere at the time."

"Can you go back to research if you want to?"

"One never catches up."

"I thought you'd invent something, cure something . . . you know . . ."

He leaned into the table. "I earned more —" He controlled what looked like a flare of shame. "That is, Sybil got used to it."

She took the criticism of his wife as a tribute.

"One does," she said. "I've been cowardly, too."

"You had other faults," he said sharply.

He approached and receded, alternately dense or ethereal, like Claro changing shape. She liked his mental reserve, his orderly yet passionate spirit, his swift, awkward gestures. She was tempted to plunge into a risky conversation, to connect the untold stories of their broken engagement. But it was too soon. The idea hung in the forefront of her mind while talk passed around it.

"Why so sad?" he asked.

"I find it painful. Being with you. Perhaps I shouldn't have phoned."

"Because I've become — what? Detached?"

"Oh, no, to the contrary." She leapt into it. "Stubborn, perhaps, but colorful and emotional." She thought he dutifully acknowledged his wife's opinion of him.

"Not emotional," he said pedantically. "You were the emotional one."

But his eyes glowed with pleasure. He wanted to be found out; he enjoyed, as she did, the little dissections, the sweet careless intrusions.

They talked about their children and their children's faults.

"Rolf's almost a different generation from the others . . . he's dictatorial, you see, obtuse . . . He has all Marek's bad qualities and so few of his good ones. I should like to be able to talk to him, but he only wants me to mend his shirts."

"Does he get on with Marek?"

"I haven't a clue."

"That's odd."

"Do you think so?"

"Not knowing, that is."

"I suppose they talk about engineering."

"How you say it."

She pushed away her plate, crossing her arms on top of the table.

"You're angry with me, Sephony," he said mischievously, and she remembered how their arguments ended in laughter.

"I'm not contemptuous of engineering," she said.

"Of course you are. It excludes you."

"They use me."

"Marek?" he asked.

"All the family."

His pale eyes spun, she was sure he was accusing her of something general, something harsh and true. Into the protected moment, the safe conversation, their past sent prickly charges like infra-sound hooks, nicking and scratching them.

"I have to go," he apologized.

She waited.

"Next Tuesday?" he asked.

"That would be lovely."

"We'll try Mother Huff's."

She met his eyes, briefly, victoriously, holding time in her hands, reeling it in.

At home she was self-conscious. Except for Simon (whom she tended through a terrible case of glandular fever that lasted well into October) the family paled into shadows. She sensed the children through the mesh and toil of their deep reserve: their unarticulated needs, their fear of the unfamiliar. Her own self enticed and obstructed her narcissistically on many levels — she thought of herself as a temporary being; she thought of herself in the third person.

But with Aaron, every Tuesday afternoon, she sprang into the world. Circumscribed by small units of place and time — a restaurant, a table, a plate, two hours — they freely traveled lumpy wooded trails, their talk abstract and personal, ending in glades or in swamps. It was easy to be perfect friends under such strict conditions, easy to be free on an island. When

episodes from the past threatened to escape they grew respect-
fully silent; they both recoiled.

They were at Gill's again, on a chilly November day.
Aaron wore a gray padded jacket piped in dark green; hers was
lilac and hyacinth. Their plates were nearly empty, they were
content. Aaron licked a fingertip and wiped the face of his
memory band, smiling boyishly at her.

"No one else makes that gesture," she said affectionately.

"And you still hide your thumbs in your fists."

She laughed. A question slipped forward, a tiny disk of a
secret sliding along her tongue and falling out, her restraint
dissolving like a wafer.

"Do you know why I couldn't marry you?" she asked.

He stopped moving, his finger arrested as if she had
struck him. Air whistled from his bones; he was dry paper
crumpled in the corner of a dusty room where webs softened
the walls and torn lace gowned the bed.

"Tell me what you thought," she went on, "immediately
after I rushed off that day in the park."

He leaned back, hugging his chest, his pale eyes veiled.

"No," he said.

"I'm sorry, how would you begin?"

"Is that why you wanted to see me," he asked bitterly, "to
dredge that up?"

"Don't you want to know?"

He stabbed peas with his fork, methodically, a single tine
into each.

"I've fantasized this conversation so often," she said softly.

"But I haven't."

"Ah."

"Not that I didn't imagine meeting you again," he said
quickly, tensely, "not that I didn't wonder . . ."

"Well, I was irresponsible. I hurt you, I broke it off."

"Quite." Fear flickered in the cool green eyes.

She had imagined leading the conversation by degrees
along certain paths, but the guarded man who resisted was not
the Aaron in her imagination.

"Can I tell you why I behaved so badly?"

"I assure you I've had no difficulty understanding why you broke our connection."

"What did you think?"

"Obviously, while I was away at school you met Marek." He mashed the peas, satisfied, judgmental.

"Oh, no," she said, startled by his version. "I didn't meet him until a year or more afterward."

"Ah . . . well . . . then you didn't love me." He looked away.

"That wasn't it."

Aaron tensed. "You can't justify that abrupt good-bye," he said angrily.

"I was such a coward, so dependent on my parents."

"The same old excuse . . . your parents said you were too young. Really, Sephony."

"Oh, that was a lie, but I couldn't think of anything else to say."

His eyes lost their accusing glint. "All right, Sephony," he said warily, "tell me." He leaned forward, his face resting in his hand, two fingers framing his eye in a characteristic vee.

"My parents took a firm stand against you, irrational but firm, and I was powerless to oppose them."

"Why?"

"They hired an investigator to study your family records."

"Indeed!" Aaron sat erect.

"I have an awful suspicion that what I'm about to tell you is something you don't know."

"Go on."

She hesitated. "They found out that your great-grandmother was a Mino," she said gently.

Aaron was all bones, the air gone from his body again, a punctured balloon that whistles, shrinks, and disappears in the sky.

"A Mino," he said.

"Yes."

"What does that matter?" he asked, defensively.

"It doesn't — they all died out. But my parents weren't rational."

"Apparently neither am I."

"You didn't know . . . I'm so sorry. Are you all right?" She took his hand; it was inert.

"I don't see why my family didn't pass on the information, it has absolutely no genetic significance." His voice cracked. "But they didn't. There you have it." He looked at her sadly and withdrew his hand, framing his eye again. "What did they say, exactly? How did they put it?"

"That your family was . . . that their grandchildren would be tainted."

"Did you believe it?" His voice was strangled.

"Not at all."

"Then why didn't you tell me?"

"I was loyal to them. And so ashamed. I couldn't bear for you to think badly of them."

"You didn't seem to mind them thinking badly of *me*."

"They forced me to choose — my father was adamant — 'We'll tear you out of our hearts,' he said."

"Because of a horrible prejudice," he said passionately. He paused. "I must have some of it myself . . ."

"I only knew I'd be cut off from them if I married you — and I couldn't bear it." She twisted a strand of hair round and round her index finger.

"So you sacrificed me. Sacrificed us."

Baskets of fire, charred limbs, Isaac on the mountain.

"Could you have defied your parents?" she asked hurriedly. "If it were the other way around?"

"I loved you. I don't do that easily or lightly. I think I could have done something. With my parents I think it would have been possible."

"Yes, with them . . . you're right. And how are they?"

"They died six years ago, I'm afraid."

"Oh, so young. In an accident?"

"They had cancer — they took euthanasia together."

"How awful for you. They were such good friends to each other, so graceful. I loved thinking they'd be my parents."

"And they were disappointed to lose you. Why didn't you bring in scientific proof, invite a geneticist to tea?"

"I was nineteen."

"Oh, Sephony." His voice carried thirty years of anguish. "Why didn't you tell me?"

The wraith of a hand hovered over her plate, spread its fingers, and vanished. She looked at Aaron. The finely chiseled face was crumpled and worn.

"I treated you abominably," she said sadly.

"I thought I knew you," he said.

"I was a frightened rabbit."

"What can I say? It's easy to take a position when one hasn't been under fire."

"My mother burned your cassettes," she said. "All the sounds of your voice . . . vaporized them in my room."

"Was she afraid my voice would contaminate you as well?"

His bitterness stung. "I felt I'd lost the battle of life, that whatever I did from then on would be cheap and automatic."

"Has it been?" he asked.

She couldn't answer — it was too distressing.

"Has it?" he insisted.

"Yes," she said flatly, "in a large sense."

"Marek?"

"I'm not being fair to him. Or to the young."

"Perhaps you're being too fair."

"I feel loyal to him."

"Loyalty — your prime mover."

"He's a decent person. I trust him. But a whole dimension of myself has folded inward, out of sight."

"My life isn't so different." He sighed.

"I must have been prejudiced," she said. "I didn't think so, until you said it. Contaminated by those videos. How could we help it? And my parents were even closer to the period . . ."

She paused. "Those hordes of albinos, all limping and pale and disgusting like slugs, and furious young people, furious diseased children . . . we called them barbarians, didn't we?"

"Oh, yes, animals and monsters."

"I could tell you your family history," she said hesitantly.

"Go ahead." He slumped in his chair and folded his arms across his chest.

"Your great-great-grandparents were exposed to the minoxine."

"Which city?"

"Norwich."

"The worst. Where it all started. Go on."

"Your great-grandmother had the heart defect and the implant. She lived in the warren, had two children by an uncontaminated man, and died at twenty-five. Her son was affected but her daughter — your grandmother — was normal. She had four children, all normal."

"Which grandmother is this?"

"Your father's mother."

"She was always very old," he said softly, "very old. I have the eyes, don't I?"

"Yes, I suppose you do."

She saw he was tired; they shared a great weariness. "I thought I acted out of cowardice and obedience," she said, "but I did succumb, didn't I . . . to the little 'what if' that creeps into the unscientific mind."

"Yes."

"Prejudices don't die, they just aren't mentioned."

"Quite," he said, "and yet I can't — I wish I were a better person . . . I can't forgive you."

"I don't expect you to," she said heatedly. "I can't forgive myself." Shame warred with innocence. "Something happened two months ago," she said. "Something truly extraordinary." She looked at him gravely. "I might tell you someday. That's why I had the nerve to ring you up a few weeks ago."

"I'm glad you did," he said.

"Even after all this?"

He nodded.

"When I saw you at Mums's party I knew we would talk about it." She hesitated. "During my breakdown . . . did you know I had a breakdown?"

"You said something . . . a fragile state, you said."

"April . . . April was an insubstantial time. I heard a voice in my bedroom and had a vision — you can imagine. But oddly, instead of mysteries, I began thinking about you. You took over my thoughts entirely."

He looked surprised. "Shall I say I'm flattered?"

"The point is, I think, one can't expect unfinished business to remain buried."

He laughed. "That's a rather dry construction."

"How did you deal with your life afterward?" she asked.

Aaron pushed away his plate and folded his arms on the table, his shoulders hunched forward. "I studied hard. Did well. I took refuge in the larger view — you know, passionate-love-happens-in-youth type thing and then one makes a sensible marriage. I didn't have it in me to risk a second fall." He looked at her frankly, his lips tense. "I probably feel about Sybil the way you feel about Marek. We get on." He laughed with relief and guilt. "One doesn't normally talk about such matters," he said, tilting his head.

"But shouldn't we? We have a chance to thaw. Wouldn't we be immoral not to take the chance?"

"How do we take it, Sephony?" His eyes glowed with pain under pressure. "Do I take off the chains, do I let myself notice you, do we become close friends, do we fall in love again? How do we take it? Right now I'm teetering on the edge. Thaw, you say — yes, I've been frozen. We're not young, we have positions and obligations. What chance do you imagine us taking?"

"Something slow," she said. "Being friends. Talking in a normal way."

"That's dangerous."

"I don't know. I have no experience."

"Neither have I."

"But I don't want to go back."

He looked severe. "To?"

"Being frozen."

"You may be braver than I, at this point."

She was silent.

"What was that extraordinary thing?" he asked.

She tested the possibility of opening the subject. "I'll try to tell you eventually — when the effects sort themselves out a bit better. Life at home wobbles at the moment, so I mainly keep to myself."

"A general estrangement?"

"I'm neither wife nor mother, and barely a scholar. I don't know what I am . . . a traveler."

"I envy you. I sit in one place."

"Are you comfortable?"

"Too comfortable." The green eyes sparkled. "I never thought to see you as my guide."

Her skin prickled; for a moment she followed Claro down the ladder. "You never thought to see me at all," she said lightly.

"Not true."

"How do you feel?"

"Nervous. And you?"

"All churned up."

"Your cheeks are red. Your cheeks always turned red."

She looked down at her plate.

"I have to go to work," he said.

"I'll walk you."

He looked at her fondly and pushed back his chair.

At the exit desk the humpbacked man nodded and clicked his counter.

"Odd to see the same host after thirty years," said Sephony, adjusting to the modest warmth of the sun.

"He still owns the property," said Aaron.

"Not many small restaurants," she said.

"Most were absorbed by cartels, like your family."

"Can you see my brother bowing to customers?"

"It might do him good. He's a cold bastard, I hear."

"Mugs is a humanoid."

"Like your father."

"Was he?"

"I thought so. The ruling class ruling in his own home."

"You belong to it now."

"Without being a tyrant, I trust."

"Are you?"

"Far from it."

"Sybil. What sort is she, really?"

"Let's cross here." He cupped her elbow. "Placid. Competent. Ah . . . agreeable. I don't know her very well, actually. She's not content, I think. She feeds the girls too much. I hate to see them so fat and lethargic. Nice girls, good verbal ability, but no spark. Sybil gets on with women, mainly. She has good rapport with women."

"And?"

"Why do you say 'and'?"

"I hear it in your voice."

"Well, we'll have to save it for next time."

He took Sephony's shoulders lightly, nervously. They hugged briefly, cheek to bony chest. He entered the building and turned to wave from the open door.

CHAPTER ⚡ 12

ASHBRIDGE STREET was dismal — three-story cement row houses sporting badly painted doors and scruffy window boxes. Children in ragged jackets played in weedy little gardens; old people hobbled past, carrying sacks. Wreckage was strewn about: bits of crafts and home appliances, rusted pulleys and braces. House numbers were scrawled in black. Mo was terribly shy, Lela had said, almost too nervous to meet her. Sephony found his number neatly printed on the faded blue door. Nervous herself, she pressed the communicall and, hearing no internal buzz, knocked vigorously. Lela had told her he would be working.

The door was flung open by a large gaunt man with wild gray hair who seemed to retreat as he advanced. Rapid, incomprehensible greetings flowed from his mouth. He seemed friendly but his eyes darted with embarrassment.

"Wash out stark," he said, ushering her in and loping ahead, "heavy nix alighted." His hunched shoulders and jutting neck cut a path through the hallway, gooselike.

"Sorry?"

He turned. "Haven't fixed the light yet."

"Ah."

"Well, heryare." He mumbled something about the shop and waved apologetically.

She might as well be going deaf.

"May I look around?" she asked, and he said something that seemed to mean yes.

Lela hadn't told her what he did — some sort of repair, she'd said, not mentioning the most striking thing. It was a piano shop, filled with elephantine acoustic pianos herded together in varying stages of disembowelment. The clutter was comprehensive, most of it old and unrelated to pianos — dried weeds in the corners, teacups nested in wiggly columns, gargoyles, faded tapestries, and a weather scan.

She sneezed.

"Sorry, thwood," Mo said, looking doubtfully at her ear.

He was fortyish, with dark, deep-set eyes, shaggy brows, and a long nose — taller and bigger-boned than Aaron, but almost as thin. His gray clothes smelled musty. He had the penitential air of a person who burns with a single flame.

"I played an acoustic piano once when I was a child," she said.

"They make a grand sound," he said, waving his hands.

"They make me think of woolly mammoths."

He laughed boyishly. "This'n looks gnarly," he declared, heading for a huge, unlidded piano on lion's claws, "buth'-soundboard's good." Dusty, ivory-tipped keys lay exposed all the way back to the hammers. He patted the side affectionately. "An old Bechstein. The rods're fragile, but lookit those legs." She was beginning to make sense of his soup of words. A lonely shy man, he must be glad to see someone now and then to verify his existence.

He strode from piano to piano sketching their problems and history. His rapid mumbling speech was punctuated with laughter, and his eyes, shifting in all directions, shone with private enthusiasm. They were both shy, like relatives meeting for the first time. He had an accent she couldn't place, well educated, but with some regional twang.

"Do you play?" she asked.

"Not very well. We can sit here'n talk. You warm enough?"

She opened her jacket, but kept it on, sitting on a swivel stool, its velvet seat worn to silkiness and its back an iron fretwork of petals. Mo sat on a bench opposite, one knee jiggling rapidly.

Though he was big-boned, there was something fragile in his nervousness, like the leaves of an aspen tree quivering in the slightest breeze.

"Well," she said, "Lela thinks we have . . . you know — a fair amount in common."

"I went through that glass without breaking it," he offered, pointing to a smallish window.

"I went through a well."

"Who knows what we went through," he said, and their eyes met.

"Probably they aren't really openings," she said, "but our way of seeing what we can't see . . . it must be something quite different to, you know, to them . . ."

"Fermions or bosons."

"Or columns of light."

"It was a dry windy place," he said helpfully.

"And what was its name? . . ."

He shuffled his feet, eager to the point of bursting, but he wouldn't say. She was glad she'd asked and relieved that he didn't answer.

"Why us, do you suppose?" he demanded. "We must have some defect in common."

Defect? Was that it? "Perhaps we're meant to have, I don't know, some responsibility. Did you just . . . go . . . alone?"

Mo leapt up and strode around the shop. He was, in his way, as strange as Claro — a contortionist, folding his arms behind his back or in front of his chest, as if he would tie himself in knots to contain his energy. She had never met anyone so restless, so in motion even when he was still. He had the lumbering sadness of a person whose vitality was greater than his body — he couldn't use it or house it, the excess was unfocused and unsuited for life — huge quantities leaked out and electrified the air around him and seemed to make him miserable.

"Her name was Anzi," he said, his shoulders jerking backward. "She screamed like an eagle. No one in this world could be so wild. And stubborn as a rusty screw. A laugh — oh, explosions, you might say." He threw himself onto the bench again. His speech, she noticed, had become clear and his knee was quiet.

"Claro was deathly serious," she said graciously. "Sometimes he swelled as if he'd suddenly gained two kilos."

"Anzi was bloody dogmatic, always picking me up and flying me over the desert — treated me like a plegic — because the ground was hot. I wanted to stay longer and learn to fly myself."

"Oh, so did I."

"You flew?"

"Claro's people live in circles of light in trees."

"Anzi lives in the shadow of a cactus."

They sat silently, enclosed in their memories.

"Family. It's tough to tell family," he said.

"I haven't. They'd think I'm crazy."

"Did you think you were?" He thrust the question at her angrily.

"Oddly, no. I felt very . . . confident."

"I lost my memory completely there, it was like living inside a gooseberry."

"Everything is terribly strained, though," she said. "The young avoid me; my husband is sour and resentful. They can't stand not knowing . . . and I don't blame them . . . although they've always reproached me when I do something for myself, however slight." She hesitated. "Do you think we'll ever, oh — go back . . . or see them again?"

"Anzi's come," Mo said. "In the wind."

Hope shocked her. "Tell me," she said.

He got up and careened around the shop, touching things, rearranging, going off wildly yet thoughtfully. He seemed anguished and feverish.

"After I came back I was mean and grouchy," he said, "on the prowl like a starving cat in a rubbish tip — always this gnawing. One day I was scavenging in theater ruins at Waterloo and a particularly brisk wind blew up from the river." He compressed himself against a piano, his arms folded protectively. "After that I noticed how alive I felt on windy days, how grand it felt to stand outside and let a gusty wind blow right through me. I craved a really violent storm. So I kept my eye on the weather scans and when a gale boiled up in the North Sea I flew to Dornoch. Ever been to Dornoch?"

Sephony shook her head.

"The last witch in Scotland was burned there in 1727." He loped around the shop again, absently picking things up and setting them down somewhere else. "I took a room near the firth and ate dehydroes, couldn't afford anything else. Everyone was fastening up their houses and boats . . . they called me the loony on the jetty. When the rain hit I nearly got blown in the sea, but that's what I came for, right? Even from my room it was amazing — waves crashing in the street, spruces waving in the rain like giant goldenrod, the wind screaming. I was so energized I could almost fly." He threw up his hands. "In the calm I went outside. And that's when Anzi came."

"How wonderful."

"She flashed onto the jetty in the eye of the storm and again in the aftermath — right through the ion-charged atmosphere, zimming on protons. She touched me — I could almost see her." He groaned. "After the storm I restrung a Steinway and when energy built up again I zimmed out to Texas to be with a tornado. Anzi only came four times. But storms are part of my life now — hurricanes, mistral, tornadoes — the crackling of ions . . ." His eyes blazed in his dry-skinned face. "Most of the time nothing's happening or I can't afford the trip," he said, sitting on the bench and gripping the edge, "so I make do with thunderstorms. Maybe it'll happen to you."

"Do you keep hoping, with every storm, that she'll? . . ."

"Nah. I can make do with the winds — they suffice for my real purpose."

"Real?"

"Well, in a small way, making holograms. And in a bigger way helping Lela and Festy's crowd make some social structure out of their instincts for cooperation."

"That's what I meant before," she said eagerly, "some responsibility." She felt a great surge of interest.

He grinned. His teeth were crooked. "They understand the beauty in collective behavior."

"Collective?" Sephony said. "That crowd was anarchic."

"You'd hate the warrens, most likely."

"Is that where Lela lives?"

"Haven't you been to her flat?"

"She comes to me when Marek's at work."

"She lives over in Briston. They swarm like fiddler crabs there. I'll bet you've never been to any part of Dulwich." His tone was sharp and accusing.

"No," she said, "not yet."

He glared at her — suddenly not a companion, but a shabby, antagonistic man from the working class. "And you've never met any Dulls, either."

"As a matter of fact Alf, our farm manager, and his helper are Dulls . . . in a marginal way."

"So you don't think Dulls are monsters." He looked surprised.

"My family does, and almost everyone I know. They think I'm soft on that issue."

"But do you know how Dulls are created? What happens in the coops?"

"Coops? The automated nurseries? Is there something wrong with them?"

"Wrong?" he mocked. "Wrong?" He lapsed into a parody of a telepitch. "Ever since the Triangle freed our working mothers," he recited singsong, "child care is fun." He turned bitter. "It's cheaper to condition people than build good robos, isn't it?"

"We're all conditioned to one thing or another. The Dulls love machines, they love to work . . . But you're saying I don't know how it's done, what price is paid."

"Right. You don't know about Dulls who are neither fish nor fowl, who don't turn out according to plan — who get screwed up and manipulated and segregated over in Briston."

"Do you mean Lela is a Dull?"

He looked pinched. "A failed Dull. Not an emotional dwarf like Festy and the others, though. Briston has a few Lelas and lots of Festys. It's a small part of Dulwich. About three square blocks. Where the creative refuse live."

"What do you mean, 'refuse'?"

"They're kids who crawled to the top of the heap on the nursery floor. The angry ones. The lucky ones. With some individuality. They end up in Briston." He spoke rapidly, his eyes shifting focus, and she had to strain to understand him again. "They're single-wired specialists — brilliant in science or art. A lot of the agrobacteria were developed by Briston biochemists. But they're wild and silly. You saw them at the Jungle, the ones you call anarchic. They stay adolescents forever. Nothing carries over."

"This is totally different from what one hears. How do you know?"

Mo pushed up his sleeve and held out his arm. She glimpsed a green diagram just above the wrist.

"You're not looking," he said savagely, thrusting his forearm close to her face.

A diamond pattern was branded in his flesh just above the jutting wristbone, a crystal-shaped numerical pattern in glowing phosphorescent green, surrounded by delicate brown hairs.

It reproached her with its alienness, with its alien system; it roused guilt.

"Someone has to do menial work," she said, desperately, "so the Triangle breeds Dulls to enjoy it. Is that worse than forcing menial work on people who hate it?"

"You accept the Triangle without question," Mo said unhappily.

"By and large. Oh . . . I don't know."

"You don't," he said triumphantly. "I hear it in your voice.

Look, no social system is good. Never has been, never will be. But some are worse than others. Is it fair," he asked passionately, "to bioengineer human beings because they're more effective and durable than robos?"

"Bioengineer normal infants, you mean . . . with a normal intelligence?"

"Doesn't matter. Those electronic coops'll turn an infant into a moron faster than you can blink."

"Wait, though. Our young had the milkmaid . . . one of those soft, cuddly things . . . to feed from on the odd occasion. They weren't damaged."

"On the odd occasion," he said scornfully.

"I'm sorry," she said. "Partisanship gets in the way."

His shoulders twitched as if warding off flies. "You've never seen a coop — it's more than a milkmaid, it's a complete environment, a complete mother-unit. That soft sloping Mumdoll inside the big crate does everything a baby needs done for it — except love it."

"It does look fantastic on the videos, though."

"Doesn't it? Technological paradise. In the working class, sixty years ago, parents were signing up babies for the nurseries before they were born. Coops were super for Mum and Dad — twelve months of ease, no nappies and sleepless nights, just play with baby on the weekend. And nice for the babies — the coops were programmed to respond to them. The babies controlled their environment, they felt secure, they had a Mumdoll who fed them when they cried and washed their bottoms when they got dirty and sang them cute little songs. They became attached to 'her.' But it was a machine, after all, and twelve months in there marked them for life. They grew into lone ducks, devoted to machines, but independent and stubborn. Almost normal, you might say — loyal but not compliant."

"Alf must be from that generation — it sounds just like him."

"The Triangle wasn't satisfied. By the time the first generation gave birth they turned the coops into warping labs.

Machines set to rigid schedules, I mean, complex sensors deleted from the Mumdolls — the babies had to do all the adapting. Of course parents didn't ask questions, everybody trusts child care systems, and these ducks were dim already. They got docile babies and didn't have a clue what made them. Imagine a room full of plexiglas boxes stacked floor to ceiling, one baby to a box, listless, like sick rabbits. Nipple pops into mouth once every four hours for exactly twelve minutes. Baby not finished? Tough. Not hungry? Tough. Crying gets you nowhere, baby has no influence at all. In three months — a year for good measure — the Triangle has what it wants — not just an obedient working class, but automatons. And a whole social system that perpetuates itself. Imagine your own children. Imagine yourself."

"Stop!"

Mo smiled, his upper lip tight and hostile, hiding his thoughts while reproaching her for not knowing them.

"Even a bad system isn't perfect," he said flippantly.

She was angry at him, angry at what he was telling her. Bearers of bad news have their heads cut off. She was angry at being drawn in, coerced to foresee the worst.

"What happens when the machines don't work?" she cried. "Suppose a baby can't depend on its unit . . . its feeding is haphazard . . . What happens to babies whose units aren't dependable?"

A victorious look flickered in his eyes. "Some die. Others are peculiar. You see it when they're let out to crawl around. They're catatonic or they crawl in weird patterns like drugged spiders. Fixing the machine doesn't help them at that point. The totally crazy ones get lethal injections. The rest survive somehow. And a few, a very few, rise above it." His eyes darted madly, his knee twitched.

It was too painful, too personal. It violated her beliefs. His news and her instincts were about to destroy her loyalty to the system.

"The Triangle doesn't kill babies," she said, barely hearing herself. "I don't believe it . . . there's always some natural loss —" She hated the small cold statistical voice. "No, I'm sorry, I don't mean that."

"That's about it," he said unhappily.

"How do the rest turn out?"

"Your average Dulls have small vocabularies, bad tempers, poor memories, and no sense of the future. They're rigid and doctrinaire and they thrive on repetition."

"And you?" she asked, feeling as if his life lay in her hands. "You aren't a Dull and you don't live in Briston."

His shoulders sagged, his craggy face was gray and forlorn. "I don't know. Maybe I made some connection with an attendant. Maybe I was ill and got special treatment for a while. I don't know what happened."

"Perhaps that's Alfie's story . . . Alf's helper, his son, I think. You were lucky."

"In a way. But something in me will never be right, wires torn and never repaired."

She wanted to put her arms around him. "Perhaps we all of us have some wires torn. The Dulls more so."

"They're proud of themselves in a stupid sort of way," he said, "proud of the nurseries, proud of their rooms and clothes. They live for machines. Work them, repair them, nothing else. Indifferent to sex. You don't dare disagree with them, they get violent about their opinions. I feel peculiar around them, as if they're perfect robos. You'd think they wouldn't bleed. But I like them."

She thought he must feel guilty, having missed by a hair being one of them. She was embarrassed to ask personal questions, his life was a tangle of wires.

Mo squirmed on the bench, limbs folded awkwardly. "The Bristers are smarter, of course, and tough . . . and screwed up. They live in groups and swarm in the streets like a single, noisy organism. Brister women are only allowed to have one kid. Their children, after the nursery period, are adopted by Dulls." He paused and took a deep, tense breath, his shoulders hiking up to his ears. "They can't keep their young because they wouldn't fit the system. And then they're sterilized."

She absorbed the shock; more would come. Was brutality an undercurrent she'd sensed all her life, a known unknown behind safety, behind efficiency?

"Dulwich is one of the country's five controlled sectors," he growled.

In a landscape beyond fog a new city rose up as she tuned her mind to it. "I've always been afraid," she admitted. "One pushes those places out of mind."

"Well, I'll take you to Dulwich sometime."

"Are the warrens all nasty and polluted? Or is that a lie, too?"

Mo leapt to his feet. "Polluted? Just the opposite! Look at this."

He strode to a corner of the room where, behind a grand piano, the feathery heads of tall, dry weeds bent gracefully. "That's goose grass," he said with enthusiasm, "and there's coreopsis. Grows in Warrens Two and Six. Can't find it any-place else in London. Come with me some evening."

Mo looked at her steadily, his eyes focused and penetrat-ing. She had seen that expression before, that insistence and the sense of strange territory behind the eyes. A longing welled in her.

"Yes, perhaps I will," she said, tossing her head in an unaccustomed gesture.

Mo patted her arm and startled her with a look of intense sweetness. "Come see the rest of my place."

He's transferred the warren indoors, she thought — his taste for proximity — amassing things in profusion as a jay stocks its nest. Besides the grand, dusty pianos, crowded in two large rooms, were broken robos and piles of microdisks, helmets and wheels, stuffed birds, silver knives, dusty bottles, and the ever-present feathery weeds. She had to move carefully in the dim light.

"You preserve the past," she said. She touched a faded cotton curtain that had once been a gay floral design.

"Somebody has to," he said.

On the other side of the curtain was a small room. Clumps

of tall weeds stood balled in boots of dried soil. In their dry state they passed into a more permanent life — the soil webbed and knotted by roots, the sandy brown blending with the room's colors of sand and earth, wet soil and dry, age and rust. Holograms lined the walls, assemblages made of feathers, weeds, portraits of old people, parts of animals, and abstract forms. Their subject was death, and they were familiar as she would be familiar to herself if she were turned inside out.

"Did you make these?" she asked, walking from one to another.

"Yes," he said quietly.

Such delicate and precise works made by this nervous, awkward person. She looked at him closely. His hands, hanging at his sides, were large and muscular, the fingers sensitive and neatly articulated, the nails buffed and the cuticles tended.

"They're beautiful," she said.

He allowed himself a smile and folded his arms across his chest.

"Do you make them when you're nervous or calm?"

"I make hollies when the storm is building and repair pianos after." He seemed on the verge of explaining something, but lunged out of the room, scratching the back of his head. She followed him upstairs to a rough space, crudely partitioned.

"This is where I sleep," he said, "which isn't much."

She didn't go beyond the doorway. The room was surprisingly Spartan — a narrow bed with a plaid blanket neatly tucked in. A single black shoe with a cracked toe peeked from under the bed like a fragment of a thought abandoned in midspeech.

"I eat down at the block kitchen," he said. "You cook your own or buy from Jenny, who always makes extra. It's wholesome."

"You don't have to be on guard as I do," she said. "You don't live among . . . enemies."

His hands fluttered to her shoulders like clumsy birds and he shook her lightly. She saw another man, as if Mo's skin had suddenly become transparent and the other man stood behind, short and telescoped, a face beneath a face with intense blue eyes, and arms reaching for her.

"I'll tell you something," he said with a strange look.

They went downstairs again, to the room of weeds and hollies. She felt uneasy, burdened. He walked about, nervously flicking the heads of tall grasses.

"A long time ago I had a terrible job," he said.

"Doing what?"

"Those babies who die in the coops — and the ones who are killed by lethal injection . . . what d'you think happens to them?"

"The usual things, I suppose," she said, shuddering. "Cremation . . . whatever the parents want."

"Cremation leaves a bad taste in the Triangle's mouth." He glanced at her sideways, uneasily. "They bury the babies, burial makes them feel they're doing the right thing."

"And your job was . . . making little coffins?"

"They don't get coffins. I dug their graves."

"Oh." She clenched her thumbs in her fists.

"In the Jungle."

An ominous humming, the shrieking of birds. Mounds in rows.

"There's a graveyard," she said, horrified, "in a clearing."

"That's right."

Giant blocks cracked in her mind, but she kept them from splitting. "The Triangle kills babies . . ."

"Mounds in rows," he said. "Birds shrieking. Hazy sunlight slanting across the grass." His craggy face was dark and drawn; he looked at her questioningly.

She heard the humming from the earth again, the rustling of trees. The bone.

"Someone from social services used to meet me there," he said, striding nervously about the room, "and she'd be carrying a package wrapped in plastic. Just the two of us . . . she'd unwrap it while I dug. You do their work or you lose your university grant," he said bitterly. "And you shut up about it."

"You must have felt you were burying your brothers and sisters," she said.

The pyramid in her mind fell to the ground in a jagged, chaotic heap. She fled to the next room and took refuge among the pianos, walking aimlessly in the forest of objects, feeling empty and crooked.

"We're so misguided," she said.

"Belief only crumbles once," he said from across the room, "and then you're free."

"It crumbles over and over, I find."

"When the last one crumbles you'll know that's the one, the last one, the real one."

"I don't think so. I don't know. It's too abstract for now."

"When will you come again?" he asked.

"Soon."

"But when?"

"I have to wait and see."

"There's one more thing I want to tell you," he said, coming closer, "if you can take it in."

"What?" she asked warily.

His eyes were dark and sad; he made a gentle appeal.

"What is it?" she asked.

"I might be out when you come . . . I'm out most days." He hesitated. "My bio-mother is dying."

"Oh."

"I don't mean to upset you."

"It's all right." She didn't have the energy for anything new.

"Pop died from a lab virus three years ago. Mum has one now, but she won't take euthanasia, she fights dying."

"How horrible."

"Stomach and intestines."

"What's being done?"

"Acupuncture and sedatives." He became quiet and confiding. "I tell her about my travels. It's a story to her . . . she loves it."

"At least you can tell her," she said.

"She says when she dies she wants to live in the shadow of a cactus."

"Perhaps she will."

Mo heaved himself onto a piano and crossed his legs. "I carry her from bed to chair and back again. She wants to keep moving. It's terrible . . . she's a sack of bones." He ran his fingers through his hair. "She used to be such a strong, vital force."

"Like the wind."

"What?"

"A strong vital force . . . she's the wind."

His eyes darted nervously from side to side. "I was telling her the other day, I must harness the wind. She's a good listener." He slid off the piano. "Take a look at the hollies in my studio before you go. I'll be there in a tick. It's upstairs. . . . I like that . . . about Mum being the wind."

She climbed the narrow, uneven stairs. Part of herself was detached and floating above her head, waiting to sort out what she'd learned. His studio was filled with tools and equipment; the hollies glowed. She studied them all, but kept returning to one that was beautiful and ugly — a fat wrinkled cylinder like the body of an elephant minus the head and legs, lying in shallow water. Little red buttons or eyes, like fireflies, peeped and winked from folds of grayish skin.

Mo stood in the doorway, his features in shadow, dark hollows in his cheeks. "Would you like that one?" he asked shyly.

"On loan?" she asked.

"To keep."

She hesitated. "Can I buy it from you?"

"Don't be silly." He took it off the wall.

"I think it must be a self-portrait," she said.

He laughed and wrapped the hollie in red plastic. "Do you have lights for it?" he asked.

"Yes," she said, carefully taking the package.

"Unless something happens to Mum, I'll be here Wednesday afternoons."

"I'll ask Lela to come. Is that all right?"

His eyes lit with pleasure.

They went down the narrow stairs and back through the repair shop, past pianos as complacent as grazing cows. She twanged a set of open strings, the vibrations fading as Mo opened the front door. She closed her jacket. They shook hands and she walked into the chilly November evening, turning once to acknowledge him, thin and gray in the doorway.

She came home a stranger in the house. She moved through dinner, adept, by now, at speaking from a corner of her mind. Nothing trespassed, no true response crossed over to the family side of her brain — the bramble patch, she called it. The afternoon, astonishing in retrospect, isolated her. She kept it intact — fragile, ugly, and precious like Mo's hologram.

CHAPTER ⨯ 13

HOW'S YOUR FARM MANAGER getting on?" Mums demanded, stopping at the window on the landing. Beyond the lawn and the mulched border was a December garden of withered stalks and vines. Mums patted her chest, the graceful soft wool sleeve exposing her forearm where skin hung loose and crepey to the elbow. Dried paint rimmed her cuticles. Why does Mums paint circles on stones? Sephony wondered — a dry, ritual wondering, like a tired moth. Why circles, why stones?

"Alf's much better," Sephony said. "He grumbles at Alfie through the cottage intercom, pretending he's not ill — I can't even ask how he is, he just waves me off. It's very strange, you know — I could almost see his heart attack coming."

Mums's sharp stare made her wonder if she'd said too much. She hoped not. They'd relaxed over lunch, were generous with each other, companionable. Mums seemed willing, even eager, to be enfolded in her life — perhaps that's what Mums had wanted all these years, to be taken in and cradled like a child herself.

"We don't have to go up to my study," Sephony said, "if you're too tired."

"I didn't have my own room," Hilary said, "until your

father died. You were very critical when I turned his office into a studio."

"Not at all."

"Oh, yes. You thought I had no respect."

"I don't remember that — I remember how bright you made it."

"Really? Well, that's nice to hear." She sighed. "If only I'd understood the power in colors years ago — I'm certain cerulean killed him."

For a moment the ridiculous idea seemed plausible. On a wave of affection she put an arm around her mother, startled by the old-age boniness palpable through the cloth. Her mother stiffened. When had she last touched Mums? Had she really been born from this woman? The idea filled her with revulsion. She gave the shoulder a little squeeze, then moved aside. And they were getting on so well. As they climbed the open spiral staircase to the top floor she shunted off expectations. Her study was still private and unfinished; Mums, even in a good mood, was unpredictable. Sephony opened the door.

The room was irregular, a true attic room, with nooks and crannies and a sloping ceiling. Two sleek Breuer chairs flanked the east window. Her desk still filled the west alcove, no changes there. Paintings and hollies from downstairs lined the walls, Mo's hollie near her desk. Wiry Michaelmas daisies flared from vases on the windowsills. A row of jade bottles stood on a shelf, cool and milky green, a nice contrast with the rich crimson rug.

Her mother looked craftily from Aunt Bess's carpet to Aunt Bess's chairs — family heirlooms far from their rightful and honored place in the sitting room. She registered the jade bottles and the standing lamps whose white shades seemed to float in space. Her gaze returned to the carpet and she stabbed Sephony with a quick offended look.

"Well?" Sephony asked.

Mums twisted her pearls, her head to one side. "Oh, I

don't know," she drawled, "it seems rather a waste — no one sees these beautiful things up here."

"I see them."

"Ah, yes, of course. But doesn't Marek object?"

"He did at first."

"And?"

"Nothing. They're mine, after all."

Her mother squinted at her coquettishly, hungrily. "You and Marek don't seem to be yourselves lately." Her coquettish look hardened, as if she were waiting to be photographed.

"Where would you like to sit?" Sephony asked.

Miffed, Hilary focused on the room again. "You know, my dear, the carpet is awfully domineering . . . and the chairs — everything is too bold for the space. You should move them downstairs where they came from."

"I like the room just as it is, actually."

"Well . . . when Bess left you our dear Nana's carpet she never dreamed you'd — how should I say — appropriate it . . . just for yourself."

"Oh, I know, but we scarcely use the sitting room anymore . . . the furniture was embalmed in there."

"Protected, you mean, but never mind. Consider the move for aesthetic reasons, then. Since you want these things about, my dear, perhaps keep only one chair up here."

"We'll see," Sephony said to pacify her.

Standing at the desk, Hilary ran her fingers over the brainer and the fiche cube, as if to extract information from them. "You're not having mental difficulties again, are you, my dear? I mean . . . first your routines change and now the furnishings."

Sephony noticed how her mother bent at the hips, shoulders thrown back awkwardly, as if to mask pain. She tried to persuade her to sit, but Mums walked directly to the jades and picked them up one by one, holding each to the light. Framed against a cloudy sky, silver-haired in gray and yellow plaid, she was inscrutable — the shades of silver and gold and her slowness giving her a metallic, sculptural quality.

"What did you mean — you could almost see Alf's heart attack coming?" she asked.

"Something was wrong with his hands."

"You said the same thing when Simon got his glandular fever."

"Yes."

"Well, don't make too much of it — no one can predict illness. We pay the earth to be scrutinized by those wretched scanners . . . I don't know why we bother . . . I ache for weeks afterward. And then those cranks you hear about — what are they called — seers. The fact is, one's healthy one day and flat on one's back the next." She sighed creakily on an inhale and compulsively evened the jade bottles.

The gasplike sigh scraped Sephony's nerves — a small thing, like Marek's laugh or an ant crawling up her leg.

"Anyway . . . you and your hands," Hilary said.

"I haven't seen any in ages," Sephony said sadly, realizing how seldom they arrived. Life was thinner in some ways without them.

"I see eyes, of course," her mother said, "but I use them, they're a positive force. Oh, and by the way, speaking of eyes, your sister had the most wonderful idea . . . she said I should use matte varnish on my stones."

"Why, I've told you that a million times."

"You really should have some of my stones up here." She patted the shelf. "I'm surprised you don't."

The moment was fraying, growing dismally real. Hilary walked about the room, her eyes registering judgment.

"Sephony?" She appeared to be tracing an unpleasant odor. "What's that hologram? I'm sure I've never seen it before." She peered at Mo's hollie, twisting her pearls, her head tilted critically.

"What do you think of it?" Sephony asked. The cylinder slowly revolved among winking buttons and disintegrating flowers — a mysterious and oddly reassuring image of decay. Death, the hollie said, was a common denominator, a unity; death calmly flowed backward and forward.

"It's hideous," Hilary said. "What's that ghastly thing in the middle? You probably paid the earth for it."

As if someone had jammed the circuits, the hollie wobbled into a jumble of meaningless fragments.

"It was a gift," Sephony said, struggling to reassemble the image and see it whole again. "I think it's beautiful."

"Who gave it to you?"

"No one you know."

"Well, you have some very strange tastes. But forget I said anything about it. Art never was one of your strong points."

Mums seemed to have grown taller; her poisonous hairs quivered.

"I think it's wonderful that the artist manages to control his overall design," Sephony said coldly, "without killing off the spirit." She sat on the edge of her desk, angry and folded into herself.

"His. Well, we know that, at least. And are you criticizing my work?"

"Yes, I suppose I am."

"I'm too controlled, you'd say."

"You're certainly repetitive."

"Repetitive?" Mums's voice swooped and crackled. "You might as well criticize the sun for rising every morning." She dropped stiffly into a chair.

"The sun has to . . . you don't."

"Order, as any sane person knows, is the very essence of life."

"Change is also the essence of life."

"The Triangle is based on order," Hilary said with threatening finality.

"Is it? What would you say if I told you the Triangle does harmful things, that it's dark and ugly, that there's evil in it?" The words flew wildly about.

"Evil? The Triangle? Really, Sephony, someone's been filling your head with ridiculous ideas . . . you've always been very impressionable." Her eyes glinted. "The man who made that wretched hologram, perhaps."

Sephony grunted inwardly. How clever her mother was, how she twisted the rope, capable of strangling her with deadly opinions. We're Siamese twins, she thought, brain to brain and heart to heart, only I don't injure her, the power goes only one way. "Evil, yes, evil," she said. "Certain people are treated abominably . . . they want change . . . elections, for instance."

"Elections? But the Triangle has done tremendous things for this country. And you want to go back to the days of elections?"

"I didn't say that."

"No sane person would."

No sane person. The rope twisted.

Mums brushed invisible lint from her trousers.

Sephony felt vengeful. Her newborn ideas embarked on a stubborn life of their own, flapping like baby sparrows against Mums's walled mind, flapping and falling back.

"The Triangle turns some people into experimental ani-mals," she said harshly. "We close our eyes . . . we brush away the Dulls — we think they're horrible creatures and that makes us feel safe."

"We have our purpose," Hilary said, fingers tapping rest-lessly on the slender leather armrests.

"We're idle," Sephony said.

"Oh, my dear, suddenly you've become a champion of manual labor. Designing rockets isn't the only sort of work."

"But we can choose and they can't. Life's all determined in the controlled sectors."

"And they like it that way. It's what they're used to. Society would be utterly chaotic without the Triangle exactly as it is. I can't even imagine it."

A whisper came from far off, from the vaporous silence of empty rooms, from holes in the sky. "Have you ever wondered who's in the Triangle?" Sephony asked. "We don't know, do we? Perhaps there's no one in it. Perhaps it's just a flaking shape on a billboard."

"Really, my dear, I don't want to discuss it. If it weren't

for the Triangle we'd be barbarians again, with elections and religions."

"Well, there are other ideals. Some people believe in regional government, based on village life . . ." Circles of light, loaves of bread, row on row.

"Dreadful. Government by the rabble." Hilary stiffened. "I think you're hurting yourself with all that history nonsense again. You'll be right back where you started from . . . mark my words. And with the holidays coming."

"I didn't have a nervous breakdown from studying, Mother."

"Of course you did. Dr. Easton as much as said so."

"Doing nothing is worst of all."

Hilary waved a limp hand. "Well, never mind, I just want what's best for you. I work so hard to make the holidays enjoyable." Backed by the afternoon light, she looked old and tense, her eyelids heavy.

"I'm not sure which of the young will come to Christmas dinner," Sephony said, continuing the war on family ground. "Rolf may go to Scotland and Dote has an invitation from a young man in Brighton."

"One can't even count on the grandchildren these days." Hilary brushed her trousers with nervous flicks of her silky, veined fingers. She wore a petulant smile, a little smile of greed and frustration, of self-pity. "The young are only nice when they're young," she said, and sighed.

The phrase echoed into the cradle. "The young are only nice when they're young." Sephony remembered bands of light on the floor by an empty rocking chair. She remembered buzzing vibrations, wet and shameful, and boiled sweets forced on her tongue from a jar in the loo. But she'd climbed trees with sturdy legs and howled and pushed Ari's pram into the pond; she'd seen life clearly and knew her way about. Gradually she'd been weakened and silenced — erupting in little rebellions that were tallied against her. Renouncing Aaron, her greatest gesture of obedience, hadn't won her parents' love; it had only ruined her life. Anger flared up, fanning outward, leaping past her tongue, burning away the links.

"Infants, you mean." Fire roared around her; she perched on a cold, white flame. "You like people who are helpless."

"Don't exaggerate, Sephony, you always exaggerate."

"You adore lambs, Mother, but you hate sheep."

"Mother . . . Mother. Stop calling me Mother."

"You stifled me."

"What on earth are you going on about?"

"Look how you treated Ari . . . how you still do."

"Ari was a good child."

"Ari was very practical. She saw what happened to me."

"Really, Sephony, I think you should see Dr. Easton."

"You don't listen to me. You never have."

"Where did you get this taste for looking backward? Not from me, certainly, perhaps from your father. Studying history is bad enough, but rehashing your own life . . . Really, my dear, it's an illness."

"Forgetting is the illness."

"Forgetting is progress," Hilary said firmly. "It enables us to move on. Why do you think we have such confidence? If we kept examining the past we'd go round and round like donkeys."

"The past is real . . . it makes the present real. Without the past, life is flat and dishonest. Aaron and I were discussing that just the other day."

"What?"

"He said the short, narrow view makes us irritable and self-absorbed."

"Does Marek know?"

"Oh, he'd agree with you."

"I mean, does he know you see that man?"

"Ah . . . no."

Her mother's eyes darted from side to side; she seemed confused, lost. "So that's who made the hologram. Well, it explains all this . . ." She waved her arm as if to call down destruction on the room, on the day, on all travesties.

"Aaron's a biologist, Mother, he doesn't make holograms."

"It doesn't matter, I'm sure he's responsible. After all our efforts to make you happy —"

"Your efforts! He was shocked to hear why you put a stop to our marriage."

"He asked you?"

"I told him."

"Sephony! What a terrible thing to do!"

"He found it . . . very painful," Sephony admitted.

"A terrible thing for *me*, I mean." Hilary spat the words, her face a limestone mask, her eyes hooded, the gemlike slits blazing. "We only thought of your health and happiness — you could have given birth to who-knows-what. But you're spiteful, always wanting your own way . . . If you'd paid attention as a child instead of going off with that little smirk into books and trees and such, always going somewhere else instead of paying attention, you would have been much happier . . . When I think how hard I tried to establish you in the real world . . . Well, you think I'm a stupid old woman, I'm a stone around your neck, my values are wrong — I know where I'm wanted and where I'm not."

Poised, she rose to her full height, in full and furious control.

"Who knows what goes on in that twisted mind of yours," she said, and stomped out of the room.

Sephony's heart retreated from Mums's receding footsteps — down the stairs, fainter and fainter, echoing through the empty house. Was she leaving? Was the front door opening? No, of course not. She was in the sitting room, enthroned in the wing-backed chair, regal and defensive, itemizing the wrongs that had been done to her. Wryly, Sephony imagined the hooded eyes, the stubbornly raised chin. Her pleasure at inflicting pain subsided. She felt rudely independent — released from politeness into a more lasting connection. On shaky ground, perhaps, but in a different place.

She sat at her desk and cupped her chin. Little yellow birds flitted in and out of spruces and winter-bare poplars. From some angles they resembled large yellow butterflies. They landed swiftly and were gone, out of nowhere, into place, leaving silence behind, as if they had never been. She sensed again the echo of an older life, as a fierce child raised to be docile senses her true self in moments of anger. The cloth of time was being woven, patterned on both sides. Her length floated before her like an image on a scrim, an intricate pattern, abstract and floral; she searched it for some recognizable, meaningful shape.

A movement at the corner of her eye distracted her. She swiveled in her chair.

A man's hand was crawling across the Parsons table. It raised a finger as if to see, crawled, paused, looked about, crawled to the edge of the table, paused, and stopped. It was a sturdy, muscled hand with raised tendons and black hairs on the fingers below the first joints — not merely a hand, but a complete living creature, a complete spirit embodying the person. She leapt from her chair.

"Claro!" she called.

She reached for him, joyfully, blindly. The feathered hairs brushed her fingers, and he vanished.

"Claro!" she cried.

His hand crawled up the chair back where Mums had been sitting. It rested on top, fingers drumming. She approached slowly; she would caress him, hold his hand to her cheek. Again the hairs brushed her fingers and he disappeared.

She sat back on her desk. Claro's hand pressed on the seat of the Breuer chair, fingers spread, as if his invisible body were trying to lift itself. The tendons strained, the nails turned pink, the hairs quivered. It lost strength and vanished.

"Come back!" she cried, and he was on the chair again, crawling up and down. She clasped her hands to keep from trying to touch him. He was describing something, speaking in a way, asking her to pay attention.

She saw a path through the woods, pennyroyal underfoot. She wore brown, Dote wore blue, Melani wore bright yellow. Dote walked sedately, close to her, Melani skipped ahead, leapt and spun, gay as a butterfly. No queens and princesses. No powers of life and death. She ended at the boundaries of her being. The light slanted through the trees and shone on her daughters, more brightly on Melani. And Dote? Perhaps she had tied too many bitter knots already with Dote. But Melani was free. And the boys? Why weren't they in the picture?

"Claro," she whispered.

The hand was gone.

She petitioned the spirits of entrances and exits. She called his name, she implored him. She looked under the furniture, on the shelves, behind every movable object. Had something interfered? Had she chased him away? She closed her eyes.

"I promise to step back," she said aloud. "I won't contaminate them with my disappointments if I can help it — no dismal legacy bleeding down from Mums and her mother and her mother before her. I've put an end to that. I hope so." She waited. The room was hushed. From far off came the whizzing of craft and the rhythmic moaning of doves. She waited another moment and went downstairs.

"Mother, I'll make you a nice cup of tea," she called, stopping by the sitting room — Mums's profile high and stern, staring into the garden.

The silvery, elegant head turned, the hooded eyes were glazed. Was it sadness?

"Tea would be lovely," she said.

CHAPTER ⚡14

MAREK STOOD at the edge of the pond in a cold wind, his fishing rod between his knees. The crespin were down there on the muddy bottom, mysteriously spawning or dying or whatever they did. His sense of them living a secret life on the bottom, refusing to be caught, perversely comforted him. The water was choppy and olive green.

He baited the hook with wormets and threw in the line. The trees were bare, the grass was a brave, winter green. A moist wind stung his cheeks. Earlier in the morning the sky had been dusty with snow, like some kind of pollution, more like ash. It melted immediately. He was contemptuous of people who romanticized winter, who lifted their faces to a pathetic flurry, saying, "Look at that. It's snowing."

No goal in life. Why was he fishing on such a cold day? Crespin didn't swim about in cold weather, they probably hibernated. He hadn't made a proper study of the breed, had stocked the pond blindly, as if he were determined to fail. He shifted his line. The pond had the wrong balance; he should have set up a polycultural system.

He thought of Sephony before she tore a hole in their lives, remembering her puttering in the vegetable bed, popping over to ask him how the feeding was getting on. Odd how scenes from the past surfaced lately, not like him to think about the past, that was Sephony's department. Perhaps if they took a holiday she'd stop treating him as if he were invisible, tell him where she'd gone and what she was doing now. All that empty space around her, shutting him out. As the months went on he felt he was the absent one.

Getting into bed with her at night was intolerable, his hands and hips weighing into the mattress, nearly touching her narrow body humped under the covers. Every night he wanted to strangle the air, take circumstances by the throat, unravel time. They said good night as if leaving on separate journeys and slept facing opposite walls.

Sometimes she was indifferent, sometimes she was cranky. He didn't mind that. Never minded a change. He minded being excluded. He could probably bear any story. A lover, that was the usual story. Aaron, probably. A man could die from the cold of being excluded. What did she do tucked away upstairs? And all those trips to London. She came home looking so pleased and generous, as if she'd brought gifts, but it was all for herself, no surprises for him or the children. She'd given up on them all.

The children were withdrawn, didn't eat as much as they used to. Subsistence is enough, she had muttered one evening when someone complained about lamb wafers and raw veggies. And yet, if he had to describe her, he'd have to admit she seemed, he could almost call it happy. She looked well, had good color, seemed strong and resilient.

"You have no goal in life." The words surfaced with the stinging wind and persisted like old humiliations. "You have no goal in life." A young engineer in his department told him that. She was interested in him, kept inviting him to eat with her. Not much of a talker, but had a look that spoke to him. Like the cows. He understood the cows by their look, whether they were content or needed new pasture. That sort of thing. He didn't know what got into him, he rang her up one evening when Sephony was in London. Surprised at himself, not the sort to do anything foolish even if he was lonely. She lived about six miles away, on one of those collective farms. Her room was small and dim, furnished with floor pillows and mattresses. He had sat cross-legged on a pillow, uncomfortable about his age and weight. Her voice was monotonous, she talked slowly, hypnotically about her friends who coupled and recoupled — that's how she put it; he couldn't tell if she admired them or was disappointed, he felt a bit out of water. And then, in a burst of confidence, he talked about work, the farm, and Sephony. Not much about Sephony, he had a sense of loyalty. The girl was attentive, she heard his complaints and offered in the same monotone, "You have no goal in life." Just that. He didn't ask what she meant. He crawled to her and kissed her face, on his hands and knees like a cow, kissed her face repeatedly. And then he left.

Something tugged on the line. The pole arched to the water. Alert and unbelieving, he crouched in a brief, exhilarating struggle. A crespin thrashed in the cold air. He smacked its head against a rock. It weighed about a kilo, round-bellied, with a bright red dorsal fin. He wiped his hands on the ground, baited the hook, and cast again. He was neither a killer nor a provider, but he took pleasure in catching a fish — an invisible opponent, a modest struggle, a modest victory. In slow succession he caught three more crespin, each a substantial size. Whistling, he stripped a branch and thrust it through their gills. Four bluish-gray bodies dangled, fat and stiff, their red fins translucent and brilliant.

He threw them in the kitchen sink and cleaned them, enjoying the messy work. Would Sephony be pleased? Dead fish, bloated fish. He could hear her say it.

Simon came into the kitchen — dark and nervous like Sephony.

"Caught some crespin," Marek said, "would you believe it?"

"I thought they hibernated in winter."

Marek wrapped them carefully and placed them on the bottom shelf of the refrigerator.

"If it's not a fluke we can sell fishing rights and make a profit for a change," Marek said.

"I don't understand what anyone sees in fishing," Simon said apologetically.

"Don't you?"

"It's boring."

"Gives your mind a chance to do nothing in particular," Marek said.

"I don't have time for that," Simon said.

"Your mother back?"

"Didn't she come home last night?"

"Said she'd be back today."

"What does she do in London?" Simon asked politely.

"Haven't a clue," Marek muttered.

"Have you asked?" Simon looked at him with unusual directness.

"Have you?"

"Melani did. She said, 'This and that.' "

"Ah. This and that," Marek said.

"Well, she seems all right, doesn't she?"

"Oh, quite all right."

Simon looked embarrassed. "You don't talk to each other, do you?"

Marek was tempted to give an easy, blustering answer, but settled for the suffocating truth. "We don't talk at all. She goes about as if she's in some other world and I'm only some kind of shadow." His language surprised him.

"Don't you think you could, well, I shouldn't be giving you advice, but, draw her out? It seems to us you should be the one to find out where she went that time."

"It doesn't matter," Marek muttered.

"We think one day she'll go again," Simon said bitterly, "and not come back." He looked young and pinched, his hair thinning prematurely, his ears large.

"You're all quite grown up," said Marek, crisply.

"What has age to do with feeling terrible?"

"You don't need her in the way a child needs her, you can manage." Marek felt stubborn, cold.

"There's alone and there's alone. We don't want to manage alone."

"No, of course not." Marek relented. He did not know how to deal with his children's emotions. "So you talk among yourselves," he said.

"Sometimes."

What was Simon's expression? Was it guilt? There was silence between them. "That's good," Marek lied. "Good you have each other to talk to."

"I'd better go study," said Simon, embarrassed.

"Right," said Marek. "Tell the others about the fish."

"Will do. Congratulations."

Marek grabbed his coat and went outdoors.

He walked through the pastures, hands deep in his pockets. Harry and Douglas nipped his heels possessively. They scattered the sheep, exciting ewes and lambs into frenzies of antiphonal bleating. The cows silently faced away from the wind, heads pointing south. He liked the cold, it gave him something to resist. Winter was a friend in misery; he was in deep freeze, the weather confirmed it, but he was not despondent.

Sephony was hanging her coat in the hall when he came home. She did not look at him straight on, but busied herself with changing into soft shoes.

"Had a nice time?" he asked.

"Mmmm," she said.

"See anyone?" he asked casually, skipping over the sensitive issue of whether he had a right to ask.

"Pardon?" She blinked, standing on one foot, her finger inside the heel of a shoe.

"Did you see anyone interesting?" He felt neutral; she might be a business acquaintance.

"Reb Nacht."

"So you still keep up with them."

Sephony shrugged and put on the other shoe.

"Would you sit with me?" he asked.

She looked at him sharply.

He resisted the impulse to take hold of her shoulders and shake her until secrets tumbled out of her mouth.

They went into the orange room and she sat in a pillow that molded itself to her thin body. Marek sat heavily in the recliner.

"I caught four crespin today," he said.

"Did you?" She blinked.

"Looks like winter is the season to catch them."

"Who would have thought so?"

"I cleaned them already."

She put the backs of her fingers over her mouth.

"Why are you laughing?" he asked.

"It doesn't matter."

"Hated to think stocking the pond was a waste."

"Four fish don't make a season," she said, still amused.

"If I have a week's success I'll sell fishing rights to the locals."

"Meaning a lot of strangers around?"

"Alf's well enough to tend them. Fishermen aren't a noisy lot."

They sat quietly.

"You still take an interest in the farm?" he asked.

"I walk, yes, in the early mornings."

"How's Reb Nacht, the old buzzard?"

"He's fine."

Lodged in the orange pillow, she was one of those puzzles made of lucite cubes, precariously balanced, facets blinking and sparkling. A light glowing gently within encouraged him to speak, but the reflected light warned him to go easy.

"You look well," he said.

"Kind of you to notice."

The cubes shifted, the lights danced, and he imagined for a moment that he was connecting with her, but the lucite softened and the real person appeared and he lost confidence.

"I don't understand you anymore," he said.

"What do you expect?" she asked, from a distance, her eyes cool and focused. She was not hostile, she was simply inquiring.

He felt old, he grew heavy and fell. "What do I expect? I expect us to have a life. I expect you to notice the children. I expect us to be a family. What else is there?"

"It's oppressive," she said.

"The family?"

"They're a suit of stones."

"Not the children. Not me."

"I fight against reverting to what I was before. I'm so tired of being split."

"Between?"

"Oh . . ." She looked about wildly as if birds were in the room.

He made an effort to keep up with her. "In the meantime, aren't we all changing? Not your mother, I don't expect her to be anything but awful, but the rest of us, me and the children?"

"I don't know."

"You don't notice us?"

She was silent.

"You don't mean to say" — he hesitated to draw out the thought for fear of encouraging her — "you don't care about us."

"Right now I don't care." She nodded mechanically. Her expression was pained and cold.

"I don't believe you."

"You've never had to protect yourself from the habits of maternal love," she said.

"But after all these years."

"It's been all right for you to be self-centered."

"You can't not care."

She was silent and looked stubborn.

"It's not natural," he said.

"In me, you mean," she said.

"I'm not so self-centered as all that."

"You scarcely know yourself."

"You're punishing us," he said angrily, "at least the young are innocent."

"They aren't young anymore."

"But they suffer."

"Do they?"

"Simon says they do."

"They'll survive."

"Is that so?" he asked vindictively. "They're adults, so they don't suffer. You're an adult."

"I'm not going back to that life," she said bitterly. "There's a whole world to consider."

"But our family is here. Our house. The farm."

"And that's enough?" she asked sharply. "You're content?"

"Life is tolerable," he growled.

"You've often imagined something else."

He thought of his designs for acoustic barriers, stored in crystals. "Doing something useful." He hesitated. "Even in a small way. Being, well, of consequence."

"Yes."

"You're looking for that?"

"In a way."

She was a figure imposed upon a figure, Sephony the stranger and Sephony on the orange pillow. He didn't know how to acknowledge them both.

"What else do you do besides Reb Nacht's group?" he asked.

"In London, you mean?"

"Yes."

She blinked. Her face closed, then opened. He was surprised to be aware of the change. He never used to notice different expressions on her face. She was Sephony, that's all. It was painful — noticing, registering, analyzing the changes in her eyes alone, windows with such a variety of messages; he marveled that he could understand them, and in the next moment doubted that he did. How much did one invent when one was interpreting the expression in a person's eyes?

"I see Aaron for lunch," she said calmly. "You remember Aaron."

She saw Aaron for lunch. That was nice. Something was expected of him, he was supposed to feel something, jealousy, perhaps. It didn't matter.

"What else do you do?" he asked.

She blinked and ran her fingers through her hair.

"I have other friends," she said.

"Who?"

"There's Lela."

The name meant nothing, but a vagueness in her eyes and a softness of voice engaged him in the intimate, ambiguous atmosphere of a dream.

"Have I met her?"

Her eyes lit with amusement. "No, you haven't."

"Is she from the group?"

"Which group?"

"Reb Nacht's."

"Lela is a student at the Technicon. I pay her tuition."

"I didn't know you went in for charity."

"It's not charity, it's repayment."

There was a cave and she sat in the entrance. Shadows behind her quivered and danced, merging into globs, splitting away to dance alone, re-forming and splitting. They loomed up to the ceiling and across the walls — bodies, arms, trees — rolling and waving, merging and splitting.

"How do you know her?" he asked, frightened.

"She helped me out of the Jungle," Sephony said. "I would have been arrested for certain, perhaps even died or gone mad."

Her statement was cold and airless. They were both weightless, drifting in space. She might slash her thigh with a kitchen knife. He could drown in a glass of water. They would dance, bubbles escaping from their lips. Rise up, sink, it was all the same.

"People can't get in the Jungle," he said.

"I accidentally came up from underneath," she said.

"Ah. From underneath."

"From another world."

"Ah."

"Called Domino."

"Ah." He cleared his throat. "What are you talking about?"

"Domino is another space, another dimension. All caves and tunnels and such, but large like outdoors. It's quite extraordinary. Light comes from phosphorescent rock and there's water and vegetation and various sorts of odd creatures. Some of them look human."

"And you were there."

"Yes."

The recliner was exceedingly uncomfortable. "That's where you were?"

"Yes."

His brain was being pulled apart, tufts of cotton flying in all directions, puff, puff, plucked and thrown.

"In an imaginary . . ."

"A real —"

". . . world that you say is underground?"

"Not underground . . . ah, outside."

He sighed. "How did you get there?"

"Through a hole in the larder floor."

Her concreteness silenced him for a moment.

"And the metergun in the potato bin?" The absurd question implicated him; he was guilty of participating in her story.

"Oh, I was so startled," she said. "He was playing games, appearing and disappearing. Trying, I suppose, to get my attention. I wonder what he ever did with the chickens."

"Who?" he asked, chilled.

"He has several names," Sephony said slowly. "I called him the chicken man at first, but he has other names." She hesitated. "Amos, Dartri . . ." A tiny, mysterious smile played at the corners of her lips and he suspected, oddly, that she had not told him the man's name.

"And this Amos — can I call him that? — he was here, in the house, in the kitchen?"

"And then we went down the ladder and on into Domino," she said with a little sigh.

"How far down?"

She winced. "It's not really down, I'm trying to tell you, it just seems that way."

"Where's the hole now?" he demanded.

"It closed up."

"Just like that."

"You don't believe me."

"I'm not saying I don't believe you," he snapped. "I don't know what to believe. What if you were in my place?"

"That's why I haven't said anything."

"But you can't expect me to just believe it, can you?"

"Reb Nacht does."

He was shocked that she had confided in someone else. "You told him, did you?"

"Rumors of other worlds troubled him; he half believed in them. I convinced him this one is real."

He would find some logical explanation. If he asked enough questions and was patient, he would discover what she meant, even though he might never learn where she had been.

"What did this Amos creature look like?"

"Like an ordinary person in most respects. But he can fly and get fat or thin at a moment's notice."

"So he has wings."

"No. They transport themselves."

"They."

"Well, it's a world."

"Ah, of course. A world." Dr. Easton would know if episodes of hallucination were likely to recur. "And where were you actually, I mean, when you imagined or dreamed you were underground, where were you, where was your body?"

"I knew this was going to be impossible," she said irritably.

"You don't realize you imagined it?" he shouted. "You appear normal, you act normal, but you say crazy things. You sit there talking, as if you'd been to Paris, about four days

underground with a man who flies. And I'm supposed to believe it? Sephony, I'm not your Reb Nacht whose mind is full
of burning bushes. I live in the real world."

"Not underground, another dimension. I'm not going to
try to prove it." Her confidence was alarming.

"What did you do there? Where did you live?" he asked
in panic. What else did she believe that knocked at the door of
reason?

"Listen," he said, "tell me simple things, details, where
you ate and slept. Something I can understand."

"The first night I slept in a cave near a lake, the second
night, well, in the Muzids' house, which had beautiful murals,
and the other two nights in . . . with Amos and his family."

A terrible weariness drew the marrow from his bones, his
skin was collapsing. He felt humble, a petitioner at the door of
her life.

"If I ask you about it bit by bit, will you tell me?" he
asked, tiptoeing into her dream, gently, hesitantly, trying to
make no footfalls.

"I'll tell you, how shall I put it, the objective facts," she
said kindly. "I'll tell you as much as I can, but some of it is . . .
I can't share with you, can't give away. Do you understand? I'm
willing to try."

"Tell me," he said, slipping onto a pillow beside her, his
cheek in his hand. He left Marek behind in the recliner, the self
he had inhabited all his life. He did not know the man who lay
beside her, who listened to a story about creatures with three
eyes and houses with floors of light, but he was strangely
grateful.

Marek reeled in a fat, protesting crespin. Fishing was the tune
and shape of reality, which he held on to as he held the pole.
Numbers and concrete solutions were abhorrent to him; he
shunned the square, the finite, the logical, as he would shun
greasy food if he were ill. The world stood on its head while he
drew up one crespin after another, visibly, in a sequence he
could understand.

He carried a pail of fish into the house, shooing away the geese. He had never felt so alive. Whenever he opened the door to the house he created something unpredictable, opened a door into Sephony, who was in herself an entrance into another world. He felt turbulent, angry, perplexed. Good to feel young when you're middle-aged, he thought, that's when you can appreciate it. But he was edgy and losing his appetite.

He cleaned the fish and took a cup of tea into the video room. Sephony removed her earphones and switched off the crystal.

"Catch anything?" she asked.

"Six good ones."

"How are you today?"

"So-so," he said.

"And?"

He settled on a pillow against the wall and took off his shoes.

"You'll never prove anything to me, but it doesn't matter. It's your life — whatever it was, it happened to you. You see? I don't feel possessive anymore. I just want to live with you and not be excluded. I can't bear to be excluded."

"But all these years you've excluded yourself."

"Have I?"

"You had your work."

"Not worth much anymore," he muttered.

"You're bored?"

"My designs pile up in storage. Feel as if nothing I do matters. No goal in life."

"How familiar," she said dryly.

"You, too?"

"The young matter, of course, but I haven't accomplished anything. Everything I make is consumed or gets dusty or goes off on its own."

"And your studies?" Odd to be questioning his wife, as if they'd just met.

"I'm reading Neolithic history," she said cautiously. "But

studying is so protected, so self-indulgent. I should be doing something practical."

"Sephony?"

"Hmmm?"

"We agree on wanting to be useful. Could we work together?"

She looked startled.

"Running the farm, for instance. If I gave up engineering."

"Running the farm?"

"Couldn't we work together and still be independent?"

"I don't think so."

"We could do aquaculture in a serious way." Visionary enthusiasm possessed him, the two of them together, side by side. "You could be in charge of breeding."

"Really," Sephony said acidly, and he felt as if he'd stepped in sheep-dip. "When I said practical," she said carefully, "I meant, oh, education or social engineering."

"Think about it," he said.

They were silent and he felt like a disappointing child. Although he'd blundered somehow, or because of it, he wanted to be close to her.

He slipped into the murky, entranced state in which her stories gave him pleasure, making him feel alternately nourished and beaten. Everything was true and everything was a lie — Domino was a lie, how she spent the day was a lie, past and present were all lies. He was a blind man in a strange house approaching the last step of a flight of stairs. He wanted, perversely, to doubt and hate. At other times he believed every word and could imagine himself walking through the corridors and gardens of Domino. He had his favorite stories — exciting adventures in which Sephony was a character. He might even believe in Domino if only she didn't claim to have been there.

"Tell me about the nudges again," he said.

"Not now."

But he wanted to remain in the murky, entranced state.

"I was wondering," he said.

"What?"

"Whether you still see hands floating about."

"Not as often. Why?"

"I wonder if I might someday."

"Not likely." She drew into herself. "Do you want to? It's not a treat."

"I suppose I am looking for proof."

"If you saw hands, then Domino exists?"

"Something of the sort."

She raised her eyebrows. "It puts me in an awkward position."

"I know. I'm sorry." He felt clumsy.

"Working with me might be rather unpleasant," she said.

"You've changed."

"Changed?" She shrugged. "The cylinder turns a bit, that's all."

"What cylinder?"

"Oh." She brushed imaginary crumbs from her lap. "I imagine my personality as a design etched on a cylinder, a silvery, aramid cylinder, but only part of the design is on top at any one time. Sometimes the cylinder rotates a few degrees. Sometimes it revolves. Sometimes it gets stuck for years and years."

"Where is it?"

"Where is what?"

"The cylinder."

"I don't know."

"In your head?"

"No, it's too big to be in my body, really, I see it outside and feel it inside."

"Well, mine's made of thick wood and hard to turn, but it's been given a good whack and sent spinning."

She laughed. He enjoyed her new, wholehearted laugh — her mouth open wide and her teeth showing. Her lips used to turn down, making her cheeks pouchy.

He wanted to encompass her, wanted to lie with her in a pine-scented room, wanted to roll and toss on green pillows, to fill her with himself and be taken by her. He slid off his pillow and crawled the distance to her, to his own wife, pulled her gently onto the rug and embraced her.

She stiffened, her unloving body stretched out against his.

"I can't," she whispered. "I just can't."

And he had to be content with holding her, appeased by her breath and physical presence. Union was not to be taken for granted anymore. She was the house of a stranger, familiar and utterly alien, a series of soft rooms that advanced and receded. Her back was immense, his hand couldn't cover its territory; it was her whole body, her self. He stroked it obsessively, feeling turbulent and hopeful.

CHAPTER 15

SEPHONY sat with Mo and Lela on floor pillows she had made over the winter, a snarl of piano strings between them, all gauges tangled together. The shop was her refuge from home, from Marek's blind curiosity, from his childlike obsession with her stories. Auras were the subject here, the miasma she saw willy-nilly leaking from hands of friends and strangers, betraying them. In Mo's opinion she was lucky not to be chasing storms. She listed the cases, the most recent the Watleys' daughter serving wine at a party, a nasty pumpkin color leaking from her palms.

"If only you people weren't so bloody polite," Mo said.

"Could you really march up to a mother and say, My dear, some disease is leaking from your daughter's hands?"

"I'd tell someone who could . . ."

"Oh, there must be Twyla Watleys in your world, too."

"How are you going to use this new power you got, then?" Lela asked.

Sephony coiled a treble string and twisted its ends. She wouldn't call it power — talent, rather, with some promise knotted within that sparkled like dewed intersections in a spiderweb. Although for the moment she crabbily wished she'd come back with a passion for sculpting.

"It's like being born," Lela said, "you can't choose."

"Lookie here," Mo said, uncramping a wire, "we have this project . . . we keep at it, down in the warren, a couple of surgeries. You could learn to be a seer." He gave her a shaggy furtive look, yanking another wire from the heap.

Grackles limped across the lawn, pecking at worms. The top branches of the poplar quivered; budding trees and shrubs dripped. She picked up a yellow plastic mailer from Mo, the color of acid, peeled the flap carefully, and tugged out a scanner print and a fiche. Pale blue sentences in the center of the page announced:

> *Opportunities in Bioradiatics:*
> · Long-term engagements in challenging urban en-
>   vironments
> · No experience necessary
> · Training provided

An inchworm humped onto the mailer, a dainty, methodical creature. It rose, swayed left and right to survey the territory, dropped, and arched smartly to attention. Sensing food, perhaps, or a fellow worm, it proceeded with confidence but, having no sense of direction, navigated the same route again and again. Move a little to the left, she directed, but it turned right, where it had already been.

At bedtime she lay under the duvet, wondering what seers did, exactly. Marek climbed into bed with heavy enthusiasm, pulling the duvet onto himself. Cold air sliced down her leg. Brusquely, she tugged the covers back.

"My friend Mo sent me an employment notice," she said.

"You're not looking for work, are you?"

"Well, yes, I might be."

"What sort of notice?"

"Something to do with health care. In London."

He propped his head and made himself comfortable. "That's interesting. I could do with a change. You wouldn't have to go back and forth; we could take a flat in London."

"What would you do there?" she asked, recoiling from his eagerness.

"Some hydrowork, possibly . . . in sonar . . . give the farm over to a tenant . . . I've considered that off and on."

Had he? Considered giving up the farm . . . her farm? Doubtful. It was another of his private schemes, like aquaculture and putting her in charge of breeding.

"Well, it's just an idea," she said. "I've not looked into it yet."

He was so needy, like a wounded sheep. And yet he shut her out — his very nature isolated her somewhere outside him. Whenever she invited him into her life he wandered about, stepped on the delicate parts, took what he needed, and walked off, leaving her discouraged.

The door was lettered in dingy blue: Hygiene, Sector 4. Sephony handed her cassette profile to a bleak, harassed woman who pointed her to the room where Dr. Getha would meet her.

People were waiting inside, other applicants, Sephony assumed. She took off her jacket and folded it over her arm. The group as a whole emitted an ominous and fragile breath, like decaying flowers.

A woman entered wearing dark blue coveralls. Brisk and decisive, she was obliquely familiar, like an acquaintance's twin. A freckled face, an ironic smile.

"Good to see you again, Sephony," the woman said, and Sephony recognized her voice. Reb Nacht's group — the congenial cynic, Anna — but she'd had long dark hair then. Under short blond curls she looked older, her face pale and lined. Even her cynicism was muted.

"How extraordinary," Sephony said.

"Don't say anything here," Dr. Getha said hurriedly.

They went into her office. Plants hung in the windows and peeked from behind equipment, their leaves glossy and vigorous.

"My name is actually Joanne," she said. "Black-wigged Anna is a secret in this office." She laughed.

"I should think so," Sephony said.

"What did you observe in the group out there?" Joanne asked when they were settled at a table.

"They were terribly ill."

"How do you know?"

"Some miasma, a general thing . . ."

"They have terminal cancer," Joanne said. Her tone was neutral, almost brusque, but pain showed in her face and Sephony understood conflict was habitual with her, that her voice and words spoke one language and her face spoke another.

A hollie viewer stood on the table, a hooded black box. Joanne explained the intuition test in detail, a flickering smile mocking her crisp instructions. "Fifty hands," she said, switching on the consoles. "Tell me if you think they're healthy, sick, or if you're not sure."

Sephony peered into the dark box, the hood hard against her forehead. On a click a life-size hand appeared, palm up, suspended in a cold light — slender and luminous with arthritic joints. A baby's hand appeared, fingers curled upward, followed by a gnarled hand with deep cracks. They gave up their secrets and the console clicked. She felt pleasure. She felt anxiety. She gave her judgments. The sick hands drained her.

"Top marks," Joanne said, switching off the viewers. "Only three errors."

"So I've not been imagining things." Sephony rubbed her forehead.

"You weren't a seer when you came to the study group, were you?"

"No, and I'm not now, either."

Joanne grimaced. Her skin was delicate, her lips dry around the edges. A sad, urgent light flickered in her eyes. A seer, she explained, picked up tiny neurochemical signatures transmitted by cancers and viral infections, signatures discernible in hands, cheekbones, and the iris.

"And this . . . soothsaying without instruments . . . is what you call bioradiatics?"

"In a general way." Joanne smiled.

"It seems dreadfully primitive."

"Oh, you'd be surprised. Within our limits we're as accurate as scanners." She made a hesitant appeal. Dulls, she said; the work diagnosing illness was with Dulls. No official medical care was available for them — no doctors, no medication, certainly no scanners, nothing official.

Another horror on the list of things they weren't meant to know. "I hope the position is in London," Sephony said.

"And another in Liverpool."

"Which warren in London?"

Joanne looked surprised. "Warren Two." She cocked her head. "Why aren't you put off about working with Dulls? You're not the obvious sort, Sephony, if you don't mind my saying so."

"I know some Bristers."

"So that's it."

"May I visit the surgery?"

"It's not much. There's old equipment and we dispense expired medication. But we manage to set bones and treat infections. The situation is intolerable, as you must have heard. There are only four surgeries in the entire London warren for a quarter of a million people. That's about twenty-five doctors and fifty nurses, most with primary positions elsewhere. And not a single hospital."

Joanne reminded her of someone — Leuma, so beautifully expressive while guarding her feelings. She spoke about duties and salary on currents of indignation. The Warren 2 surgery was the smallest — it had a doctor and a nurse as well as the seer. It was open five hours a day, only on weekdays. No operating room, no euthanasia facilities. Six beds for emergencies. Joanne had founded that particular surgery, had exchanged a comfortable hospital post for medical politics, had gotten private funding to set it up. A small network of warren surgeries existed nationwide, locally administered.

"However did you do all that and have five children?" Sephony asked.

"Oh . . . they're ex-uteros."

"And are they all right?"

"Why, yes, of course."

"Wasn't your husband against it?"

"My husband was against everything."

"I see. And I expect the Triangle is against this."

Joanne looked at her speculatively. "For some obscure reason, the Triangle allows us to practice. It doesn't notice . . . or pretends not to. Even though replacing Dulls," she said sarcastically, "is cheaper than maintenance. They even allow me this supplemental post in Sector Four, which does double duty."

"Wouldn't you rather have someone younger?"

Joanne made nervous gestures, like a child trying to be tough. The environment was taxing at any age. Too many patients and too many shortages. Too much irritation and much goodwill. If Sephony accepted she would train with a living relic, a ninety-year-old teacher in London. After three months she'd be able to work with patients intuitively under Joanne's guidance, learning, as an apprentice, on the job.

"Mainly it's just general work around the surgery," Joanne said wryly. "Any mother could do it."

"How long have *you* been a seer?" Sephony asked.

Joanne seemed embarrassed, as if hiding a defect. "Seers wear out," she said awkwardly.

"Ah. Just like scanners."

"There you have it," Joanne said dryly, with a look of longing for something lost.

"I'll think it over."

"You're our only applicant at the moment."

"When do you want an answer?"

Joanne's smile wrinkled up into a lively squint. "In two weeks, at the latest. We need a replacement by summer."

She dreamed she fell slowly and lightly as feathers, keeping pace with a crusty yellow window, and landed in a cell where she'd been all along.

She sat on a stool. A narrow cot hung on ropes. The

window was high and barred. It was the sort of cell where prisoners invent mathematical games and scrape days on the wall with a spoon — a dusty cell, motes blurring the walls, like a cocoon.

She was so lonely, she might as well be at a party. Her body made the strangely intimate and familiar cacophony silence allows, a chaotic and formal music.

Her head passed through the ceiling, leaving her body in the cell. Her head, out in the sunlight, grew in a plot of mature cabbages.

Cabbageworms chewed complacently. The garden looked familiar — there was a net of runner beans on the left and rows of broccoli — her own cabbage patch. What if Marek came along, or Alf, or one of the children? Oh, dear. Not the ticket, very embarrassing. She heard a sinister swishing.

A harvesting robo waddled on tiny feet, wielding a double-edged knife, its slashing precise and rhythmic. Cabbages rolled in their leafy collars like heads off a guillotine. Would the robo know she wasn't a cabbage? No, of course not — it would hack at her head and catch on the bones. She looked around wildly. The robo must have been repaired; it wasn't getting stuck in clots of earth. It finished the row in front and started on her row.

"Help! I'm in the cabbages!" she screamed.

Tough roots held her neck. The knife approached down the line.

She screamed.

The blade whistled and she was in the cell again, standing on the stool, desperately rubbing a peephole in the window's yellow crust. The street outside was desolate, the windows dark, store names painted in black letters outlined in gold.

In the "Monuments" store a face filled the dark pane, an enormous face with bulging eyes. It crashed through the glass, rolled across the street, and settled on its chin. A stone head, a living sculpture of her father with his sharp nose and stern mouth. It looked in her direction, looked right up at her and met her eyes. What did it want? Would it rotor up to the

cell? It seemed to be gathering energy. Just as it lifted, a lasso
flew out and caught beneath its nose. The head struggled, but
the loop tightened and dragged it backward, through the window, into the store. The shattered window reassembled itself;
the cracks remained. Mournful eyes peered from behind the
crazed glass.

The idea of the lasso beneath the nose, just grazing the
upper lip, tormented her. If only she had a kitchen knife. The
window was dark, even the cracks were gone. She couldn't see
the head, but she knew it waited behind the pane, gathering
energy.

"I have two weeks to decide, Aaron."

"How would you organize everything? With the family, I
mean?"

"Simon and Dote say they can manage the house. I'd take
a flat in London and Melani would board at Dartington."

"You're moving quickly," he said with a suspicious, chal-
lenging look.

"And you're taking it calmly. You haven't even congratulated me."

"Congratulations," he said with mock ceremony.

"Marek wants to go with me — if I go."

Startled, he jabbed a fork into his pie, releasing a trickle
of green sauce. "And are you encouraging him?"

"No, not at all," she said. "But I can't tell him I want to
take the job, move away . . . you know . . . alone. I can't.
Unless I'm prepared to sever."

"I didn't know you were considering that," he said, his
pale green eyes flickering.

"I didn't mean I was."

"Ah," he said, drawing back, "it's just a way of speaking."

Fear dimmed the atmosphere like webs of mist. She lost
herself down one slope, he down another, both sliding backward.

"Sometimes I imagine severing," she forced herself to say.

"When's your next renewal?"

"In a year."

He leaned forward and the air cleared, sun on grass, the sky pale blue with little puffs of lavender. He leaned his face on his hand, framing his eye. "I'm fond of Sybil, we're fond of each other, we really are," he said sadly. "But we've become so . . . how shall I say . . . so wary, so well behaved. She dreads being cold and hostile. I hate being judgmental. We walk on eggshells much of the time. And then we get angry over some procedure. We shouldn't have married, we were too much alike, too comfortable."

"I might not feel so guilty," she said, "if at least *your* marriage had been all right . . ."

"Don't blame yourself, Sephony. I didn't fight for you, did I? I'm in the hell reserved for complacent fools."

"And I'm in the one for cowards. Although, I must say, I never imagined you fighting for me. You weren't the sort."

"Would you have defied your parents if I'd made a fuss?"

"I don't know," she said, startled.

"You might have," he muttered. He jabbed at a Brussels sprout. "An engineer will have opportunities in London," he said.

"Pardon?"

"Always something under construction."

"Well, Marek mentioned a new hydroworks on the Thames. He's interested in sonar cages, I think he said."

"So you actually have plans. Your plans are getting on." His eyes were pale and cold.

"I have to."

"Perhaps you'll find some common ground," he said, his voice strangled.

"No," she said, oscillating for a moment between loyalty and truth. "I had a dream the other night about severed heads . . . an awful dream. He's a good, decent person, but he imprisons me, I imprison him. Do you remember your dreams?"

"We would have done well together," he said mournfully.

"It hasn't been tested," she said.

His green eyes became pale blue for a moment; she looked

into one person and saw another. A second's expression, a shift of gauzy skin, and another smile and black hairs peeped through the neck of a tunic.

"What does your name mean?" she asked urgently.

"I haven't a clue," he said. "What a question."

"I just wondered." Her cheeks burned and her speech sounded uncontrollably high and rapid. "I'll have to look it up."

"What does *your* name mean?"

"Bringer of destruction."

"Sephony . . . Sephony . . ."

"Do you ever think of life as a pattern?" she continued, with the same high, rapid intensity.

"It has any number of patterns."

"A giant ellipse, I mean, whose ends come together in the course of one's lifetime?"

"I tend to think of fractures," he said, "that break in predictable and unpredictable directions."

She laughed.

They ate silently for a while. Their food was cold.

"Simon and Dote are old enough to be responsible for the house," she said, suddenly feeling quite confident. "They'll enjoy the freedom. And Melani will only have to go to Dartington the one year." An announcement for herself as well as Aaron.

"That's it, then," he said, "well done."

"I hope so," she said. How clear everything was, all laid out ahead with only guilt trailing behind.

"They don't approve, you know. Which is my fault, bringing them up so narrowly."

"And your mother?"

"I haven't told her anything."

"Sephony?" He pushed their plates aside and took her hands.

"I wouldn't dare say a word to Mums until every last knot is tied . . ."

"Sephony? What would you think of going on holiday by yourself?"

"What? Why — I don't know. I've never been on holiday by myself."

He looked proud and frantic, as if his life depended on what he was about to say. "Go to Cornwall," he said, "to St. Ives."

"Of all places . . ."

"I do consulting for Celtic Fisheries," he said, his words tumbling over each other, "and I have to be there next month. St. Ives isn't contaminated anymore. Go for a week by yourself and then I'll join you."

Her shirt rustled loudly, her breath came too fast. "It's not contaminated, you say."

"Officially no one's encouraged to go back," he said, "but the fishery was built there, and the military are still in Penzance. Some people never left. They're damaged, of course."

"You know, it was our summer home when I was a child," she said.

"I didn't . . ."

"One of my father's shops was on the pier, his favorite. We went every summer until I was eight."

"Ah . . . well, the area's all black and destroyed, but there's something magnificent in that landscape."

"Are the cottages rebuilt?"

"Some survived. It's safe. I know of a cottage to let." He was leaping ahead, organizing, enjoying it.

"But . . . what would I say? How would I explain?"

He brought her hands together, palm to palm, and kissed her fingertips. "This time I'm going to fight for you, Sephony. If that doesn't sound ridiculous."

"Fight whom?"

"I don't know — Marek? Sybil? Our families? What am I saying?"

"It's true the way Marek and I live together . . . you could say it's dishonest." She struggled. "I've told him I'm going to London alone. To work. That as far as I'm concerned, I'm going alone. He doesn't understand 'alone.' He says 'we.' Am I deceiving him? I'm a responsible person, after all."

"We're both responsible," he groaned, banging his forehead against her fingertips.

"Oh, Aaron," she said, taking his face in her hands, the bones so accessible, the skin like a dry leaf, "if only life could be a series of lunches — maybe that's what people should do after they've raised their families, live apart and meet for lunch. There's so much you don't know about me. You might find me awfully strange. Really. You don't know."

He took her hands away from his face. "I could know anything about you, Sephony. I'm elastic, the band around my chest is broken. I could take in anything about you and it wouldn't matter. That is, it would matter infinitely. You were freedom then and you're freedom now. I want . . . how shall I say . . . I hope . . . we can both sever at the next session — for me it's three years — and marry. If you could stand me, if I'm not intolerable."

She was joyful, torn in a million pieces. Her clothing was in shreds, hungry dogs ran off with her flesh, blood flowed in the street. She had never been so enraptured.

"Oh . . . I can't bear it," she said. "Let's walk."

They walked for hours, she didn't recognize the streets. No grief, no turmoil compared with this. They stopped in deserted doorways and little gardens and held each other. They kissed, their first kisses in nearly thirty years.

One spoke. They walked. Another spoke. Thoughts were answered by buildings and city blocks, by people who jostled them at another pace.

"You'll go to St. Ives," he said.

"And you'll follow."

"Will we tell them?"

"I don't know. Will we?"

He stopped. "Are you and Marek lovers?"

"No," she said indignantly. "Are you and Sybil?"

"No, no. I've had the odd encounter, you know, women at work. But not Sybil, not for years."

But that's not everything, she thought. The years built up their conditions and tolerances — Aaron's as well, although he made light of it. Could she tell him about Domino? Torn open and rearranged, could she risk her secrets and still have a reservoir of self? Give without giving up, release without being robbed? Would it horrify him? Did she want to offer him the full emotion, with the particulars? What would they make of it together? And what were his secrets? The questions created new questions. She pulled back. She might tell him later. In St. Ives, perhaps.

"How can I move to London with Marek now? I can't move to London with Marek." She spun on a pin.

"Tell him you go as . . . friends."

"We're scarcely that."

"Tell him not to have expectations."

"I've told him from the start that I'm going alone . . . If he comes he has to fit himself into my life."

"Ugh, what a cold construction. No wonder he doesn't accept it."

"He does accept it . . . I told you — he ignores everything I say."

"He must be dreadfully dependent on you," he said with a hard, knowing look.

"And I'm susceptible."

"Don't you find it cloying?"

"I suppose I'm used to it."

They found a bench in a tiny park surrounded by hedges and a rusted fence.

"Each of us could live alone for a while," he said.

"Are you so much closer to being severed?" she asked.

"Yes. Although I have my susceptibilities, too."

They sat together until dusk.

A wind-driven rain slashed the kitchen window, turning the dusk to night. She made lentil soup, automatically, angrily. All day she'd been in London with Marek, going from flat to flat, disoriented, as if she were running in the dark. His aggressiveness was exhausting. He took over, insisted on being noticed, made assumptions — they were to have a large new flat, he said, with all-new furnishings. The idea of moving to the city had put him in high feather; he seemed to have forgotten it was all her idea. No point bringing it up. Her mind fled to St. Ives and found confusion; Aaron vaporized. She threw onions and celery into the processor. She was a limb ripped from a tree, she was the tree, she was the wind. Her feet were unsteady, she was attached to nothing. Hands, eyes, notes in a memory band, vegetables, water, plates.

She brought a tureen of soup to the table. Marek sat down heavily, his fists on the table.

"Where is everyone?" he asked.

"Here and there," she said. She ladled soup into bowls. "What do you like about the Howberry flat?" she asked, stifling irritation. "The layout is terrible."

"Well, it doesn't smell bad," he said testily, "and it's a ground floor with a bit of garden. Where's the bread?"

"Garden? You could barely grow chives in it."

"Chester Square, then . . . good neighborhood and enough space for a workshop."

"Perhaps we should take separate flats," she said.

"What?"

"Or you could stay here."

"Come, come, my dear, if you'd rather live in Hampstead, all right. As long as you don't pick one of those foul-smelling old buildings."

"I doubt there's a flat in London that could please us both," she said, struggling to sound reasonable. "I want to live in Chelsea and you want to live in Canon's Park. You might as well stay here as go into a northern sector."

"Fifteen minutes from Canon's Park to Thames Hydro. Give or take a minute."

"An hour for me, on the tube."

"An hour to what?"

"Why, to work, of course."

"Oh, that," he said, tearing a chunk of bread, "you'll probably quit in no time flat." The room shrank around his bulk.

She set down her spoon. It didn't matter what they talked about; simply by talking she gave him permission, as it were, to violate her. She couldn't extricate herself. It was her fault that he insulted her. She was guilty, of course, she helped him to insult her.

"I think that settles it," she said, mainly to herself.

"Of all the work you could have chosen," he went on, "if you had to choose any. I must say it disgusts me."

"Disgusts you!"

"Those people. Who cares if there's one Dull more or less in the world."

"I do." A white flame sharpened her voice.

"They die right and left, got no stamina at all. I'm the one who's going to have to use them, you know. They man the rigs at Thames Hydro."

"And you won't care if they get injured?"

"More where they came from."

"They're human. And we're all responsible."

"Maybe you'd like to move right in with those people. Live right in the neighborhood. Save money on transport." He ate his soup with gusto, smacking his lips.

"Maybe I wouldn't. That's beside the point."

"You don't like them either," he said triumphantly.

She hardened herself against his influence. Why speak at all? Whatever she said to him was true, but distorted. She detested herself, detested words coming off her tongue. She was emotionally twisted, suffering an emotional torsion in which her words went to Marek while her feelings turned elsewhere.

Marek looked at her, something anguished in his expression. Shaggy hairs drooped onto his eyelids. "Frankly, my dear, I don't care if they live or die. That's a fact. Aren't planning to leave me for one of them, are you?" he asked bitterly.

Silenced, she shuddered to a halt.

He sat so close she could touch his knee, so far away he was beyond familiarity: a middle-aged man, thickening around the waist, double chin, tufts of gray hair like goose grass, a strange fleshy man. His head jutted forward, legs spread wide, hands on either side of his bowl. Getting things done, an aggressive man, sorting it all out. She saw him clearly, the color and shape of him, his good and bad intentions. She had been seeing him clearly for too long, whereas the ones she loved were luminously veiled. The others, like the young, like Aaron, walked softly, winking in and out. Only Marek, poor Marek walked through her life exposed. It wasn't fair to him to be out there, known and unprotected. They had played the game of marriage long enough, not attending to the symptoms, mistaking shadows and echoes for life.

"Please yourself, Marek," she said, "I'm going to live alone."

"I refuse to eat with a bloody maniac!" Scraping his chair furiously, he stomped out of the kitchen. She finished her meal in guilty silence.

She spent the evening idly sorting things in her study. Melani looked in before going to bed.

"How's it going?" she asked.

"Not very well, I'm afraid."

"Tell me something . . . anything."

"Something. Anything. Well . . . I think you and I are growing up at the same time. I feel about fifteen at the moment, which is very confused."

Melani sat on the edge of the desk and looked at her with clear, dark eyes.

"Why do I have to board when you move to London?"

"Dartington's very beautiful."

"But they'll be so clannish — and what about Plumsie?"

"It's only a year, Melani."

"Only . . ."

"Consider it an adventure."

"Everybody's having adventures."

Sephony winced. "And you'd like the family to be as it was."

"I'm not a baby. I see things. Simon and Dote don't. Well, maybe Simon does. But he's a selfish twit, he seems to be taking your part, but he's really taking his own."

"I see." She was shocked. She hadn't considered the children's view. "Well . . . all right . . ." She caught her breath. "The latest development is I've just told your father we're living separately in London."

"I know. I heard you through the door."

"Good grief, Melani."

"How else are we going to learn anything? You make these little announcements as if they were the most ordinary things. 'Your father and I are moving to London.' 'I'm going to work in bioradiatics.' Whoever heard of that? 'Your father is going to design sonar cages.' Whoever heard of that? And you get very busy making arrangements and don't tell us anything. I don't care . . . I know what's going on."

"Melani — my life is so complicated at the moment. I can't tell you more than that."

"Why not?"

She laughed, embarrassed. "I don't know."

"You never imagine being friends with me, that's why."

"I suppose you're right."

"Well, it's ridiculous."

Sephony laughed again, perilously close to crying. "Your mother is falling in love," she said. "I don't know what's going to happen."

Melani slid off the desk. "I thought so," she said grimly. "Well, let me know if you need any help." She kissed Sephony. " 'Night."

"Good night, Melani. Push the door to."

An ally in the family — a strange reversal, as if for a moment Melani had become her mother. Comforting, in a way, and unsettling. She rested in the comfort. Time and events made a cradle: her daughter's life, which had run distant and parallel, was converging with her own.

She went to bed and lay awake. Where was Marek? Reliving their quarrel at dinner, testing the idea of living alone, she choked on dread. He came in around midnight.

"Light the small lamp," she said.

"Did I wake you?"

"We must talk." She lay on her side, propped on her elbow.

"I'll get ready for bed first," he said.

He disappeared into the bathroom and returned in a flannel nightshirt. He threw his clothes into a corner and tucked himself under the duvet, propping himself beside her.

He smiled — a patrician smile, oblivious. He'd forgotten their quarreling. He always forgot. He howled and then it was over; he ignored consequences, made no progress, learned nothing. Like a piece of elastic he returned to some stationary condition. There were dark hollows in the corners of his smile, beyond his teeth, a look of longing. How heavy his smile was. She was much to blame for the heaviness of his smile.

"Marek," she said, wriggling backward to the edge of the mattress, "I want to sever."

"Beg pardon?" He blinked.

"Sever. I can't bear this."

"What on earth are you talking about?"

"Severing. When the next period comes round."

His eyes were marbled, restrained in their sockets by eyebrows that drooped like dune grass. His mouth was slack, his skin old and loose.

"It seemed to me," he said, clearing his throat, "that things were improving."

"Hardly," she said.

"But why now, all of a sudden?"

"Oh, Marek . . . it's the whole situation . . . you know." She watched herself from a distance, appalled.

"You-know, you-know," he snapped. "I bloody well don't know."

"I'm suffocated. We're suffocating each other."

"Nonsense," he said too loudly. "I'm perfectly happy. I'm perfectly content."

"You aren't."

"This is ridiculous. Why don't we talk about it to-morrow."

He lay down and pulled the duvet up to his chin, humped under the quilt, so close and strange, so still, she could barely see him breathe — his nose arched, his eyes wide open. The situation was already out of control; her words created another Sephony, another Marek, another relationship.

"I think about us growing old and having missed life, having missed ourselves, whatever that is," she said. The words sounded feeble; they were only words.

"But that's not all," she said. She hesitated, breaking through his silence. "There's Aaron."

He twisted halfway round, expectantly.

"We want to . . . ," she began. Who was speaking? Who was vacillating? "We're going to Cornwall on holiday," she said firmly. "And we've talked about marrying."

Marek sat up and slid back, adjusting his pillow against the headboard, taking a long time to pull the covers around his knees. Very inward, like a person in pain.

"You've seen him that often?" he asked, smoothing a wrinkle on the quilt.

His innocence shocked her.

"Yes, Marek. For months and months. I've told you."

He hesitated. "It didn't mean anything."

"It means a great deal."

"To me, I mean."

"I want to live alone. And then, possibly, with him."

"Why can't you live with me? What's wrong with me?"

"Aaron and I aren't irresponsible," she went on, not wanting to analyze him, "it's as if we had suffered . . . oh . . . a long interruption."

He waited, absorbing the blow. He was thinking it through.

"A long interruption," he said dully. "Our marriage is a long interruption."

"It seems that way," she said sadly. "A period of time that held its breath. Except for the young."

"Oh — except for the young."

"If you're going to be sarcastic . . ."

"Now that you've defined our marriage," he snapped, "you're going to tell me how to talk."

His fury was hard; he threatened her with a club of ice.

"I'm sad for both of us," she said.

"Are you, now."

"We've cheated each other. You've been deprived."

"How did you cheat me?" he demanded. "I don't feel cheated."

"I didn't appreciate you," she said.

"Don't need to be appreciated," he muttered.

"Think about your life, your work . . . If I hadn't disapproved of you all the time, if I hadn't been so critical —"

"Were you?"

"A different woman would have encouraged you in a thousand ways, she would have helped you."

"And now," he said with difficulty, "you know the difference."

She looked into his eyes — how seldom she looked there — into large brown pools where defensiveness was laced with pain.

"I can't live with you, Marek," she said. "I have no energy, no vitality."

"Can you live with? . . ." He jerked his head as if his enemy were in the next room.

"I think so." Marek pulled the truth out of her, pulled Aaron out of her. She couldn't be silent or lie, but truth, under the pressure of such reluctance, felt like deceit.

He paused. The frozen mask returned, but with a gleeful tinge. He raised the ice club.

"And what does your dear old friend think of your famous trip?"

"I haven't told him yet," she murmured.

"You told me," he said, with a twinge of triumph.

"Please, Marek . . ."

"No wonder you don't know if you can live with him. This is some poetic romance. What does he know about your moods? What did he have to put up with? He's going to like your story. A charming story, to be sure. Holiday in Cornwall, oh yes. Lunches and holidays. Is that your idea of — what did you call it? Vitality?"

"I'll tell him eventually."

"Let me know how it turns out," he said with a barking laugh. "Or shall I tell him myself and spare you the trouble?"

"Don't," she said, placing her hand on his chest — not to warn or plead, but to establish some middle ground, some connection.

"And I suppose that since you and I aren't, ah, lovers . . . that you and he are."

"No," she said, embarrassed.

"Well, then," he said contemptuously, "it's all speculation, nothing real about it."

"Let's not go into it," she said. "I simply want to sever. I'd want to in any case."

"Bloody bullshit."

"It's true."

"And what's his wife got to say about it?"

"I don't know. But that's not the point."

"I see the point, all right."

She was silent. Let him take comfort in jealousy.

"How are we going to get a night's sleep?" he cried. "How am I supposed to work tomorrow? What are you doing to me?"

He rolled onto his stomach, his eyes wide and reproachful. She turned off the lamp. Her hand automatically made its way to a place on his back below the shoulder blades where he liked to be scratched. He was such a burly child and she was abandoning him. He lay rigid, then snuggled against her, holding her with a desperate hunger. He was so heavy, he weighed against her. She disentangled herself. He sighed and rolled to his side of the mattress.

She didn't fall asleep for a long time. In the middle of the night she woke and threshed over the conversation. Toward morning she dreamed. There was a hill with a rocky, sun-parched road. Elderly people were walking up, carrying groceries. One woman limped with a cane, her wig askew, holding a sack of green apples. Children raced down the hill, two girls and two boys. They picked up rocks and hurled them. The lame woman was hit. She fell sideways, her apples rolling. The children shrieked gleefully and stooped for more rocks. The old people scattered, shielding their faces.

CHAPTER 16

SHE FLEW THE HIGH LANE west over cities and nuclear plants, over dark housing estates replicated roof to roof like dreams of cancer cells. From Bodmin Moor to the Hayle River lay a refreshing green swath of undulating pastures and forests. But the landscape worsened dramatically near St. Ives; the sky itself seemed lower and grayer, and where the town had stood were black, desolate hills.

She left her craft in a clearing near the beach and walked up the hill, carrying her duffel and a sack of groceries. The wind was keen, the path overgrown with gorse and cotoneaster. She could almost hear the explosions, see the fires, smell the gases. It was a shock, seeing it at last, like the shocking sight, years ago, of her father lying unalterably still in his cremation box. Ruins lay strewn about in all directions — gray rubble under gray sky. Stone archways clung to fragments of walls. Narrow stone steps went nowhere. Wrought iron signs lay in the grass, splotched with orange lichens. A young man limped aimlessly down the hill, cold and windblown, his stomach bloated under a dirty green pullover.

The cottage was easy to find, standing alone, decrepit and crooked, in a plot of weeds and stones. Dropping her bag by the door, she struggled with lock and wood, the doorway so low her head nearly brushed the lintel. Inside was a neat, refreshing otherness. She forced open the windows. The rooms were bright and elf-size and contained only the necessary furnishings. The spareness pleased her. She felt simple and capable, as if she were dipping in Claro's pool.

After unpacking groceries into the tiny larder, she dragged the mattress and pillows outside to air. Godrevy Island, out in the bay, was shrouded in mist. The fire-blackened and jagged landscape, from charred cliff to charred cliff, was as magnificent in scope as the sky and sea — like Domino, she thought, turned inside out. Far below, waves broke on a weedy beach. Two dark houses topped a grass-fringed dune. Solitary forms stood on the earth. What had survived the destruction of St. Ives had a majesty simply because it had survived.

Too agitated to rest, she closed the house and picked her way toward town. Down on the beach a few small figures moved about, atomized and unrelated. Up ahead a crippled child in a hooded anorak limped grotesquely, supported on sticks that hunched up its narrow shoulders. Sephony felt a sudden ache, a desire to know the child, so thin and small and struggling on its own — a little girl, perhaps, she couldn't tell — its trousers flapping and its twisted feet scraping the ground. She walked swiftly, passed the child and glanced back.

An old woman rested on her sticks, mouth slack, one foot stepping on the other.

"Good afternoon," Sephony said, shocked.

The woman stared, her faded eyes expressionless, her chin fringed in a wispy white beard.

"Would you know where the Brackett's used to be?" Sephony asked.

The old eyes made a cloudy, depressed appeal.

"The Clothing Mart," Sephony said, louder. "Do you remember where it was?" She stooped over, as if the woman really were a child.

"Oh, we had a Brackett's," the woman said in a complaining voice. "We had everything, we did."

"Where was it, exactly?"

The woman looked hostile, suspicious. "Why d'you want to know?"

"My father owned it, you see."

"Did he, now?"

"When I was a child."

The woman drew herself up and pointed with one of her sticks.

"Left at the fork, right at the war memorial, left to the bottom."

"Thank you," Sephony said.

"Nothing there," the woman grumbled. "Don't bother."

The woman's directions were reasonably good, except for the war memorial. On the harbor road, where the sea slapped a gouged breakwater, Sephony stepped around potholes and over blocks of stone. She remembered a tidy harbor and bright-colored boats and a gay parade of shops, now reduced to ragged foundation walls and mounds of rubble.

At the end of the road ragged bits of masonry marked the site of her father's store. Kneeling on grit and pebbles in a broken corner, she pressed against sooty stone, embracing memories that circulated like needles in a waking foot. An orderly store; she could still feel the cool dim orderliness of it, the summer clothing aligned in cubicles, folds rippling perfectly, all the pale, smooth fabrics of summer; Dads charming to customers but leaving her alone with his assistant, who had yellow teeth and pretended she was big for her age and always got her name wrong; the back door opening onto a nasty pumping noise.

She poked angrily in the rubble with a weathered stick. Cut off; paid off. He'd bequeathed Ari and Mugs an ongoing inheritance of shares, but she'd been cut off with a sum. Oh, Dads knew how to punish and bind. Reject a daughter and she adores you forever.

Clambering over the rubble and down a heap of rocks to the beach, she cut along the hard sand, pressing her fists into her jacket pockets. Absurd to love him in this anguished way. She should see Dads as green slime on the beach, as midges and a heated, rotten smell. But he stayed heroic, satisfied with himself, cautioning her to be wary of strangers and not throw out her old shoes until she bought new ones.

The wind iced her cheeks.

Farther up the beach two children were playing in the sand, fussing over something white, tossing it a little way into the air, alternately playing catch with it and wrestling with each other. It seemed to be a dead herring gull.

She ran to them. They looked old and pinched and wore ragged, quilted coveralls. The larger child held the gull's wings outstretched and made it dance. The smaller child threw sand at it.

"Drop it," she said sternly. "Dead sea gulls have a sickness."

The children looked up at her stupidly. Their noses were pink and runny, their hair tangled.

"What?" one asked.

"Drop it," she said. "It'll make you ill."

"Wasn't dead," the child said.

"Naw," said the other. "See?" The child pointed to a bloody spot on the gull's delicate white head.

"You killed it?" she asked angrily.

The children ran shrieking up the beach, kicking the gull like a soccer ball.

The smaller child turned and made a face. "Bugger your mum!" he shouted, and swung the mangled creature by the feet. It arched over the water and dropped headfirst, wings helplessly angled.

Barbarians — what would they kill as they grew older? Each other? She looked about furiously. Something was arriving, something was shattering or had already shattered, and where she stood was not where she had been. Odd that it should be now. In anger she and time came abreast of each other — the cylinder revealed its turning. She stood outside the social contract, an alien, clear-sighted and fuller, like Claro when he grew fat. What were the Dull children like? What could she do for them in those automated nurseries? She should visit one.

Feeling scraped to the bone, she climbed the hill by a different route. Derelict houses were jammed together on crooked little streets; wash lines stretched across dark alleys. A shirt hung upside down in the shadows, flapping in the wind — the arms stiff and the collar triangular, like a fox's muzzle. It fascinated and disturbed her, the shirt of a solitary man, like an animal's pelt. She veered across the rubbled hill to her cottage.

The mattress smelled much better. She dragged it across the doorsill and into a corner of the tiny bedroom, stretched a fresh sheet on it, and covered it with a duvet. Aaron would be here in six days. How would they look to each other, feel to each other? For years her body hadn't mattered; it was trim and functional and carried her about. It encountered another body in the dark. Sex had grown hard and resistant, it had a leathery skin. She imagined her breasts in Aaron's hands again, their knees entwined. Would they be self-conscious? Guilty? Terminal circumspection; she was suffering from it already. She looked inward and tried to force an old vision, conjuring the mental space from which hands would have flown out. No hands. Sanity and happiness were insidiously sweet; she had lost the habit of turning anxiety into surprising disturbances.

She ate a fish wafer and went out, this time to the windy north bay. Porthmeor beach was as rough and wild as she remembered it from childhood. The Fisheries Center, a boxy stone and stucco building with tiny windows, stood on concrete stilts, its narrow side edging the cliffs and its length facing the sea. Aaron had a room here — a satisfying distance from her cottage. Distances mattered; it mattered that she and Aaron had rooms apart. Although he would sleep in her bed. What if they had nothing to say when they were alone? What if they felt inhibited without a lunch table? She ran along the beach, kicking a stone, hearing his voice and her own. Life is bundled, she imagined saying to him, like a ball of flames in a child's painting of a tree or a flock of high-flying birds. Life is grains, his imagined voice said, sorted by weight on the wind so all the rough and all the fine pile up in different places. She dashed after her stone until it veered into the water. An engine hummed in the distance, a rasping sound she couldn't identify. Clouds raced in from the horizon. The sound dipped and disappeared. For an instant she heard it again far off. She walked along the stony, weed-rimmed beach, hugging her chest against the wind. Long, uneven waves crashed; the receding brown water was sucked back, leaving a widening foamy line.

She felt a familiar nervousness, a rising, oscillating energy — she couldn't put her finger on it — a sense of going somewhere, a sense of being vividly alive. She used to dampen such energy when it erupted, filled with despair as she swallowed and covered it over. What a bloody, suicidal waste. Once, in the Lake District, she'd gone partway, during those happy months after Simon was born. There'd been a mountain visible from her bedroom window whose dark peak, the highest in a jagged ridge of lavender and green hills, was famous for its view. Climb me, it said, tantalizing her. Don't be absurd, Marek had said, you're here to rest. But she'd had a sense of life itself, of who she was and what she could be, so she climbed alone one very hot morning, up the sheep-cropped, stony slope, past stunted trees, stopping to look up at the dark peak and the peaks beyond. She felt glorious, setting goals along the way, the peak growing large as she drew closer to a breathtaking view of Lake Windermere and the countryside. When she arrived at the top, exhausted, there was no view, only a dip in the path before it wound around to the next peak. She had stopped. Baffled. Had lain on the hard, cropped earth feeling old and resigned. A runner had passed, a young man with a dog, running along a beaten path, wearing shorts and sturdy boots. He had waved, the dog had wagged its tail, and they were gone, into the dip and up again. She saw them at intervals. She had clambered down, supporting herself on gnarled firs. There were green lichens on rocks along the way and a view of massed gray buildings and gray spires. The peaks died away behind her.

Claro, she whispered, and turned to see if anyone was watching. Do you hear me? I'm impatient, empty and full, I may as well be eating nudge flowers. Do you hear me? Do you ever see me? I have a vision of the Dulls and the warrens, of being useful. Of getting to know my children. Of starting from solitude and growing into . . . restoring a life with Aaron. Do I love him? Is that what one asks? So easy to say it years ago, so difficult to say it now. Sand in my shoes, face to the wind, do you hear me?

Every day the weather changed, often from hour to hour. Using old hand tools, she cleared a bit of garden on the south side of the cottage and transplanted a tiny spruce she found growing in a crevice. She made ritual visits to her father's ruins and explored the area from St. Ives to Carbis Bay, picking up news of the military installation at Penzance with its laser missiles and catchers patrolling the skies. The catchers were her only uneasiness, darting on the horizon in pairs like sinister water needles. Overall she felt alert and singular, something private settling in, a quirky sense of direction.

She had a general idea of what time Aaron would arrive. Friday, he'd said. Lovely, she'd said, and that had been enough. As if they would offend each other by attaching details to an arrangement that was so perfectly understood.

She readied all afternoon, behaving contemptibly — changing clothes twice in front of the spotted mirror. She looked terrible: her cheeks were chapped and her eyes were puffy and hollowed. But he wouldn't notice such things, her appearance was of no account. She combed her hair and when the knock finally came perversely messed it before opening the door. He stooped under the low lintel, dropping his duffel in a confusion of greetings, and they embraced, gladly, awkwardly, like cousins, his hands sliding down to her waist. After a moment he gently pushed her away. The dismissal shocked her. Head brushing the ceiling, he stepped back and made self-conscious gestures of placing and observing. His bag in the corner, his jacket over a chair. His face eclipsed itself, she couldn't make out his expression. He took refuge by a window. The day was sunny and windy; down on the beach the white-capped tide was coming in.

"You look tired," she said.

He straightened his shoulders. "Has the cottage been all right?" he asked with a nervous smile.

"I'll bring us some tea," she said.

Through the kitchen archway she watched him pace from window to window. He was all planes and angles, blades of muscle, mouth like a knife. He'd had his hair cropped, the black waves tight, silver patches arching sharply at the ears.

She brought the tray and they settled at the table, sorting utensils and food. Her chair, comfortable yesterday, was too low; she adjusted pillows at her back. He cut slices of Stilton and put them on biscuits; she poured white for them both.

"What have you been doing?" he asked.

"Walking about," she said, holding the cup in her lap. "There's a bit of wall left from my father's store. I've been digging in it — it's full of emotional rubble from my childhood."

He stretched his legs under the table, thumbs tucked in his belt. His eyes met hers for a moment, then slipped aside.

"I remember feeling important but ashamed," she said. "What is it, Aaron?"

"It's nothing. Go on."

"I can't."

"Talk, please talk."

"I can't just talk on command."

"Sephony, I feel guilty — all right? There's your confession."

"I don't need a confession. Just the truth."

"It took me by surprise. The minute I saw you."

"Ah, Aaron." She caressed his wool-padded arm, plunging into her story. "Dads's shop assistant had an imaginary daughter who was killed by a falling tree. He went on and on about it, such a pathetic old man, but I liked him. He used to call me Polly — 'How's Polly today?' No one corrected him. It was his privilege to hold my hand and grin and call me Polly . . . I think I was expected to be pleased."

"I'm glad to see you . . . I'm sorry."

"It's all right."

"I had a row with Sybil."

"Oh . . ."

"We can't sit here, Sephony. I can't sit here." He gulped his tea and scooped up some biscuits and cheese. "Let's go into the country," he said and hustled himself into his jacket.

They flew along the coast to Morvah, over charcoal slopes blemished with blackened rocks and stumps — a wasteland, scorched from sea to hilltops. The sea beat against cliffs and flowed into hollows of ruined rubbish tips, formerly tin mines, which had generated methane. They left the craft near a stone barn and walked in silence across a field, past ancient stone hedges, and down a slope marked with an arrow. At the bottom stood three stones — two stumpy pillars and a rough disk with a hole in the center.

"Is it a burial chamber, do you think?" he asked.

"It's layered," she said. "A burial chamber, fertility symbols, even a clock. People used to pass babies through the hole to ward off illness."

They walked around the stones, examining surfaces and angles, still tense. The two vertical stones keeled awkwardly toward the disk. Aaron crouched and peered up at her through the hole. His mood was dark, but a bit of mischief flickered in his eyes.

"Stick your head through," she said, "and you're inoculated against scrofula."

They walked back across the field. Ancient pillars stood guard, mysteriously preserved in isolation.

"Sybil hates anything old," he said, "the awful smell of the old, she calls it."

She took his hand. Electricity flared in her palm.

"What did you quarrel about?"

"About you, naturally."

"Oh."

"I told her you'd be here. She doesn't mind losing me — it isn't even a loss. But she does hate you, I'm afraid."

"I'm not surprised."

"I wish I'd handled it better. Life's tackier emotions baffle me."

"Does she hate you, as well?"

"I don't think so," he said uncomfortably. "It all seems directed at you." He frowned, as if human nature puzzled him. "I don't hate anyone. Do you? Do you hate Marek?"

"Oh, no. I feel a grinding irritation with him — and bitterness. It makes me feel false with almost everyone, except you."

"I didn't think Sybil was capable of hatred," he said.

"Everyone is."

They flew to Zennor and hiked up along a steep, winding trail. A clean robust vitality burned in him — she felt it beside her — an easy limber stride, agile and graceful like a rock climber, his tensions focused and eased. They stopped at the highest point. Magnificent eroded cliffs swooped down to the sea, the rock billowing like curtains. Grass grew around the summit, and tiny scarlet pimpernel. Aaron found an elfin cave. A strong wind flattened the grass.

"What does Sybil mean, the smell of the old?" she asked, crushing a bay leaf for him.

"She grew up poor in the North — her father was murdered in a random attack. She will actually leave someone's house if it smells too old."

"She stayed at my mother's."

"Never set foot inside, though, never left the garden."

"Your house must be entirely modern, then."

"Absolutely flavor-of-the-month in everything. She tele-shops incessantly, I honestly don't know how she tolerates her life."

"Let's marry her off to Marek," she said guiltily. "They can furnish a flat with all the latest plastics."

He wasn't amused. "She doesn't even hear me anymore, she grits her teeth."

"But you said she was placid."

"She is."

"Has she got asthma?"

He looked surprised. "Dreadful, year-round."

"Oh, you know," she said lightly, "asthma is the quietly angry person's favorite disease."

"Well, then — her lung capacity must improve every time she bludgeons me with sentences that begin 'You.' "

"What are you accused of?"

"Tyranny," he said bitterly. "I have some horrendous authority over her . . . which I'm not aware of. Whether I disagree or agree it's all the same — she says I'm squelching her, I don't let her breathe."

"Well, there you have it, you see."

"Very clever — she'd appreciate that. Anyway, her strategy is avoidance. She doesn't like to quarrel either."

"I don't find you at all overbearing. If anything, you're too neutral . . . and fair to a fault . . . you see both sides of every issue."

"Ah. Weak and wobbly, you mean."

They sat on a rock ledge high above the sea. Waves slapping the rocky toes of three foot-shaped outcroppings split and fell. At the horizon sea blurred into sky. The wind tugged her hair.

He put his arm around her lightly and cautiously, drawing her to him with string and bones. He seldom touched her; his gestures were sparing, as if he were afraid to loosen himself, as if a single gesture would open an emotional gate and his untended self, so carefully crafted, would flood through. As if he were afraid some ghastly irresponsibility would follow. She could see into him, imagine his thoughts, his terrors, his ambivalence. Could he see into her? She loved the flow and spill of him, although he tended to pull back like the tide. Both of them did, so attached still. Such a mix of murkiness and clarity, the future a tangle.

"What's going to happen?" he asked, stroking her shoulder with his thumb — neutrally, absently.

The foot-shaped outcroppings strutted from their billowing gown of rock and met lacy cascades of spray.

"Look at yourself," she said passionately. "Sometimes I can't tell if you have your own feelings or you mirror mine. You fluctuate, you go back and forth. You say you want to fight for me. You withdraw. You say you want us to marry. Then you ask what's going to happen." She paused, and the spray arched back. "It doesn't matter. Whatever you are, I . . . oh, it doesn't matter."

"Why are you attacking me?"

"I'm not attacking you."

"You are."

"I don't know what I am to you."

"I've told you . . . freedom . . ."

"That's not enough."

"I . . . I can't, Sephony."

"Then how can you ask what's going to happen to us?"

His elbow was on his knee, his eye framed by his fingers: he was collapsed into himself, a clothed skeleton. She waited. She would not draw him back. He would come back in his own time. For an instant Marek sat here, dense and opaque; she had no influence on Marek, no interior view. Aaron — she hesitated to say — was in a column of light.

"I know what you want to hear," he said. He leaned away slightly.

She stayed where she was. The sliver of distance between them breathed.

"It's all right, I can't say it either," she said.

The curtained sun began its long downward slide.

"Come," he said, "you'll be cold."

The wind flattened gorse and heather and tufted the sea; it slapped at their jackets and their faces. They resisted the wind, drawing closer, their arms around each other. She felt young. His thin face with the glowing eyes bent slowly, slowly. She slid her fingers into his cap of hair; he covered her ears, gently tugging at her face. She fell into a steadying warmth, fell into darkness — lightness and softness glowing, passing through them, joining them as they drank each other's breath.

"Let's have an early dinner," he said. "There's one good restaurant in Penzance."

"But the militia . . ."

"They won't bother us."

They returned to Zennor and flew down the coast, stopping at the edge of Penzance. On a distant hill, huge microwave disks swiveled ominously and pinpoints of light flashed from a tower. Swallows anticipated sunset. They walked along the harbor road to the restaurant. Three pointed spires kept guard on the beach, radiating dangerous wavelengths that caused scurrying terns to change direction and gulls to wheel away. Silver-clad militia walked in pairs, silent and blank, commanding the right-of-way on narrow pavements.

She loved him, she could say it, at least, to herself. Love opposed the metallic order that strangled the streets and poisoned the shore. She pressed against him; he kissed the top of her head. How strange life was. She knew for certain that no matter how far she traveled, Aaron would welcome her back; no matter how fragmented he was, she would restore him.

After dinner they raced the last rays back to the cottage, merry and awed, holding still at the window for the afterglow, for slender black clouds gliding across an orange and azure sky.

Finally they lay in bed, naked under the warm, soft duvet. He stroked the curves of her body from rib cage to hip, from breast to thigh. In softness of skin and crackling of nerves — in breasts, mouth, and groin — light burst under intense pressure, radiant energy that fueled itself. She returned his radiance, fire for fire: fingers and palms shaping his back, molding the clay, aching to encompass him, to receive and to give. His mouth flared like the edge of a cup, the back of his thighs sinewy. He pulled her to him, flesh into flesh, their touch, as it had been so many years before, the touch of youth and first love. She had a vision of time as a gigantic incomplete ellipse whose ends strove toward each other. They moved together. Time was erased and all life was compressed into fire and airy darkness.

She dreamed she glided through green, viscous water in a tiny transparent vessel, lighting a broad path. An old man navigated; she and Marek huddled close behind.

The dark water, like veils, parted and closed around them. Sea whips waved on the sandy bottom; a tiny geyser burbled. In a blind and intricate city of industrial waste, home to kelp and barnacles, sea perch wove through the portholes of a ghostly ship and cod frowned through jagged holes. Tiny blue fish clung to an antenna, nibbling like butterflies.

"The refuge is the trap," the old man said.

They slowed at a reef of tires, piled crazily on one another, black with blacker hollows. The light caught a heap of white lobsters violently unhooking themselves from each other, nipping as they scurried into an ancient passenger train, each car divided in half, the pieces nestled crookedly in the sand like a child's toy.

"They live in the train," the old man said.

"But they all died out," Marek said.

"They came back," the old man said.

Beautiful lace sponges fanned themselves.

Marek was dancing on the old man's shoulders. Tiny and loose-limbed, he leapt from one shoulder to the other, dancing wildly.

She woke, still drifting, floating like a pleustonic animal — a jellyfish or goose barnacle. There's no hurry underwater, she thought, no abrupt changes. Whatever arrives is filtered by water and time. The ocean is our mother. See how it swallows our refuse.

Aaron slept on his side facing her.

Marek, she thought, and woke fully, seeing a pattern in

their marriage. Her fearfulness had made him cautious. His caution had made her irritable. And so they created each other in innumerable ways — judging and ignoring, snipping off an impulse here and a plan there, until they became as they were now: two reasonably attractive bonsai trees in dry pots.

What would happen to him now that she was leaving? They had their psychological chores. He undertook to be practical; she undertook to be mystical. When she left, taking unreason with her, would he take on her psychic duties himself? Would he lose his will? Punish her? Sacrifice himself? Or would he find solace in the garden?

Aaron slept. How extraordinary to wake entwined with him, to feel his long, lean body against her. She kissed his shoulder, his arm fell around her, he murmured something. He had been her idea of love from the start, born in her young spirit, an idea her body remembered. Domino passed before her in its full weight, danger, and beauty. No refuges, no traps; she would tell him the story and they would lie together and risk understanding.

CHAPTER 17

"I'M FEELIN' CABBAGY," the man said, "wiv them awful headaches." His face was yellowish and swollen, sores in the corners of his mouth, fear in his eyes. About forty, wearing wrinkled brown coveralls.

The cubicle was close and warm; he sat sideways at the desk.

"Be sent off if I get any slower. Never know where they send you, do you?"

A blue code glowed above his wristbone — he was a Group 3, probably chemicals. He worried an index finger, flexing and pulling the enlarged knuckle. His hands were broad and thick, the nails ridged and chipped. She asked him to place his hands on the desk, palms up. She touched them, heavy and callused, and gently straightened the reluctant fingers. The rough palms shimmered like puddles in the sun; in a few minutes they ceased to be opaque. Brown oozed from the base of the thumb, becoming a delicate mauve where it flared in the hollow. That would be his kidneys.

Noises broke in — running and shouting and Joanne calling her name. She excused herself and rushed into the main room, where two limp, damp bodies were being carried in. One was coughing, the other was still.

"Fell off a hydro rig," a woman shouted.

"How long ago?" Joanne asked.

"About twenty minutes."

Sephony dashed to the pulmo and turned it on.

They laid the choking man stomach down in the capsule. Sephony set the clamps program, while Joanne, whistling some tuneless thing, regulated pressure and the air supply.

"The other guy's dead," Joanne said, "but give him prolin just in case."

The second man lay on the floor, a rescuer rocking on him, kneading his back. Sephony jabbed prolin into his arm. Foamy, bloodstained water leaked from his mouth. He was in his twenties, short and sturdy; strands of wet blond hair fell across his cheek. She waited for a gasp, a cough. She remembered, after Rolf's birth, a nurse's hand squeezing her abdomen as if it were half a grapefruit, and blood obediently oozing into a pad between her thighs.

The patients, absorbed by the emergency, swarmed around the two men, muttering to one another in their sad, clannish way. The man in the pulmo coughed and was silent, coughed and was silent, seeming to come to life and die in frightening succession. Air was forced into him, water was pressed out. It looked like torture. Joanne switched off the expel function. The man hovered, shuddering violently as if warring with death, and finally took one hoarse breath, and then another. The patients cheered him on and helped lift him out.

The other man was put into the pulmo. Perhaps he wasn't dead, merely in a suspended state, preserved by the cold water. The machine ministered to him, extracting bloodstained water, stimulating his heart, pumping oxygen. Time hung suspended in the long gray intervals between out and in. Sephony waited and held her breath, but his stillness endured, hideously.

Mr. Bunson, one of the regulars, nodded at the dead man, closure in his faded eyes. The elderly people standing watch with him also nodded slowly and sadly. She reached for the switches. Death panted off the body like a mean old crow, flapping round and round. Time was too long, too thin. She passed into some awful, ongoing condition; she wasn't a person, but a life-form with a limited span. Everything in sight was turning gray. And then Mr. Bunson stared into space, muttering to himself, his tongue darting across his gums. He gave her a knowing look, inviting or absolving her, and she felt death pass into the group, pass into her, cradling her; she joined them in closing round death, absorbing it, as if they were a single creature.

She was free to attend to the survivor.

He lay on the examining table, half-conscious. Joanne was listening to his heart.

"Let's dry him off," Sephony said.

They rolled him from side to side, tugging damp sleeves off his short, heavy arms, pulling off resisting coveralls. The man groaned and coughed and mumbled to himself. They dried him vigorously and wrapped an insulator around him. Patients got in the way, handed them things, and carried him from the table to a cot.

"He'll live," Joanne said, blotting his forehead.

"I feel awful about the other one," said Sephony.

"It's not our fault," Joanne said anxiously.

"No, of course not."

Patients carried the dead man reverently across the room and laid him stomach down on the floor near the cot. Someone composed his limbs, toes out, arms by his sides, palms up.

"Get his code," Joanne said, "and I'll ring Sector Four."

Squatting by the body, she stared at the arm. It was muscular and young, the fingers curled upward. She gingerly stroked along the rough palm and up the cold wrist. No auras from the dead. She turned the arm until an orange square showed, nestled in blond hair, and trained the beam.

She took the survivor's code also and returned the beam to its post by the door. Joanne was giving coffee to the rescuers — technical specialists by the look of them. They had hard, intelligent faces, defiant and observant. Working idealists, like Joanne, they'd come to terms with death.

She sat beside the cot. The sleeping man snored; she massaged his back. A bearded rescuer pulled up a chair. He was restless, crossing and uncrossing his legs, shifting from one haunch to the other.

"Gaffers don't give a damn," he confided, drinking his coffee, "but I can't watch a bloke drown. Not even a Dull."

Not even. It was a better attitude than most, she acknowledged grudgingly, and congratulated him on his courage.

"He'll want to go to work tomorrow," the rescuer said. "They're crazy that way." He put the cup between his knees and suctioned his ears with his palms.

"Does your head hurt?"

"Not too bad," he said.

Joanne was covering the dead man with a green plastic cloth that bunched and wrinkled over his body. There was a ragged hole near his head, the size of a fist. A cheek showed through and some blond hair. Perhaps all was not lost. Perhaps he would return from his damp journey; perhaps life had only briefly skipped out and would return through the hole. Sephony waited, willing him to breathe. A loud sucking sound brought her back. Mr. Bunson was hoovering the puddle.

He slid the vacuum nozzle back and forth, limping slightly, and suddenly the group spirit was gone and a loose, selfish clamor returned to the surgery. Joanne reached for plastos and spray. The man with the damaged kidneys asked Sephony when they could finish; she told him to please wait in the cubicle.

The survivor was half-conscious, his face mushroom white, his mouth a pale, ragged line. He was small and muscular, in his thirties, perhaps. He coughed in his sleep. She shook him and he woke.

"Feeling better?" she asked, taking his pulse.

He stared at her with eyes blank as stones. Was it the drowning that robbed them of expression? An absence flapped off him too. Death in life, that's what it was. So many Dulls looked like that.

"Would you like some brandy?" she asked.

He lifted an arm and rubbed his head with a heavy, pathetic motion, like a drugged animal.

When she brought the drink he reared up on his elbows and she held the cup to his lips. He tipped his head back, swallowed, and grimaced.

"More?" she asked.

He coughed and flopped onto the pillow. He looked thick and helpless, like an overgrown child.

"What's your name?" she asked.

"Ben," he said in a hoarse voice.

"Try to stay awake, Ben," she said. "It's better for you to stay awake."

"Sleep's good," he said.

"Can you tell me about the accident?" she asked.

"Me an' Tom," he said, making an effort. "Where's Tom?"

"Tom?"

"Me an' Tom," he said. He reared up again and looked across the room at the patients, at the four rescuers huddled in conversation, at Joanne spraying a woman's bleeding arm. Sephony moved her chair to block his view of the humped body under the cloth. Ben's eyes were bloodshot, his teeth yellow and crooked.

"That Tom over there?" He stared at the rescuers.

She nodded. "Was he your friend?"

"My friend," he said.

"I'm afraid there's not much hope," she said.

"What?" he asked.

"Not much hope."

"Tom in the water. Gotta sleep," he said, falling back on the pillow.

She stroked his stiff, matted hair. A Sector 4 team arrived in pale green uniforms, threw off the cloth, and tugged a plastic sack onto Tom, headfirst. When the plastic bunched under him they sat him up, annoyed. It sickened her. Death by drowning — any suffocation — was the worst. Let Ben sleep and not know until tomorrow.

In the late afternoon she and Joanne closed the blinds and locked the cabinets.

They sorted out night duties and watered the plants.

Lela would bring Ben some soup from the block kitchen. A tranquilizer would knock him out till morning. Sephony would be tuned to the monitor all night and Joanne would come in early.

"Shall I stay with you until Lela comes?" Sephony asked.

A shadow crossed Joanne's face. "She'll be here soon. I have to notify the guy's family. Ben's a loner, but his mate lived with parents."

"Would you like me to call?"

Joanne sighed gratefully. "No, it has to be official."

Helmeted, Sephony went out into the humid July late afternoon, trudging through the warren and across the river to the Chelsea embankment. Nothing visual to ease the spirit, no flowers or mosses, no country surprises. Every building was predictable. Her sorrow hardened into anger. She arrived home with a dinner for two that she bought along the way.

Her flat was on the twentieth floor, overlooking the Thames. She threw off her shoes; the floor was cool. Odd that she had, in a sense, taken the lead, was living alone while Aaron still shuttled between her and his family. So tied to his daughters, unwilling to leave them entirely to their mother's care, snared in the metallic threads of a double life.

She didn't hear him come in. Suddenly he was behind her, kissing the top of her head. He poured them some sherry and they sat together on the Turkestan carpet. Mo's hollie hung over a shelf of jades. She told him about the drowning.

"I'll have to take it up with Marek," she said. "Thames Hydro has no safety standards at all."

"Far be it from me to defend him," Aaron said, "but his power is limited."

"The entire management is responsible. They expect to lose a Dull here and there, as he puts it."

"He won't see it that way. You'll upset yourself for nothing."

Aaron's voice was strangled, tinged with satisfaction. He disapproved of Marek — how could it be otherwise — yet he was grateful for Marek's defects, as she was grateful for Sybil's.

"Everywhere one looks, someone or something is being sacrificed," she said.

"That's how the Triangle keeps us in line."

"One of these days someone will probe the Triangle . . . if there is one."

"Hah!"

"Is it human or syntropic?" she asked.

"I'm not sure. A few years ago I thought I was close to finding out."

"Joanne's certain it's syntropic."

"So was I."

"And now?"

"The closer I get, the more it recedes. The type of secrecy seems to be human, but the large-scale mistakes are — how should I say — arbitrary and rigid."

An anxious voice underlay his functional voice, sliding away from the political subject as a wildly independent counterpoint slides away from a twelve-tone line. His forehead wrinkled; he looked terribly worn. If only he weren't so conscientious, so scrupulous.

"What is it this time?" she asked.

He was a long time answering. "Severing is immense."

"Yes," she said irritably. "When you think too much."

He sought her eyes. "Are you annoyed with me?"

"No . . . not with you."

"I think I was freer of the family before," he said unhappily.

"You don't have to be free."

He looked into space, abstracted into himself. "You're right," he said, referring to some internal argument, "sometimes I just can't make the effort."

He made her feel as if she were insisting. There was an implied threat, ever so slight, that if she insisted he would break away, but she wasn't insisting, he only made her feel as if she were, it was all his invention imposed on her.

He put his arm around her. "I'll stay the night," he said, "and you won't feel so haunted."

After dinner they walked along the embankment. Shops were closed for the night, crates heaped in front. Bits of dry refuse eddied around the lampposts. A patrol boat sped through the barge lane, its siren shrieking. She stopped to weed a neglected patch of hybrid geraniums. The dead man lay in her mind, a vacant humped thing.

"We don't get any younger," she said, pulling up frothy clumps of mustard. "How many years do we have?"

"Don't be morbid."

"I like living alone. But we haven't all that much time."

He cleared his throat. "I've got to help the girls through their revisions," he said.

Carefully she pulled up jewelweed, trying not to jostle the explosive red pods. She sensed his mind hurtling forward, racing through plans.

"That's three weeks," he said. "At the beginning of August we can live together. If you still want me."

She stayed bent over for a moment, hiding her gladness, letting his words ring and register with the slap, slap of water and the bright liberated flowers. She saw his shoes and the bottoms of his trousers, his feet shifting on the pavement. She straightened, dropping the weeds. "Of course I do," she said. He stepped into the flower bed, smiling like a boy; they kissed solemnly and took the weeds down to the river.

Before going to bed she turned on the surgery monitor. Ben was sleeping with his mouth open, making wet, snarfling sounds. He looked forlorn, a damaged creature. All Dulls are damaged creatures, she thought, beyond repair, but not beyond assistance. Aaron moved over, arm outstretched, and made room for her. She told herself to sleep lightly.

The morning was rainy and warm; she walked from the tube station with a horde of Dulls in shiny blue and brown coveralls. More blues than browns, more young than old. The age groups were divided not only by their work colors, but by their collective behavior. The blue-clad young hurried like flocks of shorebirds, detached and girded with purpose, whereas the old, who wore brown at sixty, shuffled in clusters, touching one another.

Ben was sitting in a chair with a bowl in his lap, eating cereal. Joanne must have fed him and gone straight into the lab. He was too calm.

"How are you?" she asked.

"Okay."

"Finished with your cereal?"

He held out the bowl, looking away.

"Coffee?" she asked.

"Sure."

She poured two cups from the dispenser.

He held his cup in both hands and let the steam caress his bristly, monkeyish face.

"Any soreness in your chest?" she asked.

"Nah."

"What did the doctor tell you?"

"I'm good."

She walked to the window. Rain whipped past. She sipped hot coffee.

"Tom ain't here," he said hoarsely.

"No," she said, turning.

He waited, heavy and suspicious.

"I'm sorry," she said. "The news isn't good."

"Get Tom," he said.

"He drowned. We couldn't do anything for him."

"Bad," he said.

"I'm so sorry. I couldn't tell you yesterday."

Veins swelled in his neck. Jerking forward, he leapt up, knocking over his chair, coffee flying.

He grabbed her arms, spilling her coffee. "Get Tom!" he shouted.

"No, no," she cried. "Tom is dead."

Fury darkened his minnow-shaped eyes; his mouth raged silently, a black hole.

"Tom is dead," she said firmly. "He's in the water."

He blinked his eyes. His mouth closed, a thin line in a

crumpled face. He sagged away from her. Mechanically, obediently, he righted the chair.

"I go," he said.

"I'll ask the doctor."

"I go," he said stubbornly. He sat on the chair and pulled on his boots.

In the lab Joanne was analyzing blood samples; tiny red squares coupled and shifted about the screen.

"He just had a fit," Sephony said, "and insists on leaving."

Joanne rummaged on her desk by feel like a pianist. "Here . . . I saved Tom's memory band," she said, still focused on the screen. "His parents don't want it."

They exchanged a look. "We can't force him to stay," Joanne said.

"I know."

Sephony took the lumpy orange band to Ben.

"This was Tom's," she said. "The doctor kept it for you."

What did his smile mean? Was he grateful, embarrassed?

He caressed the band with his thumb, held it to his ear for a moment, then thrust it deep in the front pocket of his coveralls. A dark lassitude hung over him like a shroud. She'd see him soon, she feared, wrapped in the green plastic cloth.

She wiped the spilled coffee, closed his file, and made up a fresh bed. Her arms were leafy, her breath light. Milling machines grated the air. Patients arrived and sat on benches against the wall. She took their histories. Did a day's work.

When everyone was gone — the surgery quiet and Joanne in the lab — she rang up Marek. His voice, of late, had developed a new tone; he talked strategically, sometimes to please, sometimes to wound, a contrived sound, on guard against its impulses.

"A man drowned yesterday," she said. "Did you know?"

"Two of them, wasn't it?"

"One's alive. He left this morning."

"Stupid buggers," he said, "don't even know how to swim."

"That's disgusting . . . you wouldn't say that about a cow."

"No point bothering me about it."

"Why are there so many accidents?"

"If you want to work with them, that's your problem."

"You're responsible for that man's death. His death is your responsibility."

"Bloody hell, Sephony, I design sonar cages. I didn't design whatever rig he fell off of."

She wanted to shake him until his neck grew soft as a swan's.

"All I ask, Marek, is that you discuss safety with someone."

"Frankly, my dear, they're subhuman. That's the standard, accepted opinion, I believe."

"Yes," she said bitterly, "that's the standard, accepted opinion."

"How are you getting on?" he asked stiffly, politely.

"Don't change the subject."

"All right. I'll bring it up at a meeting," he said. "I'll say we're wasting resources. Does that satisfy you?"

"For now."

"You expect too much."

"You're not as terrible as you pretend to be."

"That's a new line."

"It's true." She paused, feeling friendlier. "How are things at home?"

"Fine."

"Is the garden doing well?"

"Broccoli and tomatoes are coming along. Problem with cabbageworms, though."

"And the roses?"

"Oh, I don't know." His voice trailed off evasively. "Nothing's changed, I take it," he said, his voice stiff again.

"Well . . . yes, in a way. Aaron and I are living together starting in August."

"Congratulations," he said bitterly.

"It's for the best," she said.

"For you," he said.

"For everyone."

"I hadn't noticed."

"You get such satisfaction out of being miserable."

"Oh, it's jolly good fun," he snapped.

"I'm sorry, Marek."

"The hell you are." The phone clicked.

Vindictive, he was vindictive, he punished her by suffering. He clung to misery. Why couldn't he look for contentment, why didn't he take his fair share? He was an open mouth — a big baby groveling on hands and knees, crying for love and instruction. He wanted her to prop him up like a sapling. She could never get equal respect or time — equality with a woman felt like tyranny to him. His balance was her unbalance; when she stepped up he took defensive measures, ridiculed, instructed. Naturally, now, she fought back and there it was, the battle that justified his fears.

Was he going to be ill? Have an accident? Or, like Joanne's ex-husband, would he become division head and marry a woman with a smile like a shark?

She went into the lab. Joanne sat on a stool at a high table, her chin in her hands, sidelight catching the curly blond head and gentle, mocking expression. How concentrated Joanne was, how unencumbered. Whereas she was under siege; she and the children behaved like cubist hollies, their planes shifting and drifting. That's how it will be, she'd said, brutally principled. Your mother is taking a flat in London — you must visit on the weekend. And they came occasionally, singly or in pairs, and were so nervous and uncommunicative — their mother's flat, they muttered — as if a great-aunt had invited them to tea.

"Your personal life doesn't seem to get in the way," she said. "The children and all . . ."

Joanne tilted her head and squinted.

"Work governs," Sephony said, "you never have to make intimate compromises."

"Of course I do . . . I'm not celibate."

"Oh?"

"I've had a lover for years, we don't live together, of course . . . a woman named Phoebe." She laughed sweetly through clenched teeth.

"You *are* brave." Sephony pulled up a stool and looked closely at Joanne. Fine lines feathered away from eyes that were sad even when she laughed. "You take such risks."

"Well, they feel like necessities."

Joanne reminded her of a porcupine, protected by folded spikes — a practical soul, generous to everyone, yet intact like a stone.

"How's Melani?" Joanne asked.

"She came Saturday morning . . . in and out, you know. She's magnificent if you're not her mother hearing her boast about riding Plumsie nonstop . . . if you don't know what . . . oh, what confusion lies behind it. It's almost like giving birth to her again . . . she's ripping herself out of me."

Joanne pressed her lips into a downturned smile. "A horsewoman . . ."

"How did your youngest rebel?"

"With subtlety. She collected plant specimens that could never be dusted."

They laughed.

"I used to think of myself as a sieve hanging in the kitchen," Joanne said, "a red aramid sieve with perfect holes."

"Letting life run through us," Sephony said.

"Well, our youngest daughters won't do that, and they won't see women as lumps in each other's lives, will they?"

Lumps. The word hovered and spread, giving birth to metaphorical and real lumps, medical and sexual lumps, breasts and silences and tumors. They talked haltingly, swiftly, gathering their mutual history, sharing evasions and obstructions. Horrid things connected: tumors and genital mutilation, sexualized body parts, people as obstructions, suppression and pain. They spat out memories and ideas on waves of despair. No more excising, they swore recklessly, as if two critics could change the world, no more gratuitous contempt, no self-hatred.

No mutilation of the spirit, Sephony thought, looking

beyond; no death in life. A fullness is what she wanted. A mystical spot on a forest path where one stands surrounded by dead branches of living spruce. On a foggy day the spot is dull — dry branches, brown-needle carpet, dark moss — everything muted and separate. Then the fog thins and sunlight filters through, animating the dead. Pale moss glows on a decaying log, needles turn bronze, and silvery branches overlap in a shining lattice that delicately connects deep into the forest.

There's life in death, she thought, but it takes the light to see it.

CHAPTER ⚞ 18

BORROWDALE SECTOR in the Lake District had the spottiest weather; from each window she looked out at a different day. A threat of rain to the south over Sty Head, but northeast, out the living room window, the morning was brisk and fine. Puffy clouds rose and fell over the hills; Derwent Water shone between trees. A leisurely cloud shadow slid down a green and lavender slope, over a gash of bleached earth in the shape of a rabbit. Trust Joanne to be generous, giving them this weekend in her cottage for Melani's birthday.

"Wake her," Aaron said, "we should get moving."

She was impatient too. The hills beckoned, the world underfoot, the smells of sheep and juniper. The window tamed the landscape. Sephony imagined eighteenth-century travelers, women in boots and long skirts, traipsing over the fells, peering at crags and chasms through little smoky folding mirrors that reduced vistas to the scale of postcards. She yanked open the window.

Melani pattered into the front room barefoot, wearing a baggy shirt, yawning and stretching, looking, with her close-cropped curls, like an athletic boy. Sixteen, a milestone.

"Happy birthday," Sephony said, kissing her on both cheeks.

"Happy birthday," Aaron said.

From the flat above came music and a baby crying, Joanne's grandson. Melani plopped cross-legged onto the rug, radiant and nonchalant when she saw the gifts, taking her time with the wrappings and guessing outrageously. Aaron's gift was a collection of essays on the philosophy of science. From Sephony, a jade owl on a silver chain. Melani hung the owl around her neck and stroked it.

"Thanks . . . both of you . . . for thinking I'm wise," she said. She leapt up and kissed them on the top of their heads and ran to her room.

They waited for her outside. The cottage was two-story gray stone with a half-finished wing sticking into the lawn like a foot in a cast. Construction materials stood under the trees — plastic-covered sheds, an enormous blue trencher, bound roof shingles, and lengths of red drainpipes. Behind the house was a pasture bordered by saplings, and beyond were the velvet-textured Cumbrian hills, sheep-cropped and undulating.

Melani trotted down the steps, a black and yellow anorak tied around her waist by the sleeves. Claro's colors, Sephony thought. They set off to the lakeside café for breakfast. The pasture was spongy and pocked with stones. A stream wound beside them. Rounded hills shaded into the distance like a child's drawing of waves.

"The rabbit looks well content," Sephony said, pointing. Its head lay high up the slope and its feet touched the tree line.

"Rabbit?" Aaron asked in mock dismay. "With that spindly neck? It's a turkey."

"Turkeys don't have ears," Sephony said, jabbing him lightly in the ribs. He danced away.

"Six legs," Melani said. "What has six legs?"

"Where do you want to go?" Aaron asked her.tape0

"Watendlath," Melani said.

"I'm perfectly happy to climb Loughrigg," Sephony said. "It's ages since I tried, and it does have a grand view."

"I'm not being polite."

She was, though. Melani had emerged, quite suddenly, it seemed, from the cocoon of childhood, clear-eyed and considerate. A tiny ache dimmed Sephony's motherly pleasure, like a blip of cloud biting the moon. She felt a bit obscured, a bit decrepit.

"I opt for Loughrigg," Aaron said.

"But it's not your birthday," Melani said, laughing.

They crossed over the stream on a little humped bridge. The café, crowded already, was run by two serious, scruffy children who looked no older than twelve. A dog lay on the floor by the counter. A sign said Don't Feed the Dog, He's Too Fat. Young people, their pale city faces on August holiday, threw him chips and bits of sausage.

They took their coffee and cereal packets outdoors to a crumb-covered table shaped like a lily pad, brushed it off with serviettes, and ate with hearty appetites. Breakfast tasted of travel, of lake and heather, of morning sun and fat dog. It was perfectly dreadful and delicious.

Power inflatables whined across the lake. A black catcher darted on the peaked horizon, the aftershocks of its flight grating against the hills long after it disappeared.

"Let's go," Melani said.

They walked a kilometer along the footpath, craft whiz-zing overhead, and kept their eyes open for the old trail marker. Sephony saw it first, nearly hidden by ferns, a tiny white arrow pointing up. They filed onto the trail as into a tunnel, rocky and steep underfoot, branches closing around them, the forest world protective and serene. A steep climb, then the trail lev-eled into a winding grade.

Sephony felt free from discretion, free to worry aloud. "What's happening at the house?" she asked, hanging back with Melani, close behind Aaron. She almost said *home*. "No one talks anymore."

"Simon and Dote are throwing me a party," Melani said. "I'm not supposed to know."

"That's lovely," Sephony said. "Were they annoyed you came with us?"

"Nobody says anything directly, it's all sniffing and darting."

"So we're not invited," Aaron said dryly, up ahead.

"No old folks."

"What else?" Sephony asked.

Melani hesitated. "Well, you'll see eventually . . . Dads and Simon planted some pear trees."

"Where?"

Melani picked up a stick and swatted a young maple branch, sending its oversize leaves into a frenzy. "In the flower garden."

"Ah," Sephony said, anticipating some delicate brutality. "What did he take out?"

She swatted another maple branch. "Well — everything," she said miserably.

"Oh."

"I tried to stop them."

"Not the rose garden . . . he didn't destroy the roses . . ."

"Uh-huh."

"You mean my whole garden is gone?"

"I couldn't figure out how to save anything —"

"Of course not," Sephony said protectively, "you don't want to get embroiled . . ."

"By Sunday lunch the garden was nothing but clods and furrows. And then they set in pear trees."

"The roses were prizewinners . . . the Blue Wedgwood." She felt the blow exactly as it had been struck.

"And it's still your property," Aaron murmured from up ahead.

"Maybe Alf saved some," Melani said hopefully.

"Dote wasn't involved?" Sephony asked.

"Dote never helps with anything. Anyway, she isn't as mad at you as Simon. Simon is so bloody jealous."

Sephony winced.

Melani threw down the stick and gave her a quick hug. "Don't cry, I think your new life is rather jolly."

"I wish one of my children found it jolly," Aaron said, turning to wait for them on a mossy hummock.

"Doesn't Gretta?" Melani asked.

"Not that I'm aware of."

"She should buck up," Melani snapped. "I don't under-stand these people who're made of two strings and cry at the drop of a hat."

No crying at the drop of a hat, Sephony thought, not Simon, Dote, and Marek. In vengeance they were erasing her influence; they were kneeling in the brown garden. What were they doing with their memories? She saw them digging, saw robos and family destroying all her years of planting and tend-ing. Marek, uprooting her. Good-bye, then, Marek, and crack-crack, clumped roots leapt out, crack-crack, and Marek moved over, a great hulk, and the young filled the space. Her heart pounded. She placed her hand over it. There, there, she said. And there they were, the four of them, four adult children, four people, not stones in a dry riverbed.

The trail widened at the edge of a brook.

"You're angry, too, my love," Sephony said tentatively as they balanced across.

"But only about boarding next year."

"Not *only,* but never mind. We've been through that — your father can't —"

"I wasn't asking you to break any agreements."

"It's only for a year and then you're off to university."

"Right." She jammed her fists in her pockets, looking shy and defiant, as if she were teetering on the edge of a confession.

Gradually the trail wound upward through deep forest. Light glanced off fallen spruce in crosshatched glades and caught the ragged strands of a spider's web quivering between laced branches.

A clearing opened onto a cliff overlooking the lake, and they sat on a ledge, Melani in the middle. Far below, on the glassy water, puffy tree-covered islets lay neatly doubled like walnut shells. Two pale sandbars made a giant moth. A river zigzagged through a pasture. Cooling towers spewed white smoke.

"Could I live with the two of you next year?" Melani asked bluntly.

A burden lifted. Sephony looked closely at her daughter before answering. The confident child shone through the hopeful adult. She was staying loyal to everyone, trying on new situations like new clothes, turning this way and that, checking front and back for fit and appearance.

"Oh, my dear," Sephony said.

"I don't want to intrude . . ."

"I never thought you'd want us."

Aaron bent sideways and sifted through the ground cover. Would he mind losing some freedom, making some adjustments? For a moment she checked her happiness. Was Melani calculating the lesser of two evils? Did it matter? Melani and Aaron got on, the only ones in both families with a sense of humor. Aaron found what he was looking for, blew it clean, and ceremoniously presented Melani with a lacy fungus medallion.

"Glad one of your mother's children doesn't consider me an ogre," he said wryly.

"Burrow's a good school for her," Sephony said, "better than Dartington. We could try for a flat near Burrow."

"She'll have to get Marek's approval," Aaron said.

"Don't worry about that," Melani said.

Sephony squeezed her hand. The hillside rabbit was quite close now, just across the lake, a shadow gliding over the legs, sun glinting on the head, its satisfaction changing to astonishment, ears straight up, its neck a wide-open mouth.

"Look at the rabbit," Sephony said. "It's singing."

"Mountain goat," Aaron said.

"Fox," Melani said, putting the medallion in her pocket.

They climbed again, high-spirited, Melani in front, climbing up past blowdown and stone hedges into cooler air. Just as they fastened their jackets, the forest vista disappeared. Rain fell and the trail turned swampy; they had to leap from stone to stone. Fat twigs rolled in the mud like snakes and low branches swept the water.

Eyes stinging, they slogged upward from hedge to spruce, drunk from exertion, altitude, and wetness. No more decorous leaps onto stones; giddily they sloshed through mud and water, drenched inside and out, and careened up the final slippery pine-clad slope, noisily grabbing saplings and one another, and ended near the ice-blue glacier lake in the mountain village of Watendlath.

Pinpoint flashes from a tower pierced the curtain of rain; the streets were empty. Aaron remembered the way to the café. Hanging their dripping jackets in the anteroom, they wondered, in a fit of embarrassment, what to do about the puddles.

A robo glided toward them, small and silver, as rare and perfect as Reb Nacht's. It showed them to the loos, where they dried sufficiently with blowers, and then to a table by the rain-shrouded window. In fluty tones it recited the menu and took their order. They were the only patrons.

As the rain let up, the hills beyond the glacier lake emerged, rivulets coursing through eroded channels and branching around stones. A silver radar dish, like the one in Penzance, swiveled lazily. The beacon flashed.

"What's the radar for?" Melani asked.

"Northern surveillance," Aaron said.

The robo brought oat wafers and tea in a lovely old ceramic pot with a swirled design and a chipped spout.

Melani lowered her voice, her dark eyes shining. "Do you ever think about changing things . . . the way the Triangle is, I mean?"

"Yes."

"In a big way, I mean."

"For instance," Sephony asked.

"Destroy the coops. End space migration. Get rid of the cruel things."

"Cruelty is built into the system," Aaron said.

"Well, it doesn't have to be. You shouldn't accept that. When I'm a scientist I won't accept that." She fingered the jade owl — the beak, the rough feathers.

"I don't think you can put an end to space migration," Aaron said, "but there's radical work you could do in biology."

The rain stopped. Over the hills the clouds were breaking up, separating in thick gray layers.

"Radical has to be major," Melani said with adolescent finality. "Tell me what's happening in biology."

"Not on your birthday." He grinned.

"What a relief." She pushed back her chair. "I'll walk around a bit . . . do you mind?"

"We'll meet you here," Sephony said, "or by the lake."

"Keep away from the fences," Aaron said.

Outside, she loped past the window with long strides, damp trousers clinging to her shins.

"I'd like to see her at Sussex," Aaron said. "The immunology group is developing pollutant-absorbing antibodies — frightfully important and with a subversive appeal."

"Is she clever enough?"

"Oh, yes. Can't you tell?"

"No. Can you — with your own?"

"I'm afraid so . . ."

"Perhaps Gretta could live with us, too," she said.

Aaron squirmed. "I can't break up the family," he said evasively.

It was the truth and not the truth. She waited.

"Melani would eclipse her," he said.

"Quickness isn't everything," she said. "Gretta has other qualities."

"Sephony?" He leaned forward, framing his eye in his fingers. He seldom made that gesture of discomfort anymore. "Can I ask you a very personal question? Very off the subject?"

"You can ask," she said, half-bantering, half-serious.

"Whatever was that man's real name?"

"What man?" she asked, startled.

He retreated into himself, neutrality and hope in the framed green eye.

"The man in Domino," he said cautiously, self-consciously. "The one you called Amos."

"Ah, Aaron."

"I'm sorry. The question escaped."

The sun was coming out. Across the glacier lake, gullies spilled down the violet hills. A man passed, dressed in metallic cloth, head down, his stride urgent. On the peak the radar dish turned. Village and pastures quivered in silence. Someday the hill might explode, the forest burn, the lake leap like a geyser and overflow.

Gently, she took his hand away from his eye and held it in both of hers, his fine brown hand, lean and long-fingered, the skin a bit loose and speckled now. Her hand was soft and stubby, the fingernails clipped to the quick, the skin white and veined. Hands growing old together.

"His name," she said, "means the same as yours."

"What does my name mean?" he asked.

"It means 'light,' " she said.